A CALL TO INSURRECTION

★ BOOK IV OF ★
Manticore Ascendant

DAVID WEBER &
TIMOTHY ZAHN
with THOMAS POPE

A Novel of the Honorverse

A CALL TO INSURRECTION

Copyright © 2022 by Words of Weber, Inc., Timothy Zahn, and Thomas Pope

A Baen Books Original

Baen Publishing Enterprises
P.O. Box 1403
Riverdale, NY 10471
www.baen.com

ISBN: 978-1-9821-9237-2

Cover art by Dave Seeley
Maps and illustrations by Thomas Pope

First printing, February 2022
First mass market printing, January 2023

Distributed by Simon & Schuster
1230 Avenue of the Americas
New York, NY 10020

Library of Congress Catalog Number: 2021050936

Pages by Joy Freeman (www.pagesbyjoy.com)
Printed in the United States of America
10 9 8 7 6 5 4 3 2 1

A CALL TO
INSURRECTION

PROLOGUE

1542 PD

HEREDITARY PRESIDENT TRUDY MCINTYRE had never been what Lucretia Tomlinson would have called a handsome woman. But there were pictures from two decades earlier that had captured a smoldering fire, a defiance, and a sense of righteousness that had more than made up for the lack of physical beauty.

Now, sixteen T-years since McIntyre's world and people had been ruthlessly torn away from her, much of that fire had faded.

Much, but not all. And if the fire hadn't aged well, the moral righteousness certainly had.

"... I know you must be getting tired of hearing from me," the image on the display said, "as I'm sure your father did before you, as well as all the other directors that have graced the PFT boardroom. But it's important to me—and to many others—that the crimes of Gustav Anderman aren't forgotten. For sixteen T-years the people of the Tomlinson System have been crushed under his heel, denied their God-given rights to liberty and free expression.

1

"I know that after all this time our small and distant problems probably don't even register on PFT's agenda. That's why I've sent this message directly to you, Director Tomlinson. To remind you of what was once yours, and to plead with you to do whatever you can to make right what Gustav Anderman once made wrong.

"I hope to hear from you at your earliest opportunity. I hope even more that you'll do whatever you can to persuade the Solarian League to take action on behalf of your people, your colonists, and your world.

"Thank you for your attention and consideration. I know that if we work together we can return the Tomlinson System to the freedom and shining glory that your grandfather first envisioned for us.

"With respect, Hereditary President-in-Exile Trudy McIntyre."

The final image froze, a final mute plea in those aging but still fiery eyes.

With a sigh, Tomlinson blanked the screen. She'd been Chief Director of the Board for the transstellar corporation Preston, Fagnelli, and Tomlinson for the past four years. In that time she'd received no fewer than six other messages from McIntyre, all of them pleading with her to take some kind of action against Anderman and his so-called Andermani Empire.

The hell of it was that Tomlinson *had* tried. She'd sent a dozen formal protests of her own to the Solarian League, both to official agencies and to Anderman's former employers and fellow mercenary chiefs. She'd sent notes to some of the other transstellar corporations, suggesting the possibility of bringing sanctions or other economic levers to bear on the Andermani. She'd even sent messages to Gustav Anderman himself, appealing to his better nature or at least to his current reputation and his future legacy.

The League bureaucrats unanimously declared the situation Not Their Problem. None of Anderman's old friends—or enemies—were interested in stepping up to the challenge, at least not for the funding PFT's Board was willing to offer. The transstellars were likewise uninterested in rocking any boats.

Many of the latter group, in fact, hinted broadly that PFT's concerns were well beneath their interest level, as was PFT itself.

As for Gustav, the old man had started speaking exclusively German nine years ago. That said a lot right there about his perception of either reputation or legacy. Or, for that matter, reality.

Part of the problem was the distance. The Tomlinson System was a long way from the League, and despite the old saying, absence usually made the heart simply wander off. Probably one reason the rest of the transstellars had never taken PFT seriously, as well. Owning an entire star system—Preston—sitting on the edge of the Core worlds carried a certain amount of prestige, but the fact that their only other system had been at the back edge of nowhere hadn't added a lot to that status. And of course, since Anderman moved in PFT didn't even have that much.

The painful bottom line was that if McIntyre's situation barely registered in the upper levels of PFT, it didn't register at all anywhere else.

Added to that was the fact that the situation was anything but clear-cut. Anderman had indeed conquered the Tomlinson System, but the records suggested that McIntyre had launched the first attack of that brief war.

Technically, of course, McIntyre had actually launched her attack against the Nimbalkar System, with which Tomlinson had had long-standing tensions and which had only recently been annexed by Anderman.

McIntyre claimed that the attack was merely a response to Nimbalkar's previous aggressions and, furthermore, that her commanders had believed the ship they attacked was a local warship running a false Andermani ID. None of that had mattered to Gustav, of course, who'd used it as an excuse to attack and subjugate the offending system.

Unfortunately, it hadn't mattered to anyone else, either. League officials were reluctant to get involved with something so muddled, and the few who might have been sympathetic to McIntyre's plight knew far better than to cross someone with Anderman's expertise and firepower.

Tomlinson's grandfather had been the one who pushed for and ultimately set up the Tomlinson colony seventy years ago. It was *his* legacy, or it was supposed to have been. Gustav Anderman had taken that from him.

And his granddaughter Lucretia would be damned if she was going to let him get away with it.

In which case, she thought bitterly as she pulled up the report she'd been reading when McIntyre's message was delivered, she was indeed going to be damned. Right now she was Chief Director of PFT, with all the authority and power that entailed; but that stint would only last another eight T-years before it rotated to the heads of one of the other two families. At that point, under the corporation's rotation rules, it would be a full twenty-four years before it came back to her. Or to her successor, if she didn't live that long.

The bottom line was that if she didn't succeed in freeing her grandfather's colony from its oppressors this time around, she would probably never get another chance.

Gustav would win. And he wouldn't just win against the authority and against the property of PFT. He would also get away with building an empire by sheer force of arms.

And those were *not* lessons humanity needed to be learning right now.

Her intercom pinged. "Director, your eleven o'clock is here," her secretary's voice came over the speaker.

Tomlinson frowned, pulling up her schedule. She didn't have an eleven o'clock appointment.

Or at least she hadn't when she checked four hours ago upon arriving in her office. Now, somehow, that slot had been magically filled. Filled, moreover, by a name she didn't recognize.

Freya Bryce.

"One moment, Zaimal," Tomlinson said, punching the name into her computer. Everybody who was anybody was in PFT's files, along with most people who weren't anyone at all.

The list came up: twenty-seven Freya Bryces were on the planet at the moment. They were ordered by prominence, and Tomlinson ran her eye quickly over them. The first four were definitely people of some moderate power and influence, and she wondered briefly which of them could have figured out how to bypass the normal roadblocks and come calling on PFT's chief director on the spur the moment. Running a quick eye over the four photos so she'd recognize her visitor, she again tapped the intercom. "Send her in."

"Yes, Director."

A moment's pause, and then the door across the office swung open and a young woman walked in. Youngish, anyway, probably late thirties or early forties, Tomlinson estimated. She was slender, in an athletic muscular way, with short black hair and wearing the kind of business suit that definitely put her in the upper one percent of society.

And she wasn't any of the top four Freya Bryces on the list.

Tomlinson stifled a curse. That's what she got for not looking deeper before she let the unexpected visitor in. Despite the carefully engineered roadblocks, average citizens with a charity to plead or an axe to grind still sometimes managed to find their way into even the very pinnacles of power.

Still, there *was* that suit. She might as well hear the woman out. "Good day, Ms. Bryce," Tomlinson said courteously, waving her to the chair at the front corner of the desk. "Please, have a seat."

"Thank you," Bryce said as she walked toward the indicated chair. Her stride was measured and confident, her voice polite and well-modulated. But Tomlinson could hear a hint of dark steel beneath the courtesy. "My apologies for breaking in on you this way," the visitor continued as she lowered herself gracefully into the chair. "But time is short, and your official waiting list is tiresomely long."

"Then we'd best get to it," Tomlinson said. "What exactly are we discussing this morning?"

"The topic foremost in your mind at the moment," Bryce said. "Your namesake colony world of Tomlinson."

Tomlinson drew back a little in her chair, the odd

feeling in her back turning decidedly eerie. How could this woman possibly have known that she'd just screened McIntyre's message? "Tomlinson?" she asked carefully.

"As in the message you just received from former President McIntyre." Bryce smiled slightly. "And no, I'm not psychic. I know you received McIntyre's message because I arrived on the same ship that brought it to you."

"Interesting coincidence."

"Not really," Bryce said. "I was speaking with her about her problems before I—and the message—boarded the ship."

"You're a friend, then?" Tomlinson probed.

"A friend to Tomlinson, perhaps," Bryce said. "Not so much to McIntyre herself. I talked with her; now I'm here to talk with you."

"About Tomlinson?"

"Yes," Bryce said. "And how we—or rather *you*—are going to get it back." She raised her eyebrows invitingly. "That *is* what you want, is it not?"

There were a half dozen ways of summoning security to her office. Tomlinson was sorely tempted to use one of them. She'd been over this ground again and again without finding any foothold. Anyone who claimed it was possible was naïve, delusional, or a flat-out con artist.

But there *was* that suit. If this was a con, at least the woman knew how to play the game. It would probably be worth another couple of minutes of her time just for the entertainment factor.

"What I *want* isn't the question," she said. "I've put a lot of thought and effort into it. So have a lot of other people. Every avenue has been a dead end."

"I know," Bryce said. "But if I may be so bold, none of those people has been me."

"And you are . . . ?"

"Who I am is of no consequence," Bryce said. "What matters is that I represent certain parties who would be interested in freeing Tomlinson from Gustav Anderman's hands."

"I hope that doesn't mean you're one of McIntyre's alleged army of freedom-fighters."

"Hardly," Bryce said dryly. "After sixteen T-years I imagine the fires of defiance have dimmed considerably, especially given the relative unpopularity of McIntyre's rather heavy-handed leadership style. No, my associates aren't driven by any such high-minded ideals, but by the very practical fact that we have issues with the way Gustav is growing his empire. We feel that a reminder of the uncertainties of life would be in order."

"Ethical lessons don't qualify as high-minded ideals?"

Bryce gave a small shrug. "There may be some personal aspects, as well," she conceded. "The point is that we're offering the means to deliver Tomlinson back to you."

"To *me*," Tomlinson said, leaning a little on the word.

Another small shrug. "I think we can agree that McIntyre need not be brought back into the equation. The fact that she launched a reckless and unprovoked attack on an Andermani ship demonstrates a serious lack of fitness to govern."

"I thought the details of that incident were unclear."

"Not as unclear as McIntyre pretends," Bryce said. "But her stupidity isn't the issue. The issue is the people of Tomlinson, and the fact that PFT hasn't lifted a finger to right the wrong that was done to them a decade and a half ago. This is your chance to become a hero, not just to your namesake world but throughout all of human history."

"And you can make all this happen?"

"We can," Bryce said firmly. "In partnership with you."

"Of course," Tomlinson said, smiling cynically. There it was. *Partnership*: a code word that nearly always directly preceded a request for money. "And how much would this partnership cost us?"

"I have records for the last profits PFT received from Tomlinson before McIntyre surrendered to the Andermani," Bryce said, pulling a data chip from her pocket and placing it on the desk in front of her. "I also have records for the much higher profits those exports have brought in over the last sixteen T-years. Even adding in the additional shipping costs, I estimate you'll recover your expenses within three to four years."

Silently, Tomlinson reached over and took the chip. Just as silently, she inserted it into her tablet.

Silently, but with her heart suddenly thudding, she ran her eyes down the pages. She didn't have those precise numbers memorized, of course, but Bryce's figures seemed reasonable. Was a four-year recouped investment really all it would take to bring Tomlinson out of its current exile? "And what would these funds buy me?"

"It's going to buy you what you need," Bryce said. "What you've never been able to get from the League or any of Gustav's former mercenary friends. Strategic and tactical skill. A full support and logistics structure. A shipping system in place to begin bringing

Tomlinson's exports to market until you can make your own transport arrangements." She paused. "And, of course, a battle fleet."

Tomlinson jerked her eyes away from her tablet to the other woman's face. "A *battle fleet*?"

"Surely you don't expect Gustav to release Tomlinson just because we ask nicely," Bryce said with a small smile. "No, of course you don't. That's why you've been trying to find a military or paramilitary force willing to take him on."

"There are plenty of groups who are willing," Tomlinson said stiffly.

"Are there?" Bryce countered. "Fine, let me rephrase. That's why you've been trying to find a force who's willing to take him on for the money your Board is willing to spend."

Tomlinson felt her stomach tighten. That was indeed the sticking point. Even more so than Anderman's intimidating reputation.

"Plus the fact that any such group would want overwhelming odds before they even considered such an action, which means you'd need three to five separate forces," Bryce continued calmly. "All of whom would want to be paid." She raised her eyebrows. "But really, Director. A paltry couple of billion credits to a corporation of PFT's wealth and power?"

"It's not just the money," Tomlinson gritted out, all the memories of all the arguments flooding back over her. "We've got the money, and we're a planetary government. We could buy the ships and crew them without raising a single eyebrow. But certain Board members are ridiculously skittish about the whole idea. They think PFT should be above such things."

"Even at the cost of your one out-system possession?"

"Even there." Tomlinson swallowed a curse. "They don't understand. Or they don't care."

"Not surprising, really," Bryce said. "None of them is the granddaughter of the man who founded the colony. They don't have the same roots you do."

Tomlinson felt her eyes narrow. Was this stranger actually *sympathizing* with her? "It's not a question of roots," she said stiffly. "It's a question of right and wrong."

"Or, to put it another way, a question of ways and means," Bryce said. "Tell me, how far are you willing to go to regain the Tomlinson System?"

The alarm bells in the back of Tomlinson's mind, which had been doing a slow cadence ever since this woman walked into her office, picked up their pace. "Meaning?"

"Meaning something far less dark and sinister than you're undoubtedly visualizing," Bryce assured her with a small smile. "It will take less money than you think, but that money will have to be quiet and completely off the books." She raised her eyebrows. "Is that an area you're willing to discuss?"

Tomlinson eyed her, the familiar mental image of blind Justice and her scales floating in front of her eyes. PFT had a reputation among the business community and the League for straight dealing. Tomlinson herself had a similar reputation among her own people.

But on the other scale was freedom for the people of their long lost colony. Justice for the wrong that had been done. A return to the days when PFT truly could claim the status of a major transstellar corporation.

"Tell me more," she invited.

"We know of a fleet that's available," Bryce said. If she was at all surprised that Tomlinson was flirting with the edge, it didn't show in her face. "All we need is the cash to buy it from its current owners—untraceable cash, of course—and we'll be in business."

"Those owners are ... ?"

Bryce shook her head. "Sorry, but for the moment that's confidential. Once you're aboard—officially or perhaps a bit less so—I'll be able to give you more details."

"Before any money changes hands?"

"Of course," Bryce said. "If you agree, you'll be paying the owners directly. None of it will touch my hands."

Tomlinson chewed the inside of her cheek. Which still didn't mean this wasn't a con, of course. But the odds of that were steadily decreasing. "What kind of fleet are we talking about? I trust you're not talking about some hand-cobbled corvettes some third-rate dictator is trying to unload."

"Hardly," Bryce assured her. "What would you say to a few surplused League naval ships?"

Deep in her gut, Tomlinson felt a twinge of disappointment. "I would say we've already looked into that, and they were way pricier than anything the Board was willing to spend. Also way pricier than anything I could cover from our accounts without it being instantly flagged."

"Well, yes," Bryce agreed. "*If* you buy them from the League. If you buy instead from a private party—" She shrugged. "You see, not all League ships get resold once the SLN's done with them. A fair percentage get sent to the breakers."

"And some of them get lost along the way?"

"It happens," Bryce said with another shrug. "It also happens that my associates know of one such graveyard. All we need is the money to buy the ships, and Tomlinson is as good as back in your fold."

"What about crews?"

"As I said, the support system is already in place. All we need are the ships. For that, we just need a relatively miniscule amount of PFT's money."

Tomlinson looked back at her tablet. Not because she needed to see the numbers again, but because she was afraid that if she looked at Bryce the other woman would read straight down into her soul.

Tomlinson, back in the PFT fold. Lucretia Tomlinson, the savior of a whole world.

And, perhaps, the chance to be the first person in recent history who'd ever made Gustav Anderman blink.

And all for just a couple of billion credits.

It sounded too good to be true. The question was, *was* it too good to be true? "And what do your associates get out of it?"

"I already told you," Bryce said. "They don't like the way the Andermani Empire has been expanding of late. They'd like to cool things down a little out there."

"So that your associates can move into the region with their own agenda?"

"They may have interests out there," Bryce conceded. "But that's not something either of us need to know. All you need to know is that they have no interest in Tomlinson itself other than returning it to you. All *they* need to know is whether you're interested in the same thing."

"And if we did this, that would be it?" Tomlinson

asked. She'd seen this hidden hook gambit many times before. "PFT would be under no further obligation to them?"

"Exactly the opposite," Bryce said. "Once you've regained Tomlinson, my associates hope you and they can work further on other mutual projects. There's one in particular that they're expecting will pay high economic dividends in the near future. A partnership with PFT could be advantageous to both parties."

Tomlinson took a deep breath. "All right, then," she said. "I'll obviously need more information on this ghost fleet of yours before I can release any funds. But I can get things started here while you move on that part."

"Of course," Bryce said. "There are some specifications on that data chip. Nothing that could possibly identify individual ships or mark their location, of course, so don't bother trying. There'll be more data later; this is just something to whet your appetite and give you an idea of the ship classes you'll be getting."

"If I agree, what sort of time frame are we looking at?"

"Once I have your commitment, we can probably pull everything together in a year, possibly two."

"That long?"

Bryce smiled. "Patience, Director. Some of that will be travel time, but most will be the straightforward but somewhat tedious tasks of bringing the ships out of mothballs, rearming them, and training the crews on the new hardware and systems. Charging into combat against Gustav Anderman without proper preparation would be utter folly. As Trudy McIntyre has already proved."

Tomlinson hissed out a sigh. She knew better than to

let impatience override her brain. But that didn't mean it didn't sometimes happen. "Understood," she said.

"Don't worry, that year will fly by," Bryce said. "Now that I have your assurances, I can start making the other arrangements."

"Yes," Tomlinson murmured, the image of Justice and her scales disappearing and the faces of the Board taking its place. If they found out what she was doing...

She shook the last lingering shadow of doubt away. A couple of billion credits was indeed miniscule in comparison to the company's assets, easily hidden until Tomlinson herself decided when to reveal the truth.

And really, a small deception in the service of justice and freedom could hardly be faulted.

"I presume you'll allow my representatives to come along for the purchase?" she asked.

"We wouldn't do it without them," Bryce assured her. "As I say, my associates and I won't be dealing in that aspect at all. The ships will be PFT's, free and clear, to do with as you see fit."

She rose to her feet as gracefully as she'd seated herself. "The data chip also has my contact information. Most of the numbers are off-planet, so plan your timing accordingly. Message me when you've made your decision. I'll be contacting you with more details in a few months. With luck, we'll be ready to make the purchase and start the training at that time."

"Good," Tomlinson said. "One other thing."

"Yes?"

"You said you'd talked to McIntyre," Tomlinson said, eyeing her closely. "So why didn't she mention you in her message?"

"Because she had no idea I was coming to see you," Bryce said. "I went to her solely to learn her interpretation of the incident sixteen years ago, and to see if she might be a useful ally in our recapture of her former world."

"And?"

Bryce's mouth tightened, just noticeably. "As I said earlier, I don't believe she needs to be involved. Good day, Director Tomlinson. We'll be in touch."

☆   ☆   ☆

The support system is already in place, Bryce had told Tomlinson. *All we need are the ships.*

As usually happened in the real world, it wasn't quite that easy.

Commodore Catt Quint and her Quintessence Mercenaries weren't where Bryce's information had said they would be. It took Bryce another two weeks of poking around Kenichi until she got another tip, and then it was five weeks' more travel before she could finally track down the commodore.

And when Bryce *did* finally catch up with her, it wasn't in a nice spacers' lounge or corporate office. It was, instead, in a marginally sleazy bar on Dzung, seated at a table with a half dozen less marginally sleazy types.

It was just as well, Bryce reflected as she worked her way through the crowd, that she'd left that ten-thousand-credit business suit back on her ship.

Still, it was clear from the start that Quint was exactly the person Bryce was looking for. There was a toughness and steel in her face and body language that none of her pictures had managed to capture, along with a confidence that allowed her to sit among rough-looking men without a hint of nervousness. On top of that was a keen sense of global awareness: Bryce could tell the commodore had spotted her before she was even halfway across the room.

She would be ideal for what Bryce had in mind. The question now was whether she could be roped in as easily as Tomlinson had been.

Bryce was pretty sure she could. After all, the files had revealed the big fat red button plastered across Quint's psyche.

And Bryce knew exactly how to push it.

She was still five meters from Quint's circle when the two men closest to her pushed back their chairs and stood up. "Yeah?" one of them challenged as they turned to face her.

Mentally, Bryce offered them a salute. With their backs to her, the men must have been given a warning of the approaching stranger, but Bryce hadn't seen even a hint of a signal. The group was good, all right. "I'm here to see your chief," she said, nodding past them in Quint's direction. "I have a proposition for her."

"I'll bet," the first man growled. He let her get another two steps, then held out his hand in silent order. The second man, a smarmy grin of expectation on his face, stepped forward, hands raised for a good, solid, intrusive frisking.

Normally, Bryce was of the same mind as some of her other colleagues: the less attention one drew to oneself the better. But in this case, she was pretty sure that the commodore watching silently from the other side of the table would be more responsive to a different approach.

The big man's hand entered Bryce's personal space,

his fingers aiming for her upper rib cage. Bryce let him get another few centimeters, then reached over and intercepted the hand, putting on a fingerlock that brought him to a jerking halt. His other hand darted under his jacket, and Bryce caught a glimpse of a pistol at his belt.

Unfortunately for him, his gun hand was the one currently locked in her grip, and before he could get his other hand to the gun Bryce had relieved him of the weapon. Still maintaining the fingerlock she flipped the gun in midair, caught it by the barrel, and sent it arcing smoothly toward a landing on the table directly in front of Quint.

Or rather, that was where Bryce had aimed it. Instead of the crunching rattle of metal on wood, there was merely the subdued slap of metal on flesh as Quint's hand darted out and caught the weapon in midair. "I think you dropped something," Quint said mildly, lifting the gun a couple of centimeters.

"Just trying to cut through the small talk," Bryce said. "In the future, you might want to instruct your men to start a frisking with their off hand."

"Or to hand off their weapon beforehand?" Quint suggested.

"Even better," Bryce said, releasing her grip. He gave her a look that was half glower and half speculation, but made no move to pick up the frisking where he'd left off. "Sorry about the theatrics," Bryce continued. "But I spent a lot of time hunting you down, and I wanted you to take me seriously."

"Consider yourself serious," Quint said. "Taylor: the lady needs your chair. Grimling, get her a drink. Scotch?"

"Scotch is fine," Bryce said as the slightly less bulky man seated next to Quint stood up and stepped away from the table. "And for the moment I'd prefer to keep this just between the two of us. Can I buy your people a round?"

Quint gave her a measuring look, shrugged, and gestured. "Everyone to the bar," she said. "Tell Georgio the lady will pick up the tab on her way out."

Silently, the other men and women at the table got up and made their way through the crowd. "Let's make this quick," Quint said as Bryce settled into the vacant chair beside her. "You're either looking for a job or you're looking to hire me. Either way, you're out of luck. The Quintessence Mercs are out of business."

"So I heard," Bryce said. "Temporarily, I hope."

"Don't count on it," Quint said, a bitter edge to her voice. "Sometimes you're the windshield, sometimes you're the bug. This time, we were definitely the bug."

"It happens," Bryce said with a shrug. "Still, the bug usually doesn't pick itself off the windshield and make it back to its home leaf. Very impressive that you were able to do that."

"We were lucky," Quint said. "Usually once a battle-cruiser is wrecked that's it. But I have good men and women, and they were able to get us home." Her lips compressed briefly. "Rather, I *had* good men and women."

"Is that what you're doing here?" Bryce asked, nodding at the crowd around them. "Trying to get some of your competitors to take them on?"

"I don't have competitors anymore," Quint said. "But yes, that's the plan. Like I said, they're good people. They deserve good jobs." She cocked her head. "Right—I missed that possibility, didn't I? You wouldn't happen to be hiring, would you?"

"As a matter of fact, I would," Bryce said. "How many battlecruisers do you think you could crew right now?"

Quint snorted. "How many have you got?"

"Four."

Quint's mouth started to open into a laugh. It froze halfway, her face abruptly stiffening. "You're serious."

"Deadly serious," Bryce assured her. "Four moth-balled battlecruisers, plus probably a few smaller ships."

"Probably?"

"I haven't personally inspected the merchandise," Bryce said. "But the sellers know what they're doing, and they're certainly going to keep their prizes in good shape. Of course, I'd want you to check everything thoroughly before any money changes hands."

"Of course," Quint echoed, still studying her. "What group are you with?"

"My associates aren't mercs," Bryce said. "No, wait—we're supposed to say *Contingency Management Firms* these days, aren't we?"

"If we're being pedantic," Quint said. "Or bureau-cratic."

"Words of a feather," Bryce said philosophically. "Regardless, that's not who we are. My associates are merely a group of interested individuals who want to deliver a message."

Quint smiled faintly. "There are courier ships for that, you know."

"They're looking for something a bit more difficult to ignore," Bryce said. "I dare say diplomatic subtleties are lost on a man like Gustav Anderman."

Quint's face froze. "*Anderman?*"

"Sixteen T-years ago he took over a system that was owned by someone else," Bryce continued, pretending she hadn't noticed the abrupt change in mood. "That someone has decided it's time they took the system back. All they lacked were ships, which is where my associates come in, and crews, which is where you and the Quintessence come in." She raised her eyebrows slightly. "Assuming you *want* to come in."

"Mmm," Quint said, a polite but noncommittal tone. "Tell me more."

Translation: where the hell was Bryce going to find four battlecruisers no one else wanted? "Obviously, I can't go into details until you're officially aboard," she said. "Hypothetically, though, there are ways that ships can, shall we say, go missing. Ships that various regional navies, such as the SLN, are decommissioning, for instance."

"The SLN," Quint echoed, her voice flat.

"Hypothetically, why not?" Bryce said. "They have a huge navy, and a fairly impressive turnover of their ships. When they're done with something, it might be sent to, oh, say, Cormorant for salvage."

"I've heard about the stacks at Cormorant," Quint said thoughtfully. "Lots of ships there, lots of groups running the various reclamation yards. Not just SLN decommissions, either."

"No, not at all," Bryce said. "The majority of the stacks are privately owned, as I understand it, a lot of them mothballed for later reactivation or sale or reclamation. Huge backlog for the latter service, too—I hear it takes a lot of time and effort if you want to pull a ship apart into salvageable pieces instead of just blowing it to dust."

"Paperwork, too, I imagine."

"Oh, definitely paperwork," Bryce agreed. "So many ships, so much paperwork. It's a wonder that inventory slated for reclamation doesn't accidently get sent to a different stack in an entirely different orbit."

"Yes, I can see how that could be a problem," Quint said. "And with such a huge work backlog, it could be years before anyone even noticed that the next ship on their list had somehow gone missing."

"Assuming the list itself wasn't also accidently corrupted," Bryce said with a shrug. "In which case, someone could just tow the missing ship out of orbit, or cannibalize other ships in the stack for parts so that it could fly on its own, and no one would ever realize what had happened. As I said, mothballed or sold ships come in and out all the time. No one would even notice if the wrong one drifted away."

"A shame," Quint said, nodding in commiseration. "The SLN *does* so like to keep its books in order."

"I'm sure it doesn't cost *that* much to bring the books back into line."

"Ah," Quint said. "In which case, no one would be looking for the missing ship because no one would know there was anything *to* look for."

"Exactly," Bryce said. "It's odd, sometimes, how some mistakes just sort of work themselves out."

"Hypothetically, of course."

"As I said," Bryce agreed. "In the real world..." She waved a hand. "Who knows how things actually work?"

"Truth is sometimes stranger than fiction," Quint murmured. "Four battlecruisers, you say."

"Four battlecruisers," Bryce confirmed. "I need an answer, Commodore."

For a long moment Quint gazed back at her. Then, almost unwillingly, the commodore's eyes drifted across the room, settling on some of her officers.

Bryce had always been good at reading faces, and the play of subtle emotions across Quint's spoke volumes. The Quintessence had always been pretty much aboveboard, with all the right paperwork, all the right rules of engagement, and—most important of all—all the right tax receipts. What Bryce was suggesting was a serious step over a line Quint had taken pains not to cross.

The commodore's career and future were at stake, and for some people that would have been enough. But Quint was also shouldering the burden of her people: not just the officers and crew, but the ships full of dependents who traveled in the civilian vessels of the mercenaries' fleet train.

Finding jobs for competent mercs was relatively easy. Finding jobs with competent and legitimate groups was somewhat less so.

Finding jobs with groups willing to take whole groups of families in tow was probably a nightmare.

Bryce felt her lip twitch with the fresh reminder of the sort of place she and Quint were in. She doubted very much that the commodore had started with bottom-of-the-barrel places like this. Quint's emotional kaleidoscope came to a slow stop, and she looked back at Bryce. "Yes," she said, her voice gone suddenly soft and deadly. "Yes, I'd like very much to come in on this."

"Excellent," Bryce said, suppressing a smile. People, dependents, and careers were all useful tools. But for something like this, nothing beat a big fat red button.

Big fat red button, successfully pushed.

"Let's move it back one question, then," she continued. "The one about crews."

"Yes, I remember." Quint pursed her lips, her gaze defocusing. "I can fully crew one immediately. Assuming I can rehire the handful of people I've let go already, which shouldn't be a problem. If I strip my support ships, I can fully crew one more, or put skeleton crews on all four. Class and origin?"

"Not sure of the class," Bryce said. "The sellers have been a bit cagey about the finer details. But they're definitely surplused SLN."

"Well, we can get those details when we bring in the money," Quint said. "Are the ships still armed?"

"The beam weapons may still be in place," Bryce said. "Not sure about that. No missiles, though. But my associates have a line on replacements."

"What's our time frame?"

"We're hoping to get this moving in the next T-year or two," Bryce said. "That includes everything: rearming, crew acclimation and training, and travel to the Andermani Empire."

A corner of Quint's lip twitched at that last. "I'll need a retainer fee. Fifty percent, up front."

"I can do better than that." Bryce pulled out a data chip and set it on the table. "Once you pick that up, you and the Quintessence are on our payroll, at the same scale as you had on your last two jobs. The account the passcodes access should cover salaries and operating costs, plus a healthy cushion in case of unexpected costs or delays. We'll eventually need a full breakdown on those extras, of course."

Quint nodded. "Don't worry, my quartermaster is a wizard with receipts."

For a moment she gazed hard into Bryce's face. Then, she reached over and picked up the data chip. "I'm still not convinced you're not blowing smoke, you know," she warned.

"The funds in that account should convince you otherwise," Bryce said. "Welcome aboard, Commodore. Now. I'll be heading off-planet tomorrow morning, but if you can give me some idea of your travel schedule for the next few months I'll be back in touch with you at my earliest opportunity to see how the recruitment is going. Once you've got your crews, we'll move to pick up the ships and get started on the rest of the prep work. If you need me before that, the chip also has my contact information."

"We'll be ready," Quint promised. "I'll message you if things go quicker."

"Excellent," Bryce said, offering her hand. Quint took it in a nicely firm, no-nonsense grip and pumped it twice before letting go. "Again, Commodore, welcome aboard. I'll look forward to our next meeting. And I'll take care of that tab on my way out."

She stood up, an uncharacteristic hesitation spinning through her mind. She really shouldn't do this, she knew.

But the button was *so* big and *so* red and *so* satisfying to push. "And if you decide you really don't want to go up against Gustav Anderman," she added, "be sure to let me know."

"Don't worry about that," Quint said, the same ice settling over her face again. "Don't worry at all."

☆   ☆   ☆

It was always instructive, Bryce reflected as her air car lifted into the Dzung night sky, to see exactly how mercs obeyed an order from their commander. In this case, to see how expensive they would go with the drinks Quint had said someone else would be paying for.

A crew with trust issues would likely aim low, figuring that they might still get stuck with their own tabs. A crew that was used to their commander meaning what she said was more likely to go all out, knowing that if the promised payment didn't come through they'd at least get the entertainment value of watching her beat the welsher into the sawdust.

In this case, it looked like the Quintessence crew trusted their commodore up to the very highest prices on the menu.

Bryce gave a mental shrug. It wasn't like it was her personal money, after all. And the fact that she'd found a competent commander and a loyal crew for the attack on Anderman should make her superiors at Axelrod very happy indeed.

Probably happier than Jeremiah Llyn was making them.

Of course, professional rivalries aside, it was hardly a fair contest. Bryce's targets had been low-hanging fruit: a corporate head desperate to atone for the misdeeds of her predecessors, and a mercenary chief desperate for employment. Plus, in both cases, that heady mix of revenge and moral indignation that made people so willing to be manipulated.

Llyn's part of the job, in contrast, was a much steeper climb. There was no moral component to an attack on the Star Kingdom of Manticore, which meant he had to troll the blacker depths of the galaxy for the necessary firepower. Not simply the minimal firepower necessary to keep Andermani attention focused inward, as Bryce was going for, but a force strong enough to overwhelm the Manticoran defenses.

And, moreover, to overwhelm them quickly enough that the takeover could be presented as a fait accompli to all the nations around it. A protracted war might give the Andermani and Havenites enough time to drag their attention away from Axelrod's carefully engineered distractions and persuade them to intervene.

Still, uphill climbs were Llyn's specialty. If whoever he hired had the ships and the competence, they should make short work of a force as aged and inexperienced as the RMN. Once Llyn was confident the attack was ready to go, it would be Bryce's job to get her diversionary force over to the Andermani Empire and start making trouble. Hopefully, the Haven diversion would also be in place to happen at that same time.

And then, whatever Axelrod wanted with the Manticore System, they would have it.

☆   ☆   ☆

It hadn't worked out that way.

Not even close.

BOOK ONE

1545 PD

CHAPTER ONE

"*HERR MAJOR?*"

Major Kau-jung Kleinberg looked up from the report on his pad and cocked an eyebrow at Oberbootsmann Taschner. "Yes?"

"We've just picked up something a little odd, *mein Herr,*" Taschner said, gesturing at her display. "It may be nothing, but..."

"One moment." Kleinberg put away his pad and gave himself a push in the petty officer's direction. It wasn't much of a trip, given the *Komet*-class attack shuttle's diminutive size, but it gave him a good excuse to get out of his chair for a bit. He caught the handgrip on the back of Taschner's flight couch and peered over her shoulder. "Show me."

"As I say, *mein Herr,* it may be nothing," Taschner said, "but we're picking up what looks like a location transponder."

"Out *here?*"

"*Ja, mein Herr.*" She craned her neck to look up at him. "You see my concern."

He nodded, frowning at Taschner's displays. At the moment the shuttle was fifty-four million kilometers from the battleship *Preussen*, finishing up a *Raumbatallion* training exercise in The Cloud and awaiting pickup.

It wasn't like there wasn't anything out here that might need a location transponder, of course. The Tomlinson System's asteroid extraction industry was concentrated in The Cloud, which meant scores of platforms located throughout its volume, some tiny, some impressively large, and with the simmering unrest in the system, Potsdam had wanted to establish an on-going presence among them. The Komet's current search-and-rescue exercise was one of the Imperial Andermani Navy's points of presence, this one in particular halfway around The Cloud from the system's sole inhabited planet and *Preussen*.

Except that the transponder Taschner had spotted, positioned at one-zero-seven, zero-one-three and approximately twenty thousand kilometers away, didn't seem to connect to any of the known platforms or currently active vessels.

"As you can see, *mein Herr*, it's closing on us," Taschner continued. "Actually, it's crossing our track. Velocity relative to the primary is approximately seventy-one thousand KPS. Track is one-niner-seven, relative, which means it will pass well astern of us."

And given their relative positions and vectors, an interception was out of the question. If they'd been in a proper ship with a proper impeller drive . . . but if wishes were horses . . . "Shindler?" Kleinberg called to the shuttle's pilot. "Can *anyone* intercept it before it enters The Cloud?"

"Negative, *Herr Major*," Hauptbootsmann Ning Schindler said, shaking her head.

Kleinberg grimaced. The fact that he'd expected the answer made it no more palatable. "Get me the flagship," he ordered.

"*Ja, mein Herr*," Taschner replied. She tapped keys, then spoke into her mic. "*Preussen*, Shuttle Alpha." She waited a moment, then looked up over her shoulder at Kleinberg. "Hot mic, *Herr Major*."

"*Preussen*, Major Kleinberg," he said into his throat mic. "I need to speak to the officer of the watch, please."

☆   ☆   ☆

"I think Kleinberg is right, *meine Kapitänin*," Fregattenkapitän Syin-ba Greuner said, looking at the icons on SMS *Preussen*'s main plot.

"It would explain quite a lot," Kapitänin der Sterne Florence Hansen agreed, frowning at the same icons. She looked up at her superior, Flotillenadmiral von Jachmann. "We knew they were getting matériel past us, *mein Herr*. We just hadn't figured out how."

"*Someone* certainly should have," Baron von Jachmann said, looking pointedly across at Korvettenkapitän Simon Bajer, Hansen's Assistant Tactical Officer. Bajer, Hansen noted, kept his own eyes firmly on his console.

Not surprisingly, and undoubtedly not for the first time. Native-born Tomlinsons were a rarity aboard *Preussen*, continually performing balancing acts with the rest of the ship's company. But Bajer was a highly intelligent officer, the sort who thought things through, and if he was willing to put up with the pressure, Hansen was glad to have him aboard.

She certainly had no interest in contributing to

that pressure. "If by *someone* you mean *me, Herr Flotillenadmiral*, then you're correct," she said. "It *is* a classic smuggling ploy, after all."

"I didn't mean *you, meine Kapitänin*," Jachmann assured her.

"Whether you did or not, the responsibility for such lapses ultimately rests with me," she said firmly.

And really, just because the ploy was classic didn't mean it was used very often anymore. Most smugglers simply hid their contraband aboard incoming ships where customs agents weren't likely to find it, or else used false manifests. Once through customs, the cargo would be transferred to a warehouse and either wait for someone to claim it or be passed on by friendly stevedores.

But here in Tomlinson all customs inspections were under Imperial Andermani Navy control. That meant all incoming cargo had to pass through a single authorized platform, and the Empire's severe penalties for smuggling loomed over any would-be smugglers. Under the circumstances, dropping a pod or two on a ballistic course for pickup was the smarter and safer choice.

"Maybe that means they're getting desperate," Greuner offered.

Jachmann grunted. "Maybe it means they're about to launch something big."

For a moment no one spoke. Because Jachmann was probably right.

The uptick in violent rebel activity in Tomlinson had come as a bit of a surprise. Up to about eighteen T-months ago local resentment of and resistance to the system's involuntary integration into the Andermani Empire had been gradually fading, and Tomlinson had seemed to be on track to finally accepting that integration peacefully. But then, for no obvious reason, violent incidents had spiked sharply. Vandalism, attacks on infrastructure, even assassinations had spiraled upward.

Emperor Gustav had deployed *Preussen*, the transport *Kriegsmädchen*, and a small, rotating screen of lighter units to Tomlinson as it became obvious that the Free Tomlinson Front—known somewhat sarcastically to everyone else as the Freets—were unusually well-armed. The division of Imperial Army troops aboard *Kriegsmädchen*, supported by *Preussen's* embarked *Raumsbatallion* and the entire squadron's light craft had made their presence felt quickly in hopes of stamping out this rekindling of armed resentment.

But the rebellion had stubbornly refused to gutter out. The fact that it could persist even with so many of its weapons being seized showed clearly that arms shipments were somehow being smuggled in.

More worrisome was the fact that, while many of the small arms appeared to have been manufactured somewhere in the Tomlinson System, an even larger percentage were of Solarian manufacture. But no one had been able to pinpoint how the Freets were sneaking them in.

Until now.

"Do we have anyone in position to intercept the beacons?" Hansen asked.

"No, *meine Kapitänin*," Greuner admitted. "Not short of The Cloud, at any rate. They're traveling at just over seventy thousand KPS. *Rotte* is on the way to pick up the Alpha Shuttle, but won't reach position in time."

"We may not be able to catch it before it crosses

the perimeter of The Cloud," Bajer said, "but at its present velocity, it would require almost a full T-day to completely transit The Cloud, and we have a solid track on it. *Rotte* will reach the inner belt in six and a half hours, and tracking it won't be a problem."

"Tracking it without being detected by whoever is *waiting* for it may be," Hansen pointed out.

"True, *meine Kapitänin*," Bajer conceded. "But The Cloud is a very large volume, and very little of it is actually exploited. We don't know how large this consignment might be, but it's unlikely they'd be smuggling in any smaller shipments than they had to. There isn't that much traffic to Tomlinson, so they need to deliver as many weapons as possible in each drop. That means whoever is waiting for them has to have the power to grapple with and decelerate cargo containers or be large enough to rendezvous with them and trans-ship their contents."

"Or both, *meine Kapitänin*," Greuner agreed. "It shouldn't be difficult to follow the beacon through and identify any ship that's close enough—and large enough—to be the receiver."

"And Tracking is confident about this identification?" Hansen asked, waving a hand toward the blinking crimson icon on the display.

"*Jawohl, meine Kapitänin*," Greuner replied. "*Periwinkle* is the only ship that could have jettisoned cargo pods on that vector."

"I see." Hansen studied the numbers. Judging from *Periwinkle*'s low deceleration numbers—she was slowing at barely eighty gravities—she was exactly the sort of down-at-the-heels tramp someone would choose for a clandestine delivery like this.

And now that her need to release her contraband on a precise vector was known, the sloppiness of her approach to Tomlinson finally had an explanation.

She'd made her alpha translation well outside the hyper-limit, and she'd obviously been in the wrong place when she did. That wasn't uncommon, given the difficulties in making a precise n-space translation after any lengthy voyage in hyper, but her error had been larger than most, bringing her into n-space halfway around the hyper-limit's circumference from the planet.

She'd followed up that translation with some fairly incompetent astrogation, crossing the limit with more velocity than she should have, especially on a heading that would have taken her nowhere near Tomlinson. And then, to ice the cake, she'd taken the better part of an hour to realize how badly off course she was and begin correcting.

Only now it was clear to everyone that she'd spent that hour getting into position to release her cargo pods on the proper heading. She must have dropped the pods just before she made her course correction.

Of course, thanks to her original "error" she'd had an additional four light-minutes to travel, and a lot of negative velocity to kill, once she got herself turned around and pointed toward Tomlinson.

She was currently just over sixteen light-minutes out and had just made turnover and started her deceleration. At her eighty gravities max, she'd need another seven and a half hours for her zero/zero insertion into Tomlinson orbit.

Hansen gazed at those numbers, then smiled a thin, cold smile.

"I believe Korvettenkapitän Bajer has analyzed these people's operational plan correctly, *Herr Flotillenadmiral*," she said, nodding acknowledgment to Bajer before turning to Jachmann. "That means *Periwinkle* will be continuing to Tomlinson orbit to deliver her legitimate cargo. And *that* means that *Preussen* is the spider at the heart of the web. We don't have to pursue them at all. Simply wait until they deliver themselves to us."

"Understood, *meine Kapitänin*," Jachmann said. "I'll order *Rotte* to intercept the contraband."

"I'd recommend not doing that just yet, *Herr Flotillenadmiral*," Hansen said. "We don't want them worrying that they've been discovered. Not yet."

"A good point," Jachmann said. "Very well. We wait."

"In which case, *meine Herren*," Hansen said, letting her eyes sweep over the bridge, "we have several hours of waiting ahead of us. Fregattenkapitän Greuner, you'll bring the ship to Readiness Two in five hours. In the meantime, continue to monitor the targets." She smiled thinly. "And all of you might want to make sure your current paperwork and other minutia is in order. Once we raise our wedge, there will be precious little time for anything routine."

☆   ☆   ☆

A com chimed softly in a dimly lit office aboard Station Beta, Tomlinson's secondary orbital platform. The door plaque read *Intra-System Communications Center*, and once upon a time it had been an important communications node.

Now, ever since the Imperial Andermani Navy had descended upon Tomlinson in force, it was only marginally manned. The bulk of the system's important communications went through *Preussen* and the Army's communications center aboard *Kriegsmädchen*. ISCC Beta had been reduced to managing the important but boring and routine communications of the asteroid extraction platforms and the ships that served them.

The com chimed again, and the watch manager punched the acceptance button. "ISCC Beta," he growled in acknowledgment.

"Fred?" the voice on the other end replied.

The watch manager stiffened. "There's nobody here with that name."

"Oh, damn! I'm sorry, I've punched the wrong combination."

"Not a problem," the watch manager assured him. "You'd best try again."

"Right. A thousand apologies." There was the soft tone of a disconnect.

For a long moment the manager gazed at the com, pondering the code phrase which had just been passed, mentally running through his instructions as to what he was supposed to do next. Fortunately, there were enough com relays built into the system to make it very unlikely anyone would ever be able to identify either end of the message he was about to send.

Turning to his console, he began tapping keys.

☆ ☆ ☆

"Herr Leutnant—status change on Target Alpha," Stabsgefreiter Mei-chau Thörnrich said sharply. "Target is altering course and acceleration."

"On the board," Leutnant der Sterne Kevin Selavko ordered, spinning his chair to face the senior tactical petty officer of the watch. The data was coming up . . .

Selavko felt his teeth clench. The smuggler's freighter, which had been puttering along at an eighty-gee deceleration, had altered course by 130 degrees, shifting away from the distant planet and heading for the hyper limit.

And she had run her acceleration up to two-point-three-seven KPS squared. Two hundred forty-two gravities.

Two hundred forty-two.

For a brief moment Selavko and Thörnrich exchanged disbelieving looks. Then, Selavko jabbed a combination into his com.

"Kapitänin's quarters, Oberbootsmann Pang," a voice replied.

"I need to speak to the Kapitänin immediately," Selavko said.

"Einen Moment, bitte," Kapitänin der Sterne Hansen's steward said, and a second or two later, Hansen's voice spoke in Selavko's earbud.

"Yes, Leutnant?"

"Meine Kapitänin, Target Alpha has just altered course. Significantly."

There was a moment of silence as Hansen checked her repeater displays. "I'll be right there," she said.

"Shall I raise the wedge, *meine Kapitänin?"*

"No," Hansen said, and he heard a hint of a frustrated sigh. "There's no point."

"Of course, *meine Kapitänin,"* Selavko acknowledged. His earbud clicked, and he turned back to the bridge tactical displays.

Watching their quarry make its escape.

☆   ☆   ☆

"How did they guess?" Flotillenadmiral Jachmann demanded, floating stiffly beside Hansen in the relatively spacious CIC that only Andermani battleships could provide. Behind them, keeping a respectful distance and an even more prudent silence, were Bajer and Greuner.

"I hardly think they *guessed*," Hansen growled. "It's far more likely they were warned."

"But how?" Jachmann asked, fighting back his anger and bewilderment. "Kleinberg reported directly to us, and we haven't reported it to anyone else."

"Are you suggesting there might be a traitor aboard *Preussen*?" Hansen countered.

Jachmann winced. It was a question he'd been trying not to think about. But now that his Kapitänin der Sterne had brought it up, there was no avoiding it.

"There may be another explanation, *Herr Flotillenadmiral*," Bajer spoke up hesitantly from behind them.

"What sort of explanation?"

"At three light-minutes distance there was a lot of spread on Major Kleinberg's com laser, *mein Herr*," Bajer said, "Anyone within a cone thirty kilometers across at *Preussen*'s position could have received it. And his transmission was encrypted but not coded."

"And your point, Korvettenkapitän?" Hansen asked.

"I'm wondering about the coms that were stored in the Isle City Army depot during that Freet attack last week," Bajer said.

"What about them?" Jachmann demanded. "The attackers were after weapons. The coms were in a locked cabinet that wasn't touched."

"We *assumed* the cabinet and coms weren't touched," Bajer pointed out. He was wilting a little under the heat from his superiors' glares, but his voice was steady. "If they were—if someone got in and either swapped out one for a lookalike or else just downloaded the encryption—"

"Then they could just sit back and listen in on our conversations," Hansen interrupted acidly. Bajer winced, but it was quickly clear that her anger wasn't directed at him. "All they needed to do was get the stolen com close enough to *Preussen* to pick up the edge of Major Kleinberg's transmission."

Jachmann swore under his breath. "I would say, Kapitänin der Sterne Hansen, that this is not our day for demonstrating Andermani glory."

"Or even marginal Andermani competence," Hansen said sourly. "I recommend we send out an immediate order for all units to reset their coms to the Zeta-17 encryption protocol."

"So noted," Jachmann said, making a note on his tablet. "After that I suppose there will be nothing else but to write up our formal reports."

"I suppose we will, *Herr Flotillenadmiral*," Hansen agreed.

"Excuse me, *meine Kapitänin*," Bajer spoke up again. "But if I may, I don't think the day has been a total loss."

"How do you conclude that, Korvettenkapitän?" Jachmann asked.

"It's true that we failed to intercept *Periwinkle*," Bajer said, "and we must assume that the Freets were also able to alert whoever would have rendezvoused with the contraband. That makes it unlikely that we'll intercept anyone at that end of the loop, either."

"Unlikely in the extreme," Hansen agreed stolidly. "Still waiting for the *not a total loss* part."

"I say that because *this*—" he gestured at the display "—tells us a great deal about the sophistication of whoever is supplying the Freets."

They all turned to look at the icon moving across the display. The previously anemic freighter had pushed its acceleration up a notch and was now heading toward the hyper limit at a preposterous 244 gravities, thirty-eight gees higher than *Preussen* could have produced at her standard eighty percent impeller setting. In fact, even with a *zero* safety margin, the battleship's maximum acceleration was only 252.7 gravities.

Which meant *Periwinkle* was a purpose-built and very expensive vessel whose operators had taken pains to make appear as dilapidated as possible. Factoring in the Solarian weapons pipeline, the inescapable conclusion was that whoever was out there stirring the Tomlinson pot had some very interesting connections indeed.

On one level that was worrisome. But on another, it offered a small glimmer of hope. Someone that connected could hardly throw money and influence around this way without leaving a few fingerprints somewhere. Hopefully, once this was handed off to the Intelligence experts in Abteilung III, they could start hunting for those fingerprints.

"Certainly an interesting enemy we seem to have made," Hansen commented into the silence. "Let us hope we can draw him out of the shadows soon so we can see exactly what he's made of."

"Most definitely," Jachmann agreed. "Two other points occur to me. First, even if *Preussen's* impeller nodes had already been hot, we still couldn't have generated an intercept. Nor could any of our other ships. If *Periwinkle* had held her course for Tomlinson only twenty or thirty minutes longer, perhaps. But as it was..." He shook his head.

"Yes, I'd already soothed my professional conscience on that one," Hansen said. "Your other point?"

"That the Freets' communications capability is highly efficient," Jachmann said. "Not only did they intercept Major Kleinberg's transmission, but they then got the information to their own communications node promptly enough to alert *Periwinkle*."

"*And* while *Periwinkle* was still almost five light-minutes out from Tomlinson orbit," Bajer added. "Not only are their communications efficient, but also impressively powerful."

"Yes," Hansen said, her voice thoughtful. "Well, *meine Herren*. Information gained; opportunities lost. Gains, and losses."

She fixed each of them with a long, cool look. "I trust that we will emerge from our next encounter with our mysterious enemy with our balance sheet showing only gains. Do I make myself clear?"

"Very clear, *meine Kapitänin*," Bajer replied for all of them.

"Good," Hansen said. "Return to your posts. I expect to have your individual reports on this incident on my desk within the hour."

☆   ☆   ☆

Deep inside Queen Elizabeth, the baby kicked. Those kicks had been getting harder lately as the due date came closer, paradoxically moving both too quickly and too slowly.

For once, though, Elizabeth hardly noticed the fluttering in her abdomen. The report she was currently reading held every single iota of her attention.

Finally, feeling an odd mix of anticipation and dread, she looked up at the two men standing motionless in front of her desk. "She's here, you said?" she asked.

"Yes, Your Majesty," Prime Minister Julian Mulholland, Baron Harwich, said, his nod as stiff as his posture.

"She's waiting in the anteroom," Defense Minister James Mantegna, Earl Dapplelake, added. "I'll warn Your Majesty that she's a bit nervous."

"As well she should be," Elizabeth said, waving a hand at the report on her tablet. With her other hand she touched her intercom. "Send in Dr. Tolochko, please."

"Yes, Your Majesty."

Elizabeth looked past Harwich and Dapplelake as the door opened and a youngish looking woman with a surprising amount of gray in her hair stepped tentatively inside. "Your Majesty," she said, her voice shaking noticeably as she ducked her head in an abbreviated bow.

"Dr. Tolochko," Elizabeth greeted her gravely in return. "I've just read your report. It's quite interesting."

"Yes, Your Majesty," Tolochko said. "I mean, thank you, Your Majesty."

Dapplelake made a small sound in the back of his throat. "Perhaps you could lay out the full story for Her Majesty," he suggested.

"Oh." Tolochko's eyes flicked to him, back to Elizabeth. "It's . . . rather technical."

"That's all right," Elizabeth assured her. "Your report had your conclusions, but I'd like to know the reasoning that led up to them."

"Yes, Your Majesty." Tolochko took a deep breath. "It's been known for a long time that the Manticore

System has some serious navigational hazards. The worst is the major disruption zone that covers nearly half of the Manticore-B hyper limit. That one has required a permanent astrogators' warning for incoming traffic to stay clear of the danger zone. Fortunately, there's not much activity into that system, and practically none from outside the Star Kingdom. There's a similar hazard at the Manticore-A hyper limit, much milder and not nearly as dangerous. It can produce translation scatter—"

"Her Majesty is familiar with those details," Harwich interrupted, a bit tartly.

"That's all right, My Lord," Elizabeth said before Tolochko could respond. "I *did* ask Dr. Tolochko for her thought process."

"Thank you, Your Majesty," Tolochko breathed. Her nervousness, which had been fading while she was talking science, now came rushing back full force. "I—as I was saying, it can produce translation scatter and tends to wear down impeller nodes. Normally not fatal, though. Fortunately."

"Yes," Elizabeth said, giving the young woman her best encouraging smile. She vaguely remembered most of this from her school days, but Tolochko's impromptu refresher course was doing a good job of clearing out the cobwebs. "Please continue."

"Yes, Your Majesty." Another deep breath. "When these were plotted many years ago, they were put down as evidence of a gravitic fault. Gravitic faults are areas where grav waves fold tightly together in hyper and—well, and create just this sort of hazard. They're not all that common, but they *are* a well-known phenomenon. The people who studied the Manticore hazards assumed that was what was causing them, mapped them for travel purposes, and then never gave it another thought."

"Until you came along?" Elizabeth prompted.

Tolochko seemed to brace herself. "Yes, Your Majesty. We've known for awhile that the intensity and danger associated with the fault in Manticore-A has been growing, and my preliminary analysis of recent survey data indicates that both regions may be shifting position as well. That analysis, plus my earlier research, has convinced me." She drew herself up, her posture and expression taking on a mix of trepidation and defiance. "I don't think they're a set of gravitic faults at all. I think they're the resonance zones associated with a wormhole junction."

"And no one believes you?" Elizabeth suggested.

Tolochko blinked, some of her defiance evaporating. Apparently, she'd expected the same scorn and outright dismissal from her sovereign as she'd received for the past ten years from the Star Kingdom's scientific community. "Well... no, Your Majesty, they don't. I've written four papers—well, that doesn't matter. But I'm sure I'm right. If you'd like, I can go through the details—"

"That's all right," Elizabeth said, keeping her voice neutral. "I think I've heard enough. Thank you for your time, Dr. Tolochko; please wait outside."

"Yes, Your Majesty," Tolochko gulped. With another bow, she hurried from the office.

Elizabeth waited until the door closed behind her, then looked back at Harwich and Dapplelake. "I take it you believe her?" she asked.

"I don't know if I personally do," Dapplelake said. "But *someone* out there apparently does."

"It's the only thing that makes sense," Harwich agreed heavily. "There's no other reason to hire Gensonne and his mercenaries to attack us unless there was something valuable here. A wormhole junction certainly fits the bill."

"And no one but Tolochko has thought about that possibility?" Elizabeth asked.

"In all fairness, it *does* violate all known wormhole theory," Dapplelake said. "I'm hardly an expert, but I did check out some of the objections to Tolochko's theory before I brought her and her report here. Among other things, the problems in Manticore-B are more powerful than anything associated with any known wormhole."

"Not to mention that current theory says you can't have a wormhole in a multiple star system," Harwich added. "I've had Lady Calvingdell and SIS sifting through the Volsung data files for any hints, but it doesn't look like Gensonne knew why he'd been brought in to attack us."

"Not surprising," Elizabeth said. "If someone suspected the Manticore System was playing host to a wormhole, they would certainly keep that information to themselves. I assume you came prepared with a recommendation?"

"Yes, Your Majesty, we have two," Harwich said.

"Neither of which is exactly a show-stopper," Dapplelake said under his breath.

"First would be for us to hire a survey ship and take a look for ourselves," Harwich said, throwing a sideways look at Dapplelake. "Unfortunately, those are quite rare, horrendously expensive, and generally booked years in advance. Second would be to bring in some experts from the League and try to pick their brains."

"Without telling them what we think they're looking for?" Elizabeth asked.

"Yes, that's the problem with that one," Harwich conceded. "If they have the intelligence and expertise we need, *someone* in the group is bound to figure it out."

Elizabeth pursed her lips. "Would that necessarily be a bad thing?"

The two men looked at each other. "It would rather paste a target on the Star Kingdom's back, Your Majesty," Dapplelake said after a moment.

"Of course it would," Elizabeth agreed. "But the people behind the Volsungs already know about it. Or it certainly appears they do, unless we want to postulate that our modest little star system is home to *two* unsuspected, incredibly valuable prizes. Perhaps telling the rest of the galaxy about it wouldn't be such a bad thing. There aren't very many star nations out there who'd try to take it away from us—not openly—when they could expect the Solarian League to take a dim view of it. And Haven and the Andermani have to be aware of the strategic implications of a wormhole this close to them."

"Though *close* is of course a purely relative term," Harwich murmured. "Especially for the Empire."

"Granted," Elizabeth said. "Regardless, I think we could expect both of them to take an even dimmer view of anyone who *did* try. So in some ways, telling everyone we can about it might be our best protection."

Dapplelake and Harwich frowned thoughtfully at one another. Then Harwich nodded.

"There might very well be something to that, Your Majesty," he said. "I wouldn't want to *depend* on the notion that anyone who'd be willing to seize it by force in the first place would be deterred by the threat of Haven or Gustav, but it's certainly possible. My concern is that if whoever hired Gensonne realizes we've figured out what they're after, they might accelerate their timetable."

"Though there's a limit to how much they *can* accelerate it, given the distances and communication times involved," Dapplelake pointed out. "Even if word of our suspicions gets out—and it'll take months for them to even hear about it, most likely—they'd probably need quite some time to rearrange their plans in any significant way."

"Which doesn't mean they *couldn't* do it, though," Harwich warned.

"Agreed," Dapplelake said. "And if they recognize the potential upsides for us of our making the existence of any wormhole public as clearly as you do, Your Majesty, they probably *would* decide to throw the dice—if they can get everything moving—as quickly as possible. They'd want to take us over before any of those positive factors could get in their way."

"I see your point," Elizabeth said. "I expect it could be argued ether way, but keeping it a secret isn't likely to *hurt* us any. Not where whoever already knows about it is concerned, anyway. We're not going to have any choice about going public in the end, though, so I think we'd all better start thinking about how we handle that if—or rather, *when*—one of our guests does figure it out. In the meantime, we keep a lid on it. Which brings us back to how we keep any of the smart, well informed people whose brains we need to pick from figuring out why we really invited them. At least for as long as we can."

"We can certainly start by pitching it as an examination of the Manticore gravitic fault," Dapplelake suggested. "The fact that it's stronger than most of the handful of faults that have been discovered and mapped should make it interesting enough to persuade at least some of them to make the journey. Framing it that way would at least start them out looking a different direction."

"Through probably not for long," Elizabeth said.

Harwich's lip twitched. "No, Your Majesty, probably not."

Elizabeth nodded, running the options through her mind. As Dapplelake had warned, neither of them was leaping off the page at her.

But they had to do *something*. Someone out there already knew or suspected, and that someone was unlikely to be deterred just because Gensonne had gotten his nose bloodied. "I agree a conference is our best bet," she said. "As you suggest, My Lord, we'll tell potential attendees that the gravitic faults are shifting—which appears to be true based on the data analysis Dr. Tolochko has done—and that we need to get a better handle on them before they become a serious navigation hazard."

"Very good, Your Majesty," Harwich said. "Shall I start making a list of people and organizations we should invite?"

"Yes," Elizabeth said. "Get Dr. Tolochko to help with that. In fact, you might as well tell her now that she's going to be heading up the conference."

It wasn't often that she saw two such simultaneous flashes of stunned disbelief. But Harwich and Dapplelake managed it. "Dr. *Tolochko?*" Dapplelake said. "But she's—"

"Young?" Elizabeth offered. "Yes, she is. She's also the only one who spotted this and kept at it. She's got the credentials and the perseverance, and she speaks the technical language of the people we're inviting." She raised her eyebrows. "Unless you'd rather one of those who've been ignoring her for the past decade be put in charge."

"Hardly, Your Majesty," Harwich said wryly. "Certainly not when you put it that way. Dapplelake?"

Dapplelake waved a hand. "You're the one who found her. You should be the one to tell her she's been promoted to this freshly built hot seat."

"You're too kind," Harwich said.

"Good," Elizabeth said. "And while Tolochko and Lord Harwich build their list, you, Lord Dapplelake, will start organizing the trip itself."

"Yes, Your Majesty," Dapplelake said. "I presume the purpose of the voyage will *not* be common knowledge?"

"Absolutely not," Elizabeth said. "We start by downplaying the urgency. Dr. Tolochko's analysis indicates that the shift has been gradual, and was only noticeable over decades of readings. No rush, no worry, no drama."

"Hence, a routine little conference," Harwich murmured, nodding.

"Exactly," Elizabeth said. "We also downplay the guest list so people won't realize what a high-powered crew we're trying to put together."

"Yes," Dapplelake said. "Though I doubt anyone

outside that specific area of the scientific community would recognize any of the names anyway."

"True," Elizabeth agreed. "Anything else?"

"One other question, Your Majesty," Harwich said, his voice suddenly hesitant. "The rest of the Cabinet. How much of this do we tell them?"

That was, Elizabeth realized, a damn good question. And it spoke to how distracted her pregnancy had made her that she hadn't even thought about it.

Unfortunately, she didn't have much choice. There were Cabinet ministers she could trust to keep such an explosive secret through the months and possibly the years until the conference actually began. There were others she couldn't trust to keep it past dinner time. "We tell them the cover story I just gave you," she said. "Nothing more."

"Yes, Your Majesty," Harwich said carefully. "You realize that when they *do* find out...?"

"There will be hell to pay," Elizabeth said, nodding. "Yes, I know. But better hell to pay tomorrow than hell to pay today. We know someone out there is gunning for us, and if their timetable *can* be moved up, I'd rather not find out the hard way."

"Nor would we, Your Majesty," Harwich said. "Nor would we. Very well. We'll get on this right away."

"Thank you, My Lords," Elizabeth said. "And when you're finished with that, you might take a few minutes to think about what a wormhole in the system is likely to mean for us. Economically, culturally... and militarily."

CHAPTER TWO

JEREMIAH LLYN SCOWLED. *Where am I going,* he quoted the old adage to himself, *and what am I doing in this handbasket?*

The whole Manticore project had been a complete fiasco. What was worse, the chaos hadn't just engulfed his own part of the plan, but everyone else's as well.

The Volsung attack on Manticore had failed. Gensonne and his mercs had been subsequently destroyed, but not nearly as cleanly as Llyn had hoped. There were still a couple of loose ends out there: one of them a Volsung ship that had managed to evade the Danak ambush, the other the still-unidentified force that had destroyed the Volsungs' main base at Walther.

The Barcans who'd been sent to take over the Star Kingdom as its new puppet government were another loose end. They'd been chased back home and were cowering there, but the Grand Duke was still clamoring for explanations and additional payments. Unfortunately, their force had identified its point of origin during their brief pass through Manticoran space, and sooner or later the Manticorans would undoubtedly send someone there to find out what the hell had been going on. Closing off that line of inquiry would mean more expense, either in bribes or perhaps in sheer ruthless destruction.

All points which the project manager at Axelrod's Solway station had taken care to list in excruciating detail during the other's genteel, almost civil, tongue-lashing. Llyn had had to sit there and take it, just as he'd had to sit there and accept that he'd been bounced off the main Manticore campaign and transferred to the far less interesting Andermani diversion. But he was a professional, and knew how to take orders.

Which didn't mean he agreed with a single damn bit of it.

Yes, the Volsungs had had their butts handed to them. But their defeat wasn't Llyn's fault. Their record had offered no hints of tactical incompetence, and on paper they'd still been more than a match for the Manticorans. The only reason they'd lost was that the Manticorans had managed to pull off a couple of incredibly lucky tricks that had cost the Volsungs two of their battle-cruisers, which had unnerved them enough to break off the battle.

Still, it could have been worse. If the Haven and Andermani diversions had gone off on schedule, with the Manticoran goal as yet unachieved, the diversions would have had to be repeated at a later date, which would likely have raised suspicions all the way back to the League.

Fortunately, they'd been planned to take place months after the Manticore conquest, close enough to the event to draw those governments' attention away from their neighbor but not so close as to make anyone wonder why there was so much carnage happening in the same sector at the same time. That built-in delay had enabled the

Axelrod agents in charge to put those operations on hold while the architects on Solway worked out a new strategy.

Haven would keep. The Andermani, unfortunately, wouldn't. That particular diversion had relied on the manipulation of two separate and equally unsuspecting people—PFT Chief Director Lucretia Tomlinson and Quintessence Commodore Catt Quint—neither of whom realized exactly what they were being used for.

In theory, that was a good thing, allowing Axelrod to hit the Andermani with someone else's money and someone else's ships while keeping Llyn's bosses deeper in the shadows. It was also saving them a tidy sum in out-of-pocket expenses.

But that anonymity and manipulation had carried potential risks, and those risks had now come home to roost. Director Tomlinson had paid for a loaded gun, and that loaded gun was now cocked, ready to fire, and inexplicably still sitting on the table. She was beginning to wonder if she'd been had, and if that suspicion ever became certainty she would likely start making dangerous enquiries. If Llyn was to head that off, she had to see results, and soon.

At the same time the loaded gun was itself becoming increasingly frustrated at sitting on the table for the past year.

Freya Bryce was good at her job. Once she'd gotten Axelrod's order to stand down she would have worked hard to stretch out the timeline: putting Quint and her crews through extra training, probably pausing now and then to upgrade their ships with new missiles and ECM suites that she'd "just" been able to get her hands on, and all the rest of the standard Axelrod repertoire for such things.

But by now even Bryce was almost certainly running out of wiggle room. The gun that was Commodore Quint *was* going to come off the table and be fired, and soon.

It would be Llyn's job to make damn sure it was pointed in the right direction when that happened.

The timing wasn't ideal. The next operation against Manticore was still a long ways away. But if there was one thing Gustav Anderman had never been accused of it was being oblivious to danger. Abteilung III, the Andermani Department of Naval Intelligence, was incredibly good, and if they got wind of Quint and her force the hoped-for diversion would end up as a stomping in the dark, with Quint on the underside of the boot.

Still, if the object was to keep Gustav's eyes turned inward toward his own back yard for the next few years, even a rout would serve Axelrod's purposes.

It wouldn't do much for *Quint's* purposes, of course. But in the grand scheme of things, that was irrelevant.

The Quintessence's new fleet was floating just outside the hyper limit of FF-M-341-019/B: four refurbished SLN battlecruisers and their two heavy cruiser escorts, plus the three light cruisers, fifteen destroyers, and nine other support ships and civilian family transports that had survived Commodore Quint's last disastrous job.

Mentally, Llyn shook his head. Four battlecruisers plus a small group of escort and support craft against Gustav Anderman's five battleships, six battlecruisers, and dozens of smaller warships. It was probably a good thing that when Gustav decided to retire and relocate he'd picked a spot way the hell out at the edge of known space. A private fleet that size could make even major Solarian League worlds nervous.

The Quintessence ships were dark except for running

lights, their nodes reading cold. Llyn's hail was met by a polite but perfunctory welcome and directions to Quint's new flagship *Retribution*. The shuttle pilot took him the last few kilometers to the specified battlecruiser, where he was met by a large lieutenant with a neatly trimmed beard and an equally perfunctory greeting.

Llyn was used to not always being welcomed with enthusiasm and open arms. Still, the overall coolness here was a bit disquieting.

Commodore Quint was sitting behind her desk when the lieutenant keyed open the hatch. Bryce was with her, seated in a guest chair at one of the front corners. Both women were gazing at Llyn as he stepped into the office, their expressions as neutral as the lieutenant's face and the com officer's voice.

Neutral, but Llyn could see the tension lines in both women's necks and cheeks. A new metaphor flashed into his mind: not a cocked gun sitting on a table, but a full-grown tiger asleep in an oversized cat bed.

And Llyn's job was to pick up the tiger, pat it on the head, and make friends with it.

Nice kitty.

"Good evening, Commodore, Ms. Bryce," he greeted them as the lieutenant closed the hatch behind him. "I must say, your fleet out there looks quite impressive."

"You *must* say that, must you?" Quint countered. "Well, then, I must say the following. I don't like this, Mr. Llyn. I don't like it at all. An immediate corollary is that I don't like *you.*"

"I understand," Llyn said in his most soothing voice. "It's never easy—"

"No, I don't think you do," Quint cut him off. "Ms.

Bryce and I have been working this project for nearly three years, through every problem and roadblock that the universe could throw at us. Now that it's finally about to get underway, I find it highly objectionable that she should suddenly be shouldered aside for—" she waved a stiff hand toward him "—the likes of *you.*"

"I understand," Llyn said again. He glanced at Bryce.

And took a second, longer look. It wasn't just Quint who was feeling this way, he realized suddenly. Bryce was wondering the same thing, and apparently with much the same suspicion and animosity.

"But you're laboring under an incorrect assumption," he continued. Time to go full-wedge diplomatic. "Ms. Bryce isn't being kicked off her project. *I'm* being kicked off *mine.*"

For a brief second a flicker of surprise replaced the suspicion and antagonism on Quint's face. "Really," she said in a flat voice.

"Really," Llyn assured her. "And if you think about it, all the really hard work in setting you up with your new ships has been done. It's now one hundred percent your show, and all Ms. Bryce or I will be doing is observing and maybe feeding you some last-minute intel if and when it becomes available. Having watched Ms. Bryce in action, I think you'll agree that would hardly be the best use of her time or talents."

"But a perfect fit for yours?" Quint asked.

Llyn shrugged. "The life of an employee is to go where our superiors believe we'll do the most good."

"Uh-huh," Quint said. "So she gets the next big job and I get the screw-up?"

Llyn smiled faintly, suppressing the reflexive surge

of annoyance. He was *far* better at this kind of Axelrod black op than Bryce, and he had the history and records to prove it.

But he was also realistic enough to concede that, while the Volsung screw-up wasn't his fault, the fact that he'd hired them in the first place was. *Live and learn,* the old adage advised.

Learn and live was Llyn's more pointed version. It was never a good idea to assume you could survive the same mistake twice.

But the question of whether the title of screw-up applied in this case was irrelevant. Part of Llyn's competence was knowing how to play to an audience's expectations and preconceptions in order to get the job done. "I don't think I'd go *that* far," he said, putting a hint of embarrassment in his tone. "This is just the decision our superiors have made, and we have no choice but to adjust to changing circumstances."

"Uh-huh," Quint said again. She still wasn't happy about the sudden personnel switch, but with the implied insult to Bryce—and to Quint herself—now mollified she was beginning to come around, albeit reluctantly. "So when is the changeover?"

"Right now," Llyn said, watching Bryce out of the corner of his eye. No change in her expression, but he could see the slight tightening of the muscles of her hands where they rested in her lap. Quint might be starting to accept this, but Bryce herself wasn't.

"Right now, as in today?" Quint asked.

"Right now, as in within the hour," Llyn said. "I know this is all very sudden, but the timing is critical. So critical, in fact, that we don't even have time for Ms. Bryce to get to her personal ship and run up the nodes. She and I will have to swap ships: she'll travel aboard mine, and I'll take over hers."

"You're taking over her ship, are you?" Quint asked, flicking a glance at Bryce.

"Yes," Llyn said. There'd been something in that glance, but he didn't have time to chase it down now. "If you can detail someone to transfer my luggage from my shuttle and replace it with hers, she can be on her way."

"No problem, Mr. Llyn," Quint said, standing up. "I'll see to it personally."

"Thank you, Commodore." Translation: she wanted to do her own quick inspection of what he was bringing aboard her ship.

Which was fine. Llyn didn't have anything dangerous or secret, or at least nothing that even a serious search would spot, and he needed a moment alone with Bryce anyway. "With your permission, I have a few last-minute instructions for Ms. Bryce."

"Certainly," Quint said dryly. "My office is yours."

She walked behind Bryce and left the office. As the door closed, Llyn caught a glimpse of the bearded lieutenant still standing outside, with no indication that he might be leaving any time soon.

Quint's office might be Llyn's office, but Quint's ship wasn't. Not yet.

"*Seriously*, Llyn?" Bryce growled. "They're pulling me off this *now*?"

Llyn turned back to her. With no further need to keep up the illusion of corporate unity, Bryce's face had gone dark and hostile. "They're not pulling you off, Freya," he said. "They're putting you in—"

"Yeah, I heard your soap bubble," she cut him off. "I don't believe it any more than Quint did."

"Well, you'd better, because it's true," he said. "You want to listen now? Or would you rather read the text on your way?"

She scowled. "Fine. What's the deal?"

"A moment," Llyn said, reaching into his jacket pocket. A merc commander didn't usually bug her own office, but there was no point taking chances.

"It's okay—I've already got a blocker going," Bryce said. "Quit stalling."

"We need to get someone on the ground," Llyn said, passing over the implied insult. "That's going to be you."

"How are they sending me in?"

"We don't know yet," Llyn said. "Your orders are to proceed as quickly as possible or a little faster—their exact words—to Solway for a skull session. They'll presumably have some ideas by the time you get there, but they'll want your input to help tailor the role if necessary."

"With the usual escape clause built in so that Axelrod can keep their fingers clean if something goes sideways?"

"Of course," Llyn said. "We're expendable. They're not."

A brief shadow passed across Bryce's face. It was a shadow, and a thought, that Llyn knew quite well.

No matter how valuable Black Ops agents were to Axelrod, no matter how well they'd served over the years, if it came to a choice between them and the company's standing, they would be abandoned without a second thought, to sink or swim as best they could.

So far it hadn't happened to either him or Bryce. But it had happened to others. Not very many, but it *had* happened.

"Any other questions?" he asked.

The shadow faded from Bryce's face. "Just one. Why me and not you?"

Llyn scowled to himself. Too many failures, too, could be grounds for leaving an agent twisting in the wind. "My face—or at least a variant of it—has been seen by too many Manticorans. My voice, even staged or altered, is on too many recordings. Even the best disguise can be cracked, and it's been deemed too dangerous for me to take another shot at them."

"So you weren't lying," Bryce said, sounding mildly surprised. "You *are* being kicked off your project."

"I'm not off the project," Llyn said stiffly. "I've been transferred to another theater. Not the same thing."

"Sure," she said, a faint smile creasing one cheek. "The great Jeremiah Llyn; and you don't like it any better than the rest of us, do you?"

"You don't have to like your assignments," Llyn growled. "You just have to do them. Any other questions?"

"I presume everything else is in the file?"

"Yes." Llyn pulled an envelope from his inside jacket pocket and handed it to her. "Your ID and other papers, and the data chips that should explain everything else you need to know. My captain's name is Rhamas; he'll get you to Solway and handle any last-minute details you might think of."

"I've heard of him," Bryce said, fingering the envelope a moment before putting it away. "One other thing. You talked earlier about switching ships with me. I don't actually have one at the moment."

Llyn felt his eyes narrow. "What are you talking about? What happened to *Docent*?"

"One of the nodes went iffy while we were install-
ing the new launchers and Sandor took it to one of
the Cormorant maintenance stations for refurbishing.
Quint offered me a berth on *Retribution*, and it was
so convenient to be right here on board that when the
refurbishing was finished I told Sandor to go back to
Transfer Three and wait there until we got the green
light for the operation or until they needed him and
Docent somewhere else."

"Really," Llyn said between clenched teeth. Technically, Bryce was within her operational discretion to
dismiss her captain and ship. But joining a force of
mercenaries about to go into battle without a means
of quick escape if things went sideways was foolish
in the extreme.

Unfortunately, her short-sightedness had now spilled
over onto him. Unless he wanted to swing by Transfer
and get *Docent* back, which would add extra delay
to his already strained timing, he was stuck in the
no-escape box she'd walked herself into.

Unless that had been the plan all along.

Axelrod Black Ops agents were the best of the best,
their very anonymity and lack of public recognition
perversely driving a quiet but vigorous internecine
competition. In an operation as carefully compartmen-
talized as the Manticore project most of the agents
didn't know more than their own part of the job,
which helped alleviate any overt one-on-one rivalry.
But a few agents held multiple strings, and of course
someone had to have a grip on all of them. Right
now, Llyn's boss was that someone.

But if Bryce didn't have all the strings, she had almost
certainly deduced the presence and general parameters

of many of them. She knew what had happened with the Volsungs at Manticore, and might have anticipated that Axelrod would decide to shift Llyn elsewhere. With the Haven diversion on hold, the Anderman theater was the only logical place for them to shift him.

Was she angry that after all her prep work the glory of the actual battle was about to be taken away from her? Or was it more childish, a way to make Llyn sweat a little without his usual hole card?

Or was it an even longer game? Was Bryce trying to slowly erode Llyn's position and reputation in a bid to succeed to his rank in the Black Ops hierarchy?

Bryce certainly would never sabotage an operation. That would be unthinkable, not to mention fatal to her own career. But bringing about a successful result while working against Llyn beneath the surface was entirely possible.

Bryce was well-respected, but she wasn't the *most* respected. But she was definitely one of the most ambitious.

"I hope that's not a problem," Bryce said, her voice one hundred percent sincere and respectful. "If you'd like, I could swing by Transfer on my way to Solway and tell him to meet you somewhere."

Which she couldn't, of course, given the imperative nature of her orders. Which of course she knew. "That's all right," he told her, matching her sincerity and mixing in a perfect facsimile of nonchalance. "I've lived in worse places than a warship cabin. I'll get by."

"Okay," Bryce said, standing up. "I'd better get going. Don't want to keep Captain Rhamas waiting."

"No, you don't," Llyn said. "Watch yourself, and good luck. We need this one."

"You'll get it." Flashing a tight smile, she left the office.

Llyn scowled after her, wondering briefly if he should screen Rhamas and warn him about his new passenger. A waste of time, he decided—even if Bryce had designs against Llyn himself, Rhamas was certainly not in her sights. Messing with him could wreck her mission, and her reputation, before it even started.

No, Llyn's best strategy at this point was to ignore Bryce and concentrate on making sure the Andermani part of the operation was a resounding success.

And, of course, not getting himself killed in the process.

☆   ☆   ☆

He was sorting his clothing into the various cubbies in his cabin when he had an unexpected visitor.

"Settling in?" Quint asked, pausing just inside the doorway.

"Getting there," Llyn assured her. "Ms. Bryce on her way?"

"Heading toward the hyper limit at an impressive two hundred thirty gees," Quint said. "Your friends have interesting ships."

"Yes, they do." Llyn raised his eyebrows. "Fast *and* untraceable."

Quint's lips twisted in a wry smile. "Touché," she said. "Can't blame a girl for trying." The smile faded. "Or can you?"

"Not at all," Llyn assured her. "In your place, I'd have done the same thing. We're both people who like to know who we're working with. Sorry I can't be more forthcoming."

"Not a problem," Quint said. "Your people are paying

well for the privilege of being anonymous." She held out her hand. "I brought you a present."

"What is it?" Llyn asked, frowning as he took the data chip.

"Everything about my new fleet," she said. "Stats, weapons systems, personnel—the works."

"Really," Llyn said, frowning a little harder. "Why?"

"You said earlier that you might have advice and fresh intel along the way." She shrugged. "Advice is always better if you know as many of the parameters as possible."

"I agree," Llyn said, eyeing her. A hard, pragmatic merc chief. In some ways, she was just like the Volsungs' Admiral Cutler Gensonne.

In other ways, she was an exact polar opposite.

"Thank you," he said, tucking the data chip into a secure pocket. "As soon as I'm finished here I'll get started on it."

"Good," Quint said. "Dinner's in the wardroom at nineteen hundred. We'll expect you there."

"You—? Excuse me?"

"You said we're both the type who like to know who we're working with," Quint said. "Might as well start out over a good meal."

She nodded briskly and left the cabin.

For a long moment Llyn stared after her. He was used to not trusting people, and being not trusted in return. And civility and smiles aside, he certainly didn't trust Commodore Quint. Not yet, anyway.

But at the very least, this trip was starting to look very interesting. Very interesting indeed.

CHAPTER THREE

"I TALKED TO THE FLORIST this morning," Commander Lisa Donnelly said as she carefully speared a crouton with her fork. "Those roses we wanted have come in."

"That's the last of them, right?" Lieutenant Commander Travis Long asked, cutting off a piece of fish.

"As far as I know." Lisa smiled impishly. "Sorry yet that I said yes?"

"Hardly," Travis assured her, reaching across the table to squeeze her free hand. "However, I'm starting to think it was easier to plan the attack on Walther than this wedding."

"Be grateful we didn't have to rent a church or hall," Lisa said. "That would have added an entirely new layer to the proceedings."

"Um," Travis said, putting the bite of fish in his mouth. He still didn't know why *Damocles*'s commander, Captain Hari Marcello, had offered his home for his XO's wedding.

Granted, Marcello's wife came from money, the house was tastefully regal, and the great room was more than adequate for the modest ceremony Travis and Lisa had

68

planned. But it still seemed odd, and Travis wasn't yet sure if he was comfortable with the arrangement.

With the wedding only a week away, though, he'd better get comfortable with it in a hurry.

"So is Basaltberg the new buttered toast?" Lisa asked.

Travis blinked. "What?"

"You know, like something is the greatest thing since buttered toast," Lisa said, her expression studiously casual. "You keep comparing things to the attack on Walther. I'm just wondering if that's your new standard for complication, like buttered toast is the standard for greatness."

"I don't keep saying that," Travis protested, frowning as he searched his memory. As far as he could recall, he hadn't even mentioned Admiral Basaltberg and the joint Manticoran/Andermani attack on the Volsung base since he'd told Lisa all about it two months ago. "When else did I say that?"

"When we were ordering the cake."

"I wasn't talking about difficulty there," Travis protested. "I just said—" he broke off, feeling his face warming as the full memory clicked.

"Right," Lisa said, her eyes twinkling. "You said the cake would feed the entire crew of an Andermani battleship. Then there was that Czech waiter at Puffin's Roost—you said his accent was thicker than Andermani German. Then there was—"

"Okay, okay," Travis cut in. "Point taken. Sorry, but that whole thing was . . . well, it made a huge impression on me, okay? Not just the battle itself, but also realizing how pathetically unprofessional and out-of-date the whole RMN is."

"Careful," Lisa warned. "Talk like that will get you

thrown off your ship and dumped into a classroom. Oh, wait," she added, brightening. "You've already done that."

"Not necessarily," Travis said, trying hard to get a little dignity back. A waste of effort; Lisa was an expert at stripping away such things.

But only the surface dignity, the layer Travis automatically put up as armor against the world around him. She never touched the inner dignity, the core of humanity and the essence of what made him who he was. He'd pondered that long and hard, and had eventually concluded that she simply didn't want him trying to pretend he was anyone but the man she knew him to be, no matter how slightly skewed from reality the image and pretense might be.

Which Travis was fine with when it was just with her. With Lisa, he was perfectly comfortable opening himself up completely. It was the rest of the world he was still a little leery of. He'd been shot at too many times to leave the personality armor at home.

"Or at least maybe not permanently," he continued. "A guy I know in BuPers says I'm going to be getting new orders, possibly for a battlecruiser."

"Really," Lisa said, sitting up a little straighter. "Which one?"

"That part he was a little vague on," Travis said. "I think they're still shuffling people around and are looking to see where I would fit best." He considered. "Or looking for a captain who's willing to take me."

"Oh, come on—Clegg's report on you can't have been *that* bad."

"I don't know," Travis said, wincing a little at the memory of all those strained or outright hostile encounters he'd had with *Casey*'s commander on that last voyage. "Just because we won doesn't mean all the personal problems went away. She probably gave the credit for the victory to the Andermani—which she would be totally right to do—and warned them that anyone offering me a berth should make it a wide one."

"I think she was probably fairer than that," Lisa said. "But anyway, a battlecruiser would be good for you. Not that *Casey*'s not a plum assignment, but TO on a battlecruiser is the real launching spot for a major command."

"Especially after . . . ?" He paused, raising his eyebrows invitingly.

"Fine," she said, sighing in mock defeat. "After Walther. Fair warning: I hope you've got all that out of your system, because after today I don't want you talking any more about Basaltberg or the Andermani or Walther—"

She broke off, lifting her uni-link and keying it. "Donnelly," she said, her voice going all brisk and professional.

The speaker was set for directional, and Travis couldn't hear what the person at the other end was saying. But suddenly Lisa's throat tightened, and he saw some of the color drain from her face. "On my way," she said, standing up as she keyed off.

"What is it?" Travis asked, standing up as well and beckoning urgently to the waitress.

"They're activating Response Alpha," Lisa said, her voice grim. "Perimeter just reported a hyper footprint. Two contacts, twelve light minutes out, just off a least-time course for Manticore."

Travis hissed under his breath. Twelve minutes until an ID beacon or voice transmission could arrive. Twelve minutes for the RMN to scramble to a war footing, hoping for the best but fearing the worst.

Twelve minutes before they knew if they were once

again about to be thrown into a battle for the Star Kingdom's survival.

So far it was just two ships. But that didn't mean there weren't more lurking out in the darkness.

"*Damocles* still on ready-60?" he asked.

"Yes," Lisa said as she headed toward the café door. "Sorry."

"Yeah, yeah, go," Travis said. The waitress held out her tablet with the bill, and he punched in the payment. "Hang on," he said, hurrying to catch up. "I'll drive—you might need to talk to people."

☆   ☆   ☆

"Systems are coming up on schedule," Marcello's voice came from Lisa's uni-link as Travis burned through the sky toward the shuttle landing field. "Where are you?"

"Close, Sir," Lisa said, looking out at the cityscape below and doing a quick calculation. "About two minutes from the dock."

"Very good, Commander. There's a shuttle prepped and waiting, with another dozen aboard or on their way. ETD, about five minutes. Is your fiancé with you?"

"Yes, Sir. We were just at lunch."

"Hammering out the final wedding details, no doubt. Well, tell him I wish I could bring him aboard, but this time around we've got our full complement."

"Understood, Sir," Lisa said, looking sideways at Travis. The uni-link's speaker was on directional, but the echo effect inside closed spaces sometimes opened up the range of audibility.

But if Travis had heard, he gave no sign. His full attention was probably split between his driving and doing the same mental countdown Lisa was on when the intruders' ID beacons or voice messages would arrive.

"And remind him to go easy on the accelerator," Marcello added dryly. "He gets hit with a police override it'll not only make you late, it'll ruin his squeaky reputation. See you soon, XO."

The captain's voice clicked off, replaced by the feed from the secure com net designed to keep all the officers, those already aboard as well as those on their way, abreast of the ship's status. Lisa listened closely to the mix of brisk conversation and system reports from *Damocles*'s various departments, paying special attention to the tones and stress levels of those voices.

But the months of status and planning revisions the RMN had instituted since the last time unknowns had entered the system—not to mention a double boatload of drills—had paid off. While everyone she could hear was clearly alert, no one seemed anywhere near the edge of panic. They, and *Damocles*, would be ready whenever the intruders' signal reached them.

Assuming whoever was out there *wanted* to talk. The Volsung Mercenaries who'd come to wipe out the Star Kingdom two years ago hadn't. Maybe this new batch of invaders wouldn't, either.

On paper, of course, a pair of ships barely qualified as a threat, especially with the Royal Manticoran Navy in far better shape now than it had been during the Volsung attack. But Lisa knew better than to let that fool her. Just because they could only see a single battlecruiser didn't mean there weren't more ships out there, either hiding behind the main ships' wedges or else sweeping in on ballistic vectors from other directions with their wedges down, completely invisible until they reached sensor range. Whatever the intruder said or didn't say, the RMN was still going to a war footing.

Lisa would be part of that defensive line. Travis wouldn't.

Again, she sent him a sideways look. A minute and a half from the shuttle; maybe half a minute until the ID signal reached them. Just enough time to land, exchange a quick kiss, and race off in their separate ways.

Or *would* he kiss her? Travis was a little awkward about public displays of affection, especially when they were both in uniform and surrounded by other RMN personnel. Even with her possibly going to her death, would he unbend enough for a final kiss?

For that matter, did she even *want* him to kiss her?

She wanted him to, of course. Wanted it desperately. But at the same time, all the novels she'd read while growing up, all the dramas and tear-jerkers she'd seen in her teenage years, had generated a quiet but firm voice in the back of her head warning her that a dramatic good-bye kiss was a sure omen of impending death for one or both of the participants. If Travis kissed her, did that mean she was doomed to die, alone, in the cold vacuum of space?

Nonsense, of course. Utter melodramatic, illogical, hack-writer nonsense.

But the voice refused to go away.

"Should be here," Travis murmured.

Lisa shook away the horrible image of herself floating lifeless through the wreckage of what had once been her ship. He was right: the ID should have arrived a few seconds ago. Right now Admiral Carlton Locatelli and Defense Minister Dapplelake were pondering their new information, perhaps listening to whatever message had come along with the ID. Pondering the Star Kingdom's response...

Abruptly, the conversation from *Damocles* cut off. There was a brief pause—

"—best wishes from His Majesty, Emperor Gustav of the Andermani Empire," a hearty, heavily accented voice boomed from the speaker. "The Emperor feels we are long overdue for an official visit to our neighbors in the Star Kingdom of Manticore, as we've also been negligent in our obligation to greet and pay our full and proper respects to Her Majesty Queen Elizabeth the Second. I trust our arrival is not at an inconvenient time; as you of course know, the realities of distance are not conducive to advance notice.

"Please respond at your convenience as to which approach vector and orbital lane you wish us to use. I will look forward to meeting in person and in due course with your Queen and other officials. Repeating: Greetings to the Star Kingdom of Manticore. I am Admiral Gotthold Riefenstahl, Graf von Basaltberg, commanding a diplomatic mission aboard SMS *Zhong Kui*. I bring you best wishes from His Majesty, Emperor Gustav of the Andermani Empire—"

Belatedly, Lisa realized the speaker was still on directional and keyed it to general. "Travis—"

"Yeah," he breathed. His eyes still focused forward, but they now held a completely sandbagged look.

Apparently, he *had* been able to hear the focused speaker.

Lisa let the message run another full repetition anyway before keying it back to directional.

"Well," she said. For once, she couldn't think of anything else to say.

"I'll be damned," Travis said, sounding completely sandbagged. "Of all the people in the galaxy…"

"I assume that *was* him?" Lisa asked.

"Oh, yes," Travis assured her. "Admiral Basaltberg. Big, bluff, and incredibly competent."

"And condescending?" Lisa suggested, remembering some of Travis's stories about *Casey*'s time with Basaltberg.

"Hardly at all, really, and only when we deserved it," Travis assured her.

"Okay." Lisa took a deep breath, still listening with half an ear to *Damocles*'s status feed. "Okay. The captain's ramped us down to Readiness Two, but I still have to get aboard."

"I know," Travis said as he dropped the air car toward the pad.

"One other thing," Lisa added as her brain began to come on-line again. "About your promise earlier. I guess that if you *really* feel the need to talk about the Andermani some more, I'm okay with it."

"Thanks," Travis said dryly, giving her a lopsided smile. "It's good to have official permission."

"You're welcome," Lisa said. "Hey, that's just the kind of person I am."

And with the danger past, and her private fears put back to sleep, she was *definitely* going to get that good-bye kiss.

☆   ☆   ☆

Unlike most of the room number plaques in the Admiralty Building, the one for Room 2021 wasn't accompanied by any additional name or department ID plates. Most of the Navy personnel who passed by probably didn't really notice, while those who did probably assumed it was an office so deep in the bowels of BuPers that its occupant didn't rate anything but a room number.

But then, Senior Chief Charles "Chomps" Townsend thought as he pushed open the door and headed inside, he'd always liked assumptions, especially those the assumer didn't even realize he or she was making. Such assumptions formed the underpinnings of many magic tricks—and way too many political speeches—and were an equally useful tool to anyone in intelligence work.

Which was handy, because behind the door of Room 2021 was the nerve center of Delphi, the Star Kingdom of Manticore's almost-brand-new Special Intelligence Service.

Flora Taylor was sitting at her usual gatekeeper desk in the small anteroom, smiling pleasantly and keying open the inner door for everyone who was authorized to be there, and merely smiling pleasantly at everyone who wasn't. "Hey, Flora," Chomps greeted her as he closed the door behind him. "The boss in?"

"*Lady Calvingdell* is in, yes, Senior Chief," Flora said, her tone a couple of degrees cooler than her smile. For all the casual camaraderie between Delphi's personnel, Flora still insisted on maintaining proper decorum where the SIS chief was concerned. She'd reprimanded Chomps for his attitude once or twice, then apparently given it up as hopeless.

"Thanks," Chomps said, circling the desk and heading for the door behind her. The room's bank of sensors and facial-recognition programs had already given him the once-over, confirmed he was allowed inside, and put up a subtle green bar at the bottom of Flora's computer display. The door's lock snicked off as he reached it, and he pushed his way through.

He'd expected to find a beehive of semi-chaotic activity. To his surprise, there were only six other men and women in the large main room, all busily working at their computers, while Clara Sumner, Lady Calvingdell, stood behind them with her arms folded across her chest. She half turned as the door opened, saw it was Chomps, and jabbed a finger toward another computer halfway across the room. He nodded acknowledgment of the order and angled toward it as Calvingdell also headed that way.

They reached the computer at the same time. "Townsend," Calvingdell greeted him, waving him to the chair. Her face was tense, but there was an extra glint to her eyes. "I appreciate you coming in on such short notice."

"No problem, My Lady," Chomps said as he carefully lowered his Sphinxian bulk into the chair. The Navy acknowledged the presence of Sphinxians in the Academy, but he never entirely trusted the furniture to have gotten the memo. "What's going on?"

"First, you need to hear the following message," Calvingdell said, leaning over his shoulder and tapping a key. "It came through from the battlecruiser that hit the hyper limit about an hour ago."

Chomps had just enough time for a startled look—a *battlecruiser?*—when a familiar voice boomed from the speaker. "Greetings to the Star Kingdom of Manticore. I am Admiral Gotthold Riefenstahl, Graf von Basaltberg, commanding a diplomatic mission—"

Calvingdell let the message play out, then keyed it off. "We've compared the message to recordings Captain Clegg brought back from Walther," she said. "The analysts say it's a ninety-nine-plus probability that this is indeed the man you met there."

"I agree, My Lady," Chomps said. "Not just the

voice, but the intonation, cadence, and phrasing. If this is a trick, it's a very good one."

"Yes," Calvingdell said grimly. "But I'd expect nothing less from our friend Smiley."

Chomps scowled. *Smiley*—the Delphi nickname for the master manipulator and casual murderer who'd already crossed the Star Kingdom's path at least three times. Would the man *really* have the chutzpah to try for a fourth? "Impersonating an Andermani admiral is a pretty risky move," he pointed out.

"So is bringing in a mercenary gang to attack a sovereign star nation," Calvingdell countered. "Don't worry, Locatelli is just as paranoid as I am, and it's his job to get the RMN ready in case this *is* a trick." She smiled thinly. "It's *our* job, on the other hand, to be ready in case this really is the Andermani reaching out to us."

Chomps nodded. He saw now where this was going. "Understood, My Lady. Do you want me to be part of the welcoming committee, or just hang around at meetings and parties."

Calvingdell frowned. "What in the world gave you the impression that you'll be attending parties with the upper brass, Senior Chief? No, I just want you to write down everything you can remember about Basaltberg. Not just what's in your official report, but every nuance of conversation, body language, likes, dislikes, sense of humor, and everything else."

"Okay," Chomps said mechanically, his mind still back on the first part of her answer. "With all due respect, My Lady, I assumed you'd want me to put all that into action. It's a lot easier for me to read Basaltberg directly than for you to try to teach someone else how to do it."

"That's what Long will be there for," Calvingdell said. "Long *and* Clegg."

"I'm better than Travis at that sort of thing," Chomps persisted. "And Clegg hasn't got any training at all."

"I'm sure you're right on both counts," Calvingdell said. "Unfortunately, because of your unique standing aboard *Casey*, you interacted with Basaltberg way more than any of her other petty officers. He can greet senior officers like Clegg and Long like old friends without problem. But someone might notice and wonder if he did the same with you."

Chomps took a careful breath. There had to be a properly respectful and diplomatic way to say this . . .

"Yes, it's ridiculous and paranoid," Calvingdell went on sourly. "It also wasn't my decision. ONI is still unhappy about sharing their sandbox, and they don't want us hogging the spotlight on this."

Chomps huffed out an exasperated sigh. The Office of Naval Intelligence had been brought into the secret of Delphi's existence shortly after the Silesian mission, and had been glowering about it ever since. The fact that Chomps and Travis had brought back a treasure trove of data—data which ONI hadn't had a single thing to do with—hadn't helped their attitude any.

Chomps had hoped the resulting turf wars between Calvingdell and ONI Director Admiral Barnum Knox might have settled down by now. Apparently, they hadn't.

"If you'll excuse the language, My Lady, it seems to me that a royal *screw you* is in order here," he said. "Basaltberg's mission is clearly political in nature, whether it's being carried out by the Andermani military or not, which puts it squarely into our laps. Besides which, we're already in position with Basaltberg and ONI isn't."

"Indeed," Calvingdell said. "And you think I somehow missed those points in our discussions?"

Chomps winced. "No, of course not," he said. "Sorry."

"So we play nice," Calvingdell said. "Aside from the fact that they'd dearly love an excuse to shut us down, we're facing an unknown threat out there and only a fool fights over the buffet table when the avalanche is rolling down at him. Understood?"

"Understood, My Lady."

"Good," Calvingdell said. "So here's what you're going to do. You're going to give me everything you can on Basaltberg, then you're to go on leave for a couple of weeks, or until the diplomats decide they've talked enough and call it a day. Someplace outside of Landing, preferably. Sphinxians are a bit—shall we say *noticeable*?—and no one wants to risk Basaltberg spotting you in a crowd."

"How very prudent of them," Chomps muttered. "I don't suppose Delphi might be willing to pay for this forced leave?"

"As a matter of fact, we are," Calvingdell said. The small smile made a brief reappearance. "Nice to know I can still surprise you. Now get busy. Basaltberg will make orbit in about five hours, and I want you gone by then." She gave him a brisk nod and headed back toward her lurker position behind the other analysts.

Chomps watched her first few steps, a sour feeling in the pit of his stomach, as his visions of dress uniforms, elite company, and free food evaporated.

Still, he couldn't argue with her logic. For decades ONI had been the Star Kingdom's sole foreign intelligence agency, collecting data for both the Navy and the Foreign Secretary. With the latter office being largely ceremonial, though, its needs tended to get ignored as ONI focused more and more on military intel. Furthermore, the same inertia that had once affected the entire Navy had seeped into ONI as well, leaving it hidebound and heavily political, to the point where its small staff had done little except read dispatches as they came in and drool over ads for weapon systems the RMN would never have the budget to buy.

It was that lack of genuine usefulness that had prompted the creation of Delphi four years ago, and as far as Chomps was concerned it had more than proven its value.

But ONI was still there, it was still staffed by the privileged few, and—most important of all—still had more than its fair share of support in the Navy and among several influential members of the Lords. The last thing any of them wanted was a toe-to-toe fight, at least not until Delphi had proved itself beyond anyone's ability to scoff.

The mission to Silesia and *Casey*'s joint mission with the Andermani had been a good start. Basaltberg's presence here was ample proof of that. But Calvingdell clearly wanted more.

And really, it had been a long time since Chomps had had a genuine vacation. Especially a paid one. Flexing his thick fingers, he got to work.

And as he worked, he wondered.

If people like him weren't going to the grand galas being planned for the Andermani, who *was* being invited?

CHAPTER FOUR

OH, MY GOD, GAVIN VELLACOTT, Baron Winterfall, mouthed silently to himself as the recording played itself out. This wasn't happening. This *couldn't* be happening. But it was.

The recording ended. Seated at the head of the table, Prime Minister Julian Mulholland, Baron Harwich, cleared his throat. "Comments?" he invited.

Winterfall sent a furtive look around the table. Most of the men and women of the Cabinet had occupied their same posts for years and were old hands at this. In the eight months since Winterfall had been named Foreign Secretary, in fact, only two other new faces had been added.

But those turnovers had been accompanied by high levels of quiet drama. Would that drama, he wondered, find a resurgence with today's news?

"I hope everyone realizes," Olga Strait, Baroness Crystal Pine, jumped into the silence, "what a tremendous opportunity this is."

Winterfall winced. And thus it began.

Everyone else at the table was worried about military and political implications of the unexpected arrival. Crystal Pine could see only the potential profits.

Though there was no reason anyone should have expected anything different from her. The new Secretary of Industry had only joined the House of Lords five months ago, following the terrible air-car accident that had killed Jonathan Martinez, Duke Serisburg, and his entire remaining family. And while Crystal Pine's enthusiasm for her new post was evident, she still didn't quite have the niceties of proper closed-room protocol down pat.

Not all of that was her fault, of course. The death of an entire Peerage was a situation that none of the Founders had ever wanted to happen, but in the middle of the wholesale death that was the Plague Years they'd had the foresight to make sure it was addressed in the Constitution. In the aftermath of the accident, with the rest of Serisburg's family already gone, the duchy's lands had been turned over to the Crown while the vacant seat had been handed to the next investor of the original Manticore Corporation.

The deaths had been a traumatic time for everyone in the Lords, most of whom had known and worked alongside Serisburg for years. Crystal Pine had had an uphill climb against all that emotion, plus a whole lot of it's-always-been-this-way-and-I-see-no-reason-to-change-it mindset. That institutional inertia, along with Crystal Pine's lack of upper-level political experience, had naturally led to a certain animosity toward her, along with the general assumption that she would sit quietly for the first year or two as she sorted out the differences between her old local parliament and the far more tangled labyrinth that was the Lords.

But to everyone's surprise—and some people's resentment—she'd instead hit the ground running, soaking in everything like a sponge and leveraging the social and business contacts she'd made through her industrial manufacturing business into political ones. Two months after her arrival, when Baron Stallman resigned his short-lived position at Industry and the various political factions began scrambling to add the vacant Cabinet seat to their personal powerbases, Crystal Pine's immensely competent business and industry background—plus her still-neutral position vis-à-vis any of the established factions—made her a logical if somewhat half-hearted choice to replace him.

That had led to a small resurgence in animosity from some quarters. The fact that she, like the Prime Minister himself, was a loyal and frequently outspoken supporter of Queen Elizabeth was probably also a factor.

"With My Lady's permission," Katra Nessler, Countess Greatgap, put in acidly before anyone else could speak, "do you think we can hold off on matters of money and profit until we've dealt with the more immediate situation?"

"I never said anything about money," Crystal Pine countered calmly.

"No, but we all know you were thinking it," Greatgap said.

Mentally, Winterfall shook his head. The whole thing with Serisburg and Crystal Pine had only just begun to settle down when the government was hit by a second gut-punch: the resignation of Chancellor of the Exchequer Anderson L'Estrange, Earl Breakwater, and his replacement by Greatgap.

Most of the speculations about Breakwater's departure

centered around his age and health, or perhaps fallout from the same faction rivalry that had put Crystal Pine in Industry. Winterfall knew better. Breakwater had once been one of the most powerful men in government, with the kind of political muscle that had allowed him to believe he could challenge even the Queen herself.

That challenge might conceivably have succeeded. Nearly had, Winterfall suspected.

Few people knew of Winterfall's small contribution to the Queen's quiet victory in that behind-the-scenes battle. Winterfall himself knew better than to flatter himself that he'd been the factor that turned the tide. But he was also smart enough to recognize that his sudden appointment to the post of Foreign Secretary in the wake of that victory was hardly coincidence. The Queen and her supporters were grateful, and they'd made their gratitude known in a tangible way.

Not that the appointment was exactly a matter of anyone going overboard with appreciation. Up to now, the Foreign Office had been little more than a side show, barely more than an afterthought to the Prime Minister's sphere of responsibility. With Manticore's nearest neighbors weeks or months of hyperspace travel away, the Foreign Secretary was lucky if he or she got to greet a minor foreign functionary once a year, or to advise the Cabinet on some tidbit of news brought by a merchant ship. Up to now, it had been largely a ceremonial position, handed out to political cronies or to whoever was willing to put up with the boredom.

Up to now.

Now, in the space of a two-minute message, all of that had changed. The Queen and Lords knew something about the Republic of Haven and how to deal with it. None of them knew the first thing about the Andermani Empire or how to deal with *that*. They needed to figure it out, and fast.

And Winterfall was the man squarely in the middle of it all.

"In my mind, the first question we need to ask is whether these people *are*, in fact, Andermani," Greatgap continued. "We've been snoggered before by false IDs and lying bastards. *And* by empty promises of profit."

Winterfall sensed another small ripple of discomfort run around the table. Greatgap was settling into the Exchequer's position well enough, but there was an undercurrent between her and Crystal Pine that he hadn't quite figured out.

"The Admiralty's analysts are convinced," Harwich said. "And if I may suggest, this isn't the time for future speculations of any sort. This is the here and now, and we need to address more immediate concerns."

"Of course, My Lord," Greatgap said.

"Thank you." Harwich shifted his gaze to Winterfall. "I'd like you, Lord Winterfall, to screen your brother, send him a copy of this message if he hasn't already heard it, and see if he concurs with the Admiralty's assessment."

"Yes, My Lord," Winterfall said, making a note on his tablet.

Harwich's eyebrows went up, just slightly. "As in *now*, My Lord."

"Of course, My Lord," Winterfall said hastily, wincing at his momentary brain glitch. He might be new to the Cabinet, but he knew better than to try to hold a secondary conversation in the same room where others were trying to talk. "Excuse me."

Which was also just as well on another level, he mused as he hurried from the room. Winterfall and Travis hadn't been the closest of half-brothers, and the political fallout from their relationship had added a level of difficulty to Travis's slow rise through the navy's ranks. An out-of-the-blue screen might well end up being awkward or even antagonistic, and Winterfall had no desire to have anyone listening in, least of all the entire Cabinet.

Travis answered on the second ring. "Gavin," he said, his voice tight. "I assume you've heard the news?"

"Yes," Winterfall said, feeling the tightness in his chest easing a bit. Maybe with a situation that was completely outside their family looming like a hexapuma in front of them they could have a calm discussion without guilt or recrimination or baggage. "The news and the message both. Lord Harwich wanted me to play the message for you and ask if you could tell if it was really Basaltberg."

And winced again. Dropping Harwich's name, with the reminder that Winterfall was now in the upper echelons of the Star Kingdom's power, was the worst kind of self-aggrandizement.

To his relief, Travis didn't seem to notice. "No need—I've already heard it," he said. "Near as I can tell it *is* Basaltberg. Any idea what he's doing here?"

"All he said in his follow-up messages is that they're here for discussions with us, with an eye toward maybe opening full diplomatic relations."

"I guess that's doable," Travis said doubtfully. "We've got a *sort-of* relationship with Haven, and New Berlin's almost a month closer. Still a pretty hefty distance for any real back-and-forth communication."

"And of course Haven *wants* to make regular contact with its neighbors," Winterfall pointed out. "I've looked through all the archives, and as far as I can tell the Andermani have never reached out to the Star Kingdom before. I'm not sure what relationship they have with Haven, either, for that matter."

"*You've* looked through the archives? Don't you have a staff for that?"

"Oh, I've got a staff, all right," Winterfall said sourly. "Her name's Verona Blankenship, she was hired as a secretary and receptionist, and she's *extremely* not happy at having this kind of research load suddenly dropped in her lap."

"Maybe you should promise her a raise."

"I've promised her two," Winterfall said. "Assuming we all survive the upcoming all-night slave sessions, I may even be able to pry the extra money out of the Exchequer. Anyway, we were talking about Haven."

"Right," Travis said. "My point was that whether or not they've got official relationships with us or Haven, they've definitely been watching us. Did you read my report?"

"Yes," Winterfall said. "You're right, they do seem pretty familiar with the Star Kingdom. *And* with Haven, *and* Silesia, and probably everyone else in the region. Either they're paranoid or just very cautious."

"I'd guess the latter," Travis said. "Gustav Anderman was a mercenary commander in the League for a long time. You collect enough enemies, and you probably learn to watch your back."

"And all the rest of your anatomy," Winterfall said. "Speaking of enemies—or not—how were things between *Casey*'s officers and Basaltberg after Walther? Clegg's report said it was an amicable parting, but she wouldn't be the first person to tell people what they wanted to hear."

"Captain Clegg wouldn't be first, the last, or any of the others," Travis said, a little stiffly. "She's as honest and straightforward as they come."

"Sorry," Winterfall said hastily. "Didn't mean to impugn her honor."

"I'm sorry, too," Travis said. "Knee-jerk reaction. Our relationship with the government hasn't always been the most friendly. The Navy's, I mean."

"Understood," Winterfall said. "Verona and I have been through all the official correspondence—what there is of it—but you've met these people face-to-face. What's your assessment of their attitude toward us?"

"No idea what their government's attitude is," Travis said. "I'd say their navy's is probably less friendship between equals and more uncle to slightly dimwitted nephew."

Winterfall made a face. Captain Trina Clegg, commander of the advanced cruiser *Casey*, had also made the point that Andermani equipment and training was vastly superior to the RMN's. Had made it repeatedly and in great depth.

In which case... "Is there any chance they're here to pick up where the Volsungs left off?" he asked carefully. The last thing he wanted was to spark another bad reaction from his brother, but it had to be asked. "If they're *that* much more advanced than we are, maybe Emperor Gustav figures we'd be an easy addition to his real estate."

"Not a chance," Travis said firmly.

"Are you sure?" Winterfall persisted. "Like you said, Anderman was a merc for a long time. Maybe whoever hired the Volsungs decided to upgrade for their next attempt."

Travis's sigh was clearly audible. "One: you can't take Manticore with a single battlecruiser and a frigate," he said. "Even the Volsungs knew better than that. Two: there's no point in sending Basaltberg and an advance team to scope us out. They've already seen *Casey* and the RMN's combat readiness, which makes a pre-invasion survey a waste of time. And three: if the amount of data they have on the Silesian Confederacy is any indication, *that's* where Gustav is looking to extend his reach. Assuming he's looking anywhere."

"That all seems reasonable," Winterfall said.

Which didn't mean it was all necessarily true. But that would be for the Queen and Cabinet to determine.

Speaking of which, he needed to get back. Having a mostly friendly conversation with Travis was something of a new experience, but Harwich hadn't sent him out here to mend family fences. "Anyway, I have to go. We'll catch up soon, okay?"

"Sure," Travis said, in a tone that suggested he would believe it when he saw it. "Good-bye, Gavin."

Harwich and Greatgap were discussing some kind of formal reception as Winterfall reentered the chamber. The Prime Minister held up a hand as he spotted his foreign secretary, cutting Greatgap off in mid-sentence. "Well?" he asked.

"He believes it to be Basaltberg's voice, My Lord," Winterfall confirmed as he resumed his chair. "He furthermore reiterated that *Casey* and the Andermani parted on very good terms, and feels it unlikely there's any threat or danger implied by Basaltberg's arrival."

"I don't recall anyone saying there *was* a threat," Crystal Pine murmured.

Winterfall winced. "I didn't mean—"

"Whether or not anyone *said* it," Harwich came smoothly to Winterfall's rescue, "it's clear that people are *thinking* it. Otherwise Lord Dapplelake would be here with us instead of in the War Room with Admiral Locatelli and First Lord of the Admiralty Cazenestro."

"My apologies, My Lord," Crystal Pine said, ducking her head in a brief nod. "My Lords," she amended, giving Winterfall the same nod. "I didn't mean to cast aspersions. I understand that every possibility has to be taken into account."

"That's good," Harwich said. "And while the Navy deals with the military possibilities, our job is to deal with the political and diplomatic ones. You all have your assignments; Lord Winterfall, your job will be to go through the archives and see what, if anything, we know about Andermani social protocols."

"Yes, My Lord," Winterfall said. Yet another job to hand off to Verona. She might need a *third* raise. "I presume someone will also be talking to Captain Clegg? Our archives are probably somewhat out of date."

"Lord Grange will be doing that," Harwich said, nodding toward the Interior Minister. "You can pull in your brother as advisor if you want, assuming the Navy doesn't grab him first. Any questions?" The Prime Minister sent his gaze around the table. "No? Then let's get to it, My Lords and Ladies. Our distinguished guests will be here in just a few hours. If we can't impress them with our military prowess, let's try to at least impress them with our social graces."

With a flurry of quiet activity and murmured conversation the Cabinet ministers gathered their tablets and data chips in preparation for their exit. Winterfall, mindful of the task looming in front of him—and painfully aware that he'd damn well better pull this particular rabbit out of the hat—was the first one out of the room. He hurried down the corridor, mentally working out a list of which key words would be best to start his search with—

"My Lord?" Crystal Pine's voice came from behind him.

Reluctantly, he slowed, turning to look over his shoulder. The Secretary of Industry was hurrying toward him, the tails of her long jacket flapping with each step.

"Yes, My Lady?" he asked as she reached him.

"My apologies," she said, huffing a bit with the exertion. Clearly, her single-minded focus on carving out a place for herself in the Lords hadn't left her much time for outside activities or exercise. "I know you're busy, but I wanted to ask a favor."

"Certainly, My Lady."

"Two favors, actually," Crystal Pine corrected. "First: I'm naturally very interested in Andermani technology. I'm hoping you can keep an eye out for relevant information during your search and make me copies of anything you find."

"I doubt we have anything that's recent enough to be of any use to you," Winterfall warned.

"Oh, I know that," Crystal Pine assured him. "I was more looking for attitudes or protocols. How they see their tech, how willing they are to share or sell, whether they see it as an honored servant or a necessary evil. That sort of thing."

"Ah," Winterfall said, frowning. "You know, I don't think I've ever thought about technology as either servant or evil."

"It's just *there*," Crystal Pine said, nodding. "Yes, that's how most people think of it, if they think about it at all. Anyway, I'm hoping to get an hour or two to talk with them about tech purchases or trades, and having an idea of how to make my approach could save a lot of time and blind alleys."

"Understood," Winterfall said. "If I find anything that looks useful, I'll be sure to pass it on to you."

Crystal Pine inclined her head. "Thank you, My Lord."

"You said there were two favors?" Winterfall prompted, resisting the urge to glance at his chrono. He didn't have time for this.

"Yes," she said, giving him an oddly shy smile. "I'd be honored if you'd call me Olga. *Lady Crystal Pine* always sounds way more formal than I ever feel."

"I understand completely," Winterfall said, automatically smiling back. The Secretary of Industry, bending the unspoken rules of protocol for a mere Foreign Secretary? "I'd be honored in turn, Olga," he said. "And please: call me Gavin."

"Gavin," she repeated, her smile widening a bit. "Thank you for your time and your efforts. Let me know if I can help you with any of this."

"I will."

With a final exchange of nods they headed off toward their respective offices.

Olga. Gavin. Down deep, of course, Winterfall suspected the barrier-breaking was just one more aspect of Crystal Pine's campaign to solicit friends and build acquaintanceships, with the longer-term goal of making herself an indispensable part of the Cabinet and Lords.

But even with that knowledge, and with all his years of accumulated cynicism, he had to admit that it still felt good.

☆   ☆   ☆

Queen Elizabeth the Second, supreme ruler of the Star Kingdom of Manticore, was feeling extremely tired. She was also sore, in places she'd never been sore before.

But she was content as she drifted along, rising gradually out of her afternoon nap. Affairs of state, the tangled spaghetti that was politics in the House of Lords these days, even such mundane tasks as deciding what she wanted for dinner—all of that floated past like wispy clouds, distant and inconsequential and someone else's problem.

And through it all flowed a quiet happiness unlike anything she'd ever known.

Mother hormones, the analytical part of her brain reminded her. *Not real.*

She smiled. Of course it was real. It was as real as anything else in life.

Certainly as real as the two-day-old child lying on the bassinet quilt beside her.

She smiled, her eyes still closed, her thoughts and emotions stretching out toward the sleeping infant. Her son. More importantly, Carmichael's son, created inside her body from his frozen sperm.

For a moment her smile faded, the light wispy clouds overhead darkening with memory and loss. It had been six T-years since the hunting accident that took her beloved husband from her, but the pain was no less deep and unrelenting. Once, she'd thought that sense of loss would fade. Once, she'd hoped it would. Now, she realized it would be with her for the rest of her life.

But now she had his son. It was as close to having Carmichael back as she would ever get in this life.

From across the hospital suite came the sound of footsteps. Not the quiet, subtle steps of her nurses or doctors, but a more measured tread. Measured, yet at the same time oddly hesitant. Even through the happiness and the hormones she felt herself wince.

A politician.

Her eyes were still closed, and for a moment she toyed with the idea of pretending she was still asleep and making the intruder decide whether this intrusion was important enough to awaken the sovereign. But that would be childish. No, Elizabeth would wait until the footsteps stopped, give her visitor a moment to admire the sleeping baby beside her, then open her eyes. The footsteps were almost to her—

"Your Majesty?"

Elizabeth sighed inwardly. Prime Minister Harwich. And not only hadn't he waited until he was right beside her, but hadn't even taken the time to admire her son.

Unless her son was no longer there.

She snapped her eyes open, a sudden surge of hormone-fueled fear shattering the hormone-fueled contentment. If something had happened to her son—if the doctors had hurried him away for some emergency treatment while she slept—if Harwich was here to tell her the bad news and wait with her through the crisis—

David was still there, lying peacefully on the quilt. His own eyes were shut, his little lips twitching and puckering with some arcane baby dream.

Elizabeth sighed, the fear draining away and being replaced with relief and more tiredness. *Mother hormones.*

She looked up at the man gazing down at her. The Prime Minister's expression was tight, his throat working with the familiar mix of urgency and uncertainty. "Your Majesty?" he repeated.

"This had better be *really* good, Julian," she warned him.

He blinked. "This had—? Your Majesty, didn't you get my message?"

"What message?" Elizabeth asked, a horrible premonition flooding across her. Her standing do-not-disturb order while she took her nap... "No, I've heard nothing."

He took a deep breath. "Your Majesty: four hours ago two ships carrying a diplomatic mission from the Andermani Empire entered Manticoran space. Their commander—"

"*Andermani?*" Elizabeth gasped.

"Yes, Your Majesty," Harwich said. "Their commander, Admiral Gotthold Riefenstahl, Graf von Basaltberg, brings greetings from Emperor Gustav. I sent word that the Cabinet was on it and that I'd come here as soon as I could to brief you personally unless you contacted me sooner—"

"Yes, yes, I've got it," Elizabeth interrupted, fighting back a surge of anger and frustration. Even with a DND order in place, *someone* at the hospital should have passed it up the chain, at least far enough to reach someone who would have brought some common sense to the equation. "Never mind that. Why are they here, and what do they want?"

And then, her sleep-fogged brain abruptly caught up with her. The Andermani... the joint attack on the Volsung base and the retrieval of the mercenaries' data... Tolochko's possible wormhole junction... "Do you think they're here because...?" She let the half-question hang in the air.

"Because of Dr. Tolochko?" Harwich shook his head. "No, I don't think they know or even suspect. As I said, Your Majesty, it's a diplomatic mission."

Elizabeth winced. He *had* said that, hadn't he? *Mother hormones.*

"We don't know if they're hoping to establish full relations with the Star Kingdom, or whether they just want a preliminary conversation," Harwich continued. "I already have the Cabinet investigating protocol and preparing to greet our guests." He hesitated. "We haven't told them about your, ah, condition."

Elizabeth looked over at her sleeping baby. "My condition, Lord Harwich, is that I'm the queen of the Star Kingdom," she said tartly. "Thank you for the news. I presume you passed Sergeant Adler on your way in?"

Harwich nodded. "She's standing guard by the outer suite door."

"Send her in," Elizabeth ordered. "On your way out, please stop at the nurses' station and have someone start the paperwork for my release."

Harwich's eyes narrowed. "I was under the impression you were to stay another two days for observation."

"That was then," Elizabeth said firmly. "This is now. Tell the Cabinet I'll be there as soon as I can, and I'll expect a full briefing."

Harwich sighed. "Yes, Your Majesty."

"And tell them to pull out all the stops," she said. "Cabinet, Parliament, Navy—everyone."

"Yes, Your Majesty." Bowing low, Harwich turned and hurried away.

Elizabeth looked back at her baby. *Mother hormones . . .* only now, she realized, they didn't apply just to her newborn child. In a very real sense she was the mother of her whole nation.

Were Basaltberg and the Andermani here to be impressed by her child? Fine. God willing, she and the Star Kingdom would impress the hell out of them.

☆   ☆   ☆

Travis had spent a fair amount of time with Basaltberg during the Walther mission, watching the admiral interact with both his own officers and the Manticorans. And while Basaltberg had always been polite and correct he'd never been what Travis would consider jovial.

But wherever he'd been hiding his supply of good will, he was making up for it now. He seemed calm, even cheerful, as he stood with a handful of uniformed officers and another handful of civilians and endured the hastily-thrown-together welcoming ceremony.

Or maybe he wasn't really cheerful. Maybe he was just trying to be a balance for the formal rigidity of the Manticorans.

Travis himself tended toward the solemn. But even with that predisposition, the honor guard, cabinet members, and assorted Lords struck him as painfully over the edge.

Maybe that was to be expected. After all, there had been little need for full-blown diplomatic pomp throughout the Star Kingdom's existence. Official visitors had been rare, most of them from their various neighbors' navies, and had been handled by the RMN and its top brass. The civilian authorities had mostly stood watching from the sidelines on those occasions.

They were certainly making up for that lost time now. Small processionals, stiffly worded speeches of greeting, Lords and other dignitaries seemingly loaded with every bit of regalia that had collected since King Roger's time—every one of the attendees seemed intent on outdoing everyone else in ill-fitting gravity.

The one exception was the queen herself. Of everyone on the Manticore side of the welcoming ceremony she seemed the most relaxed and comfortable, as if greeting unexpected emissaries from a distant star nation was something she did every day.

What was even more astonishing was the fact that she was just two days past childbirth. Travis didn't know much about such things, but he was pretty sure that the typical woman didn't just bounce back into a normal routine this quickly.

Earlier, he'd heard someone speculate jokingly that she was so calm because she was still on drugs. He hadn't seen the comedian since then.

He'd have bet heavily that Basaltberg wouldn't spot Captain Clegg and the *Casey*'s senior officers, four tiers back from the assembled Cabinet ministers. He would also have bet that, if Basaltberg *did* see them, he wouldn't bother to come over personally when the formalities were over.

He'd have lost his money twice.

"Captain Clegg," Basaltberg greeted the captain, a pleased smile on his lips as he bowed and then offered his hand. "I'm gratified to see you returned home safely."

"A homecoming due entirely to your generous assistance against the Volsungs, Admiral," Clegg said, bowing in return and then taking his hand for a quick but firm handshake.

"You flatter me," Basaltberg said. "As well as modestly understating your own contributions to the mission. Were it not for you, I might still be searching for the traitor." His eyes shifted to Travis, and it seemed to him that the admiral's smile grew a bit wider. "Or, alternatively, the bodies of far too many of my officers and crew might well be floating through the vastness of Silesian space."

Travis felt his throat tighten. He'd offered a single suggestion, far less important and momentous than Basaltberg was giving him credit for. Was he supposed to accept the compliment at face value, knowing it was overly lavish? Surely he wasn't supposed to argue with the man out in public?

"But there will be time to reminisce about such matters later," Basaltberg continued, relieving Travis of the need to say anything at all. "Right now, I believe your military leaders would like to sit down with my military staff and me for a preliminary conversation, while our respective diplomatic staffs do likewise."

Travis suppressed a smile. Manticoran diplomats: Prime Minister Harwich, Defense Minister Dapplelake, and whoever else the Cabinet had been able to throw together into a believable diplomatic corps in the past few hours.

Plus Travis's brother Winterfall, of course. Briefly, Travis wondered how he was handling this sudden change in his job description, then put it out of his mind.

"I would like to host a reception for you, Captain, and the rest of *Casey's* officers at the end of the week,"

Basaltberg said, turning back to Clegg. "If you'd be good enough to make the arrangements from your end, I'll see to your transport to *Zhong Kui*."

"Ah—you mean Friday or Saturday?" Clegg asked, throwing a quick glance at Travis.

"Either would be acceptable," Basaltberg said, frowning slightly. "Is the offer perhaps inappropriate?"

"No, Sir, not at all," Clegg said. "It's just that... Saturday is Commander Long's wedding."

For a long moment Basaltberg just stared. Then, abruptly, the widest smile of all broke out across his face. "Well, well," he said. "My heartiest congratulations, Commander, and best wishes. The Andermani Empire is mighty indeed, but even *we* would never risk the wrath of a bride whose day has been usurped. By all means, let us postpone any formalities until all schedules are clear." He raised his eyebrows. "Provided...?" He let the word hang in the air.

And for once, Travis didn't need help figuring it out. "Absolutely, Admiral," he said. "We would be honored if you would attend."

CHAPTER FIVE

THE WEEK WENT BY QUICKLY. Each day began with extensive behind-door meetings between various groups of Manticorans and Andermani. Each afternoon ended with joint statements that were heavy on praise and mutual compliments and light on anything substantive. Each evening was filled with media and social net reaction and speculation about the statements and the closed doors.

Travis spent very little time reading, listening, or considering any of it. He and Lisa had a wedding to plan, and even with her shouldering most of the burden the whole thing sometimes seemed on the verge of collapsing under its own weight.

And then Thursday came, and with it the devastating news.

He didn't tell Lisa. He didn't dare. There would be time afterward for that.

And suddenly, it was Saturday.

The caterers were prepared. The flowers were all there. Captain Marcello's home was spotless. The guests arrived on time and matched the number of chairs that had been set out for them. The cake arrived three minutes late, but forty minutes before it was needed. Travis fit perfectly into his dress uniform, and for all the worry hanging over him didn't stumble over any of his lines.

Lisa, as he'd fully expected, was radiant.

And suddenly, it was over. The vows were spoken, the *I-do*s were said, the minister gave the pronouncement.

And Travis was married to his greatest love and his best and closest friend.

The wife and friend whom he would soon be leaving.

☆   ☆   ☆

"Chief Townsend?"

Hell. Taking a deep breath, turning on his best unconcerned smile, Chomps turned around. "Admiral Basaltberg," he greeted the other, nodding his head politely. "Please forgive my lack of a proper salute." He hefted his cup of punch and his small plate of wedding cake.

"Quite understandable," Basaltberg said dryly, holding up his own plate and cup. "An interesting ceremony. Was this typical of Manticoran weddings?"

"Pretty much, Sir," Chomps said. "Travis and Lisa wrote their own vows, so that part would be different with different couples. But the basics are all there. I take it your weddings are different?"

"Considerably." Basaltberg glanced around the milling crowd of guests, nodded toward an unoccupied corner. "If I may have a moment of your time?"

"Certainly, Sir," Chomps said, suppressing a wince. Lady Calvingdell had made it as clear as hard vacuum that he was to stay as far away from Basaltberg and the other Andermani as he possibly could.

And for most of the week he'd done exactly that. He'd started with the shoreline, worked his way inland, and had spent the last day in a little resort hotel at the edge of the forest. Saturday had arrived, and with it Travis's and Lisa's wedding, and he'd sneaked back into Landing with the intent of spending no more than two hours before returning to his exile.

So, of course, Basaltberg had somehow wheedled himself an invitation to that exact same event. And not only had he recognized Chomps, but he'd now asked for a private conversation, and Chomps really had no polite way to get out of it.

And he was pretty damn sure *it wasn't my fault* wasn't an explanation Calvingdell would be impressed by. The faster and cleaner he could extricate himself from Basaltberg and hightail it back out of town, the better.

Basaltberg led the way to the corner and turned to face him. "I presume you've heard," he said, lowering his voice, "that Emperor Gustav has requested a reciprocal visit by your diplomats, whom he wished to accompany me back to the Empire. I presume you've also heard that Lieutenant Commander Long was specifically named in that invitation."

Chomps hesitated. Normally, there was no way in hell that a mere Senior Chief would be privy to information that sensitive. As far as he knew, even Lisa hadn't been told, and he was pretty sure Travis was sweating bullets over that reveal.

But as one of Lady Calvingdell's charter Delphi members, he knew all sorts of things he shouldn't.

In this case, in fact, he and Calvingdell had had an hour-long screen trying to figure out a way to get

Chomps added to the naval side of this diplomatic mission. Unfortunately, Locatelli had been less than supportive.

Officially that was because Basaltberg knew all about Chomps's intelligence activities and sticking the Andermani with a known spy would be tactless. In actual fact, Chomps suspected, it was simply fallout from the tension between Delphi and ONI.

In Chomps's opinion, that was a spectacularly stupid reason. But Calvingdell had reluctantly abandoned the effort once it became obvious they weren't going to succeed.

Not that the concerns about the Andermani knowing he was a spy didn't have some basis in fact, of course. Basaltberg the admiral undoubtedly knew what an NCO like Chomps would and wouldn't know. Basaltberg the *Andermani* admiral, on the other hand, who had access to all the detailed intel their people routinely dug up, very likely knew more about Manticoran intelligence than he ought to.

For that matter, he might even suspect Delphi's existence. Certainly the Empire would have a feel for ONI, and there'd been enough conversations with the Manticoran brass over the past few days that Basaltberg could have concluded ONI hadn't improved since the last time the Andermani had taken a look at them. Chomps and Travis had been making up a lot of the Silesian thing as they went along, but Basaltberg might easily have spotted the differences between them and the hidebound admirals in ONI and suspected there was a new kid in town. "Yes, Sir, I'd heard that," he said.

"I had hoped *Casey* would be the escort ship to that delegation, as an example to my emperor of

Manticoran military innovation," Basaltberg continued without the slightest hint of surprise at Chomps's answer. "Unfortunately, it seems *Casey* will be in space dock for another two to three months."

"We aren't nearly as familiar with the effects of long-term voyages as you are, Sir," Chomps explained. "*Casey* spent a lot of time in Silesia, and they want to examine every cubic centimeter of her to make sure there was no structural damage or equipment degradation we need to know about for future construction."

"So I was also told." Basaltberg raised his eyebrows. "Though of course the fact that *Casey* also has a superb set of electronic surveillance equipment...?"

Chomps winced to himself. Once again, the existence of *Casey*'s high-tech spy equipment was supposed to be a secret. Once again, Basaltberg clearly knew all about it. "I was under the impression, Sir, that our people weren't going to let your people get close enough to see all that."

Basaltberg shrugged. "Some of the equipment is obvious even at a distance."

"I suppose so. As to sending her to the Empire, Sir, I imagine it would be considered impolite to park something like that in a friendly back yard."

Basaltberg chuckled, the lines around his eyes creasing with his smile. "So it would. Once again, I appreciate your discretion, Chief, as well as the discretion of your superiors."

"We'd hate to begin our relationship with the Andermani Empire on a sour note," Chomps agreed, daring to smile back. If Travis saw Andermani military skill as the RMN's goal, the casual competence of Andermani Intelligence should likewise be Delphi's.

"I presume you're familiar with our host," Basaltberg continued, his face settling back into serious lines. "Tell me, what's your opinion of him?"

"Captain Marcello?" Chomps shrugged slightly. "From everything I've heard, he's a highly competent commander. Commander Donnelly Long has served aboard *Damocles* for a number of years and has always spoken highly of him."

"That was my impression, as well," Basaltberg said. "Though of course a few moments of conversation at a wedding reception is hardly definitive proof of a man's character and abilities. I understand he and his ship were instrumental in the joint action with Haven that eliminated the Volsung forces who eluded us at Walther."

"Yes, they were," Chomps said, deciding to gloss over the fact that whoever was behind that operation had managed to snogger pretty much everyone in sight, from the Havenites to the Manticorans to the Volsungs themselves. He'd read Marcello's report, and the Havenites', and had heard Lisa's impressions of that whole incident, and he *still* hadn't figured it all out.

"Excellent," Basaltberg said. "I'm certain my Emperor would be interested in hearing his description of that battle."

"I'm sure Captain Marcello would be honored to be invited to meet Emperor Gustav," Chomps agreed, his mind kicking into high gear. If Marcello was allowed a small entourage—and if Chomps could get himself assigned to that group—Calvingdell might yet be able to sneak him aboard the expedition.

"Excellent," Basaltberg said again. "I take it there would be no problem with a ship of *Damocles*'s size making such a journey."

Chomps blinked. "You want—you mean, the whole *ship*?"

"Why not?" Basaltberg asked. "Would your queen be reluctant to lose its service for such a length of time?"

"No, Sir, not at all," Chomps assured him hastily. "It's just . . . a hundred-year-old Solarian-built destroyer is hardly representative of the Royal Manticoran Navy."

"Ships are only part of the story," Basaltberg said. "It's the men and women who form the true heart and soul of any navy. Between Commander Long and Captain Marcello and his officers I believe we would have an excellent representation of the Star Kingdom to present to my Emperor." He raised his eyebrows, just slightly.

Chomps frowned. There was something going on here, something he could sense but couldn't quite get a handle on.

Especially with the way Basaltberg was working those eyebrows. Was this another of his tests? Was Chomps supposed to know something, or understand something, or maybe read something between the lines?

Captain Marcello. Captain Marcello *and his officers*.

And then, finally, he got it.

"Absolutely, Sir," he said. "I'll be certain to make that recommendation to my superiors." He hesitated. "And if I may be so bold, Sir, may I say on a personal level that I very much appreciate your understanding and compassion."

"I thank you in turn." Basaltberg gave a little shrug. "To be honest, Senior Chief, some of my colleagues find me too much a sentimentalist."

"Again with your permission, Sir, I would disagree with the implied slight of that assessment. I've always found that a degree of sentiment, combined with logic, reason, and judgment, make the perfect combination for true leadership."

"I would agree," Basaltberg said. "Just as justice and mercy should always be present in some combination, with neither aspect ever completely sacrificed for the other." He gestured toward Marcello. "So. You will make this happen?"

Chomps smiled. And *this* one was definitely a test. Basaltberg wanted to see just how much pull and influence Manticoran Intelligence had over Manticoran politics and the Manticoran military.

Actually, Chomps had no idea how far Calvingdell's and Delphi's reach really extended into either. But for this one, he was willing to move as much dirt and heaven as he could.

Because if Basaltberg's mix of logic and sentiment could find a way to keep Travis and Lisa from having to spend their first year of married life apart, far be it from him to stand in the admiral's way.

☆   ☆   ☆

"Senior Chief Townsend," Lady Calvingdell growled, her voice stiff and painfully formal as it came from Chomps's uni-link, "the powers that be are not happy with you. They are not happy at all."

Chomps clamped his teeth together. "I really don't see the problem, My Lady," he said, matching her tone. Deference be damned—for once, on this one he was in the right. "No one who doesn't already know about us is even going to notice this, let alone think twice about it. And it's sure as hell not like we're fooling the Andermani."

"The *problem* is proper chain of command," Calving-dell bit out. "You made the suggestion to me. Fine. But then, while I'm busy working Dapplelake and Cazenestro, you jump the line and go straight to Winterfall."

Chomps clenched his teeth a little harder. If there was one thing the Navy had drummed into him, it was the whole chain of command thing. And he *had* tried.

Only it hadn't been working. The Andermani visit was winding down, Calvingdell didn't seem to be getting any traction with the upper brass, and Travis and Lisa were in danger of spending their first year at opposite ends of the universe.

And Winterfall was right there.

"Winterfall is Travis's brother, and I'm a concerned friend with a clever idea," Chomps said. "That's all Winterfall heard. That's all anyone else will hear. There's no way this is going to raise a single eyebrow. Especially since Basaltberg is already on board with it."

"Yes, and whose doing is *that*?" Calvingdell asked coldly. "What part of *low profile* did you miss?"

"I tell you, Basaltberg already knew," Chomps insisted.

"Obviously. He got that in Silesia."

"I mean my part," Chomps said. "The fact that I'm some flavor of Manticoran Intelligence. All he got in Silesia was Travis's part."

"Which of course does him no good, now that Long's gone back into the Navy," Calvingdell said. "Basaltberg needed a new name and face to connect to us. Now he's got yours. Welcome to the world of people who play the long game."

Chomps frowned at his uni-link. For someone in Delphi to have even a tentative personal relationship with a foreign officer of Basaltberg's status should be seen as a major coup. Why in hell was she so mad about that?

And then, suddenly, it clicked. For someone in *Delphi* . . .

This wasn't Calvingdell's anger raining down on him. It was ONI's. The hidebound admirals were jealous that the upstart had scored yet another point in this one-upmanship game they'd insisted on playing, and were scraping up whatever charges or mistakes they could find to try to take away some of the shine.

And the vehemence of Calvingdell's tirade strongly suggested that one of ONI's people was standing right there with her. Time for Chomps to key it back a notch.

"Well, it's not like the Andermani are going to be visiting us once a week," he muttered, trying to sound suitably chastened.

"That's sort of the definition of the long game." The uni-com hissed with a sigh. "Damn it, Townsend. I told you to stay away from Landing, and you disobeyed a direct order. I have no choice."

A tingle ran up Chomps's back. "My Lady?" he asked carefully.

"Starting immediately," Calvingdell said, her tone somehow going even more stiff and formal, "you're no longer a part of the Special Intelligence Service. All privileges and responsibilities thereof and thereto are revoked and cancelled."

Chomps stared at the uni-link. "My Lady—" He broke off, his brain frozen beyond the possibility of coherent speech. He'd been *fired*? For going to a friend's *wedding*? "Can I at least appeal?"

"I don't know yet. We'll see."

Chomps took a deep breath, exhaled it slowly. "So . . . I'm going back into the Navy?"

Actually, now that he said it aloud it didn't sound

so bad. Travis was back in, after all. Maybe they'd even serve together again someday.

"I don't know that, either," Calvingdell said. "You certainly won't be going back in immediately. I've talked to BuPers, and right now they don't have a berth for you."

"They don't have room for a senior chief?" Chomps demanded. "That's ridiculous."

"That's reality," Calvingdell said. "Remember all the enlistments in the wake of the Volsung invasion? There you go. The point is that until they find something you're on extended leave."

"Exactly how extended a leave are we talking about?"

"I don't know," Calvingdell said, some of her formality cracking a little. "I'm sorry about this, Townsend. I really am. But we have to deal with the Cabinet and ONI, and the Navy has bureaucracy, and you unfortunately have been caught in the middle."

"Yes, My Lady," Chomps said.

And as his brain began to unfreeze he started to see the sheer depth of the mud he was standing in.

His apartment was chartered to Delphi, which he was no longer part of, while the bachelor barracks in Landing were reserved for fully active personnel, which he also wasn't. In a single minute, he'd gone from a man straddling both the Intel and Navy branches of government to someone who'd fallen off both of them.

"Listen, I've spoken to a couple I know in Serisburg Duchy—Ralph and Eileen Lassaline," Calvingdell continued. "They run a little country inn called the Three Corners, and their daughter Terry's a sheriff's deputy there. The Lassalines are doing some renovation and could use an extra hand. If you're willing to help out when and where they need you, they've agreed to give you room and board until we get this straightened out."

Chomps scowled at the uni-link. So this was what he'd come to? Hired muscle? Seriously?

"Your other choice is to go back to Sphinx while you wait," Calvingdell added. "Though without knowing when you might get a hearing or assignment..." She left the sentence unfinished.

"I understand, My Lady," Chomps said with a sigh. Yes, hired muscle was indeed what he'd come to. At least if he hoped to salvage some shred of his career. "Can you send me their contact information?"

"I'll send their address and directions," Calvingdell said. "They already know to expect you."

"Ah," Chomps said. Which meant Calvingdell had known from the start he'd take the job. Typical. "I'll head out as soon as I've packed up my apartment."

"No, you'll stay put right where you are," Calvingdell corrected tartly. "You're supposed to stay out of Landing, remember? Your current hotel room is already paid for, so you can stay there. Once the Andermani are gone you can put your belongings into storage and head out to Serisburg."

For a fraction of a second Chomps considered reminding her that he was no longer in her employ, and therefore didn't have to give a damn about what she might want him to do.

But if he hadn't killed his career already, a comment like that would definitely do it. "Yes, My Lady," he said instead. "Any idea when that might be?"

"Probably another couple of weeks," Calvingdell said. "I'm sure you'll hear about their departure on the news."

Chomps sighed. In other words, she wasn't even

promising to personally let him know when it was safe to go home. Backpedaling from him for all she was worth.

"Have fun in Serisburg," she said. "I'll be in touch." The connection clicked off.

For a long moment Chomps just stared out his hotel room window, trying to make sense of what had just happened. Calvingdell and the Navy had simultaneously decided they didn't want him. The only people on Manticore who *did* want him only wanted him for his Sphinxian build, and were furthermore way the hell over in Serisburg.

If Chomps had tried to get someone as far out of sight and mind as possible, this was really close to how he would have done it.

And yet, he couldn't shake the feeling that there was more to it than just everyone being mad at him.

Maybe it was all a grand conspiracy. Or maybe someone had simply lost a bet or had their debt slate cleared.

He muttered a word he hadn't used since he was a teenager. Damn Manticoran politics, anyway.

There was a knock on the door. Frowning, he crossed the room and opened the door.

"Senior Chief," Flora Taylor greeted him calmly. Without waiting for an invitation she slipped past him into the room, deftly maneuvering her shoulder-slung messenger bag around her back to avoid brushing his bulk. "Enjoying your holiday?"

"Hardly," Chomps said, frowning again as he closed the door behind her. "Holidays are where you're supposed to be having fun."

"Or just resting from your daily labors," she said, walking to the table and sitting down on one of the two chairs. "I trust I'm not intruding?"

Chomps took a moment to glance studiously around the room. "No, I seem to be free at the moment," he said. "The boss send you?"

"*Lady Calvingdell* doesn't command my off hours," Flora said with the standard disapproving temperature drop on Calvingdell's name. "That being said, she did mention that you might want to talk."

"About my sudden and completely unwarranted exile?"

"Sudden, perhaps," Flora agreed. "But unwarranted?" She gave a little shrug. "But no, the topic today isn't exile. It's politics."

"In that case, I hope you brought a bottle in that satchel," Chomps muttered.

And to his complete surprise, and Flora's clear amusement, she pulled a bottle of whiskey out of her messenger bag. "That's what Lady Calvingdell likes about you, Senior Chief. You somehow manage to stay one step ahead of everyone."

"Sometimes apparently even ahead of myself," Chomps managed. What the *hell* was going on?

"Indeed," Flora said. "Grab a couple of glasses, will you? We need to talk about your little Serisburg exile."

☆   ☆   ☆

Two weeks of pomp, conversation, banquets, and official announcements later—and with an only marginally more relaxed closing ceremony than the one that had opened the Andermani visit in the first place—the four ships were in space.

Winterfall was sitting beside the viewport of his cabin aboard the Manticoran courier ship *Diactoros*, gazing back at the glowing spot that was Manticore

A, when his door alert pinged. "Come," he called, his voice-print order unlocking the hatch. It swung open, and he turned to see Travis step in from the passageway. "Travis," he greeted his half-brother.

"Gavin," Travis said, nodding in return as his eyes flicked across the room, taking in Winterfall's position and posture. "You know, your viewscreen can give you a much better view."

"So I was told," Winterfall said. "But I was also told they have automatic color correction. I was wondering if Manticore A's light would get visibly redder as we sped up."

"Afraid not," Travis said. "We're not going to get much past nine percent of lightspeed before we make the translation."

"Yes, that was the number I came up with, too," Winterfall said, nodding. "Still thought it might be interesting. What can I do for you?"

"I just came to tell you Admiral Basaltberg has invited the two of us and Captain Marcello to *Zhong Kui* tonight for dinner," Travis said. His tone was polite, without any friendship or animosity that Winterfall could detect. "Shuttle One leaves at eighteen hundred hours."

"Thank you," Winterfall said.

Travis nodded and turned back to the hatchway. He started to step through— "Travis?" Winterfall called.

Travis stopped and turned back. "Yes?"

For a moment Winterfall gazed at his brother, words that he wanted to say tumbling around each other in his brain. But Travis was still just looking at him, calm and official and uncurious.

An RMN officer. Not a brother.

"I wondered if Lisa was coming to dinner with us," Winterfall improvised.

"Not this time," Travis said. For a second it looked like he might actually smile, but the moment passed and there was nothing. "*Someone* has to keep *Damocles* flying."

"Of course," Winterfall said, quietly giving up. "Right. I'll be at the shuttle at eighteen hundred."

"See you then." With a nod, Travis turned again and left, closing the hatch behind him.

Winterfall turned back to the viewport, feeling a sudden fresh flow of weariness. He didn't know why he'd ever thought Travis would warm to him in the first place. Not after the way Winterfall had always treated his younger brother. And now they had four long months of travel ahead of them before they even reached the Andermani Empire.

Still, maybe that wasn't such a bad thing. They had time, and they were all cooped up together with the other three members of Winterfall's hastily assembled diplomatic team. Maybe he could find a way to break through the barriers, to find some way to reach out to Travis before they were sealed in this indifference forever.

It was only much later that it occurred to him that Travis could just as easily have screened him with the dinner invitation instead of coming by in person.

Based on the Three Corners Inn's location and rustic name, Chomps had formed an instant mental image of the place, an image he hadn't bothered to check against available pictures. As a result, he found himself surprised to find a small but modern hotel nestled at a T-junction of two old-time roads, one of which wended its way along the edge of the deep forest running down the middle of Serisburg Duchy, the other of which headed at right angles into the forest's interior.

Both roads dated to before air cars were the norm, and were now host to tufts of grass and the occasional small bush. But they were still there, a tribute to the people who'd built them and to the economic inefficiency of tearing them out.

He set his air car down in the landing area behind the inn, making sure it was well clear of the two other air cars and four ground cars already parked there. He didn't take vacations very often, but his limited experience suggested that other vacationers tended to drink more on the road than they probably did in their everyday lives, with a higher probability of bumping hard objects into other people's vehicles as they tried to get to their own. Leaving his carrybags in the trunk, he headed inside.

A middle-aged woman was sitting behind the front desk, a pleasantly welcoming expression on her face as Chomps stepped inside. "Hello," Chomps said, nodding a greeting. "I'm Charles Townsend. My—" *former boss* "—friend Lady Calvingdell sent me."

"Yes, of course, Mr. Townsend," the woman said, her smile going a little wider as she stood up. "I'm Eileen Lassaline, co-owner of the Three Corners Inn. Welcome to the absolute best part of Serisburg Duchy."

"Thank you," Chomps said, smiling back in spite of his lingering grump at what Calvingdell had done to him. The sheer enthusiasm, even surrounding a clearly canned speech, was infectious. "I was told I could help out around here in return for room and board for a while?"

"Yes, indeed," Eileen said, her eyes flicking up and down his body. "We've been trying to do some work on the east wing, and Ralph isn't strong enough to do all the heavy lifting himself." Her nose wrinkled. "And I'm not much help—injured my right shoulder as a teen and don't have a lot of flexibility in that arm."

"I'll be delighted to help in any way I can," Chomps said. "Do you want me to start now, or do I have time to bring in my bags first?"

Eileen laughed. "Oh heavens, Mr. Townsend. No, you have plenty of time to bring in your bags. *And* to settle into your room *and* to have dinner *and* to have a nice evening watching the sun go down. We're not quite so frantic out here as you are in Landing."

"Ah." From the direction of the parking lot came the faint sound of an air car setting down. "You certainly have the location for not being frantic. You get mostly hikers and birdwatchers here, I assume?"

"Mostly," Eileen said. "The duke forbade hunting in this part of Drobne Forest, so it's been a nice tourist area." Her nose wrinkled again, this time in a more ominous way. "Though now that we're part of the Queen's Lands, I don't know if that'll hold up. Lord knows there are a lot of game animals in Drobne, and a lot of people who like to catch their own dinner."

"I don't see why Queen Elizabeth would change the land usage regulations just because it's her property now," Chomps said.

"I doubt the queen herself has much to do with the matter," Eileen said sourly. "Probably some minor lord or bureaucrat who oversees her lands for her."

"And who dreams of being a major lord?"

"Or a wealthy retired bureaucrat," Eileen said.

"Especially what with the queen's new child and the Andermani—" she broke off, peering closely at Chomps. "Did you see them? The Andermani, I mean. Did you get to see any of them?"

"Yes, I saw a couple," Chomps said carefully. "I think so, anyway. They're really not any different from the rest of us." On the back of his neck he felt the subtle change in air pressure as someone opened the door.

"I suppose," Eileen said. "They talk funny, though, right?"

"It's called *German*, Mom," a pleasant alto voice came from behind him. "You must be Townsend."

"And you must be Terry," Chomps said, turning around.

He'd already noted that her voice was pleasant. Now, he saw, the rest of her was a pretty nice package, too. Terry Lassaline was taller than her mother, and chunkier, though she carried the extra weight well. She was dressed in a brown sheriff deputy's uniform, a silver star glinting on her upper chest, a hefty-sized handgun holstered at her waist on a Sam Browne belt. Her eyes flicked over him like her mother's had a moment ago, but Chomps could sense Terry's assessment went deeper than just the surface, with the full weight of law enforcement experience behind it.

And that weight didn't end at her eyes. "That's *Deputy Lassaline*," she corrected him tartly.

"Terry!" Eileen said, sounding mildly scandalized. "Mr. Townsend is our guest."

"Everyone here is a guest," Terry countered. "You want them all pretending I'm their good friend?"

"No, Deputy Lassaline is right," Chomps interjected before Eileen could object further. "I know a little something about respect for the uniform and the one who wears it. My apologies, Deputy."

"Accepted," Terry said. "Welcome to Three Corners, Mr. Townsend. Dad can definitely use the help."

"That's why I'm here," Chomps said. "So what are things like out here, law enforcement-wise?"

"Why, you looking to start a crime spree?" Terry asked. "Because I really wouldn't recommend it."

"Oh, no, nothing like that," Chomps hastened to assure her. Flora had vouched for Terry as a law enforcement officer, and the lady certainly seemed to fit the part. Unfortunately, there was really only one way to test someone's abilities in the event that push came to shove. "I just thought I'd let you know that I dealt with a lot of drunk-and-disorderlies when I was in the Navy, and I'm available if you should want any help."

"Awfully generous of you," Terry said, the temperature in her voice dropping a few degrees. "This may surprise you, but we have a fully functional legal system out here, including a sheriff and two other deputies. I think we can manage."

"I'm sure you can," Chomps agreed. "I'm just putting it out there. Sometimes extra eyes can be handy."

"Extra *eyes?*" Terry asked archly. "Or extra muscle?"

"Either."

"Yeah," Terry said. "Let's cut to the chase here. You don't think I can do my job."

"I didn't say that," Chomps assured her, wincing inside. He hated goading people this way, especially when the buttons were so visible and so easy to push. But he needed to know how well she'd been trained, and this was as good a time as any to find out. "I'm sure you're very competent. It's just that..." He waved his arms. "Sometimes you want to be able to talk someone down without having to draw your weapon."

"Ah." Terry nodded, a hint of a tight smile touching her lips. "In other words, you don't think I can subdue a suspect without shooting him."

"I just—"

"We have some big men in Serisburg Duchy, Townsend. A couple are even bigger than you."

"And one of them likes to get drunk in public," Eileen murmured from behind him.

"And you've taken him down?" Chomps asked.

"Would you like a demonstration?" Terry offered.

"Terry," Eileen said warningly.

"Actually, yes, I'd kind of like to see that," Chomps said.

"Fine," Terry said. She started toward Chomps, angling to pass him, fiddling with her gun belt buckle as she walked.

"Terry, that's enough," Eileen said, putting some steel into her tone. "Chief Townsend is a guest—"

And as Terry brushed past Chomps, she abruptly abandoned her effort to unfasten her belt. She half turned, grabbing his left wrist with her left hand, shoving the palm of her right hand against his elbow, and giving the backs of his knees a pair of light one-two kicks with the edge of her right boot.

Then, before he could even react she let go and took another step away behind him. "You have now been introduced to the floor," she announced.

"Terry!" Eileen protested.

"No, that's all right," Chomps said, turning around to face the two women. So. Clean and precise, even in a mock-combat setting. Just as important, she knew exactly how much force to apply to a given situation. Good enough. "Nice move, Deputy. Generally requires a bit better weight ratio, though."

"If I'd been serious I'd have hit your elbow instead of just pushing on it," Terry said calmly. "I find that serious pain can cancel out a weight imbalance."

"So it can," Chomps acknowledged. "Okay. I'm convinced."

"Not that you needed to be." Terry turned to face her mother. "So. Anything else interesting going on? How many guests do you have."

"Six," Eileen said, throwing a look of disapproval at Terry that miraculously turned into a look of apology as she shifted her eyes to Chomps, then resumed their glower as she looked back at her daughter. "Five one- or two-nighters, and an ornithologist who's coming tonight for some long-term studies. Actually, Chief Townsend, I believe he said he was a former Navy NCO. You and he might have some nice conversations."

"Thank you," Chomps said. "But frankly, I've had my fill of the Navy, Navy personnel, and Navy bureaucracy at the moment. Anyway, I'm here to work, not socialize."

"Speaking of which, I have Dad's shipment of bracing struts in my car," Terry said. "You want to give me a hand, Townsend?"

"Terry, he's barely even checked in," Eileen objected.

"He just said he was here to work," Terry said. "So are we working or aren't we?"

"We're working," Chomps confirmed. "I'll bring in my bags later, if that's all right."

"Whenever you want," Eileen said, giving him a strained smile. "Welcome to the Three Corners Inn,

Mr. Townsend. The absolute best part of Serisburg Duchy."

"Already loving it," Chomps assured her. "Lead the way, Deputy."

He followed her out the door and around the side of the inn. "He's working on a couple of the east end rooms right now," Terry explained. "I parked as close as I could without landing on my mother's shrubbery— it'll be easier to get them inside through one of the windows." She looked sideways at him. "You didn't have a problem back there, did you?"

"Not at all," Chomps assures her. "One of the first things we're taught to do in a new situation is assess everything around us in terms of assets and liabilities. If we wind up in trouble somewhere, you'll definitely be in the first category."

"I'm flattered. But unless you plan to get drunk and disorderly in my jurisdiction, I don't foresee us getting into trouble."

"You never know," Chomps said. "By the way, where's the other corner?"

"What other corner?"

"You're the Three Corners Inn," Chomps said, waving at the sign as they passed it. "The T-junction out there gives you two corners. I assume you're not counting your driveway. Anyone actually use those roads anymore, by the way?"

"Not as roads," Terry said. "But there are some nice trails in the area, and the road's a good place for day hikers to park. And no, we don't count the driveway. One of the major trails angles off from Drobne Cross Highway, right across the street from us. Comes right to the junction, so we end up with three corners."

"Ah. I missed that."

"You wouldn't have if you'd been here a few months ago. So why don't you want to talk to that other Navy man who's coming in?"

"Not really something I want to talk about."

"Fine. Just asking." She popped the trunk lid of her car to reveal a collection of building struts. "Can you carry one of these by yourself, or do we need to double-team it?"

They spent the next hour moving the struts from Terry's car to Ralph's work site. Ralph himself was as cheerful as his wife, thanked Chomps profusely for his help—as if Chomps was doing the family a favor instead of the other way around—and promised to call on him for anything that required muscle. When the lugging was finished Terry walked Chomps back inside, promised her mother she'd come for dinner someday soon, and then left.

An hour after that, Chomps was in his room, freshly showered from the long drive, a drink in his hand from one of the Sphinxian whiskey bottles Flora had left with him, staring out at the forest spreading majestically outside his window. The forest, and the narrow hiking trail he could now see leading off among the trees.

It was an idyllic setting. Some would call it peaceful. Others would call it inspiring, or invigorating.

Chomps called it hell on wheels. And the way things were shaping up, there was a good chance he'd be stuck here for quite a while.

He just hoped it would all be over before his whiskey supply ran out.

CHAPTER SIX

LISA'S BREATH WAS COMING in a slow rumble that was just a notch below actual snoring when Travis awoke from his light doze to realize his right arm, wedged beneath Lisa's neck, had fallen asleep.

For a minute he listened to her, imagining her face in the darkness of his cabin on *Diactoros* as he gently wiggled his fingers in an attempt to wake up the nerves without similarly waking up his wife.

He was halfway successful. The arm remained numb, but the movement didn't disturb Lisa. He relaxed the fingers and instead pressed his arm down into the pillow, hoping he could create enough of a gap with her neck and shoulders to slide the arm free.

Again, no luck. He tried again, pressing down harder this time, then gave up the effort. With a quiet sigh, he relaxed his body, pressed against hers, and tried to figure out what else he might try.

And so, of course, what movements of hand and arm hadn't accomplished the sigh did. With her final raspy breath morphing into a gentle snort, she woke up. "Travis?" she murmured.

"I'm here," he said. "It's okay."

"Sorry," she said. "Did I wake you?"

"No, no," he assured her. "But if you could just...?"

"Oh—your arm," she said guiltily as she lifted her head and shoulders off his arm. "Sorry."

"It's okay," Travis said as he pulled the arm free, wincing as the pins and needles set in. "My fault for not changing position before you went to sleep."

"Next time wake me sooner," Lisa said, rolling up on her left shoulder and resting her right hand against his chest. "Especially if it'll get me out of a dream like the one I was having there at the end."

"Another pop inspection where the whole ship is a mess and the admiral blames you?"

"That's *your* nightmare, silly," Lisa admonished, poking him gently in the ribs. "No, this one was Admiral Basaltberg going crazy and gunning down the whole bridge crew because they'd gotten lost and couldn't get him back to New Berlin."

"And you couldn't help?"

"I tried," Lisa said. "But suddenly he was speaking Chinese or Korean or something, and I couldn't understand a single word."

"Did you try speaking German to him?"

"Right, like I can remember how to speak German in a dream." She hunched up on her elbow and Travis had the impression that she was glaring down at him. "Wait a second. Are you telling me that *you* speak German in your dreams?"

"Not really," Travis hedged. "I can sometimes get some of the words, but my grammar structure usually falls apart."

"Nice save," Lisa said, mock-severely. "But watch

yourself. After all those claims about being bad with languages, you are *not* going to get workable German before I do."

"Wouldn't dream of it," Travis protested.

"Because remember, I'm still a superior officer," Lisa said, lying down again. "If we get to New Berlin before I've got this language thing licked, I'm commandeering you as my translator."

"I'll keep that in mind," Travis said. "Should I warn Gavin that my kidnapping might be in the offing?"

"No, let's let him be surprised like everyone else." Lisa paused. "How's he doing?"

Travis shook his head. "I don't know. He won't talk about it, at least not to me. But I think he knows he's in way over his head."

"Does he think anyone else on Manticore would have been more up to the task?"

"He probably thinks *everyone* on Manticore would do a better job," Travis said with a sigh.

"It's kind of sad, really," Lisa mused. "Has he ever really had a challenge?"

"Nothing remotely like this," Travis said. "He went into the Lords after his sister died and had barely gotten himself established when he was taken under Breakwater's wing. Up until then he'd been working—electrical system maintenance, mostly—and not really paying much attention to politics. For years after that he was more or less following the Chancellor's lead on everything. Now, he's suddenly been thrown into the deep end of the pool."

"Maybe you should go to him and tell him that's how we all feel when we first get this kind of responsibility."

"*Do* we feel that way?" Travis asked. "Have we ever— you and I—been in this same situation?"

"Of course we have."

"Have we?" Travis countered. "We've never been fully in charge of anything. We've always had someone over us—bosun, division head, department head, captain—who we can go to for advice."

"Not that the advice has always been good."

Travis wrinkled his nose. He'd had his share of bad superior officers through his career, too. "My point is that we've never held the full weight of anything on our shoulders, and we won't until we're captaining ships of our own. On the other hand, Gavin's carrying the full weight of Manticoran foreign policy right now."

"I hadn't looked at it that way," Lisa said thoughtfully. "No, you're right. And Basaltberg isn't making it easy on him."

"Basaltberg is worried," Travis said. "I gather Emperor Gustav wasn't in the best of health when they left New Berlin. Basaltberg's personal nightmare is that the emperor will have passed before he gets back."

"Really? He didn't show any of that while he was on Manticore."

"Of course not," Travis said. "He had his orders, and he was following them. Good thing, too. Can't you see the reaction to a grumpy, growling Basaltberg glaring at the Lords and Cabinet, with an Andermani battle-cruiser overhead?"

"There'd have been panic in the streets," Lisa agreed. "And you know all this about Basaltberg *how*?"

Travis shrugged. "I overheard a couple of the senior officers talking about it when I was aboard a few days ago."

"And they didn't think you could understand them? You *rat*," Lisa interrupted herself. "Dreams be darned—you're *way* ahead of where you said you were. Aren't you?"

"Not *way* ahead," Travis protested. "Maybe just a little."

"You rat," Lisa repeated, giving him a mock-serious punch in the ribs. "Okay, pal, this means war." She rolled over and keyed on her side table light.

"What are you doing?" Travis asked, squinting against the sudden glare.

"If you think I'm going to sleep when you're—what, three? Four?—four lessons ahead of me, you're sadly mistaken," she said firmly. "Go on—go back to sleep. Traitor."

"Oh, come on," Travis said. "Really?"

"Go back to sleep," she repeated.

"What if I made you a better offer?"

She paused, looking warily back over her shoulder. "*Are* you making me a better offer?"

"I don't know," Travis said. "Is there anything you'd like better than an hour of conjugating German verbs?"

"I guess there's one way to find out," she said, turning off the light again. "You *did* say a whole hour, right?"

☆   ☆   ☆

". . . and they signed the capitulation that evening," Quint said, taking a sip of her brandy. Her eyes were distant, Llyn noted, embracing the memory.

Over dinner he'd given her a couple of highly edited stories from his past and encouraged her to do the same. He hadn't expected the suggestion to open this kind of floodgate. For all her prestige, for all her military successes, Commodore Catt Quint apparently hadn't had anyone to talk to—to *really* talk to—for a long time.

Why she'd picked Llyn for that job he couldn't

fathom. Yes, he was playing the bon vivant, sympathetic, friendly ally sort; but surely she wasn't taken in by the act. Was she?

Maybe she'd been played that way so often that she no longer cared. She needed to talk, she wanted to talk, and Llyn was the only port in the storm.

Or maybe she was looking ahead toward her own death.

A shiver ran up Llyn's back. He'd known others who somehow sensed that a given job or trip or meeting would be their last. Sometimes they'd been wrong, but the sense of destiny and powerlessness that subsequently became a permanent part of them had been eerie.

And sometimes, they'd been right.

"Why are you doing this?"

Llyn forced himself back to the present. The lure of the past was apparently contagious. "Excuse me?"

"Why are you doing this?" Quint repeated. "I don't mean why your associates want you to do it—I know you won't tell me *that*. I mean why you?"

"You mean why me instead of Bryce? I can't really—"

"No," Quint said. "You're about to provoke a war. That begs explanation."

"I prefer to think of it as righting a wrong," Llyn said. "I assume Ms. Bryce explained the circumstances."

"Damn long delayed justice, if you ask me." Quint cocked her head a little, as if that would let her read Llyn better. "What do you have against Gustav Anderman?"

"Never met the man," Llyn said. There'd been something in her face and voice just then . . . "I take it you have?"

"No," Quint said quietly. Her face was suddenly carved stone, her eyes looking back at a more horrible memory than even the tales of carnage she'd been sharing with him. "But I will. Very soon.

"And then I'll kill him."

Llyn's first instinct was to smoothly change the subject. It was risky to let assets, especially military ones, wallow too deeply into psychological darkness.

His second instinct was to sit quietly, not move, and hear her out.

"I was six T-years old," she said, her voice gone from quiet to barely audible. "My parents were mercenaries with the Condotta Group. A few of us were in New Bombay, doing a little R and R, when Anderman and his group arrived and picked the same town for their own hellraising. I was worried, but I remember my mother telling me not to worry, that we were in the same business they were and they wouldn't bother us."

She took a long, shaking breath, followed by a long drink of her brandy. "My father told me about it afterward," she said. "Gustav Anderman himself came into our hotel. He blistered my mother for ten minutes about something he thought she'd done to his people. My father had put me in the bedroom before Anderman arrived, but I could hear the angry voices.

"And when he was done spewing his hate and anger over something she hadn't even done...he killed her."

Llyn had guessed that was where the story was going. But the last three words still sent a fresh shiver up his back. "Did your father...?" He broke off.

"Anderman let him go," Quint said. "I guess he hadn't done anything the great mercenary chief thought was worth killing him for. Anderman and his men were gone before he came back into the bedroom to get me."

"Was there an investigation? Surely the New Bombay authorities—"

"There was nothing," Quint snarled. "They took us to Police HQ so my father could give his statement. After that, nothing. Three days later we left with the rest of the Condotta, and nothing was ever done."

Llyn felt his lip twitch. Gustav Anderman's past was a colorful read, but he'd never heard anything like that about the man. Whoever he'd paid off to keep a murder off the record, he'd gotten his money's worth.

Quint took a deep breath; and with that, the shadow disappeared and the mask was back in place. "So you see, I'm just seeking justice, too," she said, giving him a hard-edged smile.

"Nice to know we're on the same page."

"But I didn't tell you that just for your amusement," Quint went on. "I have a favor to ask."

"I'm listening."

"When all this is over, if I don't succeed in killing Gustav Anderman—" She locked eyes with him. "I want you to do it."

Llyn stared at her, feeling like a rug had just been pulled out from under him. What the *hell*?

He didn't want Gustav dead. Neither did Axelrod. They *certainly* didn't want him dead at the hands of an assassin. That kind of destabilization might well plunge his Empire into civil war.

And with the military resources the sides in that war would have available, it could conceivably spill over into Silesia, Manticore, and even Haven, possibly plunging the whole sector into chaos. Clearly, Quint hadn't thought this through.

Or maybe she had. Maybe her thirst for vengeance

and justice stretched beyond the man himself into a rage that would be satisfied only by bringing down everything he'd built. The fact that her failure to assassinate him carried the implicit assumption that she herself would already be dead and in no position to gloat was apparently of no consequence to her.

She wanted Gustav's universe to burn. And she was counting on Llyn to make it happen.

And so he took a deep breath, swallowed hard like a man making a difficult decision, and looked straight back into her eyes. "All right," he said quietly. "If it's really that important to you . . . all right. I'll do it."

☆   ☆   ☆

Conversation ceased after that. Llyn and Quint finished their brandy in silence, each wrapped in his or her own thoughts. Llyn made sure she finished her drink before he did, and when she left to make a final check of *Retribution*'s bridge, he asked permission to remain behind in her private dining room until he likewise finished.

Given that he'd just agreed to commit murder for her, she was graciously accommodating.

He was down to a couple of small sips, and wondering if he should add a little more to his glass, when Amos, the commodore's personal steward, finally arrived.

"Good evening, sir," Amos said, nodding politely as he began gathering the dinner dishes together. "Pardon me, but Commodore Quint likes to have everything put away before she returns from her postprandial inspection."

"That's all right, Amos," Llyn said. "I was hoping for a chance to talk to you."

Amos's eyebrows went up a couple of millimeters. "With *me*, sir?"

"Indeed," Llyn said. "How long have you been with the Quintessence Mercenaries?"

"Not long," Amos said. "I was one of those who were hired when the commodore began gathering crews for her new ships." He raised his eyebrows. "I understand that you were the one instrumental in obtaining them for her?"

"I'd have thought a personal steward would be low on her priority list," Llyn said, ignoring the question. "A good weapons tech would seem more useful."

"Never underestimate the value of a good steward, sir," Amos said with a small smile. "Especially when that steward is also an expert scrounger. Why, the items I was able to obtain for her kitchen alone—"

"That's all right," Llyn interrupted. "Probably best that I don't know. Tell me, what was your last ship?"

"The *Jackstraw*, sir," Amos said. "Heavy cruiser of the Black Hand Consortium. Lost my job when, well, when the Black Hands ran into someone bigger and meaner."

"I remember reading about that," Llyn said, nodding. "Nice."

Amos frowned. "Nice?"

"I mean it works well because the Black Hands took so much damage in their last stand that their records were basically vaporized," Llyn explained.

"Along with much of their crews," Amos said ruefully.

"Right," Llyn said. "As last stands go, it was pretty spectacular. My point is that because the records were lost there's no complete data trail on who was actually with the Consortium and who wasn't."

Amos's eyes narrowed, just slightly. "I'm afraid I don't follow you, sir."

"Really?" Llyn asked calmly. "I thought the bread crumb trail was pretty clear. Fine, follow this. You never served with the Black Hands. You were brought aboard by Ms. Bryce—very subtly, no doubt, with Commodore Quint convinced it was her decision—to serve as an extra set of eyes and ears aboard the *Retribution*. Was invoking the *Jackstraw* Bryce's idea, or yours?"

"Sir, I have no idea—"

"Don't waste my time, Amos," Llyn bit out, dropping his voice into liquid hydrogen range. "I know Freya Bryce. She would never send her ship away and let herself be trapped under an asset's control unless she had an ace up her sleeve. I've known she had a shadow for years; now I know that shadow was you. What were her orders?"

For a pair of seconds he thought Amos was going to stick stubbornly to his cover identity. Such mindless rigidity would have given Llyn another data point on the man and possibly shifted him across that fine line between asset and liability.

Luckily for Amos, the man wasn't that stupid. "Fine," he said calmly. "Like you already said, I was supposed to keep an eye on things. There were a couple of officers in particular that Ms. Bryce wanted me to watch."

"Because . . . ?"

"Not sure," Amos admitted. "Possibly because they might oppose the commodore; possibly because they were sharp enough to see through our plan soon enough to make trouble."

"Mm," Llyn said. So it was *our* plan now. Either Amos was an enthusiastic team player, or he had a sadly overblown idea of his own importance in the grand scheme of things. Probably a delusion he'd picked up during all those years as Bryce's shadow. "And Commodore Quint herself?"

Amos's throat worked. "You heard her, sir. She wants to bring down Gustav and the whole Andermani Empire. Ms. Bryce didn't think that would be in our best interests."

"Ms. Bryce was entirely correct," Llyn agreed. "So what did Ms. Bryce want you to do about it?"

The throat twitch again. "She said that if she gave me the order, I was to kill the commodore."

"Just like that?"

"Just like that," Amos said. "She also told me that if for some reason she wasn't in position to give that order, I was to use my own judgment."

"Good orders," Llyn said approvingly. "Succinct, clear, easy to remember. Now that I'm in charge, though, there'll be a couple of changes."

"Such as?"

"You'll continue to observe the crew and report on anything odd," Llyn said. "You'll also keep a close eye on the commodore and her mental state. I presume that's why Bryce maneuvered you into the steward's slot?"

Amos shrugged. "The other option was somewhere in the impeller room where I could open the ship to deadly attack if Ms. Bryce deemed that necessary. She decided steward would give us warning sooner."

"Early warning is key," Llyn agreed. "So, watch and report. But as for any action against her, you will do nothing. Do you understand? *Nothing.*"

"But what if—?"

"Do I need to repeat myself?"

Amos's lips compressed briefly. "No. Sir."

"Good," Llyn said. "If there's action to be taken, *I* will take that action. There will be no contingency with regards to my incapacitation because there will be no incapacitation."

Amos seemed to measure him with his eyes. "If you say so."

"I say so," Llyn confirmed. "You seem unconvinced."

"No, sir, not at all," Amos said evenly. "I know my place in the food chain. And I *do* know how to take orders."

"Excellent," Llyn said, offering Amos a hint of a genuine smile. "Then we should get along just fine."

"Yes, sir." Amos held out his hand. "Take your glass, sir?"

Llyn looked at his snifter. It was indeed empty. "Thank you," he said, handing it to the other. "Good evening."

"Good evening, sir." Nodding again, Amos left the compartment.

"Yes, indeed," Llyn murmured toward the closed hatch. "We should get along just fine."

☆   ☆   ☆

"So," Ralph said casually as the evening meal wound to a close. "Any idea how much longer you'll be staying?"

"Not really sure," Chomps said. "I was told I'd be up for a hearing soon. But that was a couple of months ago. I'm starting to wonder if they've forgotten me."

"Maybe Chief Gorkich can put in a good word for you," Eileen suggested. "He finished his studies and headed back to Landing this morning."

"Yes, I know," Chomps said. He'd had a couple of short conversations with former Chief Gorkich over the past few weeks, mainly to get Eileen off his back about his lack of socializing. But the chats had been strained, and he was more than happy to see the man go. "But I doubt any of his old friends will be able to do anything. Which leaves me stuck here." He raised his eyebrows. "Unless you want me to leave, of course. I don't want to overstay my welcome."

"No, you're welcome to stay as long as you want," Eileen assured him.

"Thanks," Chomps said. "Kind of boring out here. Though I hear you had an interesting accident in the area a few months ago."

He could feel the sudden spike in tension around the table. "I don't know if *interesting* is the word I'd use," Eileen said carefully.

"Tragic, maybe," Terry muttered. "Horrible. Disgusting. Stupid. Completely avoidable."

"I suppose most accidents come under those headings," Chomps said. "So where exactly did it happen?"

"In the forest," Terry said. "Why do you care?"

"I just wondered," Chomps said. "Could you see it from here? Could *I* see the site from here? Where exactly was it?"

"You want to play tourist?" Terry demanded. She slapped her fork onto the table beside her empty plate. "Fine," she bit out, pushing back her chair. "We're here to serve. Let's go."

"What, *now*?"

"You got something better to do?" Terry retorted. "Come on, we're losing light."

Chomps looked at Ralph and Eileen. "Don't look

at us," Eileen warned. "She's been stubborn since she was a child."

"And now she's also armed," Ralph added. "Enjoy the walk, Chomps."

Two minutes later he and Terry crossed the roads in front of the inn and headed down the hiking trail into the woods.

"Watch for stray roots," Terry called to him over her shoulder. "And if you see something that looks like a giant freckled pickle alongside the path, for God's sake don't kick it."

"Got it," Chomps said, eyeing a giant freckled pickle warily as he passed it.

Forty minutes later, with the sky noticeably darker than it had been at the beginning of their trek, they were there.

"So this is it?" Chomps asked, looking around the clearing as they walked across it.

"Yes," Terry said. Her voice was no longer drill-sergeant tough, but had changed to something soft and pained and haunted. She finished crossing the clearing, then turned around and pointed behind him "There. Right there is where Duke Serisburg ran his air car into a tree and killed himself and his family. And pretty much the whole duchy along with it."

"Yeah," Chomps said, turning beside her and looking around. "That's the tree?"

"That's it." Terry pointed upward. "You can still see the scars where the impact tore into the bark."

"And nearly killed the whole tree," Chomps commented, craning his neck. The tree was the tallest one in the immediate vicinity, sticking up a good five meters above its neighbors, and was nearly four meters across at its base. Even from thirty meters below the impact point he could clearly see the deep gash where the air car had hit, and a lot of the branches above that point were twisted and leafless. "He was drinking when it happened, right?"

"That's what the autopsy showed," Terry said. "Three times the legal blood-alcohol content."

"Was that typical for him?"

"What, driving drunk on manual?" Terry growled. "How should I know?"

"You once told me you dealt a lot with drunks," Chomps reminded her. "So did you ever give him a ride home?"

"I never saw him drunk in public," she said stiffly. "What he did up in his private retreat I don't know. I *do* know we don't speak ill of the dead around here."

"No disrespect meant," Chomps assured her. "Just trying to figure out what happened."

"What *happened* was that he was flying on manual, went too fast and too low, and crashed into a tree," Terry bit out. "End of story."

"So it would seem," Chomps murmured, gazing up at the tree. He looked back behind him at the other trees rising up along the small spinal ridge that ran down the middle of the forest. From the position of the gash, it appeared that Serisburg had been flying in from that direction. He looked back at the impact tree.

And felt a small tingle raising the hairs on the back of his neck.

"There are just a few points I still don't understand," he continued. "You say he was flying drunk. But his wife was also in the car, wasn't she?"

"*And* his three children."

"Right, but they couldn't drive. She could. If he was drunk, why wasn't she the one flying?"

"Their youngest son had a bad cold," Terry said. "Maybe she was tending to him. Some people think Benjamin's sneezing might have distracted the duke at the wrong time."

"Yes, but—"

"Look, you might as well ask why he didn't engage the autopilot," Terry said. "We don't know. He loved to fly and always liked to be in charge. All we know for sure was that he hit that tree hard enough to completely wreck the counter-grav and send the car dropping straight to the ground. It's a toss-up as to which of those impacts killed them."

"Yeah," Chomps said, looking around him. The grass and local bushes had recovered from the catastrophe, but there were still a couple of deep gouges where jagged edges of metal from the crushed and half-disintegrated vehicle had slammed into the ground. "Where was he coming from at the time? His retreat?"

"Yes," Terry said, frowning at him. "Why?"

"Just wondering," Chomps said. "This is kind of an out-of-the-way part of the duchy, isn't it?"

"You should know—you're just spent two months here," Terry reminded him. "If you've been anywhere more out-of-the-way, I'd love to hear about it."

"Actually, I have," Chomps said. "It's called Sphinx. You have a map?"

Terry shook her head. "Look, I really don't want to do this. You want to play ghoul, do it on your own time."

Chomps eyed her, a second tingle running through him. "You were here, weren't you?" he asked quietly.

"At the scene of the crash. You helped pull him out of the wreckage."

"Not him, no," Terry said. There was a deep pain behind her eyes, but her jaw was set defiantly. "No, I got to pull out the children. Even strapped in and with all the airbag deployments they were . . . you want details, go look at the crash scene photos."

"I'm sorry," Chomps said. "I just want to understand."

"Then understand this," she said. "It happened. The duke killed himself and his family, and in the process changed life in Serisburg for all of us. Forever."

For a brief moment Chomps considered telling her that he, too, had gone through his share of life-changing experiences. But this wasn't the time or place. "I just want to understand," he said again. "Can you at least show me where they started from that night?"

For a long moment she stared at him. Then, some of the pain receded—or more likely was forced back by a sheer act of will—and her professional police officer's expression reinstated itself across her face. "If you like," she said, pulling out her tablet and keying it. "Here. Serisburg Point, the duchy seat and the ducal home. And here's his private retreat."

Chomps peered at the map. The direct line between the two points did indeed pass over the area where they were standing. "Any servants with them at the retreat?"

"No," Terry said. "Otherwise they would have taken the larger air car."

"And would have had a driver, I suppose?"

"Maybe," Terry said. "But like I said, the duke liked to drive." She frowned at him. "What exactly are you getting at?"

"Nothing specific," Chomps assured her. "Just noting the fact that everyone who would have known how much the duke was drinking that evening is conveniently dead."

"I don't think *conveniently* is the word I'd use." Terry sighed. "Come on, Townsend, don't you think everyone and his brother hasn't dug into this like a terrier after a rat? The rumors and suspicions were like lumps in a lump factory for weeks afterward. But no one's turned up anything to indicate it wasn't just a tragic accident."

"*Nothing to indicate* is hardly a ringing endorsement."

"The official report has been filed," Terry growled. "The case is closed, and we move on."

"To what? Drunks and disorderlies?"

For a long moment he thought she was actually going to hit him. She took a deep breath, and the fresh flame in her eyes faded into a slightly less ominous glow. "Okay, Mr. Senior Chief who knows everything," she growled. "Here's the scene. Tell me what the report got wrong."

Chomps looked up at the tree again. It was right on the edge of the clearing they were standing in, rather like the handle on a ladle. "I suppose the location of his mountain retreat wasn't exactly secret?"

"Nope," Terry said. "Neither was the fact that he was there. *Or* when he headed up there, *or* when he was coming back. When Duke Serisburg moved, he wanted the limelight to be waiting for him when he got there."

"What was the weather like that night?"

"Some low clouds," Terry said. "Nothing that should have been a problem."

"Was there an urgent meeting or something at Serisburg Point the next day?"

"Nothing on the record," Terry said. "I know—you're wondering why he headed back home in the middle of the night with a sick son and a snoot full. I wonder that myself. A lot."

"What answer do you get?"

Terry seemed to brace herself. "That the man was an idiot. An arrogant, overconfident idiot." She snorted. "Did I mention he hadn't been wearing his restraints at the time of the crash?"

"No, you didn't," Chomps said, frowning. "Not even loosely?"

"No, he'd taken them off completely," Terry said. "Hence the theory that Benjamin's coughing or sneezing distracted him. Hard to get a good look behind you when your restraints are on."

"Yes, I'm familiar with that problem," Chomps said, looking up at the tree again. The sunlight had now faded to the point that he could barely make out the gash. "Best thing for your parents' business, though, I'd guess," he said. "You must have had gawkers by the dozens swarming out here afterward."

"Try by the hundreds," Terry said sourly. "And yes, a bunch of them ended up staying at Three Corners. All in all, we'd rather host one of the duchy's bird-watcher groups. We should head back before it gets completely dark."

Chomps looked around the clearing one more time. "Lead the way," he said. "One other thing."

"Yes?" she asked as she started back along the track.

"You said I could see the photos from the scene?"

"If you really want to," she said. "There are half a

dozen from the news reports you can pull up. Knock yourself out."

"I meant the *real* pictures, the ones you and the other police took," Chomps said. "Even better, can I see the wrecked air car? I assume it's still around somewhere."

She slowed to a stop, taking her time about it, and turned to face him. "Dad calls you *Chomps*. Is that just him, or is it for general usage?"

"It's an all-purpose nickname, yes."

"Well then, Chomps, listen up," Terry said in that same tone. "This is police business. Correction: it *was* police business. Pick a tense; either way it's not for amateur busybodies from Landing to poke their fingers into."

"What if I told you something was wrong here?"

"What if *I* told you that there's always something wrong with a person's violent death?" she countered.

"Yes, but—"

"It's closed, Townsend," she said, her voice hardening. "You hear me? Closed. There's been a final report, and the residents' fear and uncertainty has faded—"

"But if there's new evidence—"

"—and we're all just waiting for whatever's going to happen now that the Crown has our duchy," Terry continued stiffly. "We don't want anyone stirring the pot, okay? Especially some amateur detective who has no idea what the hell he's doing. Clear?"

Chomps took a deep breath. "Clear," he said reluctantly.

"Good." She spun around and started back toward the inn.

Chomps followed, staring at her back. He couldn't

see the muscles through her shirt, but her whole stride and body language screamed tension at him.

The question was, was the tension because she was afraid Chomps was going to reopen a can of worms? Or was it because she *hoped* Chomps would reopen it?

He didn't know her well enough to guess which one it was. But he was going to get to know her better. A *lot* better.

Because she was his information source for this thing, and he wasn't going to let it go. Not yet. Not until he'd proven to his own satisfaction that it was indeed an accident.

Or until he'd proven otherwise.

BOOK TWO

1546 PD

CHAPTER SEVEN

"ONE MINUTE," CAPTAIN Cheryl Cherise warned from *Diactoros*'s command station, her voice carrying across the bridge that stretched out in front of her as well as to the observers floating in the back section behind her.

Winterfall took a deep breath, feeling his heartrate picking up for probably the fourth time in the past hour. One minute until transition from hyperspace, with all the nausea and discomfort that entailed. One minute from the New Berlin star system, home of the capital planet of Potsdam, heart of the Andermani Empire. One minute to finding out whether he could do the job the Queen and Cabinet had entrusted him with.

One minute to the beginning of the path that could lead Manticore and the Andermani to peace or animosity . . . or possibly even war.

He looked across the open area, his eyes skipping past his team, and focused on Travis. His brother looked calm and collected, as if they were just popping across town instead of on their way to meet with the head of a star nation that by all reports was powerful enough to rival even Haven.

But of course, Travis could afford to be calm. None of this was on him. He was just here to say hello to the Emperor, offer a detail or two of the Walther battle that Basaltberg might have forgotten or glossed over, and maybe collect a medal that he and Lisa could pass down to their children. He wasn't the one responsible for whatever negotiations Gustav might decide to throw at him. All Travis had to do—

Winterfall felt his stomach tighten. All Travis might have to do was stand aboard his outmoded and outclassed ship someday and face off against the Andermani Navy if his brother screwed this up.

Stop it! he ordered himself sternly. He might be walking on eggshells here, but it was hardly going to end in war, no matter how badly he might screw up. It was just a matter of taking things one step at a time.

Starting with the translation back out of hyperspace. Travis had warned the downward translation was usually worse than the upward one they'd experienced on their way out of Manticoran space, but Winterfall was ready for it.

Ten seconds later *Diactoros* made translation.

And Winterfall discovered to his dismay that he wasn't.

Fortunately, he had the bag ready, and got to it in time, which saved him from the absolute shame of vomiting in zero-G. But there was still plenty of embarrassment left as he heaved his guts.

Still, as he slowly recovered, he could see that several of the others weren't in the greatest shape either. Most, he suspected, were simply better at hiding it than he was.

Travis, naturally, barely even seemed to acknowledge the event.

"Signal coming in," the man at the com station called. His voice seemed odd, as if he was fighting his own gastric distress.

"What, already?" Cherise asked, sounding surprised.

Winterfall blinked back fresh tears, trying to settle his stomach and get his mind back in gear. Potsdam was a solid twelve light-minutes from where they'd crossed the hyper limit, which meant that even if the Emperor had signaled the second he picked up their footprint it should be at least another eleven minutes before they heard anything. So how could they be hearing anything this soon?

"Found the ship, Ma'am," someone else called. "It's about twenty light-seconds inward—practically on top of us. Looks like a destroyer."

Winterfall squared his shoulders. As Foreign Secretary, he was technically the master of the entire mission. He ought to join this conversation. "What are they saying?" he asked. His voice came out only a *little* slurred.

"No idea," the com operator said. "The signal's encrypted."

"Obviously intended for Basaltberg and *Zhong Kui*," Cherise said.

"Catching up on eight months' worth of news," Winterfall said, nodding.

"Or eight months' worth of military updates," Travis said.

Winterfall frowned across the lounge. "You think there's trouble?"

"I don't know," Travis said. "But that ship sure

looks like it was waiting for us specifically—as far as I know there are no other systems along this vector where an Andermani ship might have come in."

"*Zhong Kui*'s signaling back to the destroyer, Captain," the com operator put in.

"And it's only been eleven T-years since their last war and annexation," Travis added. "They might be having trouble with unrest."

Winterfall winced. "You mean eleven years since the last war we know of," he pointed out.

"There's that, too," Travis conceded. "Andermani history over the past thirty years has been a little . . . unstable."

"So it has," Winterfall murmured. It had only been thirty-four T-years ago that Gustav Anderman and the mercenaries of Liegnitz, Ltd., descended on the Old Chinese-founded world of Kuan Yin and rescued the colonists from slow starvation. The grateful populace had accepted him with open arms, and apparently had no problem with his subsequent program of turning their world into a modern version of Old Prussia. Over the next three decades New Belin had grown to become the six-system Andermani Empire as various star nations had, in their turns, attacked Anderman, been defeated, and been subsequently annexed.

At least, that was the story from the official Andermani history in Manticore's files. Other reports were less charitable to the old mercenary chief. The records from Tomlinson, for instance, claimed Anderman had overreacted to a simple misunderstanding, and had followed up the unwarranted conquest with continued harassment and heavy-handed suppression of the locals. The documents filed with the Solarian League by the so-called ABC alliance of Angelique, Babel, and Cantiz accused Anderman of naked aggression against their own peaceful worlds.

No doubt Emperor Gustav himself would repeat the claim that everyone in his empire lived under a fair and just rule. But if there *was* lingering unrest, Travis would be far better than Winterfall at analyzing the official military information and the more subtle signs embedded in them.

"Signal from *Zhong Kui*," the com operator said.

"My Lord?" Cherise invited.

Winterfall swallowed. *Master of the mission.* "Put it through," he said.

"Lord Winterfall," Basaltberg's voice came over the speaker.

Winterfall felt a shiver run through him as he threw another look at Travis. A ship waiting at the hyper limit for them; encrypted messages going back and forth; and now the admiral's voice as dark and subdued as Winterfall had ever heard it.

"I'm afraid it falls to me to deliver bad news," Basaltberg continued. "Three weeks ago, His Excellency Emperor Gustav passed from this life to that which lies beyond. His Excellency Emperor Andrew now sits on the throne in his stead.

"Gott schütze den Kaiser."

For a long moment the bridge and lounge were silent, the dead air filled with shock and disbelief. Travis found himself staring at the viewscreen, at the distant fire of New Berlin's sun and the hovering dot marking *Zhong Kui's* position. This couldn't be. It just *couldn't*. Not after they'd come all this way at the Emperor's invitation.

But it was. Basaltberg's fears, Basaltberg's premonitions, had come true.

And suddenly, for all intents and purposes, the Manticorans were adrift without a wedge.

What were they supposed to do now?

"The cortège has begun its voyage through the Empire," Basaltberg continued. "Emperor Andrew accompanies his father's remains aboard SMS *Friedrich der Grosse*, allowing all to say their final farewells. I have orders to intercept them mid-journey and join her escort through its return to New Berlin. I'm afraid—" He broke off, and Travis winced in sympathetic pain at the ache in the admiral's voice. "I'm afraid that this leaves you in something of an uncertain position, Lord Winterfall. I'm certain that Emperor Andrew will be willing to meet with you when he returns, but right now all such matters are necessarily suspended."

Winterfall took a deep breath. *Hold it together,* Travis mentally urged his brother. *You can do this. Just hold it together and find an answer.*

"I understand entirely, Admiral," Winterfall said, with just the right mix of sympathy for Basaltberg and the somberness appropriate for an outsider who had no personal claim to mourn. "If I may suggest, we of the Star Kingdom of Manticore would like to join you in your journey, that we might be present to pay our own respects to your late Emperor. Would that be acceptable?"

There was a moment of silence. Even in his grief at the shattering news, Travis knew, Basaltberg would nevertheless be running the logic, the politics, and the diplomacy though his mind. Deciding whether or not the presence of foreigners at such an intimate time and event would be proper, or whether it would be better to let those same foreigners continue unescorted to the heart of the Empire to await Andrew's return. Travis held his breath . . .

"Emperor Gustav desired to meet you and your countrymen, My Lord," the admiral said at last. "Sadly, that opportunity has now passed. But I'm certain he would have been pleased to allow you to join with the people of the Empire in saying your farewells. I would be honored to have you accompany me as I fulfill my Emperor's final orders."

Travis let out a quiet breath. Good. They would be with Basaltberg at least a little longer, which would hopefully give them all time to catch their breath and come to terms with this unexpected development. Hopefully, Captain Marcello and the rest of the *Damocles*'s officers wouldn't have a problem with this.

Actually, even if they did, it wouldn't matter. Gavin Vellacott, Baron Winterfall, was the one in command here.

"But understand," Basaltberg continued. "While Emperor Andrew may be willing to meet with you upon your arrival, there will be no discussions or other diplomatic events. This trip is solely for remembrance and mourning."

"Absolutely, Admiral," Winterfall agreed. "We accept this honor with gratitude and humility."

"Thank you as well for your courtesy," Basaltberg said. "I'm sending the necessary navigation data to you and *Damocles*. We'll return to the hyper limit and proceed with all due speed. With your permission, I must now speak to the rest of my crew."

"Understood," Winterfall said. "We'll speak again later."

There was a tone as the com channel closed. "Captain Cherise?" Winterfall asked.

"Data coming in now, My Lord," Cherise said. "Navigation, make our new course."

"Yes, Ma'am."

"So where exactly are we going?" Travis asked, straining to look past Cherise's shoulder and read the nav display.

"Not too far, Commander," Cherise said. "One of the Andermani colony worlds a couple of weeks' travel away.

"Tomlinson."

☆   ☆   ☆

It was time.

Bajer didn't know the entire plan, of course. Only the Freedom Council's inner circle knew the *entire* plan. But he had to know more than most, given how pivotal his role was, and so he knew the equipment was in place. The rest of the Free Tomlinson rebels were ready. And the timing was perfect.

In fact, it was better than perfect. The sudden and unexpected death of Emperor Gustav—and the fact that the mysterious benefactor who had gotten this whole thing rolling four years ago had been able to inform the rebels before the official word had been released here in Tomlinson—had come at precisely the right moment.

The only worrisome part was the fact that Bajer didn't know if the reinforcements they'd been promised were actually in place. It would have been far too risky for them to send any transmissions announcing their arrival, so he just had to hope they'd hit their own timing.

Even if they hadn't, though, it wouldn't matter. Not where his mission was concerned. And if he and the others succeeded, they should be more than able to deal with the situation until the reinforcements *did* arrive. Once the Freets took *Preussen*, they'd have more than enough firepower to chase away or cripple the cruiser and destroyer that acted as the battleship's escort, as well as anything else in the system that might try to challenge them.

The Freets had always known the real problems would begin when word of events in Tomlinson reached New Berlin, and they'd expected the response to be massive and violent. But that had been when Gustav Anderman had been in charge. Now he was dead . . . and if the cortège held to its itinerary, it was just possible that there would be no response from New Berlin at all.

Yet to make any of that happen, they needed time. And that meant that the *chase away or cripple* options on *Preussen's* escort ships really boiled down to just *cripple*.

Cripple . . . or kill.

The Freedom Council on the planet below him wouldn't like that. Neither would their anonymous backer. Their initial strategy had always been to position themselves with sufficient power to persuade the Emperor to negotiate Tomlinson's freedom rather than spend the lives and ships it would cost to beat down the rebels and retake the system. Too much bloodshed at the very beginning, though, might well have driven out logic in favor of pride and anger, and the Freet leaders had warned Bajer to be as cautious as possible where casualties were concerned precisely to keep injuries to that pride to a minimum.

Bajer had always had his doubts about how well that strategy would work out, given Gustav's reputation for ruthlessness. The Emperor might have been coolheaded enough to make sure logic overrode pride, but he might just as easily have decided that challenges to the imperial authority could not be tolerated under any circumstances.

Still, it had been the best hope Tomlinson had, and Bajer had been fully prepared to roll the dice.

All of that had changed now. Gustav was gone, and how *Andrew* would react—assuming he had the opportunity to react—was anyone's guess. The Freedom Council still wanted minimal casualties, and Bajer would do what he could to accommodate their wishes. But the Council wasn't here. Bajer was, and he would do whatever he had to buy back his world's freedom. And if the cortège—

"Herr Korvettenkapitän?" a voice came from behind him.

Bajer felt his breath catch in his throat. He'd worked hard to make sure this part of the ship would be unoccupied for the next few minutes, and having finished his task there was no tactical reason why he couldn't have left.

But he'd decided at the last minute that it might be a good idea to linger a bit longer anyway, just in case the ancient Demon Murphy decided to put in an appearance. It appeared now that the additional caution had indeed been warranted.

Steeling himself, putting on his most intimidating face, he turned around.

The hauptgefreiter pulling herself along the handholds towards him had a toolkit cinched around her waist. She faltered a bit as she caught his expression, then continued forward.

"Pardon me, *mein Herr,*" she said. "I was ordered to report to Oberleutnant der Sterne Kiselev to assist in running a diagnostic on Missile Three."

Bajer ground his teeth. Not only had the stupid woman misread her orders, but she'd misread them at the worst possible time.

"I believe that test is scheduled for twenty minutes from now," he said. He was taking a big risk here, he knew—there was no reason *Preussen*'s ATO should have a lowly missile tech's work schedule at his fingertips. If she started wondering about that, there could be trouble.

"But since you're here, there's something else that needs looking at," he continued. "One of the Number Six sensor feed relays has been giving the bridge unreliable responses. Instead of waiting for someone to return from planet-side liberty, I thought I'd pull the panel myself and see what was going on in there. If you have time, I'd appreciate your assistance."

The trick to a believable lie, Bajer had long since learned, lay in not giving the target enough time to start thinking it through. In this case, the built-in Andermani reluctance to hear an order without instantly obeying it should also work in his favor.

And so it did. "Of course, *Herr Korvettenkapitän,*" she said, changing direction towards the external sensors manual relay compartment and swimming inside. She planted her magnetic soles on the deck and unsnapped the cover of her toolkit.

Bajer lingered in the passageway just long enough to see Kiselev slip out of the compartment where she'd tied the stand-alone unit into the ship's internal sensors' central net. She gave him a quick thumbs up, then disappeared toward the forward impeller room. He waited until she was out of sight, then headed into the compartment behind the hauptgefreiter.

"If you'll go ahead and open it up, I've got the test program on my minicomp," he told her as he planted his own magnetic soles firmly on the deck and pointed. "That one," he added, pointing to one of the consoles with his left hand.

Once again obeying orders without question or hesitation, the spacer turned obediently towards the indicated panel. "Of course, *Herr Korvettenka*—"

Her voice broke off in mid syllable as Bajer touched the muzzle of his silenced pistol to the back of her skull and squeezed the trigger.

Her forehead disintegrated, spraying blood, brain matter, and bone across the console, the impact of the slug jerking her forward. Not enough to break her mag soles lock on the deck, though, and so she continued to float there, bent grotesquely forward, feet anchored, globules of her blood drifting in the micro-gravity.

One instant a live, breathing human being. The next, fifty kilos of dead meat.

Bajer swallowed hard. He stared at her another moment, then dropped his eyes to the hand clenched around his gun. To his surprise, the hand was rock steady, without any sign of the emotion rippling through his nervous system. He'd never actually killed anyone before, hadn't realized it would be so . . . easy.

He certainly hadn't been ready for how it would feel, as if he'd just crossed some invisible border into another world. A shadowy world where everything looked the same, but was dismal and dark.

It took another moment for him to realize that it wasn't the world that had just changed. It was him.

He swallowed again, the taste of bile faint in the back of his throat as he looked one last time upon his handiwork. Then he drew a deep breath and shoved the pistol back inside his tunic. He unlocked his mag soles, pushed himself out of the compartment, and closed the hatch behind him. He tapped a short command code into the keypad beside the hatch to *keep* it closed, squared his shoulders, and sent himself swimming up the passage towards the next stop on his schedule.

He probably hadn't really needed to kill her, he thought as he worked himself along the handholds. She hadn't seemed all that imaginative.

But they couldn't afford to take that chance. The countdown still had twenty minutes to go, and if she'd paused to ask why the assistant tactical officer was wandering around the Damage Control Department's forward sensor compartment—or worse, if she'd mentioned it to someone else—it might have been disastrous.

Besides, it wasn't as if she was the only person who was going to die today.

☆   ☆   ☆

"I just want to know what we did to get on the Kapitänin's bad side," Hauptgefreiter Yau-bin Uhlriz grumbled.

"I suspect your underlying premise is flawed," Stabsgefreiter Mei-chau Thörnrich said calmly. "Specifically, your assumption that Kapitänin der Sterne Hansen even knows we exist."

"Of course she knows," Uhlriz said, matching the neutrality in the petty officer's voice. He and Thörnrich had known each other a long time, but protocol frowned on anything other than proper formality while on duty. "I'm just saying a little time planet-side or even on the station would have been nice. If she was going to hand out extra liberty, why couldn't she hand some *our* way?"

"Probably because Oberleutnant der Sterne Eichmann told her he couldn't possibly hold the department together without you," Thörnrich replied in a voice that managed to be proper and deflating at the same time.

"That can't be right," Uhlriz insisted. "The Oberleutnant would never lie to the Kapitänin like that."

Thörnrich looked sideways at him, and Uhlriz caught just the hint of a non-regulation smile. "Of course not," she said. "I stand corrected."

Uhlriz sent the almost-smile right back at her. They really *had* known each other too long.

But his point and annoyance remained. Kapitänin der Sterne Hansen had decided to grant extra liberty, and almost a quarter of *Preussen*'s company was off the ship at the moment. He didn't know what had spurred the CO's generosity, but could only hope it didn't wear off before it was his turn to take a run dirtside and smell un-recycled air.

In the meantime, he and Thörnrich were stuck here on duty sensor watch. With the battleship orbiting placidly around the planet, that task was about as exciting as watching paint dry.

Adding to the sense of having been left high and dry was the fact that there were only half a dozen people on the bridge. Fregattenkapitän Greuner, the head of their department and current officer of the watch, was strapped into the command chair at the center of the bridge. Occasionally he looked up, checking the displays and monitors, but for the most part his attention was focused on the document reader in his hand.

"At least all we have to deal with is boredom," Uhlriz said. "There are worse problems we could be facing."

"Such as being down on the planet facing off against some Freet lunatics," Thörnrich agreed. "Do you suppose they'll ever accept that life under Imperial rule is far better than what they had under that fool McIntyre?"

"I doubt it," Uhlriz said. "As mirages go, the false memory of *the good old days* is one of the most resilient."

"So it is," Thörnrich agreed. "More's the pity."

☆   ☆   ☆

"Thank you, Zhi-wa," Kapitänin der Sterne Hansen said, smiling and inclining her head in a respectful bow as her steward set the bottle of brandy between the pair of snifters on the dining cabin table. "That was delicious, as always."

Oberbootsmann Zhi-wa Pang smiled and bowed in return. She was in her early fifties, old enough to remember the desperate conditions on Kuan Yin before Gustav Anderman came to its rescue. For many of her generation, those memories made up the glue of the Empire's unshakable loyalty to their Emperor.

But Pang was used to the intertwining of loyalty and personal history. She'd been Hansen's mother's steward before Vizeadmiral Amanda Hansen's death, twelve T-years ago, and she'd known her current captain since Hansen was thirteen.

Long-term relationships like that weren't uncommon in the Imperial Andermani Navy. Sometimes Pang wondered if other cultures throughout the galaxy had similar roots, and if not how they managed to survive without them.

"If you need anything else, Kapitänin, please let me know," she said.

"We will," Hansen assured her, and the oberbootsmann bowed her way out of the dining cabin.

"She does take good care of you," Jachmann observed from the other side of the table.

"Yes, she does," Hansen agreed. "But then, she's had a lot of practice."

"I know." Jachmann picked up the brandy bottle and poured slowly and carefully into both snifters. "I still miss your mother, you know. Your father, too, though I didn't know him as well. We lost him too early."

"We lost them *both* too early," Hansen said quietly.

"Agreed," Jachmann said soberly. "And now we've lost the Emperor." He handed her one of the snifters, took the other for himself, and shook his head as he gazed down into it. "It's hard to imagine the galaxy without him in it."

"Though it's not as if we haven't seen this coming, *mein Herr*," Hansen pointed out. "I imagine there's always going to be a sense of suddenness when it finally happens, but it's been obvious for quite some time that even Emperor Gustav couldn't live forever."

"True." Jachmann waved the snifter under his nostrils, inhaling appreciatively, then took a small sip and settled back in his chair. "It's going to hit our people hard, you know. And God only knows how the Tomlinsons are going to react." He shook his head again, his expression somber. "There's always a tendency to test new rulers, even at the best of times, and I doubt our rowdy fellow subjects on Tomlinson will be any fonder of Andrew than they were of his father."

"Probably not," Hansen agreed, her eyes opaque as

she gazed down into her own brandy. Then she blinked and looked back up at the flotillenadmiral. "But you're right about our people. That's one reason I recommended delaying the official announcement. I want to give as many of them some solid leave time before they find out about it. There's certainly plenty of time to get ready before the cortège actually gets here."

"I'm amazed the news hasn't leaked already," Jachmann said. "There's not that much traffic into Tomlinson from New Berlin, but I'd have thought some enterprising reporter would have gotten the story out by now."

"*Onkel* Gustav was always pretty particular about how sensitive news got released," Hansen pointed out. "I don't expect that to change in the near future, at least until Andrew's had a chance to put his own imprint on things."

"I expect a lot of things are going to change," Jachmann said pensively. "It's a pity, in some ways, that Andrew's been so much in his father's shadow. Nobody's sure what to expect from him. The one opinion everyone seems to share is that no one could possibly truly fill Gustav's shoes."

"No, he was . . . unique, in so many ways." Hansen shook her head. "Mother used to have a saying. She said that when the true forest giants fall, the sunlight pouring in through the hole they leave in the canopy illuminates all sorts of secret strengths and weaknesses."

"A wise woman, your mother." Jachmann raised his snifter in silent salute to the long-dead vizeadmiral. "I wish I could hear her take on—"

The sudden, raucous scream of a shrill alarm cut him off.

CHAPTER EIGHT

"PLASMA BREACH!" The computer-generated voice blared from every speaker aboard SMS *Preussen*. "Plasma breach, Conduit Seventeen! Plasma breach! Plasma breach! Plasma breach, Conduit Seventeen!"

"Shut that damned thing off!" Fregattenkapitän Greuner shouted, and the heel of Uhlriz's hand slammed down on a button.

"Plasma breach! Plas—"

"Thank you," Greuner growled, spinning his chair towards the chief petty officer at the damage control board. That would normally have been a commissioned officer's station, but with the ship in orbit Oberbootsmann Palzer had the duty. "Palzer?"

"The sensors confirm, *mein Herr*," Palzer said tautly. "Conduit Seventeen, just forward of Frame Ninety-six. Two compartments are gone."

"*Scheiße*." Greuner shook his head, then shook his entire body, like a man throwing off the effects of an unexpected punch. "Initiate—"

"Explosion in Reactor One!" another voice—a human

one this time instead of a computer—announced suddenly over the intercom. "Explosion in Reactor One, and—"

The voice chopped off suddenly, and another scarlet damage icon glared on Palzer's panel. Then another, and another.

"Fregattenkapitän, we may have a cascade failure!" Palzer called, his face pale. "I'm showing breaches at Frames Eighty-seven and One-One-Three, as well."

Greuner swallowed hard. The failsafes were designed to shut conduits down and vent to space the instant there was any sign of a breach. Normally, they did just that, limiting damage to the immediate vicinity of the breach where, admittedly, it was usually devastating. But if they failed, if there was a cascade of breaches—

He braced himself, feeling the skeleton bridge watch's tension as they waited for his response. "I—"

His earbud buzzed with a sudden priority code and he felt a huge spasm of relief as he recognized it.

"Yes, *meine Kapitänin*," he said.

"Set condition Zulu-Three," Hansen's voice came crisply in his ear. "Until we know what's really going on, we don't need any extra bodies in the way. Then seal off Reactor One and Conduit Seventeen until we get some remotes in there. Better make that Seventeen *and* Sixteen."

"At once, *meine Kapitänin*."

☆   ☆   ☆

"All hands, Zulu-Three," Greuner's voice blared from the bulkhead speakers. "Repeat, Zulu-Three."

Bajer grabbed a handhold, stopped, and flattened himself against the bulkhead as *Preussen*'s crew responded. Zulu-Three was the least drastic of the three emergency shipboard evacuation plans in the standing orders. He wished it were Zulu-Two or Zulu-One, but there was only so much that could be expected from plasma breaches, given that the heavily armored compartments around them were designed to contain the damage.

Still, it would get about half of the remaining shipboard personnel off the ship. They'd just have to deal with the ones the order left behind.

☆   ☆   ☆

"Kapitänin on the bridge!" Palzer barked as Hansen swam onto her bridge, Jachmann close on her heels. The relief on Greuner's face could not have been more obvious as he unstrapped and thrust himself out of the command chair as quickly as he could.

"Thank you, Fregattenkapitän," Hansen said, her briskly calm formality extraordinarily reassuring. "Report damage."

"We show eleven compartments breached, *meine Kapitänin*," Palzer said. "At least two of them show breaches clear through the outer hull."

"At *least* two of them?"

"*Ja, meine Kapitänin*," Palzer confirmed uncomfortably. "With the outages spreading and much of our sensor coverage lost, I can't be more precise."

"I see." Hansen turned to the young leutnant der sterne manning communications. "Alert Station Alpha, Leutnant Selavko. Inform them we have what appears to be a cascade failure of a plasma conduit and request additional assistance."

"*Ja, meine Kapitänin*," the leutnant said, turning back to his console.

☆   ☆   ☆

Ensign Rolf Panum of the Tomlinson Emergency Services was waiting in the crash car when the alarm came through.

"This is it," he called over his shoulder to the thirty-five men and women crowded silently into the compartment behind him as he gunned the thrusters. "Game faces on."

Two seconds later, the crash car was clear of the platform and blazing across the empty space between it and the Andermani battleship. Four more TES crash cars accelerated out of their bays behind him and all five streaked toward *Preussen*.

In the old days, Panum reflected with a touch of wistfulness, the area around Station Alpha would have been alive with freighters and buzzing shuttles, bringing in supplies and trade goods. Now, with the Andermani controlling shipping in and out of their Empire—and the bulk of that shipping funneled as a matter of course to New Berlin—traffic was far sparser, and most of the satellite freight platforms had been handed over to TES as staging areas for emergency vehicles and personnel.

Unfortunately for the invaders, while they were extremely cautious about foreign shipments to their conquered worlds, they were less attentive about who got to help one of their ships when it was in trouble.

They weren't completely oblivious, of course. Normally, a crash car like Panum's would undergo close examination before being allowed to enter any Andermani warship's defense zone.

But a plasma conduit rupture threatened both the ship's interior and exterior, and the local emergency crews had faster and better access to the hull than any of the repair crews inside. More importantly, certainly from Panum's point of view, a rupture as catastrophic as the one *Preussen's* systems were reporting threatened to overwhelm the battleship's own damage control personnel, especially with so many of them on leave. With an entire quadrant of the ship at risk, even proper Andermani procedures were likely to be brushed aside, given how urgently they would need extra hands.

That was the theory, anyway. Panum and his team were about to find out whether or not it was true.

☆　　☆　　☆

"We show five TES shuttles headed our way, *meine Kapitänin*," Stabsgefreiter Thörnrich reported.

"Excellent," Hanson said. "Clear them straight through."

"A very prompt response," Jachmann commented.

"Indeed," she agreed. "And I—"

Another alarm buzzed raucously.

"Compartment Niner-Seven-One-Zero shows open to space, *meine Kapitänin*," Palzer announced.

☆　　☆　　☆

Bajer floated at the end of the tether snap hooked to the handhold at Access Bravo. The large compartment, one of four spaced equidistantly around *Preussen's* core hull, was crowded as a stream of disciplined but obviously anxious spacers funneled through it to the lift cluster. The battleship's spin section, which provided her crew with living space outside the microgravity of the rest of her hull, had four spokes, each of which contained one three-lift shaft cluster for rapid personnel movements.

Under normal circumstances, the computer-controlled lift cars were timed so that there was minimal delay transiting between the core hull and the spin section without interrupting its revolutions, but there was always *some* delay. At Zulu-Three, however, the spin section locked, exactly as it did when the ship cleared for action, which greatly speeded the lift cars' transit cycle.

At the moment, the personnel currently on duty in the ship's core hull but designated to evacuate under Zulu-Three were headed up the lift shafts to join the ship's off-duty personnel and board the lifeboats riding the groove around the center of the spin section. There were additional escape pods in the core hull itself, but they couldn't be launched without first blowing the charges that blasted away scabs of armor to clear the escape pod's launch shaft. Except under the most dire of circumstances—which clearly didn't obtain . . . yet, at least—the spin section's lifeboats were the preferred mode of evacuation.

Access Bravo wasn't actually Bajer's station under Zulu-Three, but no one seemed inclined to complain about his calming presence. Here and there, a few people actually smiled briefly at him, their expressions strained but determinedly calm, and he always smiled back with equal falsity.

"Eight more minutes, *mein Herr*," the oberbootsmann supervising the lift cluster announced, and Bajer nodded.

"Good," he said.

☆　　☆　　☆

"There they go, right on schedule," Rolf Panum said as his radar showed lifeboats separating from the mammoth battleship. Its half-kilometer length dwarfed his crash car, and the lifeboats were even tinier. "Thrusters moving them clear."

"Good," Sean Clendenin, the crash car's team leader grunted.

☆　　☆　　☆

"Evacuation complete in three minutes, *meine Kapitänin*," Greuner announced.

"Excellent." Hansen nodded.

"TES requests docking instructions, *meine Kapitänin*," Selavko said.

"Tell them to use the forward emergency ring," Hansen replied. "We'll bring them aboard closest to the breaches and have them work their way aft."

☆   ☆   ☆

"Understood, *Preussen*," Panum replied over the com. "Moving to dock now. Estimate three minutes to hard contact. Emergency One, clear."

He released the transmit button and looked over his shoulder at Clendenin.

"Three—"

"Heard it," Clendenin interrupted as the men and women behind him made their final weapons checks.

☆   ☆   ☆

"That's it, *Herr Korvettenkapitän*," the Access Bravo *oberbootsmann* announced as the final lift car completed its journey.

He and Bajer were alone now in the large, echoing compartment, which seemed even larger after the crowd that had just passed through it. Indeed, the entire ship felt somehow *empty* around them, Bajer noted, as if the vessel itself sensed the absence of almost ninety percent of its crew. Only essential engineering personnel, including every soul assigned to the Damage Control Department, the Army personnel of her *Raumbatallion*, and her command crew remained onboard.

No more than two hundred and fifty people, if Bajer's calculations were correct. And of course, a solid ten percent of that number—including Beta Section, the

Raumsbatallion's off-duty company—were holding down stations in the spin section, not the core hull.

"Excellent work," Bajer complimented the petty officer as the other began reconfiguring the lift cluster. The spin section would remain in its locked position until the onboard emergency was completely contained, and the lifts would be in damage control mode, controlled independently of the central computer net by their occupants.

"Thank you, *mein Herr*," the oberbootsmann said over his shoulder as Bajer unhooked and drifted closer to him. "I guess all the drills were—"

It was much easier the second time, Bajer thought, watching the body drift away under the impetus of the bullet, leaking globules of blood and tissue. He wiped blood and bits of brain off the control panel with his forearm and finished reconfiguring the lift cluster.

The command code he entered, however, wasn't the one Damage Control would use to activate one of the lift cars.

But that was all right. It would work just fine for the Emergency Services personnel who would be boarding soon.

☆   ☆   ☆

"Are we glad to see *you*," Maat Ditmar Muthig said as the inner hatch opened.

"Got here as quick as we could," Panum assured the petty officer, floating past him into the compartment with Clendenin on his heels. "Understand you're having a few problems?"

"One way to put it," Muthig replied with feeling. A toe push sent him drifting back to clear the way for the TES personnel. "As soon as your people have their gear onboard, we'll—"

His voice died as Clendenin arrested his own drift by gripping the front of Muthig's uniform coverall and the edge of a lethally keen knife pressed suddenly against the Andermani's throat.

"Not one more word," Clendenin said. His tone was almost conversational, but his eyes were bleak and hard. Muthig stared at him in shocked disbelief for perhaps two heartbeats. Then he swallowed hard and nodded.

"Good," Clendenin said as Panum reached out and plucked the maat's com from his ear and slid it into a pocket.

"Now why don't you and I just step over here," Clendenin continued, hooking one toe into a handhold and using his leg muscles to pull the two of them out of the way as the rest of his heavily armed team began gliding swiftly past them.

☆   ☆   ☆

"How can I help you, *Herr Korvettenkapitän*?" Bootsmann Eicher asked politely, in a tone which obviously meant *and what the hell are you doing here?* as Bajer came gliding swiftly down the passage towards Reactor One.

"I was in the vicinity and the Kapitänin asked me to get her an eyes-on situation report before I head for the bridge," Bajer told the Damage Control tech. "What do we have?"

"I'm not sure yet, *mein Herr*," Eicher replied. "We just got here ourselves, but the damage seems a bit odd. Most of it's pretty minor—a lot less severe than the remotes are reporting. And the blast pattern's weird."

"Really?" Bajer frowned. "Your crew's inside?"

"Of course, *mein Herr*."

"Then why don't you and I join them? If the damage

really is less catastrophic, I'm sure the Kapitänin will be relieved to hear it."

"She's not the only one, *mein Herr,*" Eicher said, pulling himself through the open reactor compartment hatch to lead the way. "I just can't figure—"

He didn't notice that the assistant tactical officer wasn't on his heels until the hatch zipped shut behind him. He was still trying to figure out what the hell was happening when the boarding grenade Bajer had tossed through the hatchway drifted past him.

Two seconds later, there was another explosion in Reactor One.

☆　☆　☆

Obergefreiter Schuster couldn't understand why his diagnostic unit insisted there was no plasma breach on the other side of the sealed hatch in front of his Damage Control team. According to the ship's sensor net, the breach was actually spreading, but his stupid handheld unit didn't agree.

What the *hell*?

"Well, is it, or isn't it?" Bootsmann Tischler demanded. "I'm damned well not opening that hatch until I know what's on the other side."

"All I can tell you is what the unit says," Schuster said helplessly. "And it says there's no problem, which can't be right."

"Tell me something I don't already know," Tischler snarled. He keyed his com. "Central, Tischler," he began. "Something's—"

"*Mein Gott!*" someone exclaimed, and Tischler broke off as he and Schuster spun towards the sound of the voice.

Just as a fusillade of bullets from the Emergency

Services personnel who had rounded a bend in the passageway ripped through their entire five-man team.

☆   ☆   ☆

"Gunfire!" a voice shouted suddenly from the bridge speakers. "Gunfire in Compartment Niner-Four-Th—"

The unmistakable staccato of automatic weapons fire cut the voice off, and Hansen stiffened in her command chair.

"Where was that from?" she snapped.

"Niner-Four-Three-Zero," Selavko reported in a disbelieving tone.

Hansen shot a look over her shoulder at Jachmann. For once, the flotillenadmiral looked completely nonplussed, and she didn't blame him a bit. She stabbed a button on her chair arm, activating her personal com. "Major Kleinberg?" she said sharply.

"Ja, meine Kapitänin?" the commander of *Preussen's* embarked *Raumbatallion* replied from his station aft of the spin section.

"What's Alpha Team's status?"

"Alpha Team, *meine Kapitänin?"* Kleinberg echoed, clearly confused about why his CO was asking about the duty boarding team when her ship was threatening to explode around them.

"Alpha Team!" Hansen repeated sharply. "We have gunfire in at least one compartment forward of Reactor One."

"Gun—" Kleinberg began, then cut himself off instantly.

"Exactly! Maybe there's more than just a plasma breach going on."

"I can have Alpha geared up and heading up-ship in three minutes, *meine Kapitänin.*"

"*Nein*," Hansen said firmly. "Get Bravo Team down from the spin section to secure the lift clusters and the center of the core hull and isolate whatever's happening in the forward half of the ship. I want Alpha on the ready shuttle—have them come to the forward emergency ring. If this is really an attempt to take the ship, whoever it is must have gotten aboard in the TES crash cars, and I want you coming in behind them. Use the shuttle breaching charges if you have to in order to avoid the airlocks. Once you're aboard, move aft and trap them between your people and the spin section."

"*Ja, meine Kapitänin*," Kleinberg replied. "We'll be underway in four minutes."

"Good." Hansen shifted channels. "Oberstabsbootsmann Kellerman, this is the Kapitänin," she said. "I need you and at least three people you trust on the bridge. And bring sidearms." She listened for a second, then snorted harshly. "Yes, that's *exactly* what I said. Now *move*."

She released the button and raised a calm eyebrow at Jachmann. "Any other suggestions, *mein Herr*?"

"You're not going to warn the rest of the crew about what's happening?" he asked. Stunned disbelief no longer filled his eyes, but he was clearly still trying to sort things out in his own mind.

"No," she said. "We don't know how many there are or where they are right now, and I can't warn our people without tipping them off that we know what's happening. I want Kleinberg's arrival to surprise them, if we can manage that."

"Yes, that all makes sense," Jachmann conceded.

"And if this is the Freets—and I don't see who else it *could* be," Hansen added, "they can't know the ship as well as our people do. That should slow them down. There'll be time enough to warn the rest of our people when Kleinberg's back aboard."

Jachmann made a face, but nodded. "Agreed."

☆   ☆   ☆

"Move. *Move!*" Oberfeldwebel Zunker bellowed as the Alpha Team's three squads grabbed their helmets and sent themselves shooting down the passage towards the waiting ready shuttle.

The *Komet*-class shuttle was armed with a light autocannon, but its primary function was to transport boarding teams, and it carried hull-breaching charges as well as racked GK12 rifles, the standard infantry rifle of the Imperial Andermani Army, and the SK1 assault guns that were specially designed to fire flechettes for shipboard actions. The Alpha Team was kept vac-suited for moments just like this, and they would mate with their personal weapons once they were aboard the shuttle and en route.

Hauptmann Kleinberg waited till the last member of the team was in motion, then kicked off and followed them, his brain busy as he thought about the challenge ahead.

☆   ☆   ☆

"Reporting as ordered, *meine Kapitänin*," Oberstabsbootsmann Arthur Kellerman announced as he and three grim-faced enlisted spacers entered *Preussen*'s bridge.

Even after almost forty-seven T-years, there was just a trace of Kellerman's original Old Earth North American accent in his German. There was a lot of white at his temples now, too. A lot more than there'd been when he'd been a very junior stabsgefreiter assigned to Hansen's mother, Kapitäninleutnant Amanda Hansen.

"Thank you," Hansen said, eyeing the man who'd made it his business to watch her back since she'd learned to walk. "Defensive positions."

"*Ja, meine Kapitänin.*" Nodding curtly, he twitched his head at the three spacers who'd followed him. They spread out, moving to the corners of the bridge, their SK1s held with the competence instilled by the Navy's regular small arms training.

☆ ☆ ☆

"Shuttle's separating in fifteen seconds, Hauptfeldwebel," Feldwebel Metzger announced over Hauptfeldwebel Huan Niekisch's earbud.

"Good," Niekisch said, never looking away from her own handheld. Every instinct honed in twelve years of service told her she ought to be aboard the shuttle with her CO, but her forebrain knew better. As the *Raumsbatallion*'s senior NCO, her proper place was keeping an eye on Hauptmann Waldschmidt, Beta Company's NCO. Waldschmidt was a bright enough young fellow, but this was his first deployment as a company commander. He was shaping up nicely, but any hauptfeldwebel knew her job was to buff off any rough spots on the newbie officers.

"Last trooper into the lift, *mein Herr*," she continued now, looking up at Waldschmidt. "And the Skipper and the ready shuttle are separating in thirteen seconds."

"Then we'd best get to it," Ruogang Waldschmidt said grimly, and Niekisch followed him into the central lift car and hit the button.

☆ ☆ ☆

"Separation!" the shuttle pilot announced as the ready shuttle broke free of *Preussen*. It quivered as she fired her thrusters and sent her craft outward. She had to clear the spin section to reach her assigned destination, and the shuttle rose vertically on its belly thrusters.

☆   ☆   ☆

The three lift shafts from the *Raumsbatallion*'s quarters aboard the spin section operated perfectly, sliding their lift cars rapidly up the spin section spoke to the core hull. Their doors opened, and the men and women of Waldschmidt's company started to crowd out.

The six Tomlinson-born spacers waited until the doors slid apart, then two of them opened fire on each lift car with the GK12s and SK1s they'd taken from the arms lockers.

☆   ☆   ☆

"Right on schedule," Obermaat Collette Filipov murmured.

A native Tomlinson, she was rather older than most of the Andermani Navy's second-class petty officers. She was better at her job than many of those younger maats and obermaats, but it wasn't a huge surprise that she hadn't been promoted as rapidly as they had.

She'd seemed to be having a little more trouble with that apparent slight lately, however, which was why Greuner, on Bajer's advice, had moved her from *Preussen*'s bridge crew to one of the on-mount point defense crews, where she could perhaps regain some perspective. Greuner had deferred to Bajer's recommendation, as he usually did where the handful of Tomlinsons in their department was concerned.

And so Filipov now found herself in charge of the four-person on-mount crew of Point Defense Three, the only mount manned at Zulu-Three. Where, by a strange turn of fate, all but one of her personnel happened to be fellow Tomlinsons.

"Tracking," the one non-Tomlinson on PD 3's crew reported.

Filipov eyed him. She didn't know exactly where the hauptgefreiter had come from, but she was pretty damn sure he wasn't the Andermani his papers proclaimed him to be.

"Seven seconds," someone else said, and Filipov nodded.

☆   ☆   ☆

The assault shuttle cleared the spin section and started forward.

"What the—?"

There was no alarm in the pilot's voice. There wasn't time for that. There was only confusion as she realized the point defense station had trained out. It had only begun to register that its gaping muzzle was aimed directly at *her* when it fired.

☆   ☆   ☆

"*Meine Kapitänin!*" Greuner gasped. "Point Defense Three just fired! It—it destroyed the Ready Shuttle!"

A ripple of shock and confusion ran like a fire wave through the bridge. But Hansen's face showed no emotion. Releasing her seat restraints, she gave herself a shove that sent her drifting towards Kellerman. The stone-faced petty officer extended a hand to draw her to a bulkhead handhold next to him, and she turned to face the shocked members of her bridge crew.

"I know, Fregattenkapitän Greuner," she said, her voice icy calm. "I'm sorry."

And suddenly the assault rifles at the corners of the bridge—the rifles in the hands of the men who were supposed to be protecting them—were leveled and aimed.

At them.

For a frozen moment total silence enveloped the compartment. Then, Selavko thrust up out of his seat, turning toward Hansen.

He never completed the turn. An SK1 coughed, and the burst of flechettes struck him from behind at the base of his neck.

His neck simply disintegrated in an explosive shower of blood, and his head—eyes wide and staring in confusion—sailed across the compartment.

Hansen's lips tightened. She started to say something sharp, then stopped herself. The spacer who'd fired had been unable to see Selavko's hands. He hadn't known whether or not the leutnant had a weapon.

Besides, despite all the effort she'd gone through to keep casualties to an absolute minimum, it wasn't as if Selavko was the only one of *Preussen*'s people who'd died today.

Jachmann stared at her, his face dark with mingled shock and fury, and she looked back levelly.

"What do you think you're doing?" he demanded harshly.

"I think I'm committing mutiny, *mein Herr*," she said calmly.

"That's insane!"

"On the contrary, it's *very* sane," she said. "I have my reasons, *Herr Baron*. I can't explain them to you right this moment, but eventually I will. And when I do, you'll have a choice to make."

"Choice? What kind of *choice* do you expect me to make?"

"A difficult one," she told him. "Very much like

the one Arthur had to make." She touched the ober-stabsbootsmann lightly on the shoulder. "It wasn't easy for him. In fact, he tried very hard to talk me out of this. But in the end—"

She shrugged, and Jachmann transferred his glare to Kellerman. Hansen gave him another twenty seconds or so, then looked at one of the spacers who'd accompanied Kellerman.

"Dorfman, escort the Flotillenadmiral to CIC," she said.

CHAPTER NINE

"WELL," COMMANDER ARIELLA KUPNER said quietly, floating comfortably beside Captain Muneer Jamshidi's command chair, "so far at least there's no sign anything's gone spectacularly wrong."

"Your optimism is always so comforting," Jamshidi replied in an equally quiet voice. He and Kupner had known one another a long time. He'd been a mere lieutenant—and a fairly junior one—when he joined the Quintessence, and she'd been the teenaged daughter of an officer serving under Erich and Juliana Quint, the parents of their current commodore. When Jamshidi had been given command of the *Iskra*-class battlecruiser *Spark*, he'd known exactly who he wanted for his XO.

"Hey, I *am* being optimistic," she protested mildly as she watched the tactical display. "If those people had any idea what's going on—or *supposed* to be going on, anyway—they wouldn't still be ambling along that way." She shook her head. "You know, I think this is one I'm going to feel a little guilty over."

"War isn't about glamour," Jamshidi reminded her, watching the same display. "As Commander Juliana Quint once said, war is about shooting the other guy first. In the back, if necessary."

"I know," Kupner sighed. "Doesn't mean I have to like it."

"No," Jamshidi acknowledged soberly. "It just means that sometimes we have to *do* it."

☆   ☆   ☆

IANS *Rotte* bored steadily through space.

A very appropriate verb, Fregattenkapitän Cheng Dassler decided. *Bored.*

Still, it was his duty to set an example of attentiveness on the heavy cruiser's bridge, and he was working very hard to do so. Kapitän der Sterne Xuefeng Radnitz, *Rotte*'s CO, was a methodical man who believed in doing things by The Book.

At the same time, though, Radnitz also understood the dangers of complacency and boredom which could result from being *too* methodical. At times that philosophical tension created a certain quandary for the officers under his command.

This was one of those times.

Rotte had drawn the inside position for the system patrol formation that Flotillenadmiral Jachmann had established. The heavy cruiser, the second most powerful unit of the Tomlinson garrison, had been assigned to patrol the outer limits of The Cloud, roughly 2.1 light-minutes outside the system primary. The methodical Radnitz had set things up so that it took *Rotte* eight hours—not *roughly* eight hours, not *approximately* eight hours, but *precisely* eight hours—to complete a single circuit.

Given her position over seventeen light-minutes inside the hyper-limit, she'd have plenty of time to react to anything detected incoming. Even an intruder pulling two hundred gravities would need a minimum of five hours to cover that distance, and if he wanted to decelerate for a stop at Tomlinson it would take even longer.

Radnitz would probably have preferred to leave *Rotte*'s wedge down while they patrolled in order to save strain on the nodes. But physics dictated that an unpowered orbit at this distance from the primary would take forty-nine days, a completely unacceptable number. Radnitz had compromised by dropping the sidewalls and occasionally shifting the wedge to standby until their speed took the ship too far off its designated patrol path and the crew had to relight the wedge in order to bring them back to position.

For a while that maneuver had relieved the boredom somewhat. Now, it had merely settled into another part of the ship's routine.

Meanwhile, while *Rotte* scurried along in the inner position, Fregattenkapitänin Zhelan Deutschmann's destroyer *München* had the outer one, sweeping the outer edge of the system's outermost asteroid belt, 4.1 LM from the primary. *München* had a tiny bit more acceleration, but, more to the point, she was more lightly armed. So it made sense to use her as the outer picket with *Rotte* in the intermediate position and *Preussen* covering Tomlinson itself.

The patrol pattern had been planned to position *Rotte* and *München* at a ninety-degree offset, giving them a broad sensor arc without putting the primary directly between them where it would prevent direct communication if something went sideways. Since *München*'s path was 25.76 LM in circumference, that meant she had to maintain a velocity of 16,100 KPS in order to hold position relative to the heavy cruiser. It was her job, hopefully, to spot an incoming threat in time to vector her heavier consorts into position to intercept it.

That was the theory, at any rate, and given the transit times, it was highly unlikely that anyone could make it past them undetected. An intruder certainly couldn't manage it while under power without being spotted, and even trying to slip past them on ballistic paths would be extraordinarily difficult. At the very least, the intruder would need to know the exact patrol pattern, because at some point he would need to decelerate if he intended to accomplish anything, and his window for that would be extremely narrow.

Of course, *highly unlikely* wasn't the same as *impossible*, and Dassler would have felt happier if there'd been more platforms in the outer picket. A single additional destroyer would have let them establish an equilateral triangle around the inner system, with every aspect of the approach under constant observation and all of the platforms in position to hit one another with com lasers at need. Flotillenadmiral Jachmann didn't happen to have a third escort, unfortunately, but at the least the flotillenadmiral had put the ones he did have into the right roles.

Dassler liked and respected his own CO, and he'd learned a lot about out-of-the-box tactical thinking under Radnitz's tutelage. Still, he'd always considered Deutschmann to be the more mentally agile of the two commanders.

It wasn't that she was more energetic or more devoted to her duty. It was simply that she seemed more imaginative, with a knack for deliberately shaking things up from time to time if she thought her crew was settling back onto its heels. Radnitz expected his officers to combat that sort of attitude by example; Deutschmann understood that occasionally altering routine, especially without warning, was a more effective approach.

On the other hand, she also had an annoying sense of humor and played a fanatic game of bridge in which her officers' participation was not optional.

Taking everything together, Dassler decided, methodical and sometimes boring beat the hell out of a commanding officer who spent half a watch explaining in excruciating detail which card her unfortunate subordinate ought to have played.

☆   ☆   ☆

"Weapons status?" Captain Jamshidi asked quietly.

"Green board, Captain," Commander Mattias Callewaert, *Spark*'s tactical officer, replied. "Sensors have a solid lock, and a firing solution is cycling. Confidence is high."

"Understood," Jamshidi replied.

Spark's impeller wedge was at standby as she floated in the inky lee of the largest piece of asteroidal rubble Jamshidi had been able to find with all his active sensors shut down. His biggest concern—well, after the long, excruciatingly slow ballistic approach—had been what would happen when his ship crept out of her hiding spot in the heart of The Cloud to reach her attack position. He hadn't been that worried about the actual maneuver; they knew exactly when each part of The Cloud would be under observation, and *Spark*'s wedge strength had been stepped way down.

No, at this point his concern was staying hidden long enough for his target to enter his range. Passive sensor range was fifteen light-minutes; maximum powered missile range was on the order of two light-*seconds*. He could shut down every active system and pretend he was a hole in space, but without her wedge *Spark* had to dispose of her waste heat some other way, and the thermal signature of her heat exchanger radiators would show up clearly on an alert ship's sensors. He'd shut even them down almost an hour ago, but the ship's internal temperature was climbing and he'd have to open them back up again soon.

"Range now two-point-five light-seconds," Callewaert said.

☆   ☆   ☆

"Communications check, *mein Herr*," Oberleutnant der Sterne Freundel said in a tactful voice, and Fregattenkapitänn Dassler arched an eyebrow at the com officer. Young Freundel had a certain puppyish eagerness that was rather endearing, and the XO had deliberately waited to see how long the youngster would wait before reminding him about the mandatory communications check.

"Is it really time already?" Dassler asked.

"Three minutes ago, *mein Herr*," the oberleutnant said respectfully.

"Very well, Oberleutnant. Proceed."

"*Ja, mein Herr.* Transmitting now."

Dassler nodded. Given the squadron's positions, it would take about two minutes for Freundel's transmission to reach *Preussen* and over twice that long for it to reach *München*. The communication checks were initiated on a staggered schedule, and this time it was *Rotte*'s turn to initiate the test. Next time it would be *Preussen*'s, and then it would be *Rotte*'s again before the responsibility passed to *München*.

"Range, two light-seconds," Callewaert said.

"Engage," Captain Jamshidi replied, and fusion-powered boosters flared viciously as a six-missile salvo erupted from the battlecruiser's launch cells.

☆   ☆   ☆

Bootsmann Ingrid Reitman stifled an almost overpowering urge to yawn. She wasn't actually tired, which only made the need to yawn even more maddening, but she knew how Fregattenkapitän Dassler would react if she yielded to it. She liked the XO, but he demanded alertness, no matter how boring the watch was, and he was a past master at chewing someone's ass off.

If only something would happen to break her boredom. Not anything bad, just something to wake everyone up. Focus them a bit. At least her watch would be ending soon, and she looked forward to finishing the novel she'd been reading. She'd always been a sucker for historical romances, and this one—

She stiffened as her earbud pinged. For a heartbeat or two, she was certain it had to be a mistake. Or at least a malfunction, but it pinged again and her eyes widened as half a dozen icons appeared on her display.

"Missiles!" she heard her own voice say. She was peripherally aware of heads snapping around, looking at her in utter disbelief. "Closing from three-zero-five, zero-two-one. Range at launch two light-seconds.

Acceleration four-seven-point-four KPS squared. Time-of-flight—" she swallowed "—three minutes."

☆　☆　☆

"Good telemetry, Sir," Callewaert announced.

"Very good," Jamshidi said, watching the displays with bleak eyes. Two light-seconds—600,000 kilometers—was right on the edge of the Quintessence Mercenaries' powered missile envelope. According to their information, the Andermani had a little more accel, but it didn't matter. The range might be extreme, but *Rotte*'s wedge was currently in the down part of its patrol circuit, which meant they had a non-evading target.

Of course, *Freikorps*-class ships like *Rotte* had been deliberately designed as fleet escorts, with a dedicated antimissile system designed to provide area defense to high-value units. That gave them a lot of self-defense capability on the occasions when they got to use it for their own protection, and with their antimissile system online they packed in nearly as much capability as most battlecruisers. But that system wasn't online, and Jamshidi doubted that more than one of her point-defense stations were fully manned.

"Second salvo launched," Callewaert said, and six more missiles went howling off towards their targets, only ten seconds behind the first six. *Spark*'s telemetry channels allowed her to control half a dozen missiles in a single salvo, which was the heaviest throw weight of any ship Jamshidi had ever commanded.

If she could have handled more birds, he would damned well have launched them, though. She mounted only twenty launch cells, so those missiles represented sixty percent of her total loadout, but the Quintessence's employers had provided plenty of reloads aboard the mercenaries' support ships. For their primary plan to work, the ship on his display *had* to die, and Jamshidi was grimly determined to make certain that it did.

☆   ☆   ☆

"Second salvo!" Reitman shouted through the raucous howl of *Rotte*'s battle stations alarm.

"Point defense is tracking," Oberleutnant der Sterne Metternich, the tactical officer of the watch, said in reply.

Reitman snorted in bitter amusement. No doubt point defense *was* tracking, but central control was still spinning up, and with only the single duty mount fully crewed...

"Communications, send Code Omega Alpha," Fregattenkapitän Dassler grated. "Continuous send. And append Tactical's feed."

☆   ☆   ☆

"Vector merge in twelve seconds," Callewaert said.

☆   ☆   ☆

Under the circumstances, *Rotte* did well. Even caught flat-footed, her tactical crew managed to train out both point defense autocannon and even got off one antimissile salvo. That was more than Jamshidi had anticipated her bridge crew could manage with so little warning.

But the cruiser's defense solutions were rushed, and the incoming missiles' closing velocity gave them too little time to engage so many targets.

They stopped all six of the initial launch. They stopped only one of the follow-up.

☆   ☆   ☆

Jamshidi watched the display as the tiny data code representing a heavy cruiser and seven hundred human beings vanished into an expanding cloud of cooling gas and glowing debris. He gazed at it for several seconds, then looked at his com officer.

"Send 'Clean Sweep,' Lieutenant," he said.

"Transmitting 'Clean Sweep,'" the lieutenant confirmed.

"Like you said," Kupner reminded him. "Shoot them in the back." Her tone could have been cutting, but it wasn't. If anything, Jamshidi thought, it was sad.

"Yes," he said. "Now we just have to find out if the others were equally effective." He felt his lip twitch. "Effective assassins."

☆   ☆   ☆

Fregattenkapitänin Deutschmann's face might have been forged from iron.

"Still nothing from the Flag?" Her voice was quiet.

"No, *meine Kapitänin*," Korvettenkapitän Malachi Tolbert replied unhappily.

Deutschmann's nostrils flared. She knew she wasn't going to hear anything from *Rotte* ever again, but where the hell was *Preussen*? *München*'s communication section had receipted the heavy cruiser's Code Omega with the *Alpha* suffix which indicated *Destruction Imminent*. More than that, *Rotte*'s tactical feed had been dumping into her continuous transmission right up to the instant the first missiles struck.

Deutschmann didn't know what was out there, but if it could handle that many missiles in a single salvo, it had to be both big and nasty. And it also had to have been perfectly positioned with foreknowledge of *Rotte*'s patrol pattern. Xuefeng Radnitz had never struck her as a very imaginative man, but he'd been a superior tactician and he'd run a taut ship. To take

him out that quickly, someone had to have gotten to
knife range without ever being detected, and that
meant whoever it was had been waiting for *Rotte* to
come to her, not out stalking her prey.

That conclusion has been obvious to Deutschmann
from the instant she received the cruiser's transmission, which was why she'd altered heading at two
hundred gravities acceleration ten seconds later. Unlike
Rotte, *München* had been a good ten minutes behind
schedule when Radnitz's ship was attacked, because
Deutschmann had decided to call a surprise tactical
drill. It had delayed her ship by almost half an hour,
but she hadn't worried about it, given that *München*
had more than enough acceleration to make up for
lost time.

In retrospect, it was a damned good thing she had.
Unlike the cruiser. *München*'s wedge and sidewalls had
been fully up when the Code Omega transmission came
in. She'd been able to respond instantly, and it was
highly probable that was all that had saved her and
her crew. If whoever was out there had good enough
information to ambush *Rotte* with such devastating
effect, they must also have known where *München*
was supposed to be at the same time.

At the moment, though, whatever satisfaction
Deutschmann could take in her own ship's survival
was buried in a bitter-edged corner of her mind. She
knew what had happened to *Rotte*, but *Preussen*'s
continued com silence was even more frightening.

Rotte was a cruiser; *Preussen* was a battleship.
How in God's name had anyone been able to sneak
into range to attack *her*? And how had they done it

so quickly, so devastatingly, that she'd been unable to so much as get off a transmission like *Rotte*'s?

Deutschmann didn't know the answer to either of those questions. But there was one increasingly ominous thing she *did* know. Like the rest of Flotillenadmiral Jachmann's captains, she'd been briefed about the Emperor's death and the funeral cortège's schedule. Including its upcoming appearance at Tomlinson.

She had no idea how the mystery attacker could have learned about the cortège. But the timing *couldn't* be a coincidence. The enemy's ultimate objective had to be Emperor Andrew, and that meant that somehow *München* had to stay alive against an adversary who'd effortlessly swatted a heavy cruiser and a battleship.

Because someone had to warn the new Emperor before he sailed straight into his own death.

CHAPTER TEN

"IF YOUR MAJESTY PREFERS," Prime Minister Harwich's voice drifted in through the mental fog, "we could reconvene at a more convenient time."

Queen Elizabeth snapped her eyes open, realizing only then that she'd closed them. At four and a half months old David was mostly sleeping through the night, but that pattern was broken just often enough to keep her tired and off-balance.

Last night had been one of those exceptions. He'd been especially fussy, Elizabeth had been up three times with him, and she was now paying the price.

There were others who could help with her baby, of course. Many others. They were all willing and able, some of them pushing the line of insistence right to the edge of insubordination.

But Elizabeth was David's mother, and she was damn well going to do as much of that job as she possibly could.

"I'm fine, My Lord," she assured Harwich, forcing back a yawn and resisting the urge to rub her eyes. "You were saying, My Lady?"

"I was talking about our analysis of the new grav coil manufacturing techniques Fregattenkapitän Li Gong-hu gave us," Baroness Crystal Pine said, eyeing her sovereign with the sort of veiled concern that Elizabeth had seen a lot of from everybody in the past four months. "I imagine Emperor Gustav thought it nothing more than a nice, simple goodwill gift, but it's going to make a *huge* difference in how we do counter-grav."

"Anything we can use with the new *Phoenix*-class frigates?" Dapplelake asked.

"Probably not right away," Crystal Pine said. "At the moment, the new techniques will probably be most useful for civilian projects. We've only begun experimenting with making replacement parts for our impeller drive systems, but I doubt much of this will be directly transferrable to that. I'm sure we'll pick up some very useful information on the manufacturing side, though, and we may well be able to apply some of what we learn to our assembly lines, including the ones for impeller parts. Frankly, that would be extremely worthwhile in its own right. I'm afraid we're well behind the curve for modern industrial techniques as a whole, and opening a window on that could be very beneficial. But we're still buying full impeller rings from the Solarian League for any major construction, and we will be for the foreseeable future, whatever else happens. And I'm afraid that even if we do see some unexpected manufacturing efficiencies, retooling the Navy's building slips would be too expensive and cost too much time. For now, at least."

"We also probably don't want to jump too deeply into this until we know exactly what we're doing," Harwich said.

"Agreed," Crystal Pine said. "We need to be sure we know what we're doing, and that it's going to be advantageous enough to justify the inevitable cost—and delays—inherent in any major changes to our existing shipyards before we start making them. I recommend that we start with air-car manufacturing. Once we have the techniques down pat and have figured out the benefit/cost parameters, we can decide out how much retooling is worthwhile."

"I understand," Elizabeth said, wondering if anyone in the room had missed the fact that Crystal Pine's own consortium handled the same air-car manufacturing work that she was talking about renovating.

Still, many of the Lords had interests that overlapped their governmental responsibilities and decision-making. All she and Harwich could do was keep an eye on those overlaps and watch for any blatant conflicts of interest.

"Perhaps you could work up a list of lines that would lend themselves to this kind of experiment," she added.

"I already have, Your Majesty," Crystal Pine said. "Far and away the best would be Hopstead Manufacturing in Mourncreek."

"Hopstead," Elizabeth repeated, trying to hide her surprise. As far as she knew, Crystal Pine had no interests or connections whatsoever in that particular barony.

"Yes, Your Majesty," Crystal Pine said. "Jeffrey Hopstead has three separate assembly lines, so closing down one for retooling would be a smaller impact on his overall production than for most of the other air-car manufacturers. I don't know Baron Mourncreek very well, but he seems the sort who'd be willing to try something new."

"I'd agree," Harwich put in.

"Very well," Elizabeth said. "Talk to Mourncreek, get your ducks lined up, and let's see where this goes."

"I'll get on it right away," Crystal Pine promised. "Thank you, Your Majesty."

"If there's nothing else . . . ?" Elizabeth looked around the table.

There was a flurry of head shakes. Then, Crystal Pine lifted a hesitant finger. "I have one more thing, Your Majesty," she said. "But it's not really related to this topic. More personal, really."

"Then perhaps you'd be good enough to stay behind a few minutes, My Lady," Elizabeth suggested. "The rest of you, thank you for coming. I'll look forward to hearing what else you're able to glean from the Andermani visit."

There was the usual scuffling of chairs as the assembly collected their tablets and filed past the bodyguards flanking the door. A moment later, Elizabeth and Crystal Pine were alone. "Now, My Lady?" Elizabeth invited.

"It's a small thing, really," Crystal Pine said, wincing a little. "But I was recently contacted by a citizens' group in Serisburg. They're concerned that, with their duchy now absorbed into the Crown's lands, that the name will be changed or even dropped completely."

"And they came to *you* with this?" Elizabeth asked, frowning.

Crystal Pine's nose wrinkled. "Yes, I know. My best guess is that since I'm the one who replaced Duke Serisburg in the Lords that I . . . I don't know. Owe them, I suppose."

"They *do* realize you had nothing to do with the duke, don't they?"

"I would certainly hope so," Crystal Pine said fervently. "Actually, I never even met the man. Regardless, Your Majesty, I promised the group that I'd ask you about it if I had a chance."

"And so you have," Elizabeth said. "And you can assure them that no one has any intention of eliminating Serisburg's name or identity from the Star Kingdom."

"Thank you, Your Majesty," Crystal Pine said, bowing her head. "I just . . . I hate zero-sum games. You know? Someone has to lose so that someone else gains." Her lip twitched. "If I may be so bold, Your Majesty, I dare say no one on Manticore understands that feeling as completely as you yourself do."

"Probably not," Elizabeth said, wincing. Her brother and niece having to die to make way for her own ascension to the Throne . . . "I've never much liked zero-sum games either."

"Indeed." Crystal Pine stood up. "And now, Your Majesty, I've taken up enough of your time. Thank you for your assurances. I'll be sure to pass them along to the Serisburg citizens. Good day, Your Majesty."

"Good day, My Lady."

Elizabeth watched her trace out the same path to the door as the other lords and ladies had just taken.

As she'd similarly traced out the same path that Elizabeth herself had taken?

Stop that! she ordered herself firmly. Remembering the past was vital; dwelling on it was a trap. Life happened; one accepted and learned from it; one moved on.

Still, maybe their shared history was one reason

Crystal Pine was one of Elizabeth's most fervent supporters. Both of them knew how it felt to have been thrust by violent circumstances into political life.

Elizabeth sighed as the door again closed. *God grant,* she prayed silently, *that the Crown never gains any future supporters in that same way.*

☆   ☆   ☆

Finding the public accident-scene pictures was easy. Chomps accomplished that minor chore the first evening.

Finding anything else proved to be a serious challenge.

There was nothing further than a handful of details in the public police records. There was nothing in the records of the towing company that had moved the duke's wrecked air car. There was nothing useful on the social net, or in discussion groups, or people's personal pages. He even dipped his toe into some of the conspiracy threadways, with results that were entertaining in their own grotesque way but of no help.

If he'd been at his desk in Room 2021, things might have been different. The hacking tools he'd used against so many of the Silesian Confederacy's computers were eminently adaptable to their counterparts on Manticore.

Though even if he'd had those tools available, Lady Calvingdell probably wouldn't have let him use them. Delphi's charter made it laser-edged clear that their resources were only to be turned outward, toward foreign persons and governments, not inward toward the Star Kingdom's own citizens and institutions. That particular turf was reserved for police and the Royal Investigation Division.

What really drove Chomps up the wedge was that he was within spitting distance of someone who *did* have access to all those lovely private police records.

The problem was that Terry refused to play ball. She wouldn't let him into the files, she wouldn't pull them up herself and then step outside for a cup of tea, she wouldn't even play Twenty Questions about the details he was most curious about. He tried enlisting her parents to help, and ended up in trouble with both sides: gentle, firm, and vaguely disappointed trouble from Ralph and Eileen; double-barrel verbal trouble from Terry herself.

Maybe they assumed that he would eventually give up. Not a chance.

He went into the forest and studied the accident scene a dozen times after that first visit with Terry. He studied maps, laid out flight paths, tracked the duke's activities for the month before the accident, and learned everything he could about that particular air car make and model. Given that Serisburg had imported it from the Solarian League, with all the priciness, prestige, and semi-unobtainable tech data that implied, that particular part of the investigation alone took over two weeks.

There was something there. Chomps was sure of it. Something that no one else had seen, or dots no one had managed to connect.

Or, more ominously, dots that no one *wanted* to connect.

He didn't believe that particular reading. Not for a minute. It went completely against everything he believed about his people and his nation. In his more sober moments he could only assume that thoughts like that had come from his brief dip into the twisted world of conspiracy theorists.

But if he didn't want to believe it, he also couldn't afford to simply dismiss it.

He would follow this as far as he could, to whatever set of truths he could dig up, and let the chips fall where they may.

☆　　☆　　☆

He'd been poking at the edges and provoking cold shoulders and annoyance from Terry and her parents for nearly two months when he finally got his first real break.

One of the first things he'd looked for after going through the public pictures of the tragedy was the final disposition of the air car itself. To his chagrin, the records indicated that once the investigation concluded the vehicle had disappeared.

On the surface, that wasn't particularly surprising or suspicious. Once an accident report was filed the vehicles involved were usually sent to wreckers for salvage or, if the damage was extensive enough, simply sold off as scrap.

But as Chomps dug beneath that surface things got more confusing. The car had disappeared, but there was no official bill of sale. None of the local wreckers or junk yards had a record of receiving it, nor had it surfaced anywhere outside the duchy's borders. He double-checked against towing service files, again coming up empty.

More than once he considered offering all of this to Terry and seeing if she had any fresh ideas as to what he could try. But given that most of his data had come from hacking various civilian files, that would probably land him in real trouble with her. He had no idea if her standard-issue cuffs could handle Sphinxian wrists, but he was in no hurry to find out.

Then, almost as an afterthought, he thought about checking whether there was anyone in Serisburg who rented out tow trucks. Again he came up dry; but digging further he found that there were heavy-duty tow bars that could be secured between a pair of air cars for the purpose of hauling heavy cargo. Eight such racks had been rented during the relevant time frame: six to construction companies, one to a group who did kayak tours and whose usual carrier broke down, and one to a normal, everyday Serisburg citizen.

A citizen who happened to be the late duke's vehicle maintenance chief.

A citizen, moreover, who had a secluded vacation home in the Drobne Forest foothills near a town called Whistlestop.

☆   ☆   ☆

"Do either of you know how far it is to Whistlestop?" Chomps asked casually as dinner wound to a close three nights later. "The map says half an hour, but the guidebook says it's closer to one."

"The guidebook's probably giving the distance to Emerald Falls," Ralph said. "You can't fly all the way there—too much mist and spray for safety—so you have to put down and roll or walk the rest of the way. The nearer edge of Whistlestop itself is only half an hour."

"What's in Whistlestop that's caught your interest?" Eileen asked. "Surely not the Falls—I've read that there are far more impressive ones on Sphinx."

"There are," Chomps confirmed. "I was just feeling

a little cabin-feverish and thought I'd go for an evening flight. Whistlestop is supposed to have a great little ice cream place."

"You mean Plaza Parlor?" Ralph asked, frowning. "It's good enough, I suppose, but it's a little far to go just for a hot fudge sundae."

"You're probably right," Chomps said. "But like I said: cabin fever."

"Well, watch yourself," Eileen admonished him. "Unless you go by way of Serisburg Point you'll have to cross a big chunk of forest, and the trees aren't equipped with warning beacons."

"Plus the moon is already down," Ralph added.

"I'll be careful," Chomps promised. The fact that the moon had already set was the main reason he'd chosen tonight in the first place, instead of heading out three days ago when he'd first pinpointed the car's possible location. Moonlight made things a little too bright for what he suspected would be a black-bag job.

Three minutes later, after helping Eileen clear the table, he was in his air car, flying through the dusk toward Whistlestop.

He'd already decided to take the slight detour around Serisburg Point, partly because it looked less suspicious, mostly because even with traffic monitors recording IDs there was always a little slippage that made it harder to backtrack a given vehicle through a crowd. That would come in handy if he had to leave the Whistlestop area in a hurry.

He drove around the edge of the city and continued on. The sky darkened further, the traffic fading with the light. Then the light and traffic were both gone, and he was there.

He landed on a slight slope a discreet hundred meters away and covered the rest of the distance on foot. A shallow and, fortunately, narrow creek crossed his path at one point, but he was able to jump over it without trouble.

The house had looked modest from the air. From the ground it was even more so, with rough-wood, half-log walls and a shake roof. From the size he estimated it held two bedrooms, or possibly three cramped ones. There were lights on in two rooms in the rear, both covered by translucent window shades, and a small light over the front door. A quick scan with his handheld IR reader was inconclusive, but given that interior security lights didn't make much sense out here it was likely there was at least one person home.

About ten meters to the side of the house near the front was a garage, its main door opening out onto a small graveled clearing. The garage's own IR reading was solidly cold, indicating that whoever was inside had been there long enough for his vehicle to cool down. A little ways to the side of the garage was another outbuilding, this one either a large shed or a decent-sized workshop. The former, he decided, noting the lack of any windows on the walls he could see except for a couple of ventilation slits flanking the door.

The garage was the obvious spot to keep the duke's wrecked air car. But if the Silesian operation had taught Chomps anything, it was that people trying to hide things usually did their best to avoid the obvious.

Keeping one eye on the house's lighted windows and the other on his footing, he headed for the shed. The shed door was sealed with a simple key lock.

Chomps got it open and off its hasp and slipped inside, closing the door silently behind him. He spent a couple of minutes laying masking film across the ventilation slits, then did the same to the crack under the door. Then, bracing himself, he flicked on his penlight.

Jackpot. The mess of crumpled metal and plastic spread out in several places over the floor could barely be identified as the remains of an air car anymore, but what was left of the ducal crest on one of the crumpled doors made it official.

Chomps took a deep breath. *Okay, hotshot.* He'd fought for this moment, for the chance to actually see and examine the wreckage. Time to turn that long road into something useful.

He started at the front, mindful of the sharp edges as he ran his light slowly along each part, recording everything as he went. The air car's sides were next, then the rear, then the roof. The doors were off in their own sections of floor, obviously having been pried off to recover the bodies of the duke's family. The underside was tricky, but there was enough room between the wreck and the floor for him to reach underneath with his recorder and get most of it.

After that came the interior. The air car had been some kind of stretch model, longer than a standard Manticoran vehicle, with extra-generous legroom between the two front seats and the four in the rear. Now, of course, all that room had been compressed to something less even than a sport coupe. The seats had mostly remained bolted to the floor, though one end of the rear bench had come loose and was angled across the space. All four sets of the rear restraints had been cut when the duke's wife and three children were extricated from the wreckage, but what was left of the straps had unmistakable signs of stress stretching. The entire rear cocoon had deployed, the bags now hanging limp from their nooks.

The cocoons for the two front seats had also deployed. But neither of the restraint sets had been touched.

He frowned as he ran his light over the left-hand, driver's side seat. Terry had mentioned that Duke Serisburg hadn't been wearing his restraints at the time of the crash. He'd assumed at the time she was wrong—*no* sane person headed into the sky without their restraints. But the restraints hadn't been cut, and there was no sign of any stress marks.

So why had he taken them off?

Not to look around at the family behind him, as Terry had suggested. That didn't make any sense. Even if he had a stiff neck or some other malady that made turning difficult, loosening just one of the shoulder straps should have done the trick. There was no reason to unbuckle the whole thing unless he was getting out of the seat.

That wasn't a problem if he'd had the autopilot engaged. But Terry had said he hadn't.

Something wasn't right here. Either something with the duke, or something with the car. Or something with the whole damn thing.

The black box recorder wasn't where it would have been in a Manticoran car, and it took him a few minutes to find the proper compartment. The box itself was long gone, of course, tucked away somewhere in police custody, but Chomps took a few minutes to examine the fasteners and the molded protective shell that had held it in place. The various other equipment access panels had been torn off, either by the crash or by the investigators, and the instruments, sensor clusters, and control modules were missing. Most of the openings showed heat-stress markings, either from fires due to the crash or from the investigators having to cut them out of their warped mountings.

All of which boiled down to Chomps ending up this little expedition pretty much right where he'd started. Nothing he'd seen in the wreckage contradicted the details and overall conclusion he'd seen in the public data base. Now, more than ever, he needed to see the full police report.

Still, it was always possible he'd missed something that further thought would reveal. It wouldn't hurt to take another pass through the air car's interior. He activated the recorder, starting with the front...

And frowned. Duke Serisburg had been sitting *there*. He'd unfastened his restraints, supposedly to look over his shoulder at his ailing child, lost control of the vehicle, and slammed into that monster tree near the Three Corners Inn.

But if that was what had happened...

He was still frowning at the air car when he heard the soft creak of the door hasp being opened.

Instantly, he dowsed his light and dropped to a crouch behind the vehicle. Either he'd left some gap uncovered, or the house's occupant was in the habit of coming out to the wreck every evening to say good-night. He braced himself, shading his eyes...

Abruptly, the door was flung open. For a second Chomps could see a figure framed against the faint starlight; and then, right in the center of the silhouette a light came on toward him.

Amateur. Even as Chomps tried to crouch a little

lower, his hand shading his eyes from the worst of the glare, he could take small comfort in the fact that at least he wasn't facing a trained professional. Standing with even a faint light behind him made his visitor a perfect target; and if a lurker inside the shed had missed that opportunity to take his shot, turning on a light right in front of him made him an even better target.

"Who's there?" a hoarse voice called tensely. "I know you're there. Come out. Come out with your hands up. Or I'll shoot."

Chomps sighed to himself. Except that the silhouette hadn't had a weapon, and the light sweeping across the shed wasn't showing the slight but unmistakable bobble that would have accompanied the drawing of a heretofore concealed gun. With the threat sounding almost like an afterthought, Chomps was ninety percent sure he was facing an unarmed man.

He could take him, of course. The man was starting down one side of the car, waving his light at each shadow or cubbyhole he passed. All Chomps had to do was work his way around the other side, keeping the wreckage between them, and then come up behind him.

On the other hand, if he could do that, he could just as easily sneak around the side of the car, get to the door, and get the hell out of here.

That scenario carried its own risks, of course, not least of which was the need to then make his way through unfamiliar terrain in the dark and get back to his air car before the man could chase him down. Worse, if he got driven off the right path, he might have to abandon the vehicle completely.

But there was really no way he could justify attacking a citizen who was just protecting his home and property. Keeping the wreck between him and the light, he eased toward the door. Might be a good idea to head off toward the house to throw in a little misdirection, he decided, before doubling back and heading for his car. The man with the light was at the rear of the wreck; Chomps reached the front, glanced over his shoulder to make sure the doorway was clear.

He was gathering his feet under him to make his dash for freedom when a dark shape dropped out of the sky onto the grassy ground directly in his path. Chomps barely had time to twist his face away before a brilliant floodlight blazed out from the air car, filling the shed with light.

"Police! Freeze!" a voice snapped from behind the light.

A very familiar voice.

Terry.

"Yeah, yeah, right," he muttered in disgust, holding his hands out where she could see them. Damn, damn, *damn*.

"Well, well," Terry said, the light rocking slightly as she got out of the vehicle and stalked toward him. "Chomps. Imagine my surprise."

"Hello, Terry," Chomps said. "This isn't what it looks like."

"Oh, I'm pretty sure it is," she countered. "Thank you, Mr. Devereux—you can go back inside. I'll screen you later and get your statement."

"Wait a minute," the homeowner—Devereux—said, sounding confused. "You *know* this man?"

"We have a passing acquaintanceship," Terry said. "Go ahead—I've got this."

"Well...okay," Devereux said hesitantly as he started

back along the side of the wreck. "Shouldn't I see if anything's missing first?"

"I doubt he teleported anything out before you spotted him," Terry said. "Don't worry, if he took something we'll find it when we process him. Really, Mr. Devereux—just go."

The man paused as he passed Chomps, peering briefly at him through the glare of the floodlight, then continued past and out the door.

"Turn around," Terry growled. "Hands behind your back."

"Your parents turn me in?" Chomps asked as he obeyed. "Not sure if that qualifies as probable cause."

"If I were you, I wouldn't bandy around words like *probable cause*," Terry said. "Jailhouse lawyers aren't popular in Serisburg."

"I was just asking," Chomps said mildly.

"And if you must know, Dad told me you'd said you were coming to Whistlestop for ice cream," she continued. "I was en route when Devereux's screen came in to the sheriff's department. I figured it was you, so I said I'd take it and burned air. Devereux was told to wait until I got here. I guess he got impatient."

"Or maybe worried?" Chomps suggested. "You knew he had the wreck, didn't you?"

"Of course we did," Terry said, walking up behind him. There was the subtle clatter of cuffs—

"I wouldn't," Chomps warned.

"Why, because you can break me in half? Don't even think it."

"No," Chomps said, mentally crossing his fingers. "Because if you put those cuffs on me we may never find out who murdered Duke Serisburg."

CHAPTER ELEVEN

FOR A LONG MOMENT neither of them moved or spoke. Chomps watched their shadows on the far wall, wondering what he was going to do if she didn't go for this. He could escape from her, of course—his size and training pretty much guaranteed he would win any real fight between them. But assaulting a sheriff's deputy would end any chance of ever getting back into either Delphi or the Navy.

On the other hand, probably so would being arrested for breaking and entering.

"You must have suspected it wasn't an accident," he continued into the silence. "Otherwise, why hide the wreck out here?"

"Who said anyone *hid* it?" she countered. "It was put in police impound after the investigation like every other piece of evidence. Two weeks later some idiot souvenir-hunter broke in and tried to break off the decorative grille. When someone else tried the same thing a week after that, Devereux offered to put it out here at his vacation home where no one would think to look for it."

"The fact that there was nothing official about any of it didn't bother you?" Chomps asked.

"We *wanted* there to be nothing official about it," Terry retorted. "We let him handle it all quietly, through civilian channels, in case the police records got hacked."

"So you buried both the car and the paperwork?"

"I think I just said that," Terry growled. "Which brings up another question. If the details were so well buried, how did *you* get to them?"

"I have a few specialized shovels in my tool kit," Chomps said. She was arguing with him; but she still hadn't clamped on the cuffs. "Do you want to hear what I found? Or would you rather haul me away and lock me up?"

She exhaled noisily. "I'm listening."

"The first problem was the impact point," Chomps said. "It was on a line from the duke's mountain retreat to the capital—I'm sure that was the first thing everyone looked at. But there were other, taller trees along that same line. Why did he miss all of those?"

"Maybe he wasn't drunk enough? Maybe his son wasn't sneezing behind him when he passed those?"

"Maybe," Chomps said. "But then there's the next question. If he was coming straight from his retreat, why is the impact point ten degrees off that line?"

"What are you talking about?"

"I'm talking about the fact that to hit that particular spot he needed to veer off the direct line to the capital and then change his angle again just in time to crash into the tree."

He heard her give a tired sigh. "Fine," she said

reluctantly. "There *was* some veering involved. Mostly near the end, just before the impact."

"How sharp were these zigzags?"

"Sharp enough," she said. "One of the other theories is that he unstrapped to go get something from the supply cabinet at the back—maybe some medicine for his son if you're feeling charitable, another drink for himself if you aren't. He forgot to engage the autopilot, grabbed wildly for the controls when the air car swerved, overcorrected, and crashed."

Her shadow seemed to shake itself, as if she was shaking away the memories. "And *I'm* not the who's supposed to be doing all the talking," she said, the official tartness back in her voice. "If you've got something solid, let's hear it."

"I don't know how *solid* it is," Chomps conceded. "But there are some more questions that seem to lead to suspicious answers. First: again, why that particular tree? As I said, there are plenty of other ones scattered along the way."

"You mean why didn't he hit a tree that wasn't conveniently near an inn where some traveler might see everything?" Terry countered. "Seems to me you're arguing against yourself."

"Not really," Chomps said. "Yes, it's near potential witnesses, which I agree could have been a problem. But the killer had to risk it . . . because this was the only tall tree on the path that bordered a clearing big enough for the car to fall into."

"In case the first crash didn't do the job?"

"Maybe partly," Chomps said. "But more important, I think, was that the killer needed to get to the car after the crash, either to put something in or to take something out. If he'd crashed it anywhere else it might have ended up off the ground, wedged in between the surrounding trees."

"Interesting theory, I'll give you that," Terry said. "What exactly could he have wanted to put in or take out?"

"I don't know," Chomps said. "I'd need to know exactly what was in the car that the police took out. But the obvious target would be the black box. If he was able to manipulate the records, everything you think you know about the crash could be wrong."

"Can't be done," Terry said flatly. "Black boxes can't be tampered with."

"Maybe ours can't be," he pointed out. "But this was a Solarian car. Would you even know if its black box had been hacked?"

"Solarian car; *Manticoran* black box," Terry said with strained patience. "Really, Townsend, you think we'd let the duke tool around in an air car without all the legally required safety equipment?"

"And you're sure it wasn't touched?"

"Am I suddenly speaking German?" she retorted. "Don't you think we know how to do our jobs?"

Chomps scowled. So much for that potential lead. "No, of course you do," he said. "But remember that your focus was on the cause of an accident, not evidence of a murder."

"We don't go into these things with preconceptions," Terry said stiffly. "Speaking of which, I'm hearing a lot of theory and supposition but I've yet to hear any facts."

"Let me remedy that," Chomps said. "I've got two nice little facts right inside the car. Easiest to see from the right-hand side."

"Fine," Terry said, finally stepping out from behind him and walking around the front of the car. "Show me."

"You said there were two theories as to why the duke wasn't wearing his restraints," Chomps said, following her. The cuffs, he noted uneasily, were still in her hand. "But both of them should have put him at or near his seat at the time of the crash." He pointed through the gap where the right-hand door had been before the police pried it off. "So why was his body way over here on the opposite side of the car?"

"I don't see the problem," Terry said. "It hit and then fell, remember? Plenty of time in there for the car to have canted up onto its right side and slid him over there."

"But there aren't any impact marks I can see near his seat," Chomps persisted, pointing his light at that section of the dashboard. "If he was thrown there first—"

"Son of a bitch," Terry muttered. "Give me your light."

"Sure," Chomps said, frowning as he handed it over. "What do you see?"

"There's light coming in from my floodlight," she said, squatting down and shining her light toward the area beneath the steering yoke. There was an opening there, one of the equipment access areas that Chomps had noted in his earlier sweep.

"There's probably a lot of light coming in through the various gaps," he reminded her. "That one—"

"Shut up, Townsend," she cut him off. Her voice was still quiet, but there was a sudden new edge to it. "The computer's gone."

Chomps looked back at the dashboard and all the

holes where access panels had been. "I assumed the investigators took everything."

"Everything except the computer," she ground out. "It was a complete mess, besides being so badly wedged in it would have required a cutting torch to get out. That much heat on top of the crash damage would have scrambled anything that might have still been in there. No point in taking it, especially since all the flight records were duplicated in the black box, which was in much better shape."

"I see," Chomps said. He would probably have pulled the computer anyway, just for completeness sake. But maybe that was just him. "So what happened to it?"

"Three guesses," Terry growled, getting back to her feet and thrusting his light back into his hand. She scowled at the car, then turned and stomped toward the shed door. "Come on," she said, stuffing the cuffs back in their pouch. "I think we need a little chat with Mr. Devereux."

Chomps had half expected Devereux to be frantically throwing clothing into a carrybag in preparation for a guilty dash out the back door and a mad run through the woods. Instead, he was sitting quietly on an old couch in his front room, his face expressionless as he watched his visitors cross the foyer toward him, only the restlessness of his hands as they rubbed against each other betraying his tension. "Hello, Deputy," he greeted them, his voice under rigid control. "I assume you're here about the computer."

"Yes, I am," Terry confirmed, her own tone calm and professional. "I notice that wasn't a question. So?"

Devereux shrugged, his eyes flicking briefly to Chomps before returning to Terry. "There's not much to tell," he said. "I didn't realize you'd left the computer in the wreck until it got here. I thought if I could get it out I might be able to salvage some of the records."

"We already had all the data from the black box," Terry said.

"*You* had all the data," Devereux said, smiling wanly. "I . . ." The smile disappeared and he lowered his gaze to the floor in front of him. "I was the duke's mechanic, Deputy. I didn't know much about the computer—the duke handled that—but I was in charge of everything else. I thought . . . I needed to know . . ." He trailed off.

Terry looked at Chomps. "You needed to know if the crash was your fault?" she suggested quietly.

A spasm of pain crossed Devereux's face. "Yes," he whispered. "Maybe it's silly. Probably useless even to look. But I had to try."

"How did you get it out?" Chomps asked. "Hammer and chisel?"

Devereux frowned up at him. "How did you know?"

"Detective Lassaline said the heat of a torch would have scrambled anything that was left of the data. I also noticed that one of the access ports had what looked like chisel marks around the edges."

"Yes, that's what I did," Devereux confirmed, still frowning. "You've got a good eye."

Chomps shrugged. "I try."

"Have you made any progress?" Terry asked.

Devereux shook his head. "It was pretty well wedged in there, and I only got it out a couple of weeks ago. As I said, the duke was the one who dealt with the computer—part of the whole Solarian mystique, I suppose—and I've just barely figured out how to turn it on and get to the startup sections. Or what's left of them, anyway."

"Sounds good," Terry said, gesturing to him. "Let's see what you've got."

Devereux nodded and stood up. "It's in my workroom downstairs. Follow me."

A minute and a cramped flight of stairs later—cramped for Chomps, anyway—they were in the basement. Devereux led them past the power generator and laundry room and through a doorway into a large corner room dimly lit by the diffuse starlight coming in through a pair of window wells. On a workbench under one of them were several small piles of battered and blackened electronic components laid out under the soft glow of a focused desk lamp. "You can see the kind of shape it's in," Devereux said as the three of them made their way across the room. "Even without causing any further damage when I got it out it was already falling apart."

"Which part is the computer itself?" Terry asked.

"These two parts, actually," Devereux said, pointing to a pair of fist-sized components connected by several cables to a display and what looked like a diagnostic bank. "I think they're supposed to be connected together, but as I said Duke Serisburg was the one who handled all the computer work."

"Is there a manual?" Chomps asked.

"Yes." Devereux tapped one of the components. "Right in here."

"Yeah, *that's* useful," Terry growled, pointing at a rectangular box with a half dozen ports laid out along the two narrow sides. "This the outer casing?"

"Yes," Devereux said. "Here, let me show you what I've got."

He sat down at the work bench and keyed on the various components. Terry stepped behind him, leaning slightly over his shoulder as she watched the images come up.

Keeping to the side, Chomps picked up the outer casing and gave it a close look. It wasn't quite like any other computer casing he'd seen before, with its ports and access points arrayed in vastly different configurations from their Manticoran cousins. A couple of the ports were of shapes he'd never seen before, not even during his and Travis's quiet incursion into the world of Silesian data thievery. Apparently, even general, nonclassified, civilian Solarian tech was years beyond anything in this part of the galaxy.

Or at least beyond the Manticoran and Silesian regions. Maybe Travis would find the Andermani a bit more up to speed.

Which, in the larger scheme of things, could be very good or very, very bad.

He frowned, holding the casing a little closer. Surreptitiously, he pulled out his recorder and ran it over the bent metal.

"Doesn't look very promising," Terry commented. She glanced over her shoulder, saw Chomps holding the casing. Scowling, she took it away from him and set it back on the table.

"As I said," Devereux replied. "As you can see, I figured out how to get power to it and turn it on, but I'm mostly getting what you see there: error messages and scrambled screens. But I did find some serial numbers on the computer and two of the ports, if that would be helpful."

"Could be," Terry said. "Where are they?"

"Hang on—you'll need more light," Devereux said. He reached for the lamp's control—

"Hold it," Chomps said, catching his wrist as something in one of the window wells caught his eye. "Terry, does your car's floodlight have an auto-off setting?"

"Yes, but it's not on," she said, frowning. "Why?"

"Because it just went off," Chomps told her. "I saw the reflected light on the treetops go out."

"What does that mean?" Devereux asked.

"It means someone turned it off," Terry said grimly, drawing her sidearm. "You two stay here." Hurrying across the room, she slipped through the doorway and disappeared out into the hall.

"Like hell," Chomps said under his breath. "You—stay here," he ordered Devereux as he headed off after her. He wasn't armed, but there was no way he was going to let Terry head off into a dangerous situation alone.

He had finished with the stairs and was rounding the final wall toward the front door when the windows lit up with sudden light and a violent explosion shattered the quiet of the night.

☆   ☆   ☆

"Get that thing away from me," Terry snarled at the med tech dabbing at her unnaturally rosy cheek with a sponge. "I'm fine."

"Like hell you are," one of the other deputies, Carl Broganis, snarled right back. "You're damn lucky you're not already in the hospital."

"What, for a little heat rash?"

"It's called *flash burn*, Deputy," the medic said in a tone that gave Chomps the impression that Terry already had a reputation for being a bad patient. "And we need to make sure you didn't get any shrapnel in along with it."

"So shut up and let him work," Broganis added.

Terry glared at him. But there was no real force to the glare, and after a second her eyes drifted away. Broganis eyed her another moment; and then, as Chomps had known he eventually would, he turned both optic barrels full-bore onto the civilian intruder.

"As for *you*, Townsend, you're going to spend the next week in one of my cells if I don't get some answers."

"I've already given you all the answers I've got," Chomps said. "I can't help it if you don't like them."

"Oh, we're way past *liking*," Broganis said. "We're to flat-out *disbelieving*. You just *happen* to be flying out here in the middle of nowhere, and you just *happen* to notice something wrong with Mr. Devereux's shed, and instead of screening it in you decide to take it upon yourself to land and check it out yourself?"

"You left out that I just *happen* to be a veteran of the Royal Manticoran Navy who's been trained to spot trouble." Chomps raised his eyebrows. "And that I just *happened* to be right."

Broganis's lips curled back from his teeth in what would probably have been a retort for the record books.

But he left it unsaid. After all, the proof of Chomps's statement was still smoldering behind him.

Chomps shifted his eyes over Broganis's shoulder, suppressing a withering curse of his own. The shed was pretty much gone, the parts that hadn't been scattered across the landscape by the hydrogen tank explosion burned to ashes and charcoal. What was left of the duke's car, caught in the center of the blast, had been badly charred by the blast, the remains of the ducal seal gone.

If there'd been any evidence the investigators had missed, it was pretty well gone now.

"Yeah, you *happened* to be right," Broganis growled. "Of course, if you're the one who blew up the tanks in the first place then it's not that amazing of a prediction, is it?"

"I was in the house with Devereux when they blew," Chomps pointed out. "Deputy Lassaline can confirm that."

"She also said you were alone in the shed before she arrived," Broganis countered. "You could have rigged a delay switch or something."

"He wasn't involved," Terry spoke up. Waving away the medic, she stood up. "If you're going to arrest him, arrest him. If you're not, let him go."

Broganis sent Chomps another glare. "Fine," he growled. "Go. We'll think about filing charges in the morning. As for you, Deputy, we need to get you home."

"My car's right here."

"And it's not going anywhere until it's been towed in and checked," Broganis said.

"It's a *patrol car*," Terry said with clearly strained patience. "A little explosion isn't going to bother it any."

"And you're not in any shape to do any driving anyway," Broganis added. "I'll get someone to drive you home."

Chomps cleared his throat. "Actually, I talked to her mother while the medic was checking her out. She said that maybe she should come back to the inn for the night. So that, you know, she could keep an eye on you."

"If you screened my mother—" Terry broke off, her expression completing the threat without the need for further words.

"No, no, she screened *me*," Chomps said hastily. "She heard about the explosion and knew you'd been heading to Whistlestop. I told her you were all right, but she...uh...sort of insisted."

"Well, you can just screen her back and *un*insist her," Terry growled. "I have my own place in the Point, thank you very much."

"Actually, that's a good idea," Broganis said blandly. "Vespoli will insist you take a couple of days off anyway. Might as well get some home cooking while you're at it."

"Broganis—"

"I can screen Vespoli and ask her if you'd like," Broganis offered. "Of course, *she'd* probably insist you spend those same couple of days in the hospital."

Terry glared at him another moment, then seemed to wilt. "I hate you, you know. Both of you."

"Then it's settled," Chomps said. "And since I'm already heading that direction, Deputy Broganis won't need to assign someone else to drive you."

"Like hell," Broganis retorted. "You're a suspect in a—"

"Give it a rest, Broganis," Terry said, managing to sound tired, irritated, and righteous all at the same time. "Besides, you have to wait here and oversee the arson squad. Townsend can take me."

"You sure?" Broganis asked, eyeing Chomps suspiciously.

"I already said he's in the clear," Terry said. "Anyway, anything he does from now on he'll have to answer to my mother for."

"Point." Broganis made a face. "Fine. Go on—get out of here."

"I'll go get my car," Chomps said. "Be back in a minute."

☆   ☆   ☆

Ten minutes later, he and Terry were in the air.

"How are you feeling?" Chomps asked as he turned the air car toward home. "I mean, *really* feeling?"

"I've been better," Terry conceded. "But it's really just heat rash. No shrapnel, not even any splinters. A good night's sleep and I'll be fine." She stirred in her seat. "I still don't know how I let you talk me into leaving the computer with Devereux."

"Because even with your brain bouncing around your skull you recognized it was the best move," Chomps said.

"Really?" she countered. "*I* thought it was because you Svengalied me into it."

"The two aren't necessarily mutually exclusive." Chomps held a hand up against the retort he could sense her prepping. "Look. If we'd taken the computer, we'd have needed to stash it in either my car or yours. No guarantee Broganis or the other first responders wouldn't have searched either vehicle before they let us go. As it is, no one knows Devereux's got it, and he already promised to keep it hidden and secret."

"You think you can trust him?"

"After someone blew up his shed to try to get rid of it?" Chomps nodded. "Trust me—he won't tell a soul."

"*If* the computer was what the attacker was after, and *if* he thinks he succeeded."

"Yes, on both counts," Chomps said. "You remember how you didn't realize the computer was missing until you saw a glimmer from your spotlight leaking through the opening? Well, our attacker had already shut down the light, so he didn't have that clue. You also had to squat down to make sure it was gone, which means a quick glance on his part wouldn't have done it."

"Unless he also squatted down," Terry said. "We're all very big on knees in Serisburg, you know."

"One: he didn't have time," Chomps said. "He had to shut down your light, rig the connector on Devereux's hydrogen storage tanks, and get out before you showed up to investigate. And two: if he'd seen the computer was missing, there'd be no reason to destroy what was left of the wreckage and thereby tip us off that someone was actively involved with the duke's death. No, he thinks he succeeded."

"I guess that makes sense," Terry said slowly. "But that would imply that there's something damning on the computer that someone doesn't want us to see."

"I don't see any other conclusion," Chomps said. Technically, he assured himself, that was a precisely correct statement. "All the more reason to make sure no one knows we've got it."

"And Devereux understands that? I saw you talking to him while they were cleaning me up."

"Oh, he understands it, all right," Chomps assured her. "He understands he's holding some damning evidence, he understands that his life is potentially in danger, and he's mad as hell at the thought someone might have killed his beloved duke and his family. No, he's as much on our side as you can get."

For a moment they flew in silence as Terry rested and thought, or maybe just rested. "So what's our next move?" she asked.

"We need to find out everything we can about that computer," Chomps said. "First step is to see if we can get some specs on the thing."

"Devereux said the manual was on the computer."

"Damned inconveniently, yes," Chomps growled. "But *someone* imported the car for the duke, and that someone may have access to Solarian files that might help us. That same someone might also be able to dig up useful data on the car itself."

"And if that person isn't local, he's probably in Landing," Terry said. "How early do you want to leave?"

"Whoa," Chomps said. "Those couple of days off Broganis mentioned were for purposes of healing, not road trips."

"I'm fine," Terry growled. "Besides, you'll be doing the driving."

"Not the point."

"Then what *is* the point?"

Chomps hesitated. How exactly should he bring up this particular topic, especially given her injuries and her current mood?

Gradually, he decided. Very gradually. "Tell me, when you headed out to check on your car and the shed, did you pause anywhere inside the house along the way? Or did you go straight through and out the door?"

He could feel her eyes on him. "What exactly are you implying?"

"I'm just exploring the possibilities," Chomps said evasively. "Did you pause, or didn't you?"

"I didn't pause, hesitate, or trip over my own feet," Terry growled. "Straight up the stairs, through the front room, out the door, and face-first into an explosion. Does that help?"

"Maybe," Chomps said. "I was just thinking that whoever wanted to eliminate the evidence might also figure it would be a bonus to eliminate whoever seemed to have developed a sudden interest in the case."

"Because he would have expected us to be in Devereux's front room instead of his basement?" Terry countered. "Where the dousing of my floodlight would have been a lot more obvious, and the distance to the shed a lot shorter?"

Chomps grimaced. So much for approaching it gradually. Clearly, she'd already done the math on this one. "Basically."

"Is that why you suggested taking me to the inn? To keep me away from my apartment?"

"I thought it might be a little safer, yes."

"*You* thought," Terry said darkly. "So you didn't really talk to Mom."

Chomps shrugged. "I have a mother, too. I know how they think."

"Fine," Terry growled. "Let's assume you're right on the timing. Two problems with your conclusion. One: the official investigation is long over, and none of us is interested in reopening it. That includes me. Two: killing a cop in Serisburg would buy him a lot more trouble than anyone should reasonably want."

She leaned over so that she could look him squarely in the eye. "*You*, on the other hand, are not only the one poking a stick into this particular hornet's nest, but you're also not a cop. Would you like me to do the math on *that* one?"

"No, I've already run the numbers," Chomps conceded. "Doesn't mean our mystery man wouldn't take a twofer if he could get one."

"Yeah, well, *my* problem right now is that he might also go for a fourfer," Terry bit out. "Or hadn't it occurred to you that taking me to the inn also puts my parents at risk?"

"Maybe," Chomps said. "On the other hand, this way we'll both be there to keep an eye on them. On top of that, the only one who knows we're heading there is Broganis, and we aren't being followed. I've been watching."

"Yeah. So have I."

CHAPTER TWELVE

IT TURNED OUT THAT Chomps's earlier lie to Terry had had a grain of truth in it. Her parents really *had* heard about the explosion near Whistlestop and had debated screening her to see if she was all right. Apparently Terry's boss, Sheriff Laura Vespoli, was fussy enough about personal screens that they'd decided against it, but had compromised by waiting up until Chomps returned to see if he had any information.

Which meant that they were both awake, and both fully and nervously keyed up, by the time Chomps and Terry came walking in.

"...and I'm fine," Terry assured them after the hugs were over, along with the expressions of relief and probably a couple of tears on Eileen's part. "Really. You know Broganis—he'd never have released me if he didn't think I was all right."

"But your *face*," Eileen protested, tentatively touching Terry's cheek with her fingertips.

"It's just heat rash, Mom," Terry said. "Okay, excitement over. You two should get to bed—I'm sure you have a busy day planned."

"Not so you'd notice," Ralph said, folding his arms across his chest. "All right, Terry, spit it out."

"Spit what out?"

"Back in school you occasionally wanted us out of the way when you were entertaining a young gentleman," Ralph said. "Your technique was lousy then, and it hasn't gotten any better."

"*Dad!*" Terry protested, sounding scandalized.

"And since you have your own place now," Ralph continued calmly, "I doubt that's the issue here." He raised his eyebrows at Chomps. "Though I suppose it wouldn't be remiss for me to ask what your intentions are toward my daughter."

For a moment Chomps considered deflecting the question, either with humor or a show of indignation. But having lived with these people for over four months, and having observed their interactions with each other and their daughter, he knew he owed them more than empty words. "My intentions are to keep her alive."

Their reactions were about what he'd expected. Ralph's mouth dropped open a couple of millimeters, Eileen's eyes widened, and Terry looked both startled and slightly betrayed. "He's joking, Dad," she said.

"No, he's not," Chomps said. "Though he hopes he's exaggerating a little. But just a little."

Ralph looked at Eileen, then back at Chomps. "The rest of you go into the office," he said. "More private and soundproof than the dining room. I'll make coffee."

"We want to hear everything," Eileen added, taking her daughter's arm.

They listened in silence to the interlocking reports of the evening's events. Chomps and Terry finished, and for another moment all four of them sat in the same dark silence.

"You really think you found something worth killing for?" Eileen asked at last.

"If I'm right, they've already killed the duke's whole family," Chomps reminded her. "Once you've murdered five people, one more doesn't make a lot of difference." He waved a hand. "Anyway, now that you've heard the whole story, it's time for all of us to get to bed. I know Terry's had a rough day, and I doubt yours has been any easier—"

"Hold it," Ralph said, holding up a hand. "Nice try, but just hold it."

"What do you mean?" Terry asked.

"He means," Eileen said quietly, "that Chomps knows something important that he's not telling us."

"And whether you tell us about it or not," Ralph added, "whoever's running the cover-up is still going to assume you did. That puts *our* lives in danger, too." He cocked an eyebrow. "It seems to me that if we're going to join the two of you in the crosshairs, we should at least know why."

"I don't—" Chomps began.

"Forget it, Townsend," Terry interrupted. "Remember Mom telling you I was stubborn? You want to guess where I got it?"

"Yeah, but you're also armed," Chomps reminded her. "They're not."

"Never assume, Chomps," Ralph said quietly. "Never assume."

"So?" Eileen prompted.

"Okay," Chomps said reluctantly, pulling out his recorder and connecting it to his tablet, making sure none of them could see exactly what he was doing. "Let me set it up."

With access to Delphi's computers, he could have copied the file to one of the most crack-proof systems on Manticore. Unfortunately, that access had long since been taken from him.

But all that meant was that he'd have to go with Plan B.

The transfer mark flicked on and then off, confirming the file had been sent and received. At least now there was a second copy elsewhere on the planet if the killer got to Chomps.

Though Flora would probably not be thrilled about getting all this dumped on her computer this way. Especially not in the middle of the night.

"Okay," he said, keying for the relevant part of his recording and turning the tablet around toward them. "A bit of data that, not surprisingly, the investigators missed."

"What are we looking at?" Ralph asked.

"That's the computer from Duke Serisburg's car," Terry told him. "We didn't take it out during the investigation because it was already half ruined and cutting it out would have destroyed the other half. Thom Devereux, having more time on his hands, used a hammer and chisel."

"And he found something?" Eileen asked.

"Not yet," Chomps said. "Possibly never will—as Terry said, half ruined. But *this* is what I found interesting."

He keyed for a different set of pictures. "This is the computer's casing. It's got the usual collection of ports and other access points, all of them wired either to the computer directly or through buffers or modulators of various sorts." He switched pictures again. "Here are individual pictures of the ports. See if anything odd strikes you."

He ran the pictures past them, one at a time, giving them a few seconds' view of each. He watched their faces as he did so, wondering if there was really something there or if his imagination and suspicions were playing tricks on him. He reached the end and started again—

"Hold it," Eileen said. "Back up one, will you?"

"I was just about to ask the same thing," Terry said, leaning forward toward the tablet. "That middle port. The inside looks remarkably clean."

"It does, doesn't it?" Ralph murmured. "Can we see the others again?"

Chomps nodded and ran through the pictures again, feeling a sense of relief. So he *hadn't* been imagining things.

A satisfaction that was short-lived. Confirmation that he wasn't crazy also meant confirmation that he'd found possible evidence of murder.

"So what does that mean?" Eileen asked, sounding confused. "I'm not all that good at keeping my own computer dusted."

"That's not dust, Mom," Terry said grimly. "That's debris from the crash that got jammed into the ports. All except one of them." She looked at Chomps. "Which means that at the time of the crash, there was something in that port."

"Exactly," Chomps agreed. "Something that was gone when you got there. And the only other person who could have done that was whoever engineered the crash."

"Damn," Terry muttered under her breath. "The clearing. You were right—that's why he needed that particular tree. He had to get to the car and the port."

"But what could have been in there?" Eileen asked. "Ports like those are usually for peripherals and other non-vital equipment."

"Maybe it was something that scrambled the computer," Ralph suggested. "You're assuming that all the damage in the system came from the crash. What if it was a capacitor that sent a jolt of current into the autopilot? Would the duke have been able to even manually fly the car with that section fried?"

"I don't know," Terry said. "The manufacturers make it really hard to completely take out an air-car computer, for obvious reasons. I'd think a Solarian design would be even tougher."

"And something that catastrophic would show up on the black box recordings," Chomps added. "I assume the data said the computer was running properly?"

"Yes, as was all the other equipment," Terry said. "Which is why the only conclusion we could reach was operator error."

"I assume we're reaching a different conclusion now?" Ralph asked.

"I don't know," Terry said reluctantly. "Something here is weird—there's no doubt about that. But as evidence of foul play it's awfully thin."

"Could it have been something to block the radio?" Eileen asked. "Surely the duke had enough warning that something was wrong that he could have screened for help."

"You'd think so, wouldn't you?" Terry agreed. "Of course, when we thought it was just an accident, the lack of an emergency screen didn't look suspicious. Now..." She shook her head.

"The killer must have jammed the radio and his uni-link," Chomps suggested.

"But there's no indicated that the radio was ever activated," Terry countered. "Even if the signal was jammed, the fact that he tried to screen would still be recorded."

"Unless the radio had been disabled or disconnected," Ralph said. "If no signal came out of it, wouldn't the black box see that as the lack of a screen?"

Terry shook her head. "We tested the radio. It was fully functional."

"Or at least the radio you took back to the station was," Eileen said. "If the killer took something out of the computer, couldn't he have swapped out the radio, too?"

"Even easier, our missing plug could have been a cable to the radio," Terry said. "If the computer was telling the radio not to function, the black box would just record that it hadn't been used."

"And the duke knew it," Chomps said suddenly as a flash of understanding lit up his brain. "I'll be damned."

"What?" Terry demanded.

"Whatever was happening with the computer, the duke figured it out," Chomps said. "That's why he was out of his seat—he was trying to get to the computer and pull out the mystery plug."

"Only he didn't make it in time," Eileen whispered. "Oh God. Knowing your family was about to die..."

She trailed off, and for another moment the room was silent.

"We need to find out what was in there," Terry said.

"Absolutely," Ralph said. "But there's still one question

hanging over all this: *why*? Why would anyone want to kill the duke?"

"Unfortunately, motive is usually a lot murkier than method," Chomps said. "The first thing we have to figure out is who the actual target was."

"Obviously, Duke Serisburg and his family," Terry said, frowning.

"Are you sure?" Chomps countered. "Remember, his youngest child was sick. Instead of piling everyone into the car and heading home, wouldn't it have made more sense for the duchess and the sick boy to stay at the retreat for another day or two and let him recover before returning to the capital?"

"With a cold?" Eileen shrugged. "It's certainly what *I* would have done. But why does that matter? The duke, or the duke and his family—what's the difference?"

"No, no, he's right," Ralph said, frowning. "If the killers were only after the duke, then this might have been an attempt at regime change."

"At which point his family would have been collateral damage," Chomps said.

"That's a horrible way to put it," Eileen murmured.

"Sorry," Chomps apologized.

"Welcome to the wonderful world of law enforcement, Mom," Terry said. "Check your heart and feelings at the door."

"Let's track it through," Chomps said. "Typically, the title would have passed to the duke's eldest son, with the duchess acting as regent until he came of age. How was the duke seen by his subjects? I know everyone fell all over themselves praising him after his death, but I never put much stock in eulogies."

"Not an unwise policy," Ralph said. "I'd say that

Duke Serisburg was reasonably popular; but among the groups he was unpopular with he was *very* unpopular."

"Specifics?" Chomps asked.

"Terry probably knows more than we do about the realities," Ralph said. "Most of what we get are rumors and the social nets."

"We probably fielded a dozen complaints a week about the duke or the government in general," Terry said. "Maybe a death threat or two a month."

"Did those numbers increase in the month before his death?" Chomps asked.

"The complaints did," Terry said. "No change in the death threats."

"I assume your office follows up on those?" Eileen asked.

"For what it's worth," Terry said. "Most are just people venting their spleen. We find them, warn them that overt threats of violence are considered felonies, and they usually keep their heads down after that. One or two a year are from mentally disturbed people, and we usually end up referring them to the hospital for psych evaluation."

"I suppose that list will at least give us somewhere to start," Ralph said.

"Not really," Terry said. "If Chomps's scenario is right, this thing was way too clever and subtle for your typical crazy."

"And no one who actually intends murder tips his hand by sending in a threat," Chomps agreed. "So if the target was only the duke, we may be looking at an attempt at regime change. Any other thoughts?"

"Well . . ." Ralph looked at his wife. "There *was* the duke's will."

"The *duke's* will?" Chomps echoed. "Doesn't everything go to his wife and . . . wait, are you saying he had a *separate* will?"

"That's the rumor," Ralph said. "Moot, of course, given that the whole family died. But he *was* previously married, and there were persistent rumors that he had a separate will to make sure some of his holdings went to his first wife if he died before his current wife."

Chomps looked at Terry. "Well?"

"Not my department," she said firmly. "Wills are filed with attorneys and the duchy probate court, not the sheriff's office."

"Well, then, we need to track it down," Chomps said, making yet another mental note. "See if anyone besides the ex was going to get a slice of the pie. Former employees, maybe, or friends of his who aren't necessarily friends of his wife's." He hesitated, but it had to be said. "Or maybe it covers distribution of assets that weren't held in common property."

"What kind of assets?" Eileen asked.

"Assets he might have hidden from his ex before their settlement," Chomps said. "Or possibly property or cash he was hiding from the tax assessor."

"Duke *Serisburg*?" Eileen asked, her eyes going wide. "No. Not a chance."

"Hey, even the nicest guys have secrets," Chomps said. "Sometimes they're big secrets. Sometimes they're nasty secrets."

"You have a cynical view of the world," Ralph said.

"But he's not wrong," Terry said. "So we need to see the duke's will if we can."

"And I want a list of all the duke's employees at the time of his death," Chomps added.

All three of them looked at him. "You think one of them might have been involved?" Eileen asked.

"No one would know the duke's schedule and habits better than the people who worked for him," Terry pointed out.

"I'm also not necessarily accusing any of them," Chomps added. "But the killer might have cozied up to one of them for information."

"Well, if you're looking for sources, we need to check staff members, their families, their friends, their acquaintances, and the people who do their hair and nails," Terry said. "Can't be much more than half the duchy in that list."

"So I've already cut your workload by half," Chomps said. "You're welcome."

She gave him a look of strained patience. "And you've put up with him for four *months*?"

"Plus a bit," Eileen said, giving Chomps a tired smile. "Anything more?"

"Nothing I can think of," Chomps said. "Deputy?"

"No, I think this gives us plenty to start with," Terry agreed.

"Well, then, it's been a long day and all of us need to get some sleep," Eileen said. "Terry, you can take the room next to ours."

"Actually, I think I'll take the one next to Chomps's," Terry said. "Even if the killer thinks the shed explosion fixed the computer problem, he probably knows Chomps was in there making recordings before I arrived. If we're in a loose-end-tightening mood, there could be trouble in the night."

"Whatever you think best," Ralph said. "Good-night, everyone."

"Just a second," Chomps said, hesitantly. He hadn't planned on bringing this up until they'd sorted out the will and employees. But the more he thought about the evening's events, the more he'd realized he needed to get on this aspect as quickly as possible. "We're assuming the duke's air car was deliberately rammed into the tree, and that a single killer was involved. But it's possible he had an accomplice, and that accomplice would need a staging point. Unless he wanted to hunker down in the forest, he would have needed somewhere to wait."

"What's your point?" Ralph asked.

"That the backup might have decided the inn would be the perfect spot," Terry said sourly. "That where you're going with this?"

"Oh, my God," Eileen breathed. "He was *here?*"

"Maybe not," Chomps said. "Probably not, actually. There are a lot of downsides to staying in a public place. But we can't ignore the possibility."

"No, we can't," Ralph said grimly. "Okay. Let me go dig out the registration and security records."

"Not now," Terry said. "That'll take at least an hour, and you're as tired as the rest of us. Tomorrow will be soon enough."

"Agreed," Chomps said. "I just thought I should bring it up, because..." He hesitated.

"Because we kicked over a fire ant nest tonight," Terry said. "The fire ants may not be worried about it yet, but sooner or later they will be. If you still have that old shotgun, you might want to make sure it's in reach."

"All right," Ralph said reluctantly. "But all we've got is birdshot and beanbag rounds."

"You hunt with *beanbag rounds* out here?" Chomps asked, frowning.

"A gift from Terry," Eileen said with a faint smile. "She said killing an intruder created too much paperwork. Disabling him was simpler."

"Fair enough," Chomps said. "And speaking of killing and intruders, Terry, I think you should reconsider the idea of sleeping away from your parents. They might need you."

"You might need her, too," Ralph said. "And you have the records, which makes you a more likely target. Ergo, she stays near you."

"I can take care of myself," Chomps said.

"So can we," Eileen said.

"They can," Terry seconded. "Trust me."

"Then it's settled," Ralph said.

"Yes, but—" Chomps began to protest.

"And now, we'd all better get some sleep," Ralph said. "The next few days are likely to be busy."

"Absolutely," Terry said. She arched her eyebrows. "Pleasant dreams, everyone."

"We'll try," Eileen said. "And you two . . . just be careful, all right? Both of you."

Apparently, that part of the discussion was over. "We will," Chomps said. "Good night."

Which was just as well. The better Terry was in position to protect him, the better he would be in position to protect her.

☆   ☆   ☆

"You scared them," Terry said as she and Chomps walked down the quiet hallway toward the rooms.

"You have a problem with that?" Chomps countered. The adrenaline rush of the evening's events had long since passed, leaving him tired and on edge. First exile from his chosen profession, then spinning his wheels as carpenter's assistant in the middle of nowhere, and now up to his eyebrows in a murder investigation. Not exactly the way he'd seen his life going a few months ago.

"Not with the message," Terry said. "Only with the delivery."

Chomps shook his head. "I'm too tired to soft-sugar anything. There's nothing wrong with being scared if it keeps you alert. And alive."

"I suppose," Terry said. "It's not like they can't take a shock. But next time, you feed me the bad news and let *me* decide how to hand it over."

"Fine," Chomps said. "Our very next murder case. Promise."

"Right. Our next one." She was silent for the next few steps. "I take it this isn't your first time?"

"My first time with a murder?"

"Your first time sticking your nose where it doesn't belong," Terry said flatly.

Chomps shook his head. "I just came here to help with your parents' remodeling."

"Right. I forgot." She looked sideways at him. "So who exactly should I be asking about you? The Royal Investigation Division? The Navy? The Palace itself?"

Chomps winced. "I really wish you wouldn't. There could be...unpleasant repercussions."

"I'll just bet there could," Terry said, still eyeing him. "Okay, fine. I'll let you run with it. For now. Just know that I'll be watching you *very* closely."

"Understood," Chomps said. "Thanks."

"You're welcome," she said. "But I suggest you hold

your applause until the end of the show. So what are you going to look for on the employee list? Someone who's suddenly come into money?"

"Yes, if one of them was bribed and is also terminally stupid," Chomps said, dragging his mind away from the precipice's edge and back onto the case. "I'm thinking the more likely lever was blackmail or extortion."

"So you look for a shady past."

"Right," Chomps said. "The problem being that the only way blackmail works is if those shady bits haven't yet come to light. Makes the investigation a wee bit trickier."

"Well, if it was easy everyone would do it." Terry shook her head. "I don't know, Chomps. I see all the pieces you trotted out, but I can't quite make them all fit. I think we're missing something."

"I don't doubt it," Chomps said. "Hopefully, the will and the employee shake-down will help clarify things."

"I hope so," Terry said. "We're already treading dangerous ground here, and not just from the killers. Reopening a closed case isn't exactly a politically smart thing to do. Especially when opening it also rips a scab off a gaping wound."

Chomps made a face. She was right, of course. With less than a T-year since Serisburg's death the national psyche was still adjusting to the loss. Proving murder would be legally satisfying, but that didn't mean there wouldn't be resentment from some quarters that they had to relive the trauma.

And if there was enough resentment in the highest ranks of government, it could permanently end any chance of getting back into Delphi.

"But you don't go into law enforcement to be loved by all," Terry continued. "If I'd wanted that I'd have stayed here with my mother. This is your room, right?"

"Yes," Chomps said. "Well, good-night—"

"Just a second," Terry said. Crouching down, she pulled up her left pantleg and retrieved a Drakon 6mm from an ankle holster. "Here," she said, straightening up and handing it to him. "Just in case."

"You sure?" Chomps said, gazing at the weapon. Small and compact, fairly useless for anything distant, but wonderfully suited for close combat.

"I'm sure," Terry said. "Try not to get oil stains on my mother's pillowcase."

"I think sleeping with a gun under your pillow is probably more your thing."

"Hardly," Terry scoffed. "Makes a huge, uncomfortable lump. Current procedure is to holster your weapon under the edge of the bed."

"Sounds much more comfortable."

"It is," Terry said. "And do remember that that gun's registered to me. So don't shoot anything."

"I won't," Chomps promised.

"Thanks. Unless, of course," she added thoughtfully, "it's something that *needs* shooting."

CHAPTER THIRTEEN

"HYPER LIMIT IN ONE MINUTE, *Herr Admiral*," the officer at *Zhong Kui*'s helm announced.

"*Danke*," Basaltberg replied as he swept a quick, almost casual look across the bridge displays.

Travis wasn't fooled. Casual-looking or not, the admiral's eyes were pausing briefly on each display, assessing and absorbing all the relevant data there before moving on. He'd seen that same attention to detail before, not just with Basaltberg, but virtually every other Andermani officer and spacer he'd interacted with.

Basaltberg finished his sweep and turned to his two visitors. "One more reminder, *Herr Baron*, if you will indulge me, that your part in this conversation will necessarily be brief."

"Of course, *Herr Admiral*," Winterfall said, inclining his head. "I understand fully that the purpose of our presence here is to honor the late Emperor Gustav. Be assured that I and every other Manticoran will stay strictly to the background, speaking only when spoken to, and obeying every order as given."

"I appreciate that, *Herr* Winterfall," Basaltberg said, a hint of a smile touching the somberness that had seemed etched into his face ever since he'd heard the news of his Emperor's death. "But please do not feel that you are walking on eggshells the entire time."

He shifted his gaze to Travis. "Manticore has already proven its friendship by its willingness to stand with the Anderman Empire in time of need. You have requested the honor of joining with us in our grief, and we honor that request and the respect behind it. And we're not so rigid and formal that honest mistakes cannot be understood and tolerated."

"I appreciate that in turn, *Herr Admiral*," Winterfall said. "Once again, I thank you."

"Stand ready," *Zhong Kui*'s kapitän der sterne called.

Basaltberg turned back around to face forward. Travis braced himself for the translation, noting peripherally that his brother had quietly slipped a sick bag from under his tunic and was readying it for action. The indicator ran to zero—

Travis had done enough of these to have become almost accustomed to them, though they were never going to be anything but unpleasant. Fortunately, from what he could see of his brother, Winterfall was getting through this one a little easier, too.

"Transmit our greetings to Flotillenadmiral von Jachmann aboard *Preussen*," Basaltberg ordered. His voice seemed a little thick, but the effect could as easily have been an artifact of Travis's stressed hearing as it could have been from Basaltberg's voice. "Distance?"

"Approximately 17.4 LM, *Herr Admiral*," Korvettenkapitän Jason Westgate, Basaltberg's flag com officer, reported. "Signal sent."

"Danke."

Mentally, Travis threw Basaltberg a salute. The admiral had wanted to come out of hyper at the closest approach to Tomlinson and the battleship currently orbiting it. Seventeen point four light-minutes meant *Zhong Kui* had arrived damn near exactly at its intended entry point. Yet another reminder, if Travis had needed one, of the sheer professionalism of the Andermani navy.

"Locate *Rotte* and *München*," Basaltberg continued. "If they're close enough to receive our transmissions, send greetings to their commanders, as well."

He swiveled again to face Travis and Winterfall. "While we wait for their responses, perhaps you'd like to retire to the wardroom," he offered. "There are couches there if you'd like to rest."

"Thank you," Winterfall said. He didn't sound strangled, exactly, but he wasn't much off that mark, either. "That would be . . . most welcome."

☆   ☆   ☆

"Signal coming in, *meine Kapitänin*," Bajer said, his voice taut. "It's *Zhong Kui*."

"*Zhong Kui*?" Hansen echoed, her eyes momentarily going wide. "What's—"

She broke off, her face resettling into its normal calmness. Her eyes flicked to the out-of-the-way section of the bridge where Llyn and Commodore Quint were floating, then returned to Bajer. "Escorts?" she asked.

Llyn leaned a little closer to Quint. Hansen had recovered quickly enough, but Llyn knew how to read people and rooms, and that single flash of surprise had spoken volumes. Somewhere, something had gone off page. "Trouble?" he murmured to the mercenary commander.

"I don't know," Quint murmured back, her own eyes hard on Hansen. "*Zhong Kui* is an Andermani battle-cruiser, commanded by Admiral Graf von Basaltberg. One of their best, if reputation is to be believed."

"I don't remember that ship being listed as part of the cortège."

"It wasn't," Quint said grimly. "And it's not just a matter of the guest list having been changed, either. *Zhong Kui* is too early to be part of the flotilla, and she's coming from the wrong direction."

"You think someone here got a message out?"

"I don't see how they could," Quint said. "*München's* gone to ground out past the hyper limit, but surely they're sticking around close to the vector the cortège will arrive on. As far as we know the Andermani didn't have anything else in the system."

Llyn scowled. And it wasn't like the Quintessence hadn't had ships at Tomlinson the entire time, either. Even if the Andermani had some hidden ace up their sleeves—some courier quietly sitting at the hyper limit, say—there was no way it could have slipped out without one of Quint's people spotting its departure.

"The frigate *Drachen* is with him, *meine Kapitänin*," Bajer said hesitantly. "But also...we're getting transponder IDs from two ships that claim to be from the Star Kingdom of Manticore."

"*What?*" Llyn demanded, shoving off the bulkhead toward the com station, ignoring the surprised and slightly scandalized looks he got from the others for barging into the conversation. "Which ones?"

"Mr. Llyn—" one of the Tomlinson officers began in a threatening tone.

The man stopped at a gesture from Hansen. "Bajer?" she prompted.

"There's a destroyer, *Damocles*," Bajer said, giving Llyn the same reproachful look as everyone else, "and a courier boat, *Diactoros*."

"Are you familiar with these ships, Llyn?" Quint asked.

"Very familiar," Llyn said between clenched teeth. Axelrod had kicked him off the Manticore part of the plan and sent him to the Andermani, and now the damn Manticorans had *followed* him here? What the *hell* were they up to? "A couple of years ago Manticore had a run-in with an Andermani expatriate-turned-mercenary named Gensonne."

It was Hansen's turn to twitch. "*Cutler* Gensonne?"

"Yes," Llyn said. "You know the man?"

Hansen threw an unreadable look at Bajer. "I'm familiar with one of his former associates," she said carefully.

"How familiar?" Quint asked pointedly. "And how former?"

"That's not important," Hansen said, dismissing it with a wave of her hand. "What we need to know—"

"Excuse me, Kapitänin der Sterne Hansen, but it's *very* important," Quint cut in. "If there's even a chance that another mercenary group is in play, I need to know it."

"It's all right, Commodore," Llyn said before Hansen could answer. "Gensonne and his people are out of the picture."

"You're sure?" Quint asked.

"Quite sure," Llyn assured her, his gaze shifting to Hansen. "But I was under the impression that all his former associates were with him at the end or had already been dealt with."

"All his *known* associates, perhaps," Hansen said. "For the moment, all you need to know is that the causes of both justice and irony will be satisfied when this is over."

Llyn looked at Quint, noting the subtle signs of understanding in her otherwise neutral expression. Hansen had dropped a few hints about some mysterious person high up in the Andermani government who was supposedly going to be critical in bringing this insurrection to a triumphal conclusion. But so far, she hadn't shared the details with him.

She'd shared them with Quint, of course. There was no way a competent mercenary commander would sign on to a situation like this without full knowledge of assets and liabilities. *Preussen's* senior officers had presumably also been briefed—Llyn couldn't imagine this many of them agreeing to stay with Hansen's mutiny without being given a damn good reason. But so far, for whatever reason, Hansen had decided that Llyn should be kept out of the loop.

Which was pretty ungrateful of her, in Llyn's opinion, seeing as how he was the one who'd engineered her alliance with the Quintessence in the first place. But he'd tried his best gentle probes with Quint and gotten nowhere, and had regretfully decided to cultivate his patience until Hansen was finally ready to open up. He flicked a glance at Flotillenadmiral von Jachmann, floating silently near the com station—

And paused for a closer look. Jachmann had the same hooded look as Quint. Whatever Hansen's big secret was, Jachmann was on the same page.

Llyn knew all about Gensonne's part in the coup attempt that had been orchestrated and launched against Emperor Gustav eighteen T-years ago and quickly quashed. The Axelrod reports on the incident were unanimous in their conclusion that all the conspirators had been caught and executed, with Gensonne's exile being the only exception.

But unless Hansen was just blowing dust, at least one of the treasonous fish had escaped the net.

That could be disastrous. The whole idea was for Quint and Hansen to distract the Andermani so that Axelrod could quietly take over Manticore and the still unsuspected wormhole junction hidden within its twin star system. If one of the old conspirators was planning to use the Tomlinson insurrection to rekindle their old coup—especially with Gustav now dead—it could embroil the Empire in a civil war that could destabilize the entire sector.

And speaking of the late Emperor . . .

He stole another look at Quint. On the surface she'd taken the news of Gustav's death well enough, especially considering her private goal of delivering retribution for the murder of her mother. But Llyn could see the tension around her eyes and at the corners of her mouth. The next obvious target for her to vent her rage against was the new Emperor, the twenty-three-year-old Andrew. Most of the revenge-thirsty people Llyn had known over the years would have had no problem transferring their hatred onto the villain's family.

But Quint wasn't like that. Granted, she'd wanted to gaze into Gustav's face as she killed him, to make sure he knew exactly who was bleeding away his life and why. But killing Andrew would accomplish none of those goals, and would furthermore be a violent act against a completely innocent person.

So what was she going to do?

Llyn didn't know. And that worried him, not least because if Quint looked to be going off the deep end he would have to deal not only with her but also with Amos before the politely deadly steward decided to do something on his own. He needed to get Quint alone in a corner somewhere and find out what was going on behind those eyes.

But with a long list of details that had to be completed before Gustav's cortège arrived—not the least of which was making sure *Preussen* was crewed, repaired, and ready to fight—he hadn't yet had the opportunity to do that.

He'd just have to make time. Preferably before the funeral procession wandered into the Freets' trap.

"In the meantime, Flotillenadmiral von Jachmann," Hansen said, turning to Jachmann, "Admiral Basaltberg is waiting to speak with you. Have you made your decision?"

"I have," Jachmann said, his voice even.

"And are you with me or against me?"

"First answer one question," Jachmann said. "What are your intentions toward Emperor Andrew? Does he live, or does he die?"

"I have no quarrel with him," Hansen said. "I'm sure some arrangement can be made that won't require his death."

For a few seconds she and Jachmann locked eyes. Then, Jachmann exhaled quietly and inclined his head. "Very well," he said. "I'll speak with Basaltberg."

Hansen held his eyes another moment, then gestured to Bajer. "Open his mic."

"Mic open."

"And on a ninety-second delay," Hansen added. "I don't wish to impugn your honor, *Herr Flotillenadmiral*, but in this situation one must be cautious. Even among allies."

"Of course," Jachmann said with a bitter-edged smile. "I trust the others in this compartment will also remember that attitude."

Hansen gestured. "Get on with it."

Jachmann cleared his throat. "This is Flotillenadmiral von Jachmann, Admiral Basaltberg," he called. "May the Empire endure forever. Welcome to Tomlinson. I see you've brought us some guests from the Star Kingdom of Manticore. Well done, my friend."

He chuckled. "I must say, Gotthold, your string of successes continues unabated. First your genius plan for getting weapons into attack range of Gensonne's fortified base, then the diplomatic coup of making formal contact with Manticore."

Llyn nodded to himself as an old mystery was finally resolved. He'd known someone had attacked and destroyed Gensonne's base—an Axelrod black ops force had been on its way to do exactly that, in fact, when they found that their mission had been preempted. But up to now the attackers' identity had been unknown.

"I can hardly wait to see what glories you next achieve," Jachmann continued. "I notice you're keeping to a low acceleration. Is that because your Manticoran guests aren't able to achieve anything higher? Von Jachmann, clear."

"Transmission ended, *meine Kapitänin*," Bajer reported.

"An odd question, Flotillenadmiral," Hansen said, a hint of suspicion in her tone. "Why else would they be running a slow acceleration?"

"I don't know," Jachmann told her. "Hence, the question."

"Seems to me we have a bigger question to deal with," Quint put in grimly. "Our plans don't allow for dealing with an additional battlecruiser."

"Don't worry, we'll get rid of him," Hansen promised. "One way, or another."

☆   ☆   ☆

"It's a puzzlement, *Herr Admiral*," Fregattenkapitän Guiying Schlamme said to Basaltberg, pointing to the mark on the bridge's main tactical display. "If it's *München*, there's no reason for her to be there instead of on patrol. There's certainly no reason for her to ignore our hails or leave her transponder off. But if it's someone else, one would expect them to at least have shown a reaction to our arrival."

Travis felt a touch of air against his skin as his brother floated closer to his side. "Not getting the subtext here," Winterfall muttered. "Can you fill me in?"

"There's a ship at that marked position," Travis muttered back, wondering if the problem was the subtext or the language. Travis's own German proficiency was reasonably good—better than he'd expected when he first started his studies, in fact—but while Winterfall had been conversing quite fluently in his hosts' language over the past two or three weeks Travis had always had a sense that his brother was still a bit uncomfortable with it. "About six light-minutes away, sitting right at the hyper limit. It's running a *very* minimal wedge, just barely above standby, which suggests a degree of nervousness."

"If they're nervous about being seen, why have the wedge up at all?"

"At a guess, because they're not just nervous about being seen, but also about being attacked," Travis told him. "A wedge on standby takes time to fully spin up, and until then the ship's vulnerable from every direction."

"And they also can't run or dodge," Winterfall said, nodding in understanding. "So they're walking a compromise between invisible and defenseless." He smiled slightly as Travis gave him a look of mild surprise. "I'm in politics, remember? Compromise is what we do. So what's the admiral's plan?"

"He's still weighing the options," Travis said. "We could head over to check her out, but if she rabbits we'll probably lose her. We could ignore her and continue in toward Tomlinson, but that would eventually put her at our backs, which no one really wants."

Winterfall muttered something Travis couldn't catch. "I just noticed. She's sitting right where Emperor Gustav's cortège is supposed to arrive, isn't she?"

"Very good," Travis said with a flicker of new respect. He hadn't expected his brother to pick up on that. "And yes, that's probably Admiral Basaltberg's biggest concern." He hesitated. "That, plus the fact that, even if that's *München* out there, we can't seem to locate *Rotte* at all."

"*Herr Admiral,* we have a reply from *Preussen,*" Westgate announced.

"*Danke, mein Herr,*" Basaltberg said. "Let me hear it."

"This is Flotillenadmiral von Jachmann, Admiral Basaltberg," a calm, measured voice came from the flag bridge speaker. "May the Empire endure forever. Welcome to Tomlinson…"

Travis listened as the rest of the message played out. Westgate clicked it off, and for a long moment Basaltberg remained silent. Then, slowly, he swiveled to face Travis. "Lieutenant Commander Long," he said, his voice suddenly and unexpectedly formal. "Your analysis, *bitte*?"

Travis felt his chest tighten. His *analysis*? Where could he even start? He didn't know this Flotillenadmiral von Jachmann. He had no history with him, no personal knowledge of him—hell, he barely had the language down, let alone the military and civilian cultural protocols. What was he supposed to say?

"Easy, Travis," Winterfall murmured. "You've got this."

Travis sent his brother a quick look.

And in that taut moment he suddenly realized something he should have spotted from the beginning. This feeling of having been thrown into the deep end of the pool—this lack of stable footing and sense of a huge and undeserved weight dropping onto his shoulders—was the reason Winterfall seemed so uncomfortable. Because it was the way he himself had been feeling the entire time since they left Manticore.

Only Winterfall was carrying the possible diplomatic future of the Star Kingdom. All Travis had to deal with was a single tactical analysis.

He took a deep breath and turned back to Basaltberg. Maybe the admiral wanted his thoughts *because* he had no history with Jachmann. There was nothing to distract him from the message and its wording.

Winterfall was right. He *did* have this.

"I'll do my best, *Herr Admiral*," he said. "I assume first that the opening sentence, *may the Empire endure forever*, is an all-is-well code phrase?"

"It is," Basaltberg said. "The question is whether it was given legitimately or under duress."

Travis nodded. That aspect he'd already figured out. "My first question would be why he brought up the Volsungs in the first place. It was a solid Andermani victory, certainly, but it seems to me his thoughts and concerns should be on the cortège and his duties in that regard, not military history. Certainly not military history that Emperor Gustav wasn't personally involved in."

"I agree," Basaltberg said. "Anything else?"

Travis hesitated. If he'd misjudged Basaltberg—if the man wasn't the honest and honorable soldier he thought—then he was about to land himself, Winterfall's diplomatic mission, and possibly the entire Star Kingdom in trouble. "Yes, *Herr Admiral*," he said. "Flotillenadmiral von Jachmann said that you'd come up with the strategy of sending missiles on ballistic courses against the Volsung base."

"And I didn't?"

"No, *Herr Admiral*." Travis looked him straight in the eye. "I did."

"You did, indeed," Basaltberg said, inclining his head toward Travis, a small smile creasing his lips. "Have no fear, Commander. In every report, in every hearing, I always strive to give full credit where it is due. So it was with the Volsung battle."

He looked at Winterfall. "Which is, after all, why

Emperor Gustav wished to meet you and your fellow officers in the first place."

"But not everyone would have taken the time to read that report," Travis said as he finally picked up on Basaltberg's logic. "If Flotillenadmiral von Jachmann is acting under duress, he might have thought that detail might slip past his watchdogs."

"Yes," Basaltberg said, his voice going cold. "And when combined with the verbal all-clear signal, that leads us to the conclusion that his keepers are fellow Andermani officers."

"But that would mean mutiny, *Herr Admiral*," Schlamme protested. "How could such a thing happen?"

"I don't know," Basaltberg admitted. "But perhaps Flotillenadmiral von Jachmann gave us one final clue. Lieutenant Commander Travis's tactic involved slipping missiles in on ballistic courses. Perhaps whoever moved against *Preussen* invaded the system the same way."

"Which would imply the Freets have additional backing and resources," Schlamme said. "Or it might warn that a new player has entered the game."

"And either way, we have no idea what we and Emperor Gustav's cortège are facing," Basaltberg said grimly, turning to Travis. "Commander Long, I need you to send a message to *Damocles* and *Diactoros* ordering them to drop their acceleration to zero. I'll do the same with our two ships."

"Understood, *Herr Admiral*," Travis said as Westgate detached a mic and handed it to him. If there was trouble with *Preussen*, the last thing Basaltberg would want was to get closer to her and farther in from the system's hyper limit. "*Herr Korvettenkapitän?*"

"You're connected," Westgate confirmed.

"Danke." Travis keyed the mic. *"Damocles,* this is Lieutenant Commander Long. I need to speak to the OOW immediately."

"Damocles," Lisa's voice came back in the properly formal tone of an official conversation. "Commander Lisa Donnelly Long."

"Admiral Basaltberg needs you and *Diactoros* to drop acceleration to zero," Travis told her.

"Zero acceleration, acknowledged," Lisa said crisply. "Signaling Captain Cherise now. Timing?"

Travis looked questioningly at Basaltberg, got a nod in return. "As soon as you can," he told Lisa.

"Acknowledged," she said again. "Reconfiguring wedge now."

Travis turned to look at the tactical display, mentally counting out the seconds. He'd reached fifteen when *Damocles*'s icon suddenly turned red. *"Damocles* acceleration at zero, *Herr Admiral,"* Schlamme confirmed. *"Diactoros* acceleration . . . also zero."

"Signal *Drachen* to suspend acceleration, then do likewise," Basaltberg ordered.

It took a bit longer for a ship the size of *Zhong Kui* to go to zero acceleration, but the usual Andermani efficiency was again on display. Ninety seconds after *Damocles* dropped into ballistic trajectory, the entire four-ship group was likewise.

Though the staggered time frame in which that had taken place meant that the four ships were now strung out over a long stretch of space instead of being in a compact travel formation. If there was an enemy out there waiting to pick them off one by one, the uncomfortable thought flicked through Travis's mind, Basaltberg had just handed him a golden opportunity—

"Hyper footprint, *Herr Admiral!*" Schlamme snapped. "Just outside hyper limit, almost directly behind us."

"Set Readiness Two," Basaltberg ordered calmly.

"Travis?" Winterfall murmured, his voice tense.

Travis looked at the displays. The newcomer had made translation about eighteen light-seconds behind them. "We should know in about ten seconds," he murmured back. Automatically, he began mentally counting down the time as he watched the bridge crew coolly and efficiently move the battlecruiser toward a war footing. His count ran to zero—

"We have transponder ID, *Herr Admiral*," Schlamme said. "It's *München*."

"*München* is signaling," Westgate added. He touched a switch—

"Fregattenkapitänin Deutschmann to Admiral Basaltberg," a woman's voice came over the bridge speaker. She sounded tired, Travis thought, but fully alert. "Be advised that *Preussen* is in hostile hands and *Rotte* has been destroyed. Beware unseen enemy forces."

"Such as that one," Travis said to Winterfall, nudging his brother and gesturing toward the spot on the tactical marking the mystery ship. "Probably been waiting for *München* to come out of hyper, hoping she would drop in close enough for an attack."

"Send acknowledgment," Basaltberg ordered. His voice hadn't changed, but Travis could feel the sudden tension filling the flag bridge. "Order all ships to return at once to our entry point at their best possible speed." He keyed a set of coordinates over to the comm officer. "Also signal all ships—including *München*—that we'll rendezvous at this point."

He looked at Travis, and Travis felt a chill run

through him. "And," the admiral added, "bring the formation to Readiness One."

☆   ☆   ☆

Preussen's bridge had gone unnaturally silent. But then, Llyn thought darkly, there really wasn't much to be said. *Zhong Kui* had been warned, and was running for the hyper limit, along with the Manticorans and the elusive *München*.

And there wasn't a single damn thing any of them could do about it.

He looked at the tactical again, just to be sure. The *Norfolk*-class destroyer that Quint had sent to the hyper limit in hopes that *München* would pop back in for another intel sweep was still in position, and coincidently was lurking close to where Basaltberg had arrived.

Unfortunately, it wasn't nearly close enough to get to the admiral's force. It certainly was too far away to get to *München*.

Anyway, right now there were more urgent matters to deal with than Basaltberg's inevitable escape. Llyn had noted the fact that the Andermani and Manticoran ships had stopped their inward acceleration well *before* they received *München*'s warning. That meant that somewhere in the brief message Hansen had allowed Jachmann there'd been a signal or warning that had alerted Basaltberg to the danger awaiting him in the inner system.

Which further meant that the support Hansen had hoped to obtain from the Flotillenadmiral was no longer on the table.

From the expression on Hansen's face as she turned to her former commander, she knew it, too.

"A wasted effort, *mein Herr*," she said, her voice under rigid control. "They will still come—alerted and better prepared than they would have otherwise, perhaps, but still with no true understanding of what they face. The end will still be the same."

"An interesting analysis, Captain," Jachmann said in a voice that perfectly matched hers, "given that I was about to give you the same warning in reverse."

"My *rank* is *Kapitänin der Sterne*."

"No," Jachmann said flatly. "When you committed treason you lost the right to be treated as an officer of the Andermani."

"*Treason?*" Hansen spat out the word. "You saw the evidence of my claim."

Llyn frowned. The evidence of Hansen's *claim*? What the hell did *that* mean?

"I saw *your* evidence," Jachmann countered. "Given that it can't be confirmed out here, I have no reason to believe it."

"The confirmation is on Potsdam."

"You'll never reach Potsdam," Jachmann said. "You'll die here in Tomlinson. One way or another."

"Andrew will never push things that far."

"You may be surprised."

"I'm already surprised," Hansen said, a flicker of pain crossing her face. "I thought you were a man of honor."

Jachmann snorted. "You have no idea what true honor means. Furthermore, I never said I was joining you, Captain. I made the mewings of defeat and acceptance, and you simply heard what you wished to hear."

"If you think Andrew is the leader the Empire needs, you're a fool."

"My thoughts and opinions are irrelevant," Jachmann said. "Andrew is the rightful heir to the throne."

"You saw the—" Hansen broke off. "So that's it? You're just going to yield to some rigid tradition?"

"Of course not." Jachmann drew himself up. "When you first pleaded your case in front of me, Captain, you made a point of telling me that you'd kept casualties to a minimum. In fact, you seemed rather proud of that."

"You would have preferred a mass slaughter?"

Jachmann shook his head. "You really don't understand do you? It never even occurred to you that there was only one number of casualties I would find acceptable. The number zero."

Once again, the bridge descended into silence. Once again, Llyn knew, there really wasn't anything more to say.

This time it was Bajer who spoke first. "Request permission to relieve the Flotillenadmiral of his life, *meine Kapitänin*," he said coldly.

For a moment it looked to Llyn like Hansen was going to agree. Then, she shook her head. "You will escort the Flotillenadmiral to his quarters," she said. "I may wish to talk to him later."

"*Jawohl, meine Kapitänin*," Bajer said. He drew his sidearm and gestured, and Jachmann and his two Tomlinson guards headed for the hatch.

Llyn moved closer to Quint. "So what are we looking at?" he asked quietly.

"Your basic two-point split," she said. Her voice was calm, but Llyn could tell she wasn't any happier at how this had gone down than any of the rest of them. "Option one: Basaltberg collects his ships and Gustav's cortège and charges straight into battle. Option two: they all scamper off to New Berlin and return with everything that can fight."

Llyn winced. And given the size of the Andermani fleet, that would be a very bad thing. "Which do you think they'll go with?"

She shrugged. "Hard to say. If *I* were in charge, I'd go with number two. From what we let *München* see of our forces, Basaltberg may figure he already has enough of an edge for a likely win, so he might be tempted toward number one. But the fact that someone successfully ambushed *Preussen* and *Rotte* strongly suggests a bunch of hidden aces, and I'd be very leery about charging into anything that looks too easy. Even given that postponing a confrontation gives Hansen and the Tomlinsons more time to repair and consolidate, that's still where I'd go."

"Especially when you had four more battleships and the rest of the Andermani navy to play with?"

"Especially then," she agreed. "Actually, in this case there may be a third option. Our new Emperor Andrew might look at the situation, do some math on what it would cost him to retake Tomlinson, and decide to negotiate. Hansen is probably hoping it'll break that direction." She smiled crookedly. "As is your employer, I presume."

"It *would* make things easier," Llyn conceded. Certainly Lucretia Tomlinson and PFT were hoping Andrew would make a deal. Axelrod, for its part, didn't really care one way or the other. "You think he'll do that?"

Quint shrugged again. "Impossible to say with such an unknown quantity. My guess is that he'll *want* to follow in his father's footsteps and charge in for flag and Empire. What will happen once he's had his nose bloodied, though, is anyone's guess."

Across the bridge, Jachmann and his guards disappeared through the hatch. "Any idea what Hansen meant about a claim? A claim to what?"

Quint hesitated. "I'm sorry, but I can't talk about that. Not because I don't trust you," she added, "but because Kapitänin der Sterne Hansen has something of a mistrust for civilians. Particularly civilians whose life details are, shall we say, as sparse as yours."

"There are reasons for me to keep a low profile."

"I know," Quint said. "And if it were up to me... but it's not. Even though you provided the funding, and are therefore technically my employer, Hansen is the task force's commanding officer. In a military situation, which this is, my first loyalty has to be to her."

"That makes sense," Llyn agreed. "And I certainly wouldn't want to get you in trouble."

"I appreciate that," Quint said. "I'll tell you this much: If things work out the way Hansen expects, we'll get through this with a minimum of bloodshed. On all sides."

"I'll hold you to that," Llyn warned with mock severity. "Anyway, the excitement appears to be over for the day, so I might as well head back to *Retribution*. Are you coming?"

"I should probably stay a bit longer," Quint said. "I imagine Kapitänin der Sterne Hansen will have things she'll want to discuss. I'll send word to the shuttle to take you across."

"Thank you," Llyn said. "I'll see you at dinner."

There was no point going after *Preussen*'s officers

or crew, Llyn knew. Even if any of them were willing to talk to him, they also talked among themselves. There was even less chance he could get anything from Hansen.

But Jachmann was a different story. He also knew what was going on, and he was confined to quarters. No one to talk to in there.

Of course, given what Quint had just told him, Hansen's people were undoubtedly keeping a close watch on *Retribution*'s mysterious civilian. If Llyn was seen wandering around *Preussen* on his own, let alone caught near Jachmann's quarters, there would be some serious trouble. Not just for himself, but also for Quint. There was no way he could get to Jachmann.

But no one ever noticed stewards.

Amos had been coasting long enough, Llyn decided. Time for him to start earning his keep.

CHAPTER FOURTEEN

BARONESSE MARIJA SHENOA had known Emperor Andrew for most of his life. She'd started out as his nursemaid, moved from there into the role of guardian and companion, and somehow ended up as one of his most trusted advisors. Along the way she'd seen him happy, sad, frightened, grouchy, and every other mental and emotional state a child, teenager, and young adult could go through.

But sitting a meter to Andrew's left, close to him but not officially seated at the conference table in SMS *Friedrich der Grosse*'s flag briefing room, it occurred to her that until today she'd never seen his eyes blazing with such an icy, deadly anger.

Of course, it wasn't like he was the only one.

"Majestät, this *cannot* be allowed to stand!" Kanzlerin Wilhelmine Heilbronn, Markgräfin von Schwarzer Flügel, snarled. Her green eyes swept the table, her army uniform in stark contrast with the naval and civilian garb worn by everyone else.

In contrast, but hardly out of place. Schwarzer Flügel

had been one of Gustav Anderman's most reliable army officers since long before he settled down to empire and crown. Along the way she'd been named not only senior ground commander, but also commander of his elite Black Wing assault infantry. Now, well into her seventies, she'd taken on the additional role of kanzlerin, head of the Empire's government.

Many faced with that mix of age and responsibility would have found themselves softening. Not Schwarzer Flügel. Indeed, as far as Marija could tell, the effect had been to simply wear away the surface layers, leaving nothing but the underlying granite.

"It won't be, Markgräfin von Schwarzer Flügel," Andrew replied from the head of table. His tone was milder than his kanzlerin's and the fire in his eyes not quite so visible. Some at the table, Marija reflected, might even miss that fire completely.

And that would be a mistake.

There were people in the Empire—many people, in fact—who believed Andrew Anderman to be a pale imitation of his father. On one level such a comparison was not only justified but inevitable. Men of Gustav Anderman's stature were rare, and the shadows they cast over history were long and broad. Expecting anyone to measure up to such a standard was unreasonable, particularly when the person in question was only twenty-three T-years old.

Andrew had graduated from the *Interstellare Kriegsakademie* barely a year and a half ago and was still, technically at least, a mere leutnant in the Andermani Army. There'd been far too little time for him to build a reputation of his own, far less a reputation that could possibly rival Gustav Anderman's.

The men and women seated around the conference table knew him better than most, of course. They knew he was a quiet man, and also knew that his relative absence from the public eye hadn't been merely personality or misanthropy, but also part of Gustav's strategy of keeping potential assassins looking in a different direction.

Still, even Andrew's closest advisors and governmental leaders didn't know him as well as Marija did. And none of the traitors and rebels on Tomlinson knew him at all.

But they would learn. They would positively, absolutely, and painfully learn.

"First of all," Andrew continued, shifting his gaze to Admiral Basaltberg, "I want to offer my thanks and special commendation to you and Fregattenkapitänin Deutschmann. Without your quick thinking and perseverance we would have sailed directly into the rebels' ambush. As my father always said, knowledge of your enemy is what allows you to deal with him effectively. Now, thanks to you, we have the beginnings of that knowledge."

"I'm only happy we were able to alert you, *Eure Majestät*," Basaltberg replied, bowing his head.

But while his voice was confident, Marija could see the quiet caution in his eyes. This was Andrew's first real challenge, and even a man who'd been as close to Gustav as Basaltberg had been wasn't at all sure how the young Emperor would respond.

"What I don't understand is what insanity could have possessed Kapitänin der Sterne Hansen," Außenminister Yuèguìshù Shān said, looking at Schwarzer Flügel as if expecting the kanzlerin to magically have the answer.

Marija had seen that from Shān before, and her best guess was that it was a cultural thing. Thirty years younger than Schwarzer Flügel and steeped in the traditions of Potsdam's original colonists, Shān perhaps naturally expected her elders to carry an extra depth of knowledge and wisdom. "She was one of *Seine Majestät*'s most trusted officers."

"I would give a great deal to know the answer to that question," Admiral der Flotte Hoher Berg said heavily. The senior uniformed officer of the Imperial Andermani Navy shook his head slowly, his eyes sad. "I've known her all her life and cannot *conceive* of anything that could have driven her to mutiny and treason."

"Treason is always most painful when it comes from those closest to you," Andrew said. His voice and eyes were dark, and Marija winced at the event she knew he was drawing from his memory. He'd had first-hand knowledge of that truth when he was barely five years old.

"Indeed, *Eure Majestät*," Basaltberg said, his eyes still steady on the Emperor's face. "And as soon as we can return with a sufficient force, I will personally see to it that she pays the price."

"*Return?*" Andrew asked, the calmness in his voice gaining an undertone of challenge, his cold blue eyes taking on an extra layer of ice. "There's no reason for anyone to *return*, Admiral. We have sufficient firepower at hand to accomplish that task. Moreover, I think it would please my father if he knew he would be present when it was done."

"Majestät, I can't recommend anything that risky," Schwarzer Flügel spoke up.

"Are you implying such a mission is beyond my capabilities?" Andrew countered. "Or are you suggesting that I wait on Potsdam while officers and spacers of the Empire put their own lives at risk?" He shook his head firmly. "No. My father didn't hide behind others' lives. Neither will I."

"*Eure Majestät*, it's true your father risked his life leading his ships and his people in battle," Basaltberg pointed out. "But only before he became Kaiser. Once he assumed the crown, he recognized he could no longer do that. And he didn't."

"Oh?" Andrew cocked his head. "What about the crushing of resistance at Babel?"

"That was a special case," Basaltberg replied. "Victory was absolutely critical, and we had no sound fallback if we'd lost that battle."

"*This* is a special case," Andrew pointed out. "This is the first time the commander of a capital ship of the Imperial Andermani Navy has committed mutiny and treason. Hundreds of men and women have already been killed. Men and women of *my* Navy, who died loyal to their oaths and their duty. I will see those men and women avenged, Admiral."

"And so they shall be, Majestät," Schwarzer Flügel replied. "But that's not the chief concern here. The crucial point is that you have no heir. The succession, should something happen to you, is not at all clear."

Marija blinked. With all the talk of treason and retribution, that aspect of the situation hadn't even occurred to her. Judging from the expressions of the others around the table, it hadn't occurred to anyone else, either.

"After your marriage, after you and your Kaiserin

have produced an heir," Schwarzer Flügel continued into the slightly awkward silence, "*then* you will have the right to risk your life should you decide a situation demands it. But not before, no matter how grave the cause or critical the battle."

"I must agree with Markgräfin von Schwarzer Flügel," Berg said. "We simply can't permit you to risk your life at this moment."

"I don't think anyone aboard this ship has the authority to tell me what I am or am not *permitted* to do," Andrew said, his voice stiff.

"Perhaps not the *authority*, Majestät," Schwarzer Flügel said. "But we *do* have a moral responsibility. As members of the Imperial Council, we are required to give you our very best counsel, even if that angers you. Even if your anger is justified. No one in this compartment doubts your courage, determination, or judgment. But it's our duty, before God and the Empire, to protect the succession and the stability of the Empire your father spent so much of his life creating."

Andrew sent a questioning look at Marija, inviting her to either speak in his support or else add her own weight of words to the stack that had already been delivered. But she remained silent. Her role here was completely unofficial, and taking a side would be seen by many of them as interference in matters beyond her authority or concern.

Besides, she'd seen Andrew face down his father on many occasions, standing his ground and presenting his case with logic and forethought. She had no doubt he could do it here, too.

"You speak as if I'm motivated by impatience or anger," Andrew said. "That is not the case. I wish to mount an attack because, tactically, this is the best moment to do so. Admiral Basaltberg, remind us again of the rebels' strength."

"We've *observed*—" Basaltberg stressed the verb ever so slightly "—only *Preussen*, a battlecruiser, one heavy cruiser, and three destroyers."

"And your forces combined with our own?"

"We can field a battleship, two battlecruisers, two frigates, and three destroyers."

"So we hold a marked advantage?"

"So it would appear, *Eure Majestät*," Basaltberg said reluctantly. "But it's possible there are forces in-system we haven't yet seen."

"Possible, but unlikely," Andrew said. "On top of that is the strong possibility that *Preussen* suffered at least some damage during the mutiny. That damage may or may not have been repaired, but Kapitänin der Sterne Hansen's chain of command must also have been damaged. I think therefore we can assume *Preussen* will be at less than peak efficiency."

"That depends on how organized the rebels were, and how prepared they were to move in," Basaltberg pointed out.

"Perhaps," Andrew conceded. "But no matter how prepared they think they are, I'll put *Friedrich der Grosse* up against any other warship in space. Moreover, I think it highly unlikely the battlecruiser you observed is as powerful or as effective as our own. They must be mercenaries hired by the rebels, and no matter how competent they are they can't be as smoothly integrated with *Preussen* as our own ships are with one another. All of that taken together means we have a significant edge in combat power."

He paused, looking around the table as if daring the assemblage to correct his logic. But no one spoke. It would probably take him a while, Marija knew, to realize that now that he was Emperor he could talk as long as he wanted, make any and all points that occurred to him, and that people *would* patiently and silently wait to hear him out.

"More to the point, the longer this situation is allowed to fester, the more risk it poses to the Empire's stability," he continued. "As has been pointed out, I have no heir and am newly come to the throne. If Kapitänin der Sterne Hansen and the Tomlinson rebels aren't crushed quickly and decisively, their example may spread. Someone else may decide to challenge the Empire if I appear weak in the face of her treason.

"And finally, you're correct that there may be ships lurking in the system of which we're unaware. But by the same token, we have no way of knowing there aren't additional forces en route. Unlikely, perhaps, but no less unlikely than one of our own battleships mutinying, or the Freets acquiring the support to hire even a single battlecruiser to back their rebellion. The point is that here, at this moment, we have parity in firepower and superiority in unit quality. That may not be true if we don't strike now."

Furtively, Marija looked around the table. It was a good argument, with good reasoning behind it. But the lack of an heir was an all-but-immovable object lying across the young Emperor's proposed path, and from the expressions she could see everyone else knew it, too.

So how would any of them talk Andrew out of doing one right thing in order to do a different, even more important right thing?

At the far side of the table, Kapitänin der Sterne Yasmin Sternberger cleared her throat. Up to now *Friedrich der Grosse*'s commanding officer had stayed out of the discussion, deferring to those of Andrew's advisers with more years and experience. She was young, less than forty-five T-years old, and Marija remembered a small wave of surprise through the civilian and military establishment when Gustav personally nominated her to be *Friedrich der Grosse*'s flag captain. But the Emperor had always had an eye for talent, and didn't much care what people thought.

"Forgive me, *Eure Majestät*," she said, almost diffidently. "But I'm afraid this discussion is pointless. I'm *Friedrich der Grosse*'s captain, and as such will not expose you to danger."

A ripple of slightly discomfited surprise whispered around the table. "Excuse me?" Andrew said, his eyes narrowing.

"Majestät, there are well over two centuries of military experience in this compartment," Sternberger said. Her voice was still deferential, but Marija could sense the steel beneath it. "The reason those centuries are disagreeing with you is that even if everything you've said is absolutely accurate, it's also absolutely guaranteed that we *will* take damage in any engagement against a force so close to equal with our own. No one can predict how severe that damage will be, or where it will fall. Remember that *Bayern* was destroyed in this same star system twenty T-years ago, and damage far less severe than it absorbed could nevertheless get deep enough to kill you. Whether you accept it or not, whether you like it or not, *you*, Majestät, are truly indispensable."

"No man is truly indispensable," Andrew countered.

"And be aware that disobeying an order in the face of the enemy is grounds for court-martial and execution."

But to Marija's ears, a hint of uncertainty had crept into his voice and manner. Maybe he was finally starting to realize that there was more at stake here than just him.

"That will be your decision, Majestät," Sternberger said. "But whatever the consequences, I will not take *Friedrich der Grosse* into action so long as you are aboard."

Marija felt a sudden flicker of inspiration. "You *and* Fräulein Liang," she murmured, just loudly enough for Andrew to hear.

He sent another look in her direction, this one with a hint of surprise attached. As he'd momentarily forgotten about an heir, he'd apparently also forgotten that his fiancée was aboard.

And maybe—just maybe—that reminder would tip the balance.

He and Liang Ying Yue had met in Andrew's first year at the *Kriegsakademie*. Her family was far removed from the *Adelsstand*, but she'd won an appointment to the Academy on the basis of sheer brilliance. Marija had watched as the acquaintance grew into a friendship, and finally blossomed into something greater.

More than one voice had commented disapprovingly on her lack of noble connections when the Crown Prince's name was first linked with hers. But while Andrew and his father had not always seen eye-to-eye, Gustav had unflinchingly backed his son on this one.

Marija just wished she knew whether Gustav had supported him as his father, recognizing his right to marry someone he actually loved, or as his Emperor, a monarch aware of the need to cement his dynasty's connection to New Berlin's original colonists.

"The Kapitänin der Sterne makes a good point, Majestät," Schwarzer Flügel said. "Another option would be for you and Fräulein Liang to transfer to the Manticoran diplomatic vessel, either to be safely escorted to Potsdam or to await the battle results here at the Tomlinson hyper limit."

"The Manticorans have already offered their services," Basaltberg added, "and I can vouch for their trustworthiness."

Andrew's lip twitched, and it wasn't hard for Marija to read his thoughts. The Manticoran courier *Diactoros* could easily carry the Emperor and his fiancée. But there were numerous other civilians in his father's cortège, including Schwarzer Flügel herself, and it was unlikely that even a tenth of them could be similarly accommodated.

Andrew and Ying Yue might be sent to safety. But they would leave behind scores of other civilians to face the danger their Emperor had fled.

Across the table, Basaltberg stirred. "Whether you choose that option or not, *Eure Majestät*," the senior naval officer said, "I must inform you that Kapitänin der Sterne Sternberger won't be the only one you may have to have shot. There isn't a single officer in this compartment, or anywhere in *Friedrich der Grosse*'s chain of command, who would disagree with her decision or reach any other. I respect your logic, and I respect your courage. But I will not risk your life."

For a long moment the two of them locked eyes. Then, deliberately, Andrew pushed back his chair and stood up.

"Don't think this will be forgotten," he said in a voice of velvet-covered steel, the kind Marija had often heard him use in those often-strained discussions with his father. "Just because you're unanimous doesn't mean you're right. It *certainly* doesn't mean I'm prepared to begin my reign fighting against defiance at a time as critical as this. If you choose to defy me, there *will* be consequences."

He glared around the compartment, but every set of eyes met his without flinching. Not happily, not without trepidation, but without flinching. He sent one final, unreadable look at Marija, then gave a short nod. "We're done here."

Turning, he strode out of the compartment.

☆   ☆   ☆

The hatch leading into Emperor Andrew's private suite was large, elaborate, and clearly armored. The royal crests to either side were even more elaborate and just as clearly permanently built into the bulkheads. This was an area reserved for the Emperor, whether the Emperor was aboard or not.

Winterfall had seen enough of *Diactoros* during the voyage from Manticore to know that shipboard space was at a premium. For the Andermani to carve out this much space—and he had no doubt that the compartment behind that hatch was impressively large—meant that their Emperor was of the absolute highest priority to them.

And here he, Travis, Lisa, and Captain Marcello were about to intrude on that space and that Emperor. All at the worst possible time.

What in the *world* were they doing here?

It had seemed like a good idea at the time. Following

Basaltberg and *Zhong Kui* to Tomlinson to meet the
funeral cortège would put the Manticore delegation
in position to be available for meetings with the new
Emperor whenever he decided he wanted to take a
moment from his other responsibilities. Until that
moment Winterfall and the others would hang back,
join in the grieving to whatever extent their hosts
permitted, and just be available.

He'd had no way of knowing they would instead
land themselves in the middle of a full-fledged military
and political crisis.

And so now here they were, heading back to New
Berlin with the Andermani fleet where they would...
what?

Because, really, what would they do there? Emperor
Andrew undoubtedly had a million things to do, both
before and after he assembled whatever fleet he was
planning to send to devastate the Tomlinson rebels.
Would he really have time to spare for representatives
from a small, backwater nation?

But what else could Winterfall have done? Offered
to stay in the Tomlinson System and keep an eye
on the rebels? Ridiculous, especially since Admiral
Basaltberg had already detached two frigates for
that job, and had also sent messages to Nimbalkar
recalling several more. Offered to take messages
to warn other Andermani systems of the trouble?
Equally ridiculous, plus Basaltberg had sent ships
to do that, too.

Offered to simply leave and go home?

He eyed the two black-clad soldiers flanking the
door. Not just ridiculous, but potentially highly dangerous. Even if the Andermani didn't take it as an insult,

Queen Elizabeth would be furious if they returned to Manticore without even some preliminary meetings under their belts.

Behind the two soldiers, the hatch snicked open and a middle-aged woman stepped into the opening. *"Wilkommen, meine Freunde,"* she greeted them. "I am Baronesse Marija Shenoa, advisor to *Seine Majestät* Emperor Andrew Anderman. The Emperor will see you now." She took a step back out of the hatchway and beckoned.

"Danke," Winterfall said. Taking a deep breath, he headed inside.

The compartment beyond was somehow exactly what Winterfall had expected, yet at the same time somehow entirely different. It had all the size and grandeur he'd imagined, but was styled to be less of a throne room and more of a formal greeting lounge. Emperor Andrew sat in a tall-backed chair at the far end, flanked by two more soldiers, while four other slightly less elaborate chairs were set out in pairs between him and the hatch. Behind him were two other hatches, unmarked, probably leading to the Emperor's private compartments.

Baronesse Shenoa took them a couple of steps into the compartment and then took a step to her right and motioned them to stop. *"Eure Majestät,* allow me to present the chief representatives of the Star Kingdom of Manticore," she said, bowing to the young man. "Gavin Vellacott, Baron Winterfall, Foreign Secretary to Queen Elizabeth. Captain Hari Marcello and Commander Lisa Donnelly Long, commander and executive officer of HMS *Damocles.* Lieutenant Commander Travis Long, former tactical officer of HMS *Casey.*

May I present Andrew Gustav Gotthold Boyer-Laird Anderman, *Freiherr von Wolfenbüttel* and Emperor of the Andermani Empire."

"*Wilkommen*," Andrew said gravely as they all bowed to him the way Basaltberg had coached them. "Your names and accomplishments are well known to me. The Andermani Empire stands in your debt." He waved at the chairs. "Please, be seated."

"*Danke, Majestät*," Winterfall said, taking the right-hand seat closest to Andrew. Travis sat beside him, leaving the two left-hand seats for Marcello and Lisa. Baronesse Shenoa, meanwhile, crossed to the side of the room where a wheeled cart holding beverages and small cakes was waiting.

"May I begin by expressing our deepest condolences, and those of Queen Elizabeth, for the loss of your father, Emperor Gustav," Winterfall continued as he eased himself into the chair, noting peripherally how much space was left around the little group. Apparently, the Emperor could tailor the number of chairs to match the number of invited guests. "We were very much looking forward to meeting the legendary commander and Emperor, the man who rescued the people of Kuan Yin from starvation. In our own small way, we feel the depth of your loss."

"The Empire and I appreciate that," Andrew said. A hint of a smile touched his lips. "I especially appreciate your remembrance of what he did for the people of the planet now known as Potsdam. Most of those outside the Empire remember my father only as a great military commander. It would have pleased him to know that some, at least, recognize that he was also a bringer of life."

"*Danke, Majestät,*" Winterfall said. "The Star Kingdom has had its own brushes with planetary disaster. Those who reach into despair and bring out life and hope will always hold a place of honor in our thoughts and histories."

"A wisdom that is, regretfully, all too rare among the peoples of the galaxy," Andrew said. "May you never lose that perspective." He gestured toward Baronesse Shenoa as she wheeled the cart into the open space between the Manticorans. "May I offer some refreshment?"

He waited until each of his guests had taken a glass and a cake before choosing one for himself. "Thank you, Marija," he said, a hint of a smile briefly touching his face as he nodded to her. "You may leave us."

"Majestät," she said, nodding back. She gave each of the Manticorans a brief, thoughtful look, then crossed behind Andrew's chair and disappeared through the right-hand hatch.

"As you know, there are many items currently demanding my attention," the Emperor said, eyeing each of them with the same measured look Winterfall had just seen from the baronesse. "I realize that your primary purpose in coming here was to continue the talks begun at Manticore regarding the future relationship between the Empire and Star Kingdom, but I'm afraid I won't be able to participate in such conversations as much as I might like. Certainly not as much as my late father likely intended for himself. However, when we reach Potsdam, my foreign secretary, Außenminister Yuèguìshù Shān, will be available for more formal discussions than the brief conversations you've already had."

"We will be grateful for whatever attention your people can spare us, Majestät," Winterfall assured him. "We realize that our arrival occurred at the worst possible time, and that it puts additional strain on an already difficult situation."

"None of which you could have anticipated," Andrew assured him. "But as I say, that was *your* purpose. My father's purpose in inviting you, on the other hand, was to learn more about the two-pronged attack that finally erased the Volsung Mercenaries and their leader from the universe. My military experience is far less than his, but I would be interested in hearing those tales."

His eyes shifted to Travis. "Perhaps we can begin with you, Commander Long. I've read Admiral Basaltberg's report on the joint attack on the Volsungs' base, but no two people ever remember history in exactly the same way. I would be grateful if you would relate your memories of those events."

Winterfall felt his stomach tighten. His brother wasn't exactly comfortable in high-level political settings, and this was as high as anyone could get in this region of space. Would he be able to pull it off?

"I would be honored, Majestät," Travis said, inclining his head. "Should I begin with our arrival in the Volsung system?"

"For the moment, at least, I have plenty of time, Commander," Andrew said. "Let's start a bit earlier, when your ship first made contact with *Hamann* and Major Chien-Lu Zhou."

"Yes, Majestät." Travis took a deep breath. "We were in the Saginaw system when we were contacted by a man who called himself Charles Kane..."

☆   ☆   ☆

Winterfall had spent a great deal of time on the voyage from Manticore poring over the RMN's reports on those two engagements. But as he listened to Travis, and then to Marcello and Lisa, he found himself continually surprised by how much more detail there was to a battle than ever made its way into the official accounts.

Nothing factual had been left out of the reports, of course. But now he was getting the additional layers of sensation, emotion, anticipation, chagrin, and sometimes even gallows humor that turned a simple rendition into a vivid tapestry.

He was also struck at how strongly and permanently those facts and emotions were etched into their participants' memories. It had been over a year since the Manticorans had fought against the Volsungs, but all three of them spoke as if the battles had been yesterday.

War sometimes changes people. Winterfall had heard that adage bandied about most of his adult life, and he'd always believed it. Now, he realized it was wrong.

The word wasn't *sometimes*. It was *always*.

By the time they were finished, the group had talked for over an hour. Andrew had mostly listened in silence, occasionally asking a question or requesting clarification of some point. Winterfall had watched him closely the whole time, alert for the subtle signs that he was getting tired of the topic or merely becoming bored with his guests. But as far as he could see, the young Emperor was fully invested in the twin sagas.

"Most instructive," Andrew said when it was finally over. "I must admit that hearing personal recollections is considerably different from reading official battle reports. One final matter we need to discuss before the shuttles return you to your ships."

For a moment he was silent, again eyeing each of them in turn. "I've been told that you, Baron Winterfall, have offered any and all assistance the Star Kingdom of Manticore can provide to the Andermani Empire."

"That is true, Majestät," Winterfall confirmed.

"And do the rest of you also hold to that promise?" Andrew asked, looking at Travis, Lisa, and Marcello.

"Absolutely, Majestät," Marcello said for all of them.

"No matter the possible danger involved?"

Winterfall felt his lip twitch. Could he really make a promise like that?

Marcello didn't even hesitate. "Yes, Majestät," he said firmly.

"Thank you," Andrew said. "As you're no doubt aware, the interstellar repercussions of what will soon happen at Tomlinson could be deep and wide-ranging. I would like to ask Commander Donnelly Long and Lieutenant Commander Long to help me minimize those repercussions.

"Here is what I wish for them to do..."

☆   ☆   ☆

Llyn was in his cabin aboard Quint's flagship *Retribution*, making sure everyone else aboard the battle-cruiser knew he was there, when he got the message to meet Quint in her office.

"You definitely put in a full day's work today," Llyn commented when he was seated across the desk from her and the hatch was closed behind him. "How is Hansen doing? Has she gotten over Basaltberg's escape yet?"

"Oh, she was over Basaltberg an hour after he hit

hyper," Quint said, dismissing the question with a casual wave. "Today was mostly about what Andrew might send, and how we would want to reposition our ships in response."

"Does that mean she's over Jachmann, too?" Llyn asked.

"That one, maybe not so much," Quint conceded, pulling a bottle of brandy and two glasses from her desk's side drawer. "She really hoped he would join her in this. Though I'm not sure she ever really expected him to."

"Well, unreasonable expectations are still expectations," Llyn pointed out. "I trust that's not going to mess up your strategy too badly?"

"Not at all," Quint assured him as she poured a small amount into each glass. "It just would have been easier with Jachmann. Did Amos get back, by the way?"

"Get back from where?"

"He went over to *Preussen* with me this morning," Quint said, handing one of the glasses to Llyn. "He said he had a line on trading some spices to one of the cooks for some Cornish game hens."

"He didn't return with you?"

She shook her head. "He said it might take some extensive bargaining and that he'd come back with the XO when he was finished with his tactics discussions."

"Ah," Llyn said, frowning as if trying to chase down a vague memory. "I'm pretty sure I heard that Commander Grimling was back. If he's here, I'm sure Amos is, too."

"Probably preparing dinner," Quint said. She reached for the intercom—

Llyn winced. Except that Amos might not be in

the commodore's private galley yet. He might still be cleaning up from— "If you're going to call him, just make sure he knows it wasn't my idea," he said. "The last time I interrupted him while he was cooking he nearly took my head off."

"You're speaking figuratively, I presume?"

"Oh, yes, definitely," Llyn assured her. "Though he *was* holding a knife at the time."

"He *does* enjoy those antique Wootz knives, doesn't he?" Quint said dryly, drawing her hand back from the intercom switch and instead picking up her glass. "Well, the artistic ego is a sensitive thing. I suppose we can just wait to see what he's planned for dinner."

☆   ☆   ☆

Dinner that evening, to Llyn's complete lack of surprise, was Cornish game hens.

"Whatever you traded for these, you got the best part of the deal," Quint commented as Amos began clearing away the plates and flatware. "How many did you get?"

"We have four more, Commodore," Amos said. "I wanted to offer you at least three meals."

"Very good." Quint looked across the table at Llyn. "My natural inclination would be to spread them out so as to savor the treat. But with the Andermani return only a couple of weeks away . . . ?"

"We should probably compress the savoring a bit," Llyn agreed.

"As you wish, Commodore," Amos said. "Just let me know when you wish the next pair."

"I will." Quint set aside her napkin and stood up. "And now, if you'll excuse me, it's time for my evening inspection."

"I'll wait until you're back," Llyn said. "We can have one final nightcap before we turn in."

"Sounds good," she said. "I'll see you in a bit." Smiling at both men, she left the compartment.

Llyn waited another ten seconds, just to make sure she was truly gone. "Well?" he asked.

"I got in," Amos said. "And you're not going to believe this. Seems Hansen claims she's Gustav's illegitimate daughter."

"Does she, now," Llyn murmured. So *that* was the claim she'd mentioned to Jachmann. And, apparently, to everyone else except Llyn himself. "And, what, Gustav tossed her down the back steps?"

"Jachmann's not sure," Amos said. "He knew the Emperor pretty well, and said that doesn't sound like him. More likely he never knew about her. Either way, he got married shortly after that, and Hansen's mother decided not to tell her daughter about her heritage. The point is that, since she predates Andrew by over a decade, she thinks she has a legitimate claim to the Andermani throne."

"And merrily into the firepit we go," Llyn said, scowling. Talk about destabilizing the Andermani Empire and this entire region of space. "So if her mother didn't tell her, how did she find out?"

"That's the interesting part," Amos said. "There was a coup attempt eighteen years ago that got squashed."

"I know," Llyn said. "Our late friend Gensonne was the only one who got out alive."

"The only one we *thought* got out alive," Amos corrected. "It seems that one of the top people in the conspiracy—or possibly there are two of them; Jachmann was a little vague on that—was able to keep his name out of it and skated on the whole purge thing. He read the Tomlinson rumblings correctly, figured their insurrection needed a boost, and told Hansen about her father, with DNA matches to prove it. He also told her Gustav knew all along, of course."

"Of course. So now she wants revenge and figures the Empire can toss in the throne as extra compensation for her inconvenience?"

"More or less," Amos said. "Whether her benefactor will really push to get her the throne, or whether he'll play her just until he can put some plan of his own in motion is another question."

Llyn sipped at his glass. An insurrection that ground to a deadlock and legal battle would have been messy. Hansen had lucked out with the timing of Gustav's death, especially with the possibility that the Empire's official heir would fly straight into her arms.

But Basaltberg's arrival and subsequent escape had quashed that chance. Now, things were back to being messy.

"I presume no one saw you get into Jachmann's quarters?" he asked.

Amos shook his head. "The guards are alive and well and won't remember a thing."

"And Jachmann?"

"He's long past memories of any sort."

Llyn suppressed a grimace. It had to be done, he knew—they could hardly have Jachmann telling anyone he'd spilled the truth to Commodore Quint's personal steward. And Llyn had long since lost any squeamishness about killings.

It was just that Amos seemed *way* too satisfied with what he'd done.

"I hope you made it look like suicide," he warned. "There's going to be enough fallout over this between Hansen and her Tomlinson allies as it is."

"She'll get it smoothed out," Amos said with a shrug. "The Freets can hardly kick her out and take over themselves. Not with Quint—and you—standing by to pull the plug if they try it."

"True," Llyn said. Unfortunately, the chaos Axelrod wanted here still required someone with Hansen's position and reputation to be driving it. "I'll keep an eye on things."

"I'm sure you will," Amos said. "And yes, of course it looked like suicide." He paused, a thoughtful look in his eye. "Pity we're here instead of in New Berlin. If Hansen's contact there is planning something for Andrew—" He smiled. "I do so enjoy watching professionals at work."

"Yes," Llyn said, a knot forming in the pit of his stomach. "I'm sure you do."

CHAPTER FIFTEEN

CRYSTAL PINE'S REPORT was the last on the Cabinet's schedule. To Elizabeth's mind, at least, it was also the most interesting.

"The retrofitting work on Hopstead Manufacturing's Number Three assembly line has been completed," she said. "Jeffrey has only run it up to half speed, but he can already tell that the change will cut time and costs significantly."

A murmur of interest ran around the table, reflecting Elizabeth's own cautious excitement. The difference in complexity and power between an air-car counter-grav coil and an impeller node was impossible to overstate, but she'd been following Hopstead's progress as closely as her other time demands allowed. Anything that improved processes and trimmed down manufacturing costs—*any* manufacturing processes and *any* manufacturing costs—could only bolster the growing industrial capacity that might actually let them recognize her late brother's dream of manufacturing their own impeller rings and, ultimately, moving the entire shipbuilding process into the Star Kingdom.

Though it was clear that not everyone shared Crystal Pine's optimism. "What exactly does *significantly* mean?" Chancellor of the Exchequer Greatgap asked. "Are we talking ten percent? Thirty percent? Half a percent?"

"Right now it looks like it'll be in the eight to ten percent range," Crystal Pine said. "I'll also point out that even with the most optimistic number the costs of the refit mean that the procedure won't reach breakeven for at least two T-years, possibly longer."

"Never mind the breakeven for the moment," Director of Belt Mining Jhomper put in. "What about operating costs? Any idea yet whether there would be any savings there?"

"At this point, those numbers are a bit softer even than the efficiency ones," Crystal Pine said. "But the projection is also for an eight to ten percent savings in power."

"Interesting," Jhomper said. "Do you know if these coil reconfigurations would also work in mining craft?"

"They won't be applicable to spacecraft at all, I'm afraid," Crystal Pine said in her most tactful tone. "There are huge differences between a starship's impeller drive and the counter-grav coils in an air car. We *have* picked up a few pointers, ways in which the much larger, more powerful coils built into an impeller node could be tweaked when the time comes. But we don't have the supporting industrial base to build them yet ourselves. In the meantime, though, this has some very positive potential implications for our entire planetary industrial and freight handling infrastructure. Not just air cars and lorries, but warehousing equipment and anywhere else we use counter-grav."

"I see," Jhomper said stiffly. Despite Crystal Pine's diplomatic tone, he looked less than delighted at having been reminded in front of his colleagues about the difference between an air car and the impeller nodes that his own directorate dealt with every day.

"So this is something we can apply across the board?" Greatgap asked, stepping in smoothly in a clear effort to cover her colleague's embarrassment. "What sort of availability projections are we talking about?"

"My Lady, please remember that we're still in the early stages of this trial," Crystal Pine said. "As yet we have no data on durability, failure rate, or any other potential downsides. I recommend we proceed with this as scheduled until we have a better idea of both the plusses and the minuses."

"Well, if this is what the Andermani use, I can't imagine there being any serious downsides," Jhomper growled.

"The Andermani are hardly the Olympian gods of the galaxy," Crystal Pine replied stiffly. "More to the point, they're running entirely different manufacturing lines and procedures. It might turn out that using their coil style in our systems will create compatibility problems."

"Did any such problems show up in the simulations or lab tests?" Jhomper persisted.

"Not to my knowledge," Crystal Pine said. "But such checks aren't foolproof. They diminish the chances of unexpected problems, but don't entirely eliminate them."

"I suppose," Jhomper said. "Still, caution and tippy-toeing can only take you so far. Fortunately, belt miners are used to taking risks for the Star Kingdom."

"Even more fortunately, those risks aren't as great

as they used to be," Secretary of Education Jakob Oldham, Baron Broken Cliff, put in. "Not with all the MPARS ships out on patrol." He sent a stern look around the table. "Courtesy of Earl Breakwater, in case the Cabinet has forgotten."

Elizabeth suppressed a grimace. Breakwater was long gone from the Cabinet, but she'd always suspected he would look for a way to reintroduce his presence, even if it was only second-hand. Apparently, he'd managed to turn the normally apolitical Broken Cliff into his mouthpiece.

She wasn't particularly happy with the thought of dealing with the Ghost of Exchequers Past, but she could handle the annoyance.

The current Exchequer wasn't nearly so phlegmatic.

"The Cabinet hasn't forgotten, thank you," Greatgap said, sending a stern look at Broken Cliff. "I would also appreciate sticking to the topic at hand and not drifting into political speechmaking and ancient history."

"I simply wished to remind the Cabinet that belt mining isn't nearly as dangerous an occupation as it once was," Broken Cliff said stiffly.

"And I'm sure we all appreciate all the people, past and present, who've brought us to this glorious era," Greatgap countered.

"Very well," Elizabeth said. Time to cut off the growing tension and send everyone back to their corners. "I believe that concludes today's scheduled business. If there's nothing more—" She broke off at Crystal Pine's hesitantly half-lifted hand. "My Lady?"

"Forgive me, Your Majesty, but I have one more concern." She glanced around the table. "Though perhaps this is neither the time nor the place."

"Well, when you settle those questions, be sure to let me know," Harwich said. "With the permission of the Crown, My Lords, and My Ladies—"

"It concerns you, as well, Lord Harwich," Crystal Pine interrupted. "As well as some . . . I believe there are some risks you haven't fully considered."

"In that case," Elizabeth said before Harwich could respond, "perhaps you and the Prime Minister would be willing to stay a few more moments."

"Certainly, Your Majesty," Harwich said, his eyes narrowed slightly as he gazed at Crystal Pine. Clearly, he was sensing the oddness in her manner, too. "With the permission of the Crown, My Lords, and My Ladies, I declare this session closed. God save the Queen."

"God save the Queen," the others intoned in unison.

The rest of the Cabinet filed out, leaving Elizabeth, Crystal Pine, and Harwich still in their seats. Elizabeth watched the others leave, wanting to urge them to hurry but knowing full well that any additional strangeness to this would only pique their curiosity more than it already was.

Finally, the exodus was over. The door closed behind them all, and Elizabeth shifted her full attention to Crystal Pine. "Very well, My Lady," she said, keeping her voice calm. "What exactly is this unconsidered threat?"

"I don't know if it's a *threat*, exactly, Your Majesty," Crystal Pine said, sounding a bit less sure of herself. "But it's . . . well, it concerns the gravitic anomaly conference invitation that's been sent out to the Solarian League."

"What about it?" Elizabeth asked, keeping her

expression neutral. The announcement of the conference, and its subsequent departure, had been mostly met with a collective yawn from both the Cabinet and Parliament as a whole, the only real interest coming from those who wanted to know how much the whole thing would cost. So why was Crystal Pine bringing it up now?

"I've been digging into the guest list," Crystal Pine said. "And I'm seeing some...interesting names there." She seemed to brace herself. "Specifically, what I'm seeing is that this conference seems to be focused less on gravitic faults like Manticore's and more on wormholes."

"Interesting conclusion," Elizabeth said. "Continue."

Crystal Pine seemed taken aback. "Continue, Your Majesty?"

"You don't bring information like that to your sovereign—particularly information she already has available—without further questions, comments, or conclusions," Elizabeth told her.

"Yes, Your Majesty," Crystal Pine said. She took a deep breath. "I also noted that this conference was arranged after *Casey*'s trip to Silesia. I'm wondering... did they discover a wormhole junction out there?"

"Another interesting thought," Elizabeth said, working hard to keep the relief out of her voice. So near, and yet so far. "You'll understand that any such information would be a very deep secret, to be shared only on a need-to-know basis."

"Yes, of course," Crystal Pine said. She was playing it cool, Elizabeth could see, but it was equally clear that she considered the Queen's studied silence on the matter as confirmation that her guess was right.

"I was simply worried about some of the parties who may be coming here."

"Anyone in particular you're worried about?" Harwich asked.

Crystal Pine's lip twitched. "I notice that experts from Axelrod are included in the list, My Lord." She looked at Elizabeth again. "I've heard some unpleasant stories about their efforts—and ability—to get their hooks into local industrial bases. They have a nasty reputation for killing local innovation in order to increase dependence on their products and services, and those of their business partners. They're part of a growing trend by the Solarian transstellars to create...*debt peonage relationships,* an economist friend of mine calls them, with fringe systems like ours."

"I understand your concerns," Elizabeth said. "I think we'll be able to keep any industrial and economic espionage to a minimum, though."

"But you make a valid point," Harwich said. "Fortunately, we'll have time to make sure our critical sectors are protected from our guests. And we'll keep a close eye on any contacts Axelrod might make locally. In fact, you're one of the people we'll have doing that."

"Thank you, My Lord," Crystal Pine said. "And thank you for taking the time to see me, Your Majesty," she added to Elizabeth. "I apologize if I wandered into areas I shouldn't."

"That's all right," Elizabeth said. "Honest thought and new ideas are the hallmarks of the Star Kingdom."

"Though you probably shouldn't mention this to anyone else," Harwich added. "I know the information on the conference is technically public information, but if someone else wants to speculate, let's make them dig it out for themselves."

"And certainly keep the potential espionage part quiet," Elizabeth said.

"Of course," Crystal Pine said, giving her a small, slightly embarrassed smile. "Thank you, Your Majesty. Good day to you both."

With another small smile, she turned and left the room.

Harwich waited until she was gone. "Well," he commented. "I do believe, Your Majesty, that we lucked out on that one."

"I agree," Elizabeth said, finally allowing herself to wince.

"But you *do* realize it's not going to end with her, don't you?" Harwich continued. "Eventually, someone else *will* figure out what's really behind it . . . and that someone will probably not privately vet their speculations through you before announcing them."

"I know," Elizabeth said. "We'll just have to handle those brush fires where and when they happen."

"I'm starting to wonder if keeping this from the rest of the Cabinet was a good idea," Harwich mused. "They're going to launch into orbit when we *do* end up telling them."

"We've been through this," Elizabeth reminded him. "If our unknown nemesis has a source on Manticore, we don't want them to know *we* know."

Still, paranoia aside, it wasn't just a matter of the people who'd hired Gensonne knowing that the Manticorans suspected the reason for their interest in the Star Kingdom. There were a lot of other nations out there who might decide that even a possible gravitic anomaly was worth the risk of taking their own shot at profit and glory.

The RMN had barely been able to survive against a single attacker. There was no chance in hell they could fend off two of them.

And if one of those fortune-seekers turned out to be the Andermani themselves?

Basaltberg's reasons for visiting Manticore had been eminently reasonable, given the close cooperation they'd had with Captain Clegg and *Casey* in Silesia. But Elizabeth couldn't shake the discomfiting suspicion that Emperor Gustav might have learned something from his attack on the Volsung base and had decided this was the perfect time to size up his distant neighbors.

"Speaking of launching people into orbit," Harwich continued, "Countess Calvingdell tells me Admiral Knox was poking around Room 2021 yesterday."

"Wonderful," Elizabeth murmured. Admiral Barnum Knox had been director of Manticore's Office of Naval Intelligence for nearly twenty T-years now, and as such was as much of an institution as Susan Tarleton had been in the Foreign Secretary's office.

Tarleton's replacement with Winterfall had sent only minor ripples through the government. Replacing the well-connected Knox, in contrast, would very likely have unleashed a tsunami. That had been one of the reasons Calvingdell had been set up with the brand new Special Intelligence Service instead of simply putting her in Knox's place in ONI.

Unfortunately, that trick had merely sidestepped the conflict, and in the process changed it from a battle over a chair to a war over jurisdiction. Ever since SIS's existence had been revealed to ONI, Knox had made it his personal crusade to make sure Calvingdell stayed *precisely* within her bounds, never encroaching even a millimeter over the line from political intel to military intel.

The problem, of course, was that there was never a fine line between those spheres of responsibility. Which Knox undoubtedly knew.

"What did he want this time?" Elizabeth asked.

"The usual," Harwich said. "SIS's complete files on operations, personnel, funding levels, and all the rest."

"Did Calvingdell remind him that much of that was still classified?"

"He never saw her," Harwich said. "That receptionist— Flora Taylor—caught him before he could get in and told him he wasn't authorized for entry without Calvingdell's express permission."

"I'm sure he was eloquent in his response to *that*."

"I didn't see any actual blistering on Taylor's skin when she screened me," Harwich said ruefully. "I'd hoped he'd settle down once he accepted the fact that SIS is part of the team. Apparently, he hasn't."

"So it seems," Elizabeth said. "We'll just have to see how it plays out."

"Indeed, Your Majesty," Harwich said. "Maybe we should offer them a piece of the conference security system, task them with keeping people with roving eyes and sticky fingers from poking them where they don't belong."

"Not really their area," Elizabeth said. "But we could certainly find something for them to do. I'll work on that."

"As will I," Harwich said. "Unless you have further instructions . . . ?"

"Not for now," Elizabeth said. "Good day, My Lord."

"Good day, Your Majesty." He smiled. "God save the Queen."

Elizabeth watched him leave, a fresh sense of powerlessness threatening to overwhelm her. The conference, the wormhole, the Andermani, the threat of new attacks on her kingdom and her people. So much that needed to be done. So little that she seemed able to actually influence.

God save the Queen. It wasn't just a benediction, she knew. At its core, it was also a prayer.

Elizabeth believed that God always answered prayers.

She also knew that often the answer was *no*.

CHAPTER SIXTEEN

WINTERFALL HAD NEVER quite appreciated the term *calm before the storm* until *Diactoros* reached the New Berlin system. At that point, he learned what exactly the *storm* in that adage truly consisted of.

And that was even after he and the other Manticorans missed the first part of the flurry. As soon as the group of ships hit the hyper limit and Basaltberg transmitted the news of what had just happened at Tomlinson the Andermani took off at full acceleration toward the planet Potsdam, spitting out reams of data and lists of orders as they went while leaving the slower *Damocles* and *Diactoros* in their dust. By the time the Manticorans finally settled into their prescribed orbit—an orbit, Winterfall noted, that was far removed from the Andermani warships and the busy ant-trails of shuttles bringing in supplies and personnel—the general shock had passed and the navy settled into the grim task of ramping up for what Winterfall had no doubt would be a withering response to the Tomlinson insurrection.

Still, Basaltberg didn't leave them completely high and dry. They'd been sitting in orbit only about seven hours before the admiral sent a shuttle to take Winterfall, Travis, and Lisa to the capital city of Zizhulin.

"Are you ready for this?" Travis asked quietly as the shuttle broke free from *Diactoros* and headed toward the planet below.

"What, for diplomatic discussions in the middle of treason and betrayal?" Winterfall asked, trying to keep his tone light. "At least I'll be safe on Potsdam. *You're* the ones *I'm* worried about."

"Warfare is always a gamble," Travis admitted. "But the fact that Emperor Andrew has transferred Admiral Basaltberg to *Friedrich der Grosse* and put him in overall command of the fleet is a good sign. I've seen him in battle, and if anyone can finish this with the least amount of overall damage he's the one who can do it."

"As long as he's still not angry with the two of us," Lisa murmured.

"He'll cool down," Travis assured her. "Besides, it was the Emperor who insisted he take us along, not us."

"If that matters," she said.

"It'll matter to Basaltberg," Travis said firmly. "Don't worry, it'll be fine."

"If you say so," Winterfall said.

Still, his brother's assurances notwithstanding, this was probably the part that worried him the most. Andrew's request—his command, really—that Travis and Lisa accompany Basaltberg aboard *Friedrich der Grosse* to act as impartial observers to the coming conflict had been an unexpected capstone to their private audience with the Emperor.

Certainly there was sound logic behind the decision. With the Andermani going up against rebels in conquered territory, Andrew was clearly concerned about future Tomlinson propaganda as to the Empire's behavior during and after the battle. With personnel from Manticore unexpectedly but conveniently available, it made sense to send them along as witnesses, especially after their stories of previous battles had confirmed that they had both good memories and a firm grasp of detail.

Which wasn't to say Basaltberg had been thrilled by the idea. Even aboard *Diactoros*, where Winterfall was nominally in command, he'd noted a certain prickliness in Captain Cherise on the rare occasions when he'd intruded on her bridge. He could only imagine what the conversation between Basaltberg and the Emperor must have been like.

Winterfall had no doubt that Basaltberg would get over whatever anger or annoyance he'd left that meeting with during the two-week voyage back to Tomlinson. He was more concerned about the subtle but very real effects having two foreigners on Basaltberg's ship might have. He'd read enough of Manticore's limited collection of battle reports to recognize that anything that could distract a captain or crew member at a critical moment could mean the difference between life and death.

He didn't like the fact that his brother and his brother's new wife would be standing squarely on top of those critical moments.

Maybe Winterfall wasn't the only one thinking along those lines. Lisa, seated beside Travis, seemed to be gazing into the future with the same trepidation her brother-in-law was feeling. "You okay, Lisa?" he asked.

Her eyes came back from whatever she'd been contemplating. "What?"

"I asked if you were okay," Winterfall repeated. "You seem a little . . . odd."

"You mean odd for someone heading into a major battle?" she replied, giving him a tight smile. "Don't worry, I'm fine." She took Travis's hand. "At least *I'll* be with Travis, who knows what he's doing. You and your team are the ones who are going to be all alone down there."

"And none of *us* has any idea what we're doing?"

"I wouldn't put it *quite* that way."

"But if you had, you'd be right," Winterfall conceded. "Tell you what. You two worry about your military miracle, and I'll worry about my diplomatic one."

"Deal," Travis said with a smile.

Lisa smiled, too. But her odd expression remained.

☆   ☆   ☆

They said their good-byes at the spaceport. Then, Gavin was whisked off to Sorgenfrei Palace to meet with Außenminister Yuèguìshù Shān and palace security to arrange for his team's lodging and to work out the preliminary meeting schedule. Lisa and Travis were whisked off the opposite direction to one of the staging areas transferring supplies to *Friedrich der Grosse* and the other ships of Basaltberg's force.

And through it all Lisa glowered at herself.

She should have known Gavin would notice. She'd taken care to hide her mood from Travis, but Travis's brother worked on a different set of visual cues and she hadn't taken that variance into account. She'd covered it up all right, but she shouldn't have let him get even that much of a glimpse behind the curtain.

Especially since the whole thing was *so* stupid.

Back during Basaltberg's unexpected arrival at Manticore, she'd let all the old books and dramas of her teenage years tangle up her emotions and thoughts, to the point of wondering if getting a good-bye kiss from Travis would inevitably bring death and destruction to their relationship. Now, with the two of them about to be thrust into a looming battle far from home, those same emotional reflexes had once again kicked in.

Two weeks from now, all those old tear-jerkers whispered at her, one of the newlyweds was going to die.

"Hey," Travis said quietly. "You okay?"

"Sure," Lisa said, putting as much conviction into her voice as she could. "Why?"

"You seem worried, that's all."

"No, not at all." She smiled at him. "How can I be worried when you're right here beside me?"

"I can think of a whole stack of reasons," he said dryly. "You're sure?"

"I'm sure," she promised.

No, she wasn't worried. Her *emotions* might be worried, but *she* wasn't.

And there *was* a difference, she told herself firmly.

The transport to *Friedrich der Grosse* was waiting when their shuttle landed. Standing at the hatch, clearly waiting for them, was a short man with olive skin, curly black hair, and wearing the insignia and rank designations of an Andermani lieutenant commander.

"Greetings," he called in heavily accented English as they walked toward him, lifting a hand in salute and giving them a dazzling smile. "I am Korvettenkapitän Cristaldo Carrino, *Friedrich der Grosse*'s chief engineer. I'm told you'll be traveling with us on our mission of justice and retribution."

"*Jawohl, Herr Korvettenkapitän,*" Travis said.

"Ah—you speak German," Carrino said, shifting to that language. "Excellent. I must apologize for my English, but it's been twelve years since I left Haven and I'm afraid I haven't had much chance to practice it since then. Even back then, to be honest, my English was hardly what one might call flawless."

"German is fine," Lisa assured him in the same language, feeling only a twinge of concern. Travis was only marginally better at the language now than she was, but she still felt self-conscious about some of her grammar. "Our German is hardly flawless, either. So you're a Havenite?"

"Was," Carrino corrected, gesturing to the hatch. "But we're on a tight schedule, so if I may ask . . . ?"

"Our apologies," Travis said as the two of them picked up their pace. "I hope you weren't waiting too long."

"Not at all," Carrino assured them. "I was supervising a spare-parts shipment when word came that you were on your way. I thought it would be simplest for us to travel back to *Friedrich der Grosse* together."

He ushered them through the hatch. "Especially since I'll be the one giving Lieutenant Commander Travis his tour of the ship."

"I'll be getting a tour?" Travis asked.

"A *complete* tour, too," Carrino confirmed. "By order of Admiral Basaltberg himself."

"That would be wonderful," Travis said, and Lisa could hear the excitement in his voice. "Admiral Basaltberg has on occasion graciously permitted me to spend time aboard *Zhong Kui*, but as a foreign national there were of course many areas that were off-limits to me. This is an unexpected honor."

"It shouldn't be all *that* unexpected," Carrino said as he waved them to seats along the shuttle's starboard side. "As Emperor Andrew's personal observers, you'll need to know every corner of an Andermani battleship, and all the ways of getting from each of those corners to all the others. You'll also be getting a tour, Commander Donnelly Long. Your escort and guide will be *Friedrich der Grosse*'s assistant tactical officer, Oberleutnantin Jingyi Unterberger."

"I'd be honored," Lisa said, feeling some fresh excitement of her own. Being *Damocles*'s XO was an eminently satisfying position, but she sometimes secretly missed her earlier days as the ship's tactical officer. Meeting someone in a similar position would feel almost like going home. "I was once a tactical officer myself."

"Yes," Carrino said, smiling again, this time mischievously as he strapped into one of the seats across from them. "We know."

From the shuttle launch site and *Friedrich der Grosse*'s orbital position, Lisa had estimated it would take twenty minutes to reach the battleship. In fact, it took just over sixteen. Either Andermani shuttles were faster than the Manticoran equivalents, or Basaltberg was in a hurry. Most likely both.

Carrino had received word en route that he was to bring Travis and Lisa directly to the bridge. Along the way he gave them a quick primer on the layout and the Andermani compartment numbering system. It was slightly different than the RMN's pattern, but it was very logical and easy to remember, and by the time they reached the bridge Lisa had it down pat.

She'd expected to be impressed by the bridge, and

she was. Not only was it at least three times the size of a Manticoran heavy cruiser's, but there was also considerably more empty space. She puzzled at that a little as Carrino floated them across to Basaltberg's command seat until it occurred to her that with this many people and stations there would be a lot more people moving around, switching out one officer for another or bringing in replacements, than ever happened on a Manticoran bridge.

Basaltberg was on the intercom, talking with someone elsewhere on the ship, when they reached his station. He looked up, acknowledged them with a nod, and brought his conversation to a quick end. "*Wilkommen,* Commander Donnelly Long; Lieutenant Commander Long," he greeted them, nodding to each in turn. "I trust Korvettenkapitän Carrino has taken good care of you?"

"He has, *Herr Admiral,*" Lisa assured him. As was the case in the RMN, here the senior officer of any group was the *de facto* spokesperson. "Thank you for the opportunity for us to be part of this operation."

"Thank Emperor Andrew," Basaltberg said. "At least *this* was an order I could obey."

Lisa felt her forehead wrinkle. Had there been orders recently that the admiral *couldn't* obey?

"I'm certain you will fulfill the task the Emperor has set before you," Basaltberg continued. "The first step, as I'm sure Korvettenkapitän Carrino has already informed you, will be to learn everything possible about *Friedrich der Grosse.*" He beckoned across the bridge to a trim young woman. "Oberleutnantin Unterberger: attend."

"*Ja, Herr Admiral,*" the woman said briskly, unstrapping and giving herself a push that sent her floating to Basaltberg's chair. Her eyes flicked across Lisa's face, then Travis's, then settled on Lisa's.

"This is Oberleutnantin Jingyi Unterberger," Basaltberg introduced her. "She will be your guide, Commander Donnelly Long, and will be at your disposal for whatever you need whenever she's not on duty."

"*Danke, Herr Admiral,*" Lisa said, offering her hand to Unterberger. The woman took it and gave it a quick double shake. "*Friedrich der Grosse* is a magnificent ship. I'll look forward to learning everything there is to know about her."

"Then we'd best get started," Unterberger said with a sly but friendly smile. "We *do* only have two weeks, after all. With your permission, *Herr Admiral*?"

"You're relieved of duty, Oberleutnantin," Basaltberg confirmed. "You and Korvettenkapitän Carrino may offer full access to our guests, and may answer any questions except those which would breach security." He smiled at Lisa and Travis. "And you will deliver your charges to my dining compartment at twenty hundred. The Manticorans and I have a great deal to discuss."

☆   ☆   ☆

Außenminister Yuèguìshù Shān had a way of speaking which, combined with her normally rather reserved expression, made her just a bit intimidating. But as she and Winterfall talked she gradually opened up, and by the end of their first conversation he knew she was someone he'd be able to work with.

The preliminary schedule had been settled, Winterfall had screened *Diactoros* to get the other three members of his team transported down, and he was looking over the set of rooms they'd been assigned in the Imperial Palace when there was a quiet knock on his half-open door.

"*Herr* Foreign Minister Winterfall?" The man standing in the hallway was tall and muscular, and was dressed entirely in black. He held a helmet under his left arm and had a large and nasty-looking gun holstered at his waist. "I'm Major Basle Strossmeyer, third shift commander, *Totenkopf* Hussars. I'll be overseeing your security while you're in Sorgenfrei Palace."

"*Danke*, Major," Winterfall said. He'd worried a lot about whether his crash German course on the voyage from Manticore would prove sufficient, but he was already feeling surprisingly comfortable with the language. "Though I don't expect personal attention will be required. From what I've already seen of the *Totenkopf*, I have no fears whatsoever for our safety."

"Yes," Strossmeyer said, favoring Winterfall with a somewhat thin smile. "I should perhaps mention that the security I mentioned is not just yours. This is, after all, also the Emperor's home."

Winterfall swallowed, freshly aware of the size of the gun riding Strossmeyer's hip. "Of course," he said. "I hadn't thought about that aspect."

"Few people do," Strossmeyer said. "But of course, such thoughts aren't your responsibility, but ours."

"I can see you take that responsibility very seriously," Winterfall said. "I can't imagine anyone even attempting to make trouble here."

"Perhaps not now," Strossmeyer said, his face hardening. "But there was once a time . . ." He stopped and seemed to shake away an unpleasant memory. "But that's not why I'm here, *Herr* Foreign Minister.

Along with introducing myself, I also wanted to ask if you or any of your group have any problems I should know about. Allergies, chronic illnesses, special dietary needs?"

"No, nothing like that," Winterfall assured him.

"Any symptoms over the past ten days that might indicate disease?"

"Again, no," Winterfall said. "We were checked out by *Diactoros*'s medic when we first approached the New Berlin system a month ago, and again three days ago. We were also given broad-spectrum vaccines and antibiotics."

"Our medics will need to confirm that," Strossmeyer said. "This evening, if that's convenient."

"That would be fine," Winterfall said. "My team should be here in two hours, and we have nothing official scheduled until tomorrow morning."

"Good," Strossmeyer said. "I'll inform the medics. You'll need to postpone your dinner until after the examination."

"No problem, as long as the exam isn't too late," Winterfall said. "Außenminister Shān has arranged dinner for eight o'clock, and she doesn't strike me as the sort of person you want to keep waiting."

"Indeed she's not," Strossmeyer agreed. He gave Winterfall another small smile, this one looking more genuine. "I'll inform the medics of that factor. I presume you'll be dining in the Marble Hall?"

"Normally, yes," Winterfall said. "Tonight she said it would be just her and the four of us and we would be in the Audience Room."

"Yes," Strossmeyer murmured. "She showed you where that is?"

"Yes."

"All right." Strossmeyer gestured past Winterfall. "If I may?"

"Certainly," Winterfall said, stepping out of the way. Strossmeyer strode past him, set his helmet down on the end of the bed, and pulled out a tablet. "Let me give you a few extra parameters," he said. "Here's the palace diagram."

Winterfall stepped to his side. "Yes, she showed me that."

"Good for her," Strossmeyer said gruffly. "I'm showing you again."

He touched a group of rooms in the palace's center section's right-hand wing. "Here are your guest rooms." He shifted his finger to a pair of spaces in the center. "Here are the Marble Hall and Audience Room," he continued. "That's where you'll have your meetings and your meals. *This* section—" he indicated the palace's entire left wing "—is off-limits. Understood?"

"The Emperor's private living and working area," Winterfall said, nodding. "Yes, I understand."

"Good." Strossmeyer paused, his finger hovering over the area two rooms past the Audience Room.

Gustav Anderman's private office, Winterfall remembered. "You must have spent a lot of time there," he said.

Strossmeyer twitched his finger back. "What? No. I was never inside. I was . . . those rooms are off-limits. That's all you need to know."

"Of course," Winterfall said. "My apologies. I didn't mean to bring up painful memories."

"They're not—" His voice faltered. Slamming the tablet back into its pouch, he picked up his helmet and spun around toward the door. "I'll be back later with the medics," he said over his shoulder. "Just stay where you're supposed to and everything will be fine."

The rest of Winterfall's team arrived at five. At five-thirty Strossmeyer was back with a pair of medics. The *Totenkopf* stood silently as the doctors performed the exams, then just as silently escorted them out. At eight, when Winterfall led the way to the Audience Room for their dinner with Außenminister Shān, Strossmeyer was again standing guard.

As Shān had told Winterfall earlier, the dinner turned out to be an informal affair. The food was good, the conversation was light and of the getting-to-know-you variety instead of anything serious. Winterfall had pushed his people hard on their German lessons during the trip from Manticore, but they were still awkward enough that he found himself wincing at some of their more egregious pronunciation errors. But Shān was patient, and was willing to speak in slightly halting English when necessary, and they made it through.

What the rest of the Andermani diplomatic team would think of their visitors' lack of language skills, of course, would be another matter. If they didn't seem as forgiving as Shān, Winterfall would just have to make sure certain of his team kept their mouths shut.

Either way, he promised himself darkly, there would be some highly unflattering reports filed when they returned home.

With the morning meetings set to begin right after breakfast, Shān made sure not to push the evening activities too late. It was just after ten when Winterfall herded his charges back toward their rooms,

reminding them not to linger over bedtime preparations and suggesting that, if insomnia should strike,
they could always fill the sleepless hours with some
extra language study.

He'd returned to his own room and was undoing
his collar when there was a quiet knock at the door.
He opened it, to find Strossmeyer standing outside,
his helmet again cradled in his left arm. "Sorry to
disturb you, *Herr* Foreign Minister," he apologized.
"I came to inform you that your part of the palace
is about to be locked down for the night."

"Locked down?" Winterfall asked, frowning. "Is
something wrong?"

"No, not at all," Strossmeyer said. "It was thought
that it would be a wise step to take until the lab work
on your medical exams is finished. Unless the medics
find something wrong, this should be the only night
you'll be so treated."

"Understood, and it's not a problem," Winterfall
assured him.

"I appreciate your cooperation," Strossmeyer said.
"If any of you need anything—food, drink, extra
blankets—there are call buttons in each room that
will connect you to a steward."

"Thank you, Major, but I don't anticipate any such
needs," Winterfall said. "Certainly not food. Not after
that magnificent dinner."

"If you were impressed by *that* meal, you have
no idea what's yet in store," Strossmeyer said, almost
smiling. "Wait until the Emperor orders a banquet."

"I'll look forward to it," Winterfall said. "Thank you
for stopping by to let me know. Hopefully, the tests
won't show any problems."

"I'm sure they won't." Strossmeyer hesitated. "May I ask you a question, *Herr* Foreign Minister?"

"Of course," Winterfall said beckoning. "Do you want to come in?"

"No, that would not be permitted," Strossmeyer said. "Your Queen Elizabeth. I understand there were unpleasant circumstances surrounding her ascent to the Star Kingdom throne?"

"Yes, the sudden deaths of her brother and her niece," Winterfall said, wincing at the memory of that horrific day.

"And were your people...unsure of her?"

Winterfall felt his eyes narrow. "Are you talking about Queen Elizabeth, Major? Or Emperor Andrew?"

A small wince cracked Strossmeyer's carefully controlled expression. "Emperor Gustav was a giant among men," he said. "There are some who are...concerned, I suppose, that Emperor Andrew's youth and inexperience will make it difficult to fill his late father's shoes."

"I'm not sure anyone who's suddenly thrust into a position of authority ever feels entirely ready for the job," Winterfall said. "Queen Elizabeth rose to the challenge. I'm sure Emperor Andrew will, as well."

"Perhaps." Strossmeyer's eyes flicked around the hallway. "Still, the palace is not the same without Emperor Gustav."

"Give him time," was all Winterfall could think to say.

"Of course." Strossmeyer brought his eyes back to Winterfall and inclined his head. "Good night, *Herr* Foreign Minister. Sleep well. And...thank you."

Winterfall's last mental image as he drifted off to sleep was a picture of Queen Elizabeth at her coronation. Against all the odds and all the opposition, she'd made the throne and kingdom her own.

He could only hope Andrew would do the same.

☆   ☆   ☆

The first session of Oberleutnantin Unterberger's tour of *Friedrich der Grosse* took four hours and ran Lisa through the bridge, flag bridge, CIC, and the forward engineering compartments.

And Unterberger had been right. Two weeks would not be nearly enough time to learn everything there was to know about the massive warship.

"First thing I'm going to append to my report when we get back to *Diactoros*," Travis said as they sealed the cabin they'd been given, "is that while we're upgrading the RMN's tactics, weapons, and ship design we also need to upgrade the quality of our food."

"Admiral Basaltberg *does* set a very nice table," Lisa agreed, savoring the pleasant aftertaste of *sauerbraten* and *spätzle*. "But I doubt everyone aboard gets the same cuisine."

"Knowing Andermani, I wouldn't put it past them," Travis said as he started unfastening his tunic. "So what did you see today?"

"The command centers and forward engineering," Lisa said. "You?"

"Damage Control Central and the aft missile launchers," Travis told her. "As impressive as everything else I've seen from the Andermani. I'm getting CIC and the command areas tomorrow."

"All with Carrino's sparkling running commentary, I assume?"

"Probably," Travis said, smiling. "I still wonder what the rest of the officers and crew think of him. He's *so* different from both the original Chinese philosophy or Anderman's adopted Prussian one."

"Well, he makes *me* laugh," Lisa pointed out. "Even the ancient Prussians must have appreciated people who could do that."

"I think they do here, too," Travis said. "I spotted a lot of smiles that people were trying to hide along the way. It's just that they don't seem to know how to react. Or maybe they just don't think they could hold their own against him once they got started. How's Unterberger?"

"Detailed, methodical, and an excellent teacher," Lisa said.

"I meant sense of humor-wise."

"I'm pretty sure she's got one," Lisa said. "But she doesn't let it out to play the way Carrino does."

"You'll have to work on that," Travis told her. "If nothing else, I'd love to see a pun contest in German between her and Carrino."

"I'll see what I can do," Lisa promised. "In between getting my head stuffed with ship details."

"Yeah," Travis said, sobering. "I just can't help thinking about what Basaltberg said at dinner about unpredictability."

"*The approach to battle must always be as methodical and controlled as possible,*" Lisa quoted. "*For it is a given that once combat begins, one will inevitably face unpredictable events.*"

"*One must therefore prepare carefully and thoroughly ahead of time,*" Travis picked up the rest of Basaltberg's words, "*in order to prevent mistakes from creeping in any earlier than possible, and to give oneself the strongest platform from which to react to those elements when they present themselves.* It *does* lend itself to easy memorization, doesn't it?"

"Yes," Lisa said, a shiver running through her. "The worrisome part is that by the time we get there the rebels will have had a full month to prepare."

"Longer than that if you add in the months or years they've been planning this," Travis reminded her soberly. "Plus the fact that their commander has the same training in strategy and tactics as Basaltberg and the rest of his officers."

"Going to be like mirror-fighting."

"Pretty much," Travis said. "But we should have the advantage in both hulls and throw weight."

"Unless they have ships we don't know about."

"Unless then," Travis conceded. "But at least Basaltberg will have an advantage Hansen can't possibly know about."

"What's that?" Lisa asked, frowning.

Travis grinned impishly at her. "Us."

Lisa rolled her eyes. "Right," she said. "Two Manticorans who have no official positions and no idea what they're doing. Hansen must be shaking in her boots."

"Hey, speak for yourself about not knowing what we're doing," Travis said with mock reproof. "I, for one, intend to know every last thing about *Friedrich der Grosse* before we hit the hyper limit."

"Only if Carrino stops making jokes and starts actually teaching you things."

"Oh, he is," Travis said. "And there are other ways."

"Like calling up the specs and doing another couple of hours' work right now, you mean?" Lisa accused. "Like you and your German lessons on *Diactoros*?"

"And if I do, who's to stop me?" Travis said loftily.

Lisa tilted her head. "How about someone with a better offer?"

"You have one?"

"Oh, yes," Lisa said, smiling one of her special smiles.

Travis smiled back. "Sold," he said.

Eat, drink and make merry, the old quote whispered through Lisa's mind afterward. *For tomorrow you may die.*

In this case, it would be another two weeks.

But the thought, and the warning, remained.

CHAPTER SEVENTEEN

CHOMPS HAD HOPED THAT, given the urgency of the circumstances, Terry would loosen up a little on letting him into the classified sheriff's files.

But no. Calmly, blandly, but firmly, she pointed him to the public information databases, assured him she would look through the classified files herself, and promised to let him know if she found anything of interest.

Still, there was plenty in the public files to keep him busy for a while.

Duke Serisburg had had eight full-time employees: a chauffeur, a chef, two housemaids, a secretary, and three bodyguards. Another dozen people had regular or semi-regular access to the mansion, including landscapers, caterers for the duchess's monthly formal banquets, occasional tutors for the two oldest children, and, of course, Devereux.

The secretary would have had the most complete knowledge of the duke's schedule. But Chomps could find nothing in his past or current life situation that either indicated a need for fast cash or hinted at dark, manipulatable secrets. The bodyguards were next on his list, but again there was nothing to indicate trouble. The chauffeur and his wife were rumored to be having some marital problems, but everyone Chomps talked to agreed that most of their trouble had faded in the surge of shock and loss following the Serisburg family's deaths. The chef and maids had equally innocuous backgrounds and lifestyles.

The one bright spot was that he found the man who'd handled the import and sale of the duke's air car. The other didn't have any detailed specs on the car's computer, but he promised to get in touch with a couple of friends in Landing who did similar purchases and let Chomps know if he found anything useful.

It was a week later, and Chomps was starting through the caterer's employee list, when he got a message to meet Terry at a café near the Serisburg Point sheriff's office.

She was waiting at one of the outside tables when he arrived. "Terry," he said, sitting down across from her and glancing around. She'd picked her spot well, he noted: The streets around them had their fair share of vehicles humming along, but most of the foot traffic was on the other side of the road, leaving the two of them in reasonable seclusion. "What's up?"

"I had a request," Terry said, her face set and unsmiling. "Someone wanted to talk to you."

The hairs on the back of Chomps's neck tingled. "Does this someone have a name?" he asked, freshly aware of the Drakon 6mm tucked out of sight in its waistband holster.

"Yes—Sheriff Laura Vespoli," a hard voice came from behind him.

Before Chomps could turn a tall, blond woman stepped into view alongside him and sat down in one of the vacant chairs. Her uniform was identical to Terry's, except with a slightly fancier badge and a few extra spangles on the shoulderboards. "I gather you're the famous Charles Townsend?"

"Don't know how famous, but that's me," Chomps confirmed. There was a distinct whiff of alcohol on the sheriff's breath. "Nice to meet you."

"Oh, you're famous, all right," Vespoli growled, fixing him with the kind of withering stare Chomps normally saw only on bosuns and bosuns' mates. "I've had four complaints about you in the past week. That's a record, even for Serisburg Point."

"May I ask the nature of these complaints?" Chomps asked, keeping his voice steady. When bosuns used that stare they were usually looking for an excuse to rain brimstone down on some unlucky spacer, and he had no intention of giving Vespoli any assistance in that department.

"Harassment," Vespoli said. "Interfering with business. Generally sticking your nose where it doesn't belong and isn't wanted."

"I'm sorry to hear that," Chomps said, resisting the awful urge to ask if duchy law defined those as misdemeanors or felonies. "I'm just interested in your people and the emotional aftermath of Duke Serisburg's untimely death."

"Let me guess. You're writing a book?"

Chomps looked at Terry, hoping for a clue as to whether or not he should take Vespoli into their confidence. But her face was still unreadable.

When in doubt, don't, Chomps's uncle had always said. Not necessarily what he'd always *done*, but pretty much what he always *said*. "I've done some professional writing," he said, putting a hint of defensiveness into his tone. One of the best ways to manipulate people was to play to their expectations. "It was never my intention to cause people distress. My apologies."

"Yes," Vespoli murmured. Clearly, she'd come here ready for a fight. Just as clearly, Chomps's unexpected humility and lack of push-back had taken some of the wind out of her sails. "You have enough material?"

"I have enough to get started."

"You have enough material," Vespoli said, making it a statement this time. "I suggest you go back to Landing and start writing."

"Of course," Chomps said. "Again, my apologies."

Vespoli gave him another long, evaluating look, then stood up and disappeared back behind him. Chomps didn't turn, but instead focused on Terry's face as the deputy watched the sheriff's departure.

Finally, he saw the flicker he'd been watching for, the shift in expression that told him Vespoli was out of earshot.

"You could have warned me," he murmured.

"*You* could have stuck to the plan," she countered sourly. "You were supposed to sift through public records, not poke the good citizens of Serisburg with a stick."

"I got bored. Did Vespoli really track me down through a measly half dozen complaints?"

"Never underestimate the sheriff," Terry growled. "Sees all, hears all, tells not much, puts up with nothing. And she's serious. Stop poking or risk getting booted out of the duchy."

"I'd like to see her try."

"No. No, you wouldn't."

Chomps rolled his eyes. "Fine. I'm a bad dog. Is that all you hauled me out here for?"

"Not entirely." Terry favored him with a tight smile. "I got word about the Solarian air-car computer."

"The importer was supposed to screen *me*."

"This wasn't from the importer," Terry said. "I found a car buff on Sphinx who thinks he has the data we need."

"Who *thinks*?"

"It depends on where the computer was made," she said. "Turns out some of those ports are hard-wired and can have different options depending on which planet the car was intended for."

"Let's take a look," Chomps said, reaching for his recorder.

"Save it," Terry said, waving back the device. "It's not on any of your recordings—I already checked. The number we need is inside the computer, underneath the port."

Chomps made a face. He would have sworn he'd gotten everything they would ever need on his recorder. "Fine. Let's go see Devereux."

"Whoa," Terry said holding out a restraining hand as he started to get up. "I can't go right now—I'm on duty. It'll have to be later."

"Why? I don't need you to hold my hand."

"Yeah, and perish *that* thought," Terry growled. "Remember the whole chain of evidence thing?"

"I'm not going to touch or bag anything," Chomps said patiently. "I'm just going to take a look."

"No, you're not," Terry said. "Aside from the legalities, the last time you went up there alone we ended up with an exploded hydrogen tank and wrecked shed. We go together or we don't go at all. Clear?"

Chomps sighed. "Clear."

"Good," Terry said, her voice heavy with suspicion. "Now swear it."

"What? Terry—"

"I mean it, Chomps. Swear to me on my mother's continued good-will toward you that you will *not* go talk to Devereux alone."

Chomps rolled his eyes. "I swear I will not go talk to Devereux alone," he intoned, lifting his hand palm-forward like the people in courtroom dramas.

"Good," she said, still eyeing him. "I'm off-duty in three hours. Go back to the inn, or get ice cream in Whistlestop or something. I'll screen you when I'm ready." She stood up. "See you later, Mr. Townsend."

"See you later, Deputy Lassaline," Chomps said, just as formally. "By the way, the sheriff's starting a little early in the day, isn't she?"

Terry's lips puckered. "No earlier than usual."

"That's not a good thing," Chomps pointed out. "Also more than a little against regs."

"I know." Terry took a deep breath and sat back down. "Look. Okay, she's got some demons—some really nasty ones. Staying a little numb gets her through the day."

"And the duke let her get away with that?"

"The duke understood and winked at it," Terry said. "So did everyone else."

"I sympathize," Chomps said. "But to properly do her job—"

"Do I have to draw you a map?" Terry cut him off. "The job's all she's got left. Don't dig into that, just take my word for it. And she's careful—never drives under the influence or confronts anyone in any kind of potentially deadly situation. She does her job, and the duke's word is right up there with law, and that's that." She winced. "That *was* that, anyway. No idea what happens now."

Chomps sighed. The sad truth was, what would probably happen was nothing. Until and unless the Queen appointed someone to handle Serisburg directly, the duchy would fall under the management of the Royal Lands Administrator, who was already up to his eyeballs in other work. Unless Sheriff Vespoli stepped out of line in a very dramatic and visible way—or unless someone brought it to the Crown's attention—she'd probably be allowed to keep her job and her behavior until the day she retired.

Of course, the only line-stepping that would likely catch anyone's attention in Landing would probably be because she got someone killed.

"But that's not your problem," Terry said, in a tone that made it clear it wasn't to *become* his problem, either. "Now, I believe there's a hot fudge sundae with your name on it?"

"I believe there is," Chomps agreed. He nodded slightly back over his shoulder. "Just keep an eye on her."

"We do," Terry said soberly. "Believe me, we do."

And she undoubtedly did, Chomps thought as he headed toward his air car. Terry had will, all right. *All will, and a meter wide*, his uncle used to say.

But for all that will, and for all her law enforcement experience, she didn't understand bad guys as well as Chomps did. With all the poking around he and Terry had been doing, it was entirely possible that whoever had sabotaged the duke's air car had gotten wind of the possibility that his last attempt to destroy the computer had failed. The last thing Chomps wanted to do was hang around until the end of Terry's shift and give the murderer those additional three hours to make trouble.

He'd sworn he wouldn't go alone to talk to Devereux. But really, he'd never said he was planning to *talk*.

☆   ☆   ☆

There was no one in sight on the grounds as Chomps lowered his air car toward the spot between the shed and the house where Terry had set down that other evening. With the sun blazing down his IR scanner couldn't definitely ascertain whether or not anyone was home. Still, he'd seen Devereux's door locks, and if the man had stepped out for a minute he should have no problem getting inside.

And if someone had helped him step out, that was what Chomps's concealed Drakon was for.

No one answered his knock. The door was indeed locked, but a minute of work with his pickset and he had it open. Giving the clearing one last look, he opened the door and slipped inside.

"Hello?" he called tentatively. "Devereux? It's Townsend. Anyone home?"

There was no answer. Feeling a creeping feeling along the back of his neck, he drew his Drakon and thumbed off the safety. Hopefully, Devereux was simply down in his workshop with the door closed and hadn't heard the knock or Chomps's entrance.

Still, caution was definitely called for. Peeling himself off the door jamb, Chomps headed for the stairs as quietly as a massive Sphinxian could manage. If he ran into Devereux now, he reflected, the man would probably have a heart attack.

There was no one on the stairs or in the basement. The door to the workshop was ajar—a bad sign, given that the only way Devereux could be sitting there oblivious was if it had blocked the sound of Chomps's arrival. Clenching his teeth, holding his gun ready, Chomps crossed to the door and gently swung it open with the toe of his shoe.

Devereux wasn't there. Neither, to Chomps's relief, was Devereux's dead body.

Neither was the air-car computer.

For a minute Chomps stood at the doorway, his eyes running methodically around the room, looking for anything out of place or something that might offer a clue as to what had happened. A closer look might yield something, but if something had happened to Devereux this might be a crime scene, and he knew better than to contaminate it. Backing out, he retraced his steps through the basement, up the stairs, and out the door into the clearing.

There he again stopped and looked around. The shed was there, or at least what was left of it, looking like it had the night he and Terry had been here. Now that he was seeing the area in daylight he saw that one side of Devereux's garage had been scorched and pitted by the explosion.

He took a step closer. The garage doors were closed and there were no windows. No way to tell whether Devereux's car was there.

That, at least, he should check. If the car was gone, maybe Devereux had simply gone into town or somewhere. He headed across the grass, keeping an eye on the trees at the edge of the clearing.

He was passing the shed when he heard the sound of an approaching air car.

Reflexively, he took a long step between the wrecked

doors into the partial cover of the shed. He froze there, just inside the doors, peering up through the gaps in the roof and turning his head back and forth in an attempt to figure out the vehicle's vector. Coming from due south, he concluded, the direction from Whistlestop.

And definitely coming toward him.

He swore under his breath. Terry, probably, checking to see if he'd disobeyed her order and come out here without her. And it didn't take a genius to figure out what she would say when she found him here.

But there might still be a chance. If she was coming in low, she might not have spotted his car yet. If she hadn't, he might be able to get to it and skate off the other direction, maybe flying low along the gap in the trees around the creek he'd had to jump his last time here. He turned back to the shed doors—

Just as the thundercrack of a rifle shot shattered the forest silence and something whistled past behind him.

Navy- and Delphi-trained reflexes kicked in with a vengeance, sending him diving to the floor. There was another rifle crack, the shot again slicing through space he'd already vacated.

No chance of getting to his air car now. The shed walls would have been inadequate cover even before they'd been blast-shredded, and they were even less useful now. There was another of Devereux's heavy workbenches at the far end that might provide protection, but only from directly above, and it was bolted too securely to the floor for him to detach it to use as a moving shield.

You can run, his uncle used to say, *or you can hide.* Clearly, it was time to run.

Only there wasn't any place to run to. Not with all

that open ground. Not with a sniper floating overhead where Chomps couldn't get a clear return shot at him.

Or at least, not without making a hell of a mess.

He moved to the shed door, muttering a curse as he lined up the Drakon's muzzle on the aft part of his car where the main hydrogen tank was located. Sighting down the barrel, he squeezed the trigger.

His first two shots went through the side of the car and into the tank, breaking through the containment wall and then breeching the tank itself. He heard a faint hiss as a stream of released gas erupted from the car, scattering leaves and dust ahead of it. His third shot shattered the electronics regulator box beneath the tank, and his fourth went into the box itself. If he could create a spark at the edge of the hydrogen flow...

That fourth shot didn't do it. Neither did the fifth. Chomps clenched his teeth, knowing that the sniper had almost certainly figured out what was happening and where his target had to be standing. Bracing his hand against the door jamb, he fired a sixth shot, and a seventh—

And with a sudden ferocity, the hydrogen jet burst into flame.

Reflexively, he ducked back as the blast swept across the front and roof of the shed. A second later the inferno faded, leaving all the remaining wood in those areas blazing with a smoky flame.

And for the next few seconds, whatever infrared targeting system his attacker was using would hopefully be useless.

He ducked past the flames, leaped through the doorway, and headed to his left toward the nearest section of trees. The smoke was angling partially across the path he was taking, which should hopefully block his attacker's view as well as messing with the IR.

For the first few seconds that seemed to be the case. There were no further shots as he reached the edge of the clearing and charged into the woods, dodging trees and roots and grabbing as much distance as he could. Ten meters...twenty...halfway to his goal—

Another thundercrack sounded from behind him. This time he didn't hear the whistle of the round, which suggested it had gone wide, which hopefully meant the attacker had lost his quarry. Another shot, again wide—

And then, he was there. Bracing himself, he leaped over a final tangle of grasses at the edge and launched himself head-first into the creek.

The water was a *lot* colder than he'd expected, and for that first agonizing second he was convinced he was going to have a heart attack. But there was no time for such trivia now. The water was deep enough to not only cover him but to allow him enough buoyancy to float a little, and he took advantage of that to dog-paddle his way another ten meters downstream. There, hanging onto a submerged tree root, he buried himself in the cold water, leaving only his eyes and nose above the ripples.

And now, with his last card played, there was nothing to do but wait.

He lay there for what seemed like hours, the frigid water sapping his body heat, then his strength, then his feeling. Twice he thought he heard the sound of an air car, but the first time it was too distant to worry about and the second time he wasn't sure he wasn't hallucinating the sound.

He was half asleep, visions of hiking through the snow with his uncle drifting across his eyes, when something half-felt closed around his upper arm and he found himself being pulled out into the warm mountain air. "Townsend?" a distant voice called. *"Townsend!"*

"Yeah, yeah, don't shout," he heard another voice mutter. That one was both distant *and* slurred.

"Come on, snap to it," the first voice said. "I can't do this all by myself."

With an effort he forced open his eyes.

To find himself staring into Terry's face.

"Were you shooting at me?" he muttered, wincing as feeling started coming back into his arms and upper chest. He shifted his gaze downward, discovered that Terry had levered him into a sitting position in the creek. "You shouldn't have shot at me," he continued. He flexed his fingers, managed to close them solidly around a tree root, and started pulling.

It wasn't easy. Probably wasn't pretty, either. But between the two of them they got him out of the water and stretched along the bank. "How long were you in there?" Terry asked, checking his pulse and peering into his eyes. "Do we need to get you to the hospital?"

"I don't know," Chomps said. At least the slurring was going away. "A couple of hours." An idea belatedly sifted through the mental fog, and he checked his uni-link. "About twenty minutes," he corrected. "And no, I'm fine."

"More than can be said for your car," Terry growled. "Okay. Let's hear it."

"Which part?"

"Start where you decided to ignore my orders," Terry said. "End where I dragged your sorry butt out of the water."

By the time Chomps finished, his body had mostly recovered from the ordeal. Recovered to the point, in fact, where the air no longer felt warm but began aggressively chilling his wet skin and clothes. When Terry silently took off her uniform jacket and draped it across his chest, he didn't argue.

"Well, if we had any doubts before about this being murder, they're pretty well out the window," Terry said, a shiver running through her shoulders. Chomps started to hand her back her jacket, stopped as she waved it back. "I don't suppose you got a glimpse of the car or the driver."

"Sorry," Chomps said. "He came in at a low angle, and once the smoke started he was completely out of sight."

"And vice versa."

"Yes." Chomps pursed his lips. "He *or* she."

"That sounded significant."

"I was just wondering where Sheriff Vespoli was during the incident," Chomps said.

"That's what I thought you were wondering," Terry said darkly. "And you can stop any time."

"Why?" Chomps countered. "You've been poking around this thing for a couple of weeks now, and it wouldn't take much detective work to figure out what you were doing. Toss in an overheard screen asking an enthusiast about Solarian air-car computers, and there you go."

"Point one: She wasn't the first one at the crash scene," Terry said. "*I* was. There's no way she could have gotten there ahead of us and removed whatever gizmo you say was taken. Point two: The duke was the one who ignored Vespoli's little failings and let her stay in her job. That doesn't give her much reason to want him dead. In fact, just the opposite."

"Points taken," Chomps had to concede.

"And point three—" She punched some keys on her uni-link. "She hasn't left the two-block area around the office since she met us at the café."

"Locator histories can be faked."

"Not police ones."

She was wrong about that, Chomps knew. But now didn't seem the right time to point out that he knew how to do highly illegal stuff like that.

Anyway, there were her other two points, both of which were unfortunately reasonably solid. "So where does that leave us?" he asked.

"For starters, going back to the scene and telling the firefighters what happened," she said, standing up. "Or a modified version of it, anyway. So the computer was gone?"

"The computer and Devereux both," Chomps said with a sigh. "I'm hoping he's out enjoying Whistlestop culture and not lying dead under a log somewhere."

"I'm guessing the latter," Terry said bitterly. "Once the killer got the computer, Devereux would be the next to go." She raised her eyebrows. "Followed by you."

"Already figured that out, thanks," Chomps said ignoring her proffered hand and getting to his feet by himself. "Well. Let's get it over with."

☆　　☆　　☆

The firefighters had finished with the blaze and were packing up their equipment by the time they reached the clearing. Questions were asked, answers were given, and a whole lot of paperwork was threatened.

Fortunately, Terry's presence on the scene got some of that paperwork postponed, though probably not eliminated.

And finally, the two of them were once again alone.

"I don't suppose I could help your team search the house," Chomps said, eyeing the building.

"We don't have a *team* here, and no one's searching any houses," Terry said. "They'll do a quick person-in-distress check of the area, then call it a day." She gave him a hard look. "Which is what *you're* also going to do."

"What if there's still evidence in there?"

"There isn't," Terry said. "Even if our killer can't hit a Sphinxian at point-blank range, he's certainly competent enough to do a proper search."

Chomps scowled. But she was probably right. "Fine," he said. "So we'll have to find something else to do. I was just thinking about the joys of sitting in front of a roaring fireplace."

"The inn hasn't got a fireplace."

"No, but I'll bet Duke Serisburg's mountain retreat does."

"No," Terry said firmly. "Let me rephrase that: *hell* no."

"I want to see if someone besides the duke and his people could get in without leaving any traces," Chomps said patiently. "If I can't get in, that'll tell us something."

"Like what? Besides, the crash didn't happen anywhere near the retreat."

"My uncle used to quote an old magician's saying," Chomps said. *"By the time the magician says 'watch closely,' the trick's already done.* So: mountain retreat?"

"*Damn* it, Chomps," she gritted. "What parts of *warrantless* and *inadmissible* don't you understand? Do I have to haul you back to Point and let you dry out in a jail cell?"

Chomps sighed. "We don't have a choice, Terry," he said quietly. "Just asking a few questions put the killer onto us. Getting a warrant—telegraphing our intentions and suspicions to everyone in Serisburg—is the surest way to make sure any evidence still at the duke's retreat is gone before the paperwork's even done. And as for a cell—" He looked her straight in the eye. "Given the events of the past hour, I submit that disarming and immobilizing me would get me killed in the first twenty-four hours. Possibly the first twenty-four *minutes*."

"We can protect you."

"How? You don't even know who you're protecting me *from*."

Her gaze drifted away, settling into the direction of the twice-baked storage shed. "You really think someone else got into the retreat?"

"That's what I'm hoping to find out. But if someone else did it, so can I."

"And you think we won't need whatever we find to convict the killer? Because there's still that warrant thing."

"At this point I'll settle for figuring out who the killer *is*," Chomps said. "We can worry about convicting him later."

"Yeah, well, us *real* cops have to worry about both parts of it." Terry hissed out a frustrated-sounding sigh. "Fine. Anyway, if I let you go alone and you get killed I'll never hear the end of it from Mom."

"That's the spirit," Chomps said. "Let's go. Your car's got a good heater, right?"

CHAPTER EIGHTEEN

DUKE SERISBURG'S MOUNTAIN RETREAT was smaller than Chomps had expected: two floors, maybe three times the size of Devereux's home, with a modest four-car parking area. Apparently, the duke had been serious about this being a place to get away to, as opposed to an alternative venue in which to entertain friends or impress colleagues.

Still, the outside stonework was definitely on the elaborate side, as was the tailored landscaping.

Previously tailored, anyway. In the months since the deaths the groundskeepers seemed to have abandoned the place. Hopefully everyone responsible for the retreat's interior had gone away, as well.

Including whoever had set the duke up to be murdered.

The place hadn't been neglected to the point of leaving any of the doors and windows unlocked, of course. But Chomps hadn't expected it to be *that* easy.

He began by walking around the building, checking and observing, making careful mental notes of anything that looked like it might be the mark of a breaching tool. Finishing his first circle, he took another round, this time paying special attention to the second-floor windows and the sections of wall beneath them.

Terry spent that time at the front of the house, leaning against the side of her car with her arms folded across her chest in silent protest.

Finally, Chomps returned to the front door. "Well?" Terry asked.

"He got in around back," Chomps said. "Do you want to see it, or should I just go in and open the front door for you?"

Terry pushed herself away from the car. "Lead on."

With Chomps in the lead, they walked to the back of the house. "There," he said, pointing up at one of the second-floor windows. "The frosted glass on the lower half marks it as a bathroom, traditionally one of the favorites of the break-and-enter crowd."

"How did he get up there?" Terry asked. "That wall's sensor-pocked six ways from April. Putting a ladder or platform anywhere near it would trigger an alarm."

"Which is why he didn't use a ladder." Chomps turned around and pointed to a nearby tree—a Shelton willow, he tentatively identified it. "You can see that that branch is long enough to get someone into working distance of the window without touching the wall hard enough to trip the sensors. All he had to do was bend the branch to the horizontal, climb along it, and he was in."

"Lucky for him Shelton willows are that flexible."

"I doubt there was any luck involved," Chomps said. "Just lots of good planning."

"And some damn good fine-tuning," Terry murmured. "Especially since he had to figure out how his weight would affect the limb's dip and compensate for it."

"Oh, this guy's a pro, all right," Chomps agreed. "You might want to start a data search for the upper crust of the B and E types."

"Already on it," Terry said, punching keys on her uni-link. "And *this* part, at least, *will* be admissible."

"Right," Chomps said. "So far everything we've done has been in plain sight."

"I assume that's about to change?"

"It is." Chomps took a deep breath. "Okay. He probably used weights or guy lines to adjust the branch. Let's see how it handles Sphinxian body mass."

Given the grounds' state of neglect, he guessed that the alarm system had likewise been shut off or at least was no longer being monitored. Still, he watched Terry out of the corner of his eye for a warning as he carefully crept along the branch toward the house. The limb was dipping more than he really wanted, and by the time he got within arm's length of the window the end was scraping the wall. "Any alerts?" he asked.

"Nothing yet," Terry said, peering at her uni-link. "I assume the window has its own set of alarms?"

"It did," Chomps said, studying the frame. "Our murderer has kindly done all that disabling for us. Let me get this open and I'll come around and pop the front door for you. By the way, did you ever find out who stood to gain from the duke's secret will?"

"We couldn't even *find* the duke's secret will," Terry said sourly. "If it even exists, which I'm starting to doubt. Why are you bringing this up now?"

"Because this little exercise would seem to prove that none of the duke's staff was involved in setting him up," Chomps said. "No need to go to all of this effort if you already have a key to his retreat."

"So any household bonuses that might be in the will are off the table."

"Which would seem to leave the ex-wife," Chomps said as he worked at the window latch. "Or any boyfriends, current husbands, or hungry lawyers. Anyone like that in the picture? Or hasn't anyone bothered to look?"

"Well, *I've* looked," Terry said. "So far nothing. The ex remarried four T-years ago, and they live way the hell over in San Giorgio. I haven't found any record of them coming to Serisburg in at least three T-years."

"Does she need money?"

"Doesn't everyone? Seriously, though, they seem to be doing pretty well for themselves."

Which could be more illusion than reality, Chomps knew. But natural cynicism aside, he had to concede the ex was looking less and less like a good candidate. "Okay, I've just about got it. Go back around, and I'll let you in."

As he'd guessed, the window did indeed open into a bathroom. Not just a bathroom, though, but the duke's private spa bath suite. Even as Chomps worked his way through the window and set off across the thick white carpet he found his face warming at some of the decorations and sculptures along the walls. Clearly, the duke and duchess had had a healthy and robust relationship.

He passed through the spa and master bedroom and out into the hall. Four other, much smaller bedrooms were at the other end—the children's quarters, presumably. Midway along the hall was a wide wooden staircase leading down to the edge of a greatroom. Chomps started down, pausing halfway to give the greatroom a brief bird's-eye scan. Everything seemed a little dusty, but he didn't spot anything that was obviously wrong or misplaced. A pair of glass-fronted gun display cases flanked the fireplace, with a nice mix of modern and antique weapons. Circling around the edge of the room, he walked through the foyer to the front door. There he paused again, studying the three sets of locks on the door and the security control box set into the wall. Keying what he hoped was the off switch, he unfastened the locks and opened the door.

Terry was waiting, her hands gloved, her sour expression firmly in place. "You stop for a nap or something?" she growled.

"I was looking at the security system," Chomps said, pointing to the box. "Are you *sure* the house hasn't triggered an alarm?"

"Well, if it has, no one at the office is paying attention," Terry said, consulting her uni-link again. "Nope. Nothing. Probably set just to fire off a local alarm instead of sending to a remote."

Chomps focused on the landscape of trees and mountains stretching out behind her. "Like there's anyone out here to hear anything."

"Maybe it was reset after the accident when caretakers were coming in and out and tidying up."

"If they were tidying, their hearts weren't in it," Chomps said. "There's dust everywhere."

"It's not much fun cleaning a dead man's house," Terry said. "For the record, there's no sign of forced entry."

"I thought we agreed he came through the window."

"*You* agreed he came through the window. The stuff in the back of the house could have been a red herring."

"I suppose," Chomps murmured, an odd thought suddenly occurring to him. "I wonder if it could have been a sudden threat that caused the duke to grab his family and take off."

"You mean like an intrusion alarm going off from the rear of the house?" Terry shook her head. "No, he wouldn't run. Not the duke. You throw even a hint of trouble at him—" She broke off. "And he would go for his guns. *That's* how we see if he was reacting to an alarm."

"Doesn't look like any of them are missing," Chomps said, taking another look at the gun cases. "All the display prongs are taken."

"Did you look under the bed in the master bedroom?"

"I glanced at the edges near the headboard," Chomps said. "There was nothing obvious."

"Go double-check," Terry said. "I'll see if there's anything in the kitchen."

"Okay," Chomps said, heading back to the stairs. "And don't forget the pantry."

"You think he might have had one of those quick-and-dirty safe rooms put in?" Terry called after him.

"A lot of the Lords did," Chomps said over his shoulder. "The Volsung invasion got people worried about fifth columns, and retrofitting a pantry was one of the cheaper ways to feel safe."

"*Feel* being the operative word," Terry said sourly. "If you find a gun box and it's empty, *don't* touch it."

"Yeah, thanks," Chomps called back. "I *had* figured that out."

But she was already gone. Rolling his eyes, Chomps headed up the stairs.

There were no gun boxes under either side of the bed. Or in the nightstands, behind the headboard, in the master bath, or either closet. He left the bedroom and headed back down the hall, studying the walls for signs of a hidden compartment. Some of the Lords had put in those, too. He reached the stairs and started down—

"Chomps!"

He had the Drakon out and unsafetied before he reached the foot of the stairs. He hit the door jamb leading into the kitchen, bouncing off at an angle across the opening in case there was someone in there ready to open fire.

And came to a confused halt. Terry was standing in front of the double-sized refrigerator, staring at the closed door, a rigid expression on her face.

"What is it?" Chomps demanded, trying to look all directions at once as he crossed to her.

"Open the door," Terry instructed, taking a step backward. Her voice was as rigid as her face.

Chomps stepped up to it, feeling his teeth setting in anticipation. Keeping his gun ready, he pulled open the door—

And slammed it shut again as a horrible odor slammed into his nostrils.

"Oh, my God," he breathed.

"Relax—it's not that bad," Terry said, some of the life starting to come back into her voice. "We're not talking about a dismembered body or anything. It's just sour milk."

Chomps frowned, running the last wisps of odor across his memory. Sour milk, all right. "Yeah, got it," he muttered, feeling like an idiot.

"You're missing the point," Terry said. "There are a

half dozen cartons of chocolate milk in there. Probably Benjamin's."

"He's the one who had the cold?"

"Yeah," Terry said. "Anyway, he loved the stuff. The problem is that properly sealed milk should never go bad—that's what sterilization's for. So what happened?"

"Must have left one open when they rushed out."

"They didn't. All the cartons are still sealed. I saw that much before I closed the door."

"But one of them *was* opened to the air," Chomps said slowly. "If it still looks sealed, that means it was done surreptitiously. Something was taken out . . . or something was put in."

For a long moment neither of them spoke. "The child wasn't just sick," Terry said, her voice soft and dark. "Someone *made* him sick. Sick enough that the duke bundled the whole family into the air car and headed for home and a doctor."

"Why didn't he screen ahead?" Chomps asked.

"Why did he crash?" Terry countered. "I'm guessing it's part of the same package."

"And so he piled them all in," Chomps said, wincing, "and drove them to their deaths."

Terry hissed out a curse. "It wasn't just the duke. They wanted the whole family."

Chomps nodded. And with that, the card castle he'd been trying to build out of motive, method, and opportunity—a castle that had never been solid enough to stand up—was suddenly gone. In its place . . .

He looked at the refrigerator. "We need to go back in there," he said.

"Not *we*," Terry countered. "*I*. And this time, we need that warrant."

"We still have the problem that getting a warrant will tip our hand."

"No way around it," Terry said. "If we're right, this whole thing is a lot nastier than anyone thought. We need a proper chain of evidence. You and I will just have to stand guard over the house until Vespoli and an analysis group gets here."

"Wait a second," Chomps insisted. "Let's think this through. I saw—" he pulled up the mental image "—five cartons of chocolate milk in there. Right?"

"Six," Terry said. "There was one more off to the side."

"Fine, six," Chomps said. "If someone gimmicked them to make the boy sick—who said he had a cold, by the way?"

"It was in the report."

"I know it was in the report," Chomps growled. "I'm asking who put it *into* the report."

"I don't know," Terry admitted, frowning. "It was cold season. I suppose someone made an assumption and it just stuck."

"No one did autopsies?"

"Of course," Terry said. "But I'm guessing no one looked past the obvious trauma of the accident. Plus the duke's supposed alcohol level."

"Yeah," Chomps said. Sloppy, like so much else connected to this case. "Fine. So we—"

"Hold it," Terry interrupted, pulling out her uni-link. "Something coming through." She keyed it, and Chomps saw her eyes tracking as she read the report.

Saw her eyes falter. Saw them slow down.

"What is it?" he asked.

She closed her eyes briefly. "They found Devereux,"

she said quietly. "He was pinned under his car in his garage."

Chomps stared at her, feeling a sickness in his stomach that had nothing to do with the lingering odor of sour milk. "Damn. How?"

"They think he was working on the counter-grav and the jack slipped," Terry said.

"So they're calling it an accident."

"There'll be an investigation. But yeah, that's probably how it'll go down."

"Like hell it will," Chomps bit out. "They send you pictures?"

"They're coming through now," Terry said, flicking through various pages. "No signs of a struggle...jack fallen to the side...nothing that looks staged...a bunch of tools laid out...yeah, it looks exactly like an accident."

"The killer probably spun some sort of plausible story that got him out to the garage," Chomps said. "Maybe said there was something dangerous under his car that he needed to get rid of."

"Or there was some evidence there that would link the car to the duke's death," Terry offered doubtfully.

"Let me see," Chomps said, holding out his hand.

"Sure." Terry handed over the uni-link. "I just can't believe he fell for whatever the story was. I'd have thought having his shed blown up would have kicked his paranoia level into the stratosphere."

"So would I," Chomps agreed, scrolling through the pictures. Devereux on the garage floor, his head and torso blocked from view by the car. A closer view of the scene, showing the tools laid out neatly beside him. A close-up of the garage door, showing no forced entry.

He frowned, scrolling back a shot. The tools ...

He looked up at Terry. "He *didn't* fall for it," he told her. "He was playing along, hoping for an opening to get away. Only he never got one. But he left us a clue."

"Where?" she asked, stepping close beside him and looking at the uni-com.

"Right there," Chomps said, pointing at the tools. "Screwdrivers, wrenches, probes, disconnects ... and a chisel."

"That's a clue?" Abruptly, Terry's eyes widened. "I'll be damned. A *chisel.*"

"The tool he said he'd used to get the computer out of the wrecked car," Chomps confirmed. "And that tells us where he hid the computer."

"He put it back in the car?"

"Exactly," Chomps said. "The killer must have looked at the car some time after he blew up the shed and realized it was missing. He probably poked around for a few days, checking to see whether it had turned up in the sheriff's evidence locker—"

"Or in your room in the inn."

"Or there," Chomps agreed, wincing. "When it didn't, he realized Devereux must still have it and went to his house to look."

"But in the meantime Devereux had hidden it in the last place anyone would look," Terry said. "Because everyone had already looked there." She plucked the uni-link out of his hand. "Come on—we need to get back there."

"In a minute." Chomps pointed to the refrigerator. "This first."

Terry looked at the refrigerator, pursed her lips, then looked back at Chomps. "All right. Convince me."

"Okay," Chomps said, working through the logic. "Whoever wanted the boy sick couldn't know which box of milk they'd pull out for him, right?"

"Probably the closest," Terry said. "But the killer could hardly take that chance. You're saying he gimmicked *all* of them?"

"Right. If he injected them with something, that would have provided the opening for bacteria to get in and start the souring process."

"So we could take one carton and get it analyzed, and if it's positive for something nasty we can come back with a warrant and use that to get the other ones tested."

"With a clear chain of evidence," Chomps said. "We won't have touched or disturbed those cartons, which will presumably still hold the fingerprints and DNA of the duke's family." He raised his eyebrows. "Or, if we're lucky—"

"The killer's?"

Chomps nodded. "If we're *really* lucky."

For a long moment she looked at him, her mouth half puckered. Then, she huffed out a breath. "It still may not fly," she warned. "But you're right. The killer's already tried to get rid of the car computer. We don't want him getting to the drugged milk, too."

"Yeah." Chomps looked at the refrigerator. "I wonder why he didn't come back and clean everything out months ago."

"Maybe he figured interest in the case was dying down and didn't want to risk another intrusion." Terry hesitated, then handed him her uni-link. "Fine. But *I'll* do all the collecting and bagging. You'll stand out of the way and record everything."

"How about I record with both?" Chomps suggested, taking his own uni-link in his other hand. "A dual record's always harder to corrupt or alter. Any idea who we're going to bring this to, by the way?"

"I have a couple of ideas," Terry said. "Let's worry about that after we get the sample." She pulled out an evidence bag from the dispenser on her belt and cleared her throat. "Okay, start recording. This is Sheriff's Deputy Theresa Lassaline, recording from Duke Serisburg's mountain retreat on the seventh day of..."

Chomps watched in silence, recording Terry's every move, sorting these new bits of data into the stack in his mind. The computer was still the key, but if Devereux had indeed hidden it right under the killer's nose that key would soon be available to them.

And if his growing suspicion on what that key would show proved to be correct, he might have the pieces he needed to finally make this card castle stand.

CHAPTER NINETEEN

FOR THE PAST FIVE DAYS Winterfall had felt like he was on a treadmill that was running about two kilometers per hour too fast.

But now that the preliminaries were over, Außenminister Shān assured him, the pace would pick up.

The worst part was the names. Like everything else Andermani, the names were a mix of Chinese and Old German, which not only made for mental confusion on his part but often made it impossible to predict which of the people on the attendance lists were male and which were female. That shouldn't have been a problem, but Winterfall discovered to his private embarrassment that having a mental image of the wrong gender threw him off stride for the first few seconds of a given introduction. All the fumbling make him feel stupid and awkward, not to mention probably lowering his hosts' opinion of Manticore in general.

The titles, at least, were pretty much all German. Still, the jaw-cracking compound words were still something of a challenge.

And of course, there was so much of everything and everyone. There was the Chancellor, or Kanzlerin, a formidable woman with the equally formidable name of Wilhelmine Heilbronn, Markgräfin von Schwarzer Flügel. There was the Minister of War, Kriegminister Aeric Zimmerman, plus a vizeadmiral and flotillenadmiral who served as his advisers. There were several other ministers from the *Staatsministerium*—Interior, Finance, Justice, Research, Industry, and Transport— all of whom made appearances at the grand banquet that Emperor Andrew arranged to formally greet the Manticoran guests, and none of whom was then ever seen again.

Most of the meetings were held in the palace, usually in the Marble Hall or Audience room. A few of the larger ones took place in government buildings elsewhere in Zizhulin. Those meetings gave Winterfall and his team a chance to see a bit more of the Empire's people and architecture, at least in passing, as well as offering some welcome breathing space.

Naturally, the vehicles used to transport them across town were far better than anything Manticore had to offer.

Still, even just with Außenminister Shān, Kriegminister Aeric Zimmerman, plus their various aides and assistants, there were plenty of people involved to keep things lively. Especially since Winterfall had the sense that at least half of them thought the whole thing was a waste of time.

"It's really not that, you know," Major Strossmeyer assured him one evening as the *Totenkopf* was escorting the Manticorans back to their wing of the palace. "There are all the preparations going on for this palace wedding that's taking up a lot of everyone's attention. On top of that, Admiral Basaltberg and the fleet are just four days out from Tomlinson, and all of Potsdam's thoughts and hopes are with them. You have to expect they'll be a little distracted."

"I understand," Winterfall said, his stomach tightening around yet another magnificent dinner. Basaltberg's fleet, and Winterfall's brother and sister-in-law. In four or five days it would all be over, with probably a great many of those who left New Berlin never coming back.

And no one here would know anything about it for another two weeks.

"And of course, there's also Emperor Andrew," Strossmeyer said into Winterfall's quiet fears.

"What do you mean?" Winterfall asked.

Strossmeyer waved a hand. "The usual. The questions and concerns about whether he's truly ready to lead the Empire."

"I thought everyone was going to sit back for a bit and give him a chance to prove himself."

"Maybe," Strossmeyer said. "But a lot of that may depend on what happens at Tomlinson over the next few days. And if some of the doubters decide to take matters beyond cautious watchfulness..."

Winterfall glanced around. No one else was in earshot. "Are you talking about a coup?" he asked softly.

"I hope to *Gott* not," Strossmeyer said feelingly. "But it happened once, you know. Eighteen years ago. If it happened once, what's to stop it from happening again?"

"You," Winterfall said. "You and the other *Totenkopfs.*"

"Maybe," Strossmeyer said. "But..." He shook his

head. "It's strange, *Herr* Foreign Minister. I would have died for Emperor Gustav. Instantly, without thought or question. But Emperor Andrew...I'm not sure I could. Not anymore."

"That's your job, *Herr Major*," Winterfall said, letting his voice darken, a small voice in the back of his mind noting the irony of a foreigner as ill-equipped as he was to do his own job lecturing someone else on how to do his. "If you're not ready to do it—"

"I should resign," Strossmeyer said. "Of course. I know that. The deeper question is whether I should consider leaving the Empire entirely."

Winterfall frowned. "It's *that* bad?"

"No, no, it's not *bad*," Strossmeyer hastened to assure him. "It's just *different*. Emperor Andrew may turn out to be a great and enlightened ruler. But he's not Emperor Gustav. The *feel* of the Empire has changed." He gave Winterfall a wan smile. "Or maybe I have. *Gott* help me."

"There's nothing wrong or shameful about a person growing in a different direction than he expected," Winterfall said. "From what I've seen of you, I have no doubt you would continue to protect the new Emperor every bit as zealously as you did the old. But if you don't feel right about it, then you should definitely consider a change."

"I thank you for your advice and insights, *Herr* Foreign Minister," Strossmeyer said as they reached Winterfall's door. "Though there's still be the question of *where* I could go."

"Why not Haven?" Winterfall suggested. "The Empire already has good diplomatic and commercial relations with them."

"Which may actually argue against it," Strossmeyer said. "Goods and diplomats are not the only things that travel between our two nations. Information does, as well...and I will be a failed *Totenkopf* trying to make a new life."

"I doubt the Havenites would care."

"Some would," Strossmeyer said. "And in their faces..." A muscle in his cheek twitched. "No. And there's nothing in Silesia I would want. No, it's the Solarian League, or nothing."

"That's an awfully long trip."

"I know." Strossmeyer twitched a smile. "Unless there might be a place for a professional bodyguard in your Star Kingdom of Manticore? If not for your queen, perhaps some high official would be interested in hiring a former Andermani *Totenkopf* to handle his security."

"I'm sure someone would," Winterfall said, frowning. "But to be honest, I think that after living in the Empire you'd find Manticore a little—shall we say *rustic*?"

"Rustic may be just what I need after the stress of protecting the Empire," Strossmeyer said ruefully. "Tell me, how difficult would it be to obtain Manticoran citizenship?"

"I really don't know," Winterfall said. "We get our share of immigrants, so I know there's a procedure in place. But that's not my department, and I don't know the details. Would you be wanting to come back with us aboard *Diactoros*, or wait for passage on a future ship?"

"I don't see what purpose a delay would serve," Strossmeyer said. "As you yourself pointed out, if

I'm not wholly prepared to give my entire self to my job, it would be in everyone's best interests if I left as soon as possible."

"There's that," Winterfall conceded.

"And who knows when trade between Potsdam and Manticore will become a reality?" Strossmeyer added. "It's not as if Majestät will simply give me a ship of my own and speed me on my way."

"That would seem unlikely," Winterfall agreed. "On Manticore you're lucky if you just get a good reference from your employer. Let me look into it, check the relevant laws and statutes, and discuss it with my team. I should have an answer for you by the end of the week."

"I appreciate that, *Herr* Foreign Minister," Strossmeyer said. "Sleep well."

☆   ☆   ☆

For an hour after Winterfall turned off the light he lay awake, staring at the curtained window, noting the occasional shadows of night birds flick across the moonlight. Then, with a feeling of trepidation, he turned on the nightstand light and keyed the call button.

"Palace services," a female voice came promptly. "How may I assist you, Baron Winterfall?"

"I'd like to leave a message for someone," Winterfall said. "I don't think she's in the palace, and I don't want to wake her up. I just want to leave a message for her to get in the morning. Can I do that?"

"Of course, *Herr Baron*. You may record whenever you're ready."

"All right." Winterfall paused, choosing his words. "This is Foreign Minister Gavin Vellacott, Baron

Winterfall. I would like to speak to you on a matter of—" did he dare say *great importance*? "—some importance at your earliest convenience. As this is a delicate matter, I would beg of you to keep it as confidential as possible. End message. Did you get that?"

"Ja, Herr Baron," the woman assured him. "And the recipient?"

It was a long shot, Winterfall knew. It was also likely going way out of channels and way above his position, and given the Andermani rigidity in the matter of proper protocol it had the potential to sabotage his entire mission.

But deep within him he knew it had to be done. And this was the only way he could think to do it.

"One of Majestät Andrew's advisers," he said. "Baronesse Marija Shenoa."

☆   ☆   ☆

Winterfall wasn't expecting to find an answer to his message waiting when he woke up the next morning. Nor did one come while he washed and dressed, nor had one been delivered by the time the group assembled for the morning discussions.

Which wasn't surprising. An advisor to the Emperor would have a lot of duties, and answering a message from a visiting dignitary—or even reading it, for that matter—was probably low on the baronesse's priority list. If he got an answer within the few days it would take to track down the immigration data for Strossmeyer, he would consider that a win.

That particular morning's talks revolved around commerce issues, giving Winterfall a chance to sit back while the trade expert Baroness Crystal Pine had sent with the mission handled the Manticoran half of the conversation. Fortunately, she'd applied herself enthusiastically to her language studies on the voyage, and her German was excellent. Luncheon was served at the usual time, right on the stroke of one o'clock. Winterfall had finished his meal and was listening to the casual conversation at his end of the table when a young man he hadn't seen before stepped up to him.

"Excuse me, *Herr* Foreign Minister," the young man said. "My name is Josef Shu Tung, one of the caretakers of the Emperor's greyhounds. Außenminister Shān told me that your family has an interest in dogs, and suggested you might wish to inspect the palace kennels."

"Yes, I'd like that," Winterfall said. He'd noticed the greyhounds, of course. They were everywhere, apparently with complete run of the palace. Fortunately, they were also well-behaved, and aside from demanding a bit of attention from everyone they met they weren't a problem.

How Shān had learned about his and Travis's mother's dog breeding business he didn't know. But he was starting to get used to Andermani omniscience.

More to the point, he still had half an hour before the next session. "Would this be a good time?" he asked.

"It's entirely at your convenience, *Herr* Foreign Minister."

"Then let's do it," Winterfall said, easing his chair back and standing up.

"Excellent," Shu Tung said, smiling. "If you'll follow me, *bitte*?"

The young man led him past the Manticorans' rooms, through a short double-ell turn and into the farther palace wing. Winterfall could hear and smell the dogs well before Shu Tung stopped by an open door and gestured him inside. "In here, *Herr* Foreign Minister. Enjoy."

"*Danke,*" Winterfall said, and stepped through the doorway.

And came to an abrupt stop. Seated on a woven-mesh chair just inside the door, a happy greyhound's head cradled in her hands, was Baronesse Marija Shenoa. "*Guten Tag, Herr Baron,*" she greeted him, her voice solemn, her eyes steady on his face. "I understand you wish to speak with me."

With an effort, Winterfall found his voice. "I do, Baronesse. Please forgive me if I overstepped my bounds or intruded on your privacy in any way."

"One has to work much harder than that to offend me, *Herr Baron,*" she said with a hint of dry humor as she gestured to another chair across from her. "Please sit. And tell me of this matter of importance."

"*Danke,*" Winterfall said, lowering himself carefully onto the chair. The material looked fragile, but seemed to hold his weight without any problem. "The problem is that I don't really *know* if the matter is important or not," he continued as another greyhound trotted over and put its head in Winterfall's lap. "I had a conversation with one of our *Totenkopf* guards last night, Major Strossmeyer. Parts of our talk just seemed . . . odd."

"In what way?" Marija asked. If she thought he was wasting her time, Winterfall thought, she was hiding it well.

"He suggested while he was intensely loyal to the late Emperor Gustav, that he was uncomfortable guarding Emperor Andrew," Winterfall said as he stroked the dog's head. "He talked about resigning and leaving the Empire."

"Hardly something to be concerned about," Marija said. "The *Totenkopf* Hussars form strong attachments to their Emperor. So do the members of the palace staff and the various official ministers. A period of adjustment isn't unreasonable."

"He also talked about protecting the Empire," Winterfall said. "Not the Emperor, but the Empire."

"One and the same," Marija said. "As I said, feelings run deep. I wouldn't be surprised if some of our citizens, even highly placed ones, eventually decide to immigrate to Haven or the League."

"I actually suggested Haven," Winterfall said. "That was the other odd part. Instead, he pushed for me to invite him to immigrate to Manticore."

Marija's forehead furrowed slightly. "I hardly think a man of Major Strossmeyer's tastes would be happy on Manticore. No offense intended."

"None taken," Winterfall said. "I made that same point, in fact. But it wasn't just the words. It was also his...well, it was everything. His tone, his expression, his body language. It felt like there was something going on under the surface that I was missing. He also spoke of preparations for *this palace wedding*. Not *my Emperor's wedding* or something of that sort. The whole phraseology just felt cold and distant."

"I'm afraid you may be suffering from culture shock, *Herr Baron*," Marija said. "Andermani aren't given to expressing warmth or any other emotions, particularly to strangers and outsiders. If Major Strossmeyer is unhappy here, I'm sure Emperor Andrew will offer him alternate service, or allow him to resign his commission and take up a new life elsewhere." She smiled. "Even on Manticore, if he so chooses."

"I understand, Baronesse," Winterfall said, trying to conceal his frustration. There was still something wrong about all this—he could *feel* it. But it was equally clear that those feelings couldn't be translated into words. "Thank you for your time." He gave the greyhound a final pat on the head and stood up.

Or perhaps not quite final. The greyhound looked up at him with plaintive eyes, making little pleading sounds. "Oh, all right," Winterfall said, feeling a little embarrassed as he leaned over and gave the greyhound a more vigorous rub around her head, ears, and muzzle, making sure to dig under her collar where other dogs he'd known tended to have itches. "Yes, you're a good dog," he said. "My apologies, Baronesse."

"None needed, *Herr Baron*," Marija assured him. Fortunately, she sounded more amused than annoyed. "You seem to have made a friend in Sunna."

"She's a beautiful animal," Winterfall agreed. One final pat—*really* final this time—and he again straightened up. "Thank you again, Baronesse. And if Major Strossmeyer wants to come to Manticore, we'll be happy to save Emperor Andrew the trouble of providing him a ship." He bowed again and started to turn to the door.

"Stop," Marija said, her voice suddenly filled with broken ice.

Winterfall froze. What had he done? "Yes?" he asked carefully as he turned back.

He felt his breath catch in his throat. There was a new hardness to Marija's face, a sudden simmering fire in her eyes, a visible clenching of her jaw. "Sit down," she said, the broken ice still there. "What did you mean, happy to save the Emperor the trouble of providing a ship?"

"I apologize if I offended you," Winterfall said between suddenly stiff lips. "It was just something Major Strossmeyer said."

"His exact words, *Herr Baron*," Marija ordered. "His *exact* words."

Winterfall took a deep breath, thinking back. "We were talking about whether he could wait for some kind of commercial travel between our nations to emigrate," he said slowly. "He then said, *And who knows when trade between Potsdam and Manticore will become a reality? It's not as if Majestät will simply give me a ship of my own and speed me on my way.*"

For a moment Marija searched his face in silence. "I see," she said at last. "A small joke on the major's part, I suppose."

"Did the words have any special significance?" Winterfall asked.

"As I said, simply a joke," Marija said. "You may go, *Herr Baron*. It appears to be only a minor matter, but thank you for bringing it to the Emperor's attention."

"You're welcome," Winterfall said, completely lost now. "I'll of course be available if you wish to speak further."

"Should that become necessary, I will certainly inform you," Marija said. "You will of course not mention any of this to anyone else. That includes your negotiating group as well as ours."

"And Major Strossmeyer?"

Her eyes bored into his. "Especially not the major," she said quietly. "Thank you again. I trust your next round of talks will be fruitful."

"I'm sure they will," Winterfall said. "Thank you again, Baronesse."

And that was that, he told himself as the young greyhound caretaker led the way back down the hallway. If there'd been anything sinister or seditious in what Strossmeyer had said or done, Winterfall had alerted his hosts as a good guest should. It was their job now to evaluate and act.

And if there hadn't been anything to it, and Winterfall had just made a fool of himself, he could only hope to God that word of it didn't get back to Queen Elizabeth.

CHAPTER TWENTY

IT WAS JUST AFTER SEVEN O'CLOCK that evening when the knock Chomps had expected finally came. Taking a deep breath, he got up from the edge of the bed where he'd been sitting, crossed the room, and opened the door.

"Mr. Townsend," Sheriff Vespoli greeted him formally. "May I come in?"

"Sorry," Chomps said, not moving from the doorway. "I'm expecting someone."

"If you mean Dr. Tsai, he won't be coming," Vespoli said. Her hand, Chomps noted, was resting casually on her holstered sidearm. "He and Deputy Lassaline are on their way to the duke's retreat to retrieve the rest of the spoiled milk cartons."

"Really?" Chomps said, frowning. "I thought we were going to have this one checked first."

"Change of plans." Vespoli's gaze flicked past his arm. "You have it here?"

"I do."

"Good, because I'm here to collect it."

"I don't know," Chomps said hesitantly. "I should check with Terry first."

Vespoli shook her head. "I'm afraid I have to insist." And suddenly, her gun was clear of its holster and pointed squarely at Chomps's chest. "Hands on your head," she said quietly, "and step back into the room."

Clenching his teeth in half a snarl, Chomps obeyed. Vespoli followed, staying well out of reach, and closed the door behind her. "Over there," she said, gesturing to the corner farthest from the door and the bed. "Face the wall, please."

She waited until he was in the corner. Then, as he watched her over his shoulder, she sat down on the bed and felt under the pillows. "You're wasting your time," Chomps said. "I don't have a gun."

"Maybe not one of your own," Vespoli said. She finished with the pillows, then leaned over and ran her hand along the underside of the bed. "But Lassaline carries a backup Drakon—ah."

She straightened up, holding up the Drakon for him to see. "Serisburg Deputy gun; Serisburg Deputy hiding place." She checked the chamber, confirming there was a round in place, then holstered her own gun and shifted the Drakon to her right hand.

"And Serisburg Deputy murder?" Chomps suggested, turning back around to face her.

"I'm sorry," Vespoli said. She sounded determined, but not especially sorry. "But you know too much."

"So does Deputy Lassaline," Chomps pointed out. "You going to kill her, too?"

A flicker of pain crossed Vespoli's face. "That one's going to hurt," she admitted. "I'm just glad I won't have to do it myself."

"Your fellow murderer will do it?"

"There's no *fellow murderer*," Vespoli ground out. "I'm the one who killed them. He's just helping me clean up my mess."

"Awfully decent of him," Chomps said. "This Good Samaritan got a name?"

"Why do you care?"

"Why do *you* care?" Chomps countered. "You're about to shoot me, aren't you?"

For a moment she stared at him. Then, she gave a little shrug. "His name's Masterson," she said. "He's a special agent with the Royal Investigation Division. He's the one who first—" She broke off, her throat working. "He's the one who told me the duke was going to fire me."

"Really," Chomps said. The Royal Investigation Division. Right. "I thought the duke had a permanent wink about your drinking."

"I guess his eye got sore," Vespoli said. "He'd decided to kick me out. And not just kick me out, but publicly shame me." Her throat worked again. "This job's all I've got, Townsend."

"Yes, Terry told me," Chomps said. "So what did you do? Go to his retreat and confront him?"

Vespoli gave a little snort. "Yes, that would have been the adult thing to do, wouldn't it? And believe me, I had a speech ready that would have blistered the wood siding off his greatroom. But no, I needed a little extra courage first. So I had a drink. And another, and probably another."

She took a deep breath. "And when I finally woke up, I was sitting in my patrol car in the middle of the forest, with the wreck of the duke's air car beside me."

"Wait a second," Chomps said, frowning. "Falling-down drunk, you were still able to force him into a tree?"

"Who said anything about forcing anyone?" Vespoli demanded. "I *scared* him into the tree. I had him dodging, weaving—he was just trying to get away and protect his family. But I was too crazy drunk to care. If I could take it back...but what's done is done. You have to understand—all I've got left is my job."

"I understand," Chomps said.

So he'd been right. He almost wished he hadn't.

"So you scared him into a tree," he said. "Let's talk about Deputy Lassaline. You said Masterson's waiting at the retreat to kill her?"

"Yes." Vespoli glanced at her uni-link. "She's almost there."

"And you're going to explain how she's there getting killed at the same time she's here at the inn shooting me?"

Vespoli shrugged. "I can revise her uni-link locator history afterwards."

"That could end up being confusing."

"Not really. I know how to do it."

"Of course you do." Chomps shook his head. "I'm sorry, Sheriff. I was really hoping it wasn't you."

Vespoli frowned. "What do you mean?"

"I was hoping it was Deputy Broganis or one of the others," Chomps went on, ignoring the question. "For a while I thought it might even be Terry."

"If you're trying to stall—"

"Because it had to be one of you," Chomps said. "Only a police car has the capability of overriding another air car and taking over its controls." He shook his head. "Duke Serisburg wasn't scared into the tree, Sheriff. His car was overridden and rammed into it."

"Don't be absurd," Vespoli bit out. "There was no override. The black box would have shown that."

"Only if the override frequency and protocols were ones the black box recognized and recorded," Chomps said. "Except that this was a *Solarian* car."

She was frowning now. "So?"

"League planets are pretty crowded," Chomps said. "Lots of people, lots of jurisdictions, all of them pushing up against one another. There's no way one frequency, or even one group of them, could handle all the potential police overrides. That's why their air-car computers have a handy little port on one side to shift to the local jurisdiction's override frequency."

"I don't understand."

"No, I think you do," Chomps said. "Your friend Masterson, the one who claims to be helping you clean up your mess, is the one who started all this in the first place and has been playing you like a puppet. He was the one who got into the duke's car and slipped the frequency-shifter into the computer, then poisoned the milk in the fridge so the duke would grab his family and head for Serisburg Point and a hospital."

"No," Vespoli insisted, her voice strained. "That's impossible."

"We have the computer," Chomps told her. "More than that, we have the specs and now know what that port was for. Masterson was the one flying your patrol car that night while you were sleeping off the booze and whatever drugs he'd added to it. He would have had to put something in your patrol car's system to shift its override frequency to the new one, but that wouldn't have been a problem—all of that would have been out of sight, and no one was looking at *your* car or its black box records.

"Once everything was in place, it was pretty simple. I'm guessing he took partial control of the car right from the start, shutting off the radio but otherwise letting the duke fly it until they got near the site he'd picked out for the crash. Once it was done, he retrieved the shifter, woke you up, and spun his story. The tweaking he'd done to your override system could be pulled out over the next couple of days at his leisure."

Vespoli's face had gone progressively more rigid as he talked. "It doesn't matter," she said. "Maybe it happened that way. Maybe it didn't."

"The ironic thing is that somewhere along the way the duke figured it out," Chomps said. "That's why he unstrapped and was trying to get to the computer. I'm guessing all the swerving that Masterson said was you buzzing the car was Masterson trying to throw the duke back and forth across the car and away from the console before he could get to the shifter and pull it out."

He paused, but Vespoli remained silent. "The black box recorded all the car's movements like it was supposed to," Chomps continued, "but didn't register that the commands were coming from outside. Masterson could control the car from well outside proximity range, so your patrol car didn't show up on any of the black box's sensor records. He was also lucky in that the duke lived a few minutes after the crash, long enough for him to pump some alcohol into his blood and get it circulated enough to indicate he was flying drunk. A nice little twist of the knife, but really just icing on the cake."

"You're not listening," Vespoli said. "Maybe it happened that way. It doesn't matter. I was there, in the car, when it happened. Whether I was flying or not, it's still my responsibility."

"You weren't culpable."

"The law says otherwise." She hefted the Drakon. "And this job's all I've got. I'm sorry."

"I'm sorry, too," Chomps said. "Let me see if I've got this straight. You're going to shoot me, then gimmick Terry's uni-link to show she was here at the time—and gimmick yours to show that you weren't—then make it look like after she killed me she flew to the duke's retreat where Masterson killed her. That right?"

"Yes." Vespoli visibly braced herself, and Chomps saw her knuckles whiten as she got a firmer grip on the Drakon.

"Yeah, I don't know," Chomps said doubtfully. "It's going to look strange. Her uni-link being gimmicked twice in the same day, I mean."

Vespoli frowned. "What are you talking about?"

"I'm talking about that," Chomps said, nodding over her shoulder. "Deputy?" he called.

And as Vespoli half turned her head, the closet door swung open and Terry stepped out, her gun drawn and ready.

Vespoli, at her best, was pretty good. She could have only barely felt the subtle movement of air on her neck and cheek before she dropped to one knee and swiveled around at the waist to bring the Drakon to bear on the deputy. The muzzle steadied on target, and Chomps heard the click of the striker.

Nothing happened.

Again, the sheriff was right on it, working the slide awkwardly with her body half twisted and ejecting the bad round. As Terry moved toward her there was a second useless click—

"Don't bother," Chomps advised. "Loading the magazine with dummy rounds makes it pretty useless."

Vespoli swore and again worked the slide.

And then it was too late. Terry was right in front of her, ignoring the useless weapon and pulling the sheriff's own gun from its holster. "It's over, Sheriff," Terry said, her voice under rigid control. "You have the right to remain silent—"

"I know my rights," Vespoli interrupted, her voice suddenly weary.

"You have the right to remain silent," Terry repeated doggedly, clearly determined to follow all the protocols. "You have the right..."

This time she got through the whole list. "You okay?" she asked, looking at Chomps as she cuffed Vespoli's hands behind her and sat her down on the edge of the bed.

"I'm fine," Chomps said. "You get all that?"

Terry nodded. "Recording came out perfect." She hissed out a breath. "I didn't believe it when you said this was how it happened. I still don't want to."

"Do you know this Masterson?" Chomps asked. "Was he part of the investigation team?"

"No, and I never heard of him," Terry said. She threw a tight look at Vespoli. "He must have kept his connections here strictly to the sheriff."

"Just remember that she was a patsy," Chomps said. "Masterson was the one pulling the strings and doing the actual killing."

"I know," Terry said. "It still tracks like a nightmare."

"It's almost over," Chomps assured her. "By the way, I trust Dr. Tsai isn't *really* heading for the retreat?"

"No, of course not," Terry said. "Though if we'd known Masterson would be planning an ambush there we could have set up a welcoming committee for him."

"Don't worry, we'll get him," Chomps said. "Sheriff? Feel free to jump into this conversation any time."

"What do you want me to say?" Vespoli bit out. "I'm either a murderer or a dupe. Big damn choice."

"Third choice: you can be a Crown's witness," Terry offered. "We want Masterson, not you."

"You want both of us," Vespoli countered.

"Technically, yes," Chomps said. "But mostly because we want you to ID him once we catch him."

"You won't," Vespoli said, shaking her head. "Not a chance. He's way too smart."

"It's a small planet," Terry reminded her.

"It's a big universe," Vespoli countered. She took a deep breath, and Chomps saw a subtle shift in her expression. "What's it worth for me to help you nail him?"

"What do you want?" Terry asked.

"I want out of here," Vespoli said. "Cleared record, new name, maybe on Gryphon where no one knows me. You guarantee that and I'll get him out in the open for you."

Chomps and Terry looked at each other. "I think we can get someone to sign off on that," Terry said.

"I'm sure we can," Chomps confirmed. "Okay. Where and when?"

"He's expecting word that you've been dealt with," Vespoli said. "I'll screen him and say you must have changed your plans at the last minute and I wasn't able to get to you."

"What about me?" Terry asked. "You said he was going to take me out at the duke's retreat?"

"Obviously, we went off somewhere together," Chomps said, thinking quickly as he took his uni-link off his wrist and used his multitool to pull off the back cover. "Dr. Tsai was nervous about meeting at the retreat and insisted we go to his office instead to have Benjamin's chocolate milk analyzed. He wanted to make sure the chain of evidence was documented."

"And there will be other people working in his building, so he'll feel safer there," Terry added. "Masterson can't easily get to him, which is why you didn't screen him earlier to let him know where to find us."

"That should work," Vespoli said. "Okay. Uncuff me."

"Just a second," Chomps said, pulling out his pocket flashlight. He unscrewed the bottom, pulled out the special Delphi gadget tucked away in there, and plugged it into the uni-link's diagnostic port. "I don't know if he can access our locators, but if he can it might be just a tad suspicious if he noticed we were all in the inn together when we were supposed to be elsewhere . . . okay. You still came here, Sheriff, and probably waited for me to come back."

"And you spent a few minutes searching for the tainted milk before you screened him," Terry added.

"Right," Chomps said. "While Terry and I . . . Terry, what's Tsai's address?"

"Two Hundred West Barker Avenue in Serisburg Point."

"Thanks. While Terry and I met Tsai. Give me another second . . ."

A minute later, he'd finished entering the false location data into his uni-link. Three minutes after that, he'd done the same for Terry's locator.

"Interesting gadget," Terry commented as Chomps put it away. "Do I want to know where you got it?"

"Probably not," Chomps said, handing Terry back her uni-link. "Okay, Sheriff. You're on."

Vespoli waited silently until Terry removed her cuffs. Then, visibly bracing herself, she keyed her uni-link.

Another moment of silence. "Masterson?" Vespoli said. "It's me. We've got a problem."

Chomps listened closely as Vespoli ran through the scenario he and Terry had given her, trying to spot anything in her words or phrasing that sounded odd or out of place. If Masterson had set up a code to tip him off that they'd been compromised, this would be the time for her to use it.

Beside Vespoli, Terry leaned casually backward across the bed, craning her neck to peer at the sheriff's uni-link display. She straightened up, caught Chomps's eye, and shook her head.

So, no locator or other useful data attached to Masterson's number. Chomps hadn't expected there to be.

"...so what do you want me to do?"

The reply was audible but too soft for Chomps to make out any of the words. Masterson talked for no more than ten seconds before Vespoli nodded. "I'll be there," she said, and keyed off.

"Well?" Terry asked, wiggling her fingers in silent order.

"He wants to meet," Vespoli said, handing the uni-link to the deputy.

"So we gathered," Terry growled. "When and where?"

"Now, and at the spot—" Vespoli's throat worked. "At the spot where the duke's family died."

"Oh, yeah, that's a nice touch," Chomps murmured. "Not ghoulish or anything."

"Maybe it's ghoulish, but it's also practical," Terry said grimly. "Out in the woods he'll be able to hear a second air car coming from a long ways away, not to mention scanning for human heat signatures on his way in."

"And he knows I'm here at the inn," Vespoli said. "It won't take me long to get there."

"Longer than I can get anyone else here, anyway," Terry said. "I guess it's up to us, Townsend. Any ideas on how to sneak up on someone who'll be specifically watching for someone to sneak up on him?"

"I might," Chomps said. "Let's go see if I can borrow your parents' shotgun."

☆　　☆　　☆

Masterson made better time than Chomps had expected, especially given that the man was almost certainly staying strictly to the speed laws rather than risk drawing unwanted attention to himself. The killer must have been already on his way back from the duke's retreat, he decided, when Vespoli first called him.

"Here he comes," Vespoli warned.

"Yeah, got it," Chomps said as he climbed out of the patrol car. Making sure his borrowed shotgun was slung securely across his back, he climbed beneath the rear of the vehicle and slid as far under the thrusters as he could.

A fully heated thruster nozzle, the Delphi techs had once told him, could mask a human IR signature from anything short of military-grade detectors. The question now was whether the sheriff's trip from Serisburg Point had been enough to crank up the thrusters' heat to that level. Certainly the heat radiating down on him felt like it would be enough.

Unfortunately, there'd been no time to test it. His only clue that it had worked—or, more critically, that it *hadn't* worked—would be when Masterson opened fire on him.

He lay flat beneath the vent until the underside of the other air car came into view as Masterson settled toward the ground on the other side of the clearing. Then, moving quickly, he rolled out from under Vespoli's air car to the far side and rose into a crouch, keeping the thruster vents between him and Masterson's sensors.

The other car's door popped open, and Chomps eased an eye up over the rear of Vespoli's car. He caught a glimpse of a single shadowy figure in the car—

And ducked again as a searchlight abruptly blazed out at him.

He swore under his breath. Not entirely unexpected, but he'd been hoping he could get a quick picture of Masterson on his uni-link before he and Vespoli got into their conversation. But the spotlight now glaring into his face made that impossible.

Or at least, impossible from his current position.

He turned his head, blinking away the purple afterimage, and studied the forest. Vespoli had landed close to one edge of the clearing, putting the nearest trees no more than three meters away. If he stayed low, he should be able to stay in both the thruster's IR glare *and* the air car's shadow and make it to cover undetected.

The air car rocked slightly as Vespoli got out and headed across the clearing. Picking a good-sized target tree in the middle of the air car's shadow, Chomps got down on hands and knees and headed toward it.

No shouts or gunshots accompanied his movement. He reached the tree and crawled behind it. A line of small bushes led off to the side; using them for cover, he crawled another ten meters, far enough to be out of the floodlight's main beam. Picking another sufficiently large tree, he got behind it and stood up.

He'd moved as quickly as he could while still staying mostly silent. But even so, the clearing wasn't all *that* big, and he'd fully expected Vespoli to be all the way to Masterson's car by now.

Only she wasn't. She'd covered maybe two-thirds of the distance and was now simply standing there, facing Masterson from a few meters away, her arms folded across her chest. Chomps could hear a murmur of conversation, but the distance and the rustling leaves made it impossible for him to eavesdrop.

But if he shifted his uni-link to tight-beam, maybe its microphone could pick up their words. He got the device in hand and started making the adjustment—

And then, without warning, Vespoli abruptly unfolded her arms, dropped her right hand to her holster, and drew her weapon.

She had it about halfway to target when the sound of a shot hammered across the clearing. Vespoli jerked backward, her legs collapsing beneath her.

Chomps was already in motion, dropping the uni-link and snatching the shotgun from across his back. But it was too late. Far too late. Even as he lined up the muzzle a second shot rang out, the jolt of the round twitching Vespoli's body for a second time as she landed in a crumpled heap.

The displaced leaves were still fluttering as Chomps's return shot blasted across the clearing, the beanbag arrowing through the open door to slam into the half-seen figure there. The air car, which had been starting to rise again on its counter-grav, hesitated as the hands guiding its movements were knocked off the controls; Chomps fired again, and this time the air car dropped back solidly to the ground.

The beanbag rounds were pretty potent ones. Still, given time, Masterson would recover enough to escape. Chomps had no intention of giving him that time. He sprinted across the clearing, swearing viciously the whole way, ready to fire a third round if it seemed necessary.

To his bitter disappointment, Masterson gave him no such excuse. He was, in fact, only starting to come out of his daze as Chomps reached the air car. The gun he'd shot Vespoli with was still gripped loosely in his hand; Chomps wrenched it away, stuffed the weapon behind his own belt, then grabbed the man's arm and hauled him out of the vehicle. "Damn you to hell," he snarled, shoving his face close to the killer's, noting distantly that the man's lip was bleeding and wishing regretfully that his beanbags could have caused at least a *little* more damage.

Masterson didn't reply. Chomps hadn't really expected him to. Still holding the killer's arm, he shoved him face-first into the dirt and leaves, then pulled out a binder strap and pinioned his wrists behind him, probably tightening the strap a bit more than necessary. Then, shotgun in hand, he sprinted back to Vespoli.

The sheriff was still alive, her breath coming in short gasping bursts. Chomps grabbed her wrist, keyed her uni-link— "Vespoli's been shot," he snapped. "Get Emergency here—*now!*"

He didn't wait for Terry's acknowledgment. Pulling off Vespoli's belt first-aid kit, he popped it open and grabbed a tube of wound sealant. "Help's on its way, Sheriff," he said between clenched teeth as he pulled open her tunic and searched for the entry wounds. One was over her left lung, the other just below her heart, possibly having clipped it. Not good. "Stay with me, okay?"

"It's ... all right," she murmured, her hand weakly touching his as he got the sealant tube open. "Townsend ... it's all ..."

"Stay with me, Vespoli," he repeated, squeezing sealant onto the first wound. "Come on, damn it."

"It's ... all ... right," she repeated, her voice now almost too soft for him to hear. "This ... job ... all ... I ... had ..."

Chomps had closed her eyes and was sitting wearily beside her when Terry's patrol car dropped like an avenging angel into the clearing.

CHAPTER TWENTY-ONE

THE FLEET CAME OVER THE HYPER WALL at eighteen thousand kilometers per second, making its alpha translation in a vivid, blue wash of transit energy like a wall of sheet lightning. Ahead, the G5v primary of the Tomlinson System was suddenly a particularly brilliant star, 18.3 light-minutes from SMS *Friedrich der Grosse*.

Gerechtigkeitsgeschwader, Emperor Andrew had christened the fleet. *Justice Squadron.* Thirteen ships in tight formation, with considerably more firepower than any naval force Travis had ever seen. He gazed at the displays as he let the translation sickness abate, hoping that all the death and destruction those ships represented wouldn't be needed.

But he was fairly certain it would.

He looked across *Friedrich der Grosse*'s flag bridge. Lisa was easy to spot, her Manticoran vac suit standing out among all the Andermani vac suits. Travis appreciated the compliment the Emperor had paid him and Lisa by letting them travel into battle with Basaltberg's force, and certainly welcomed the opportunity to profit from the Empire's deep well of experience. But he still had lingering doubts about whether he and Lisa might inadvertently get in the way somewhere in the heat of battle.

Which brought up the larger concern digging at the back of his mind. Part of him was grateful to have Lisa beside him, but another part was only too well aware that not even battleships were immune to combat damage. If anything happened to her...

For a moment he just gazed at her profile, noting the curve of her lips and the way she held herself as she floated at the side of the bridge. Her eyes were focused on the tactical display before them, bright and intent, and something about her reminded him of a falcon in the moment before it stooped.

Only once before had they been together on a command deck at battle stations, and that time had ended without combat. He could hope this one would, as well, but the odds on that weren't good.

He inhaled deeply, driving the fears back. At least anything that happened to one of them would probably happen to the other as well. It was a strange thought in which to take comfort, but such were the paradoxes of the life he and Lisa had both chosen.

A trio of green icons blinked alight in the display, clustered around their translation spot, and a musical tone chimed.

"Transponder confirmation, *Herr Graf*," a sensor tech announced. "*Drachen*, *Schwert*, and *Kurzschwert*."

"Challenge from *Drachen*, *mein Herr*," Korvetten-kapitän Westgate said in almost the same moment, looking over his shoulder at Basaltberg before the admiral could acknowledge the first report.

"It's good to see that Korvettenkapitän Scherzer is as alert as ever," Basaltberg commented. "Acknowledge his challenge."

"*Jawohl, mein Herr.*"

"Tactical update, *Herr Graf,*" Fregattenkapitän Schlamme, Basaltberg's staff tactical officer said a moment later, and Travis watched as the main display updated in response to Korvettenkapitän Gangyi Scherzer's upload to the flagship. Scherzer's *Drachen* was the senior of the five frigates which had been detailed to picket Tomlinson's approaches while the rest of the fleet prepared, and it was apparent that Scherzer hadn't wasted his time waiting for the fleet's return.

"So there have been some reinforcements, *mein Herr,*" Basaltberg's chief of staff, Kapitänin der Sterne Jijun Kranz, commented.

She was right, Travis saw with a sinking feeling as he studied the displays. According to Scherzer's data, around twenty more warships had arrived to support *Preussen* and the battlecruiser which had ambushed *Rotte*. Unfortunately, none of the frigates Basaltberg had left to picket the system had been in close enough proximity to get detailed readings on the new arrivals. It was possible that even more reinforcements had crept in completely unobserved, although it was unlikely with that many pickets in place.

What *had* been spotted was impressive enough, however. Scherzer's tactical officers had tentatively identified the newcomers as three battlecruisers, five light or heavy cruisers, and twelve destroyer-range hulls.

Travis stroked his lower lip as he considered the numbers. Added to what the enemy had already had in-system, the new arrivals gave the insurgents a fifty percent advantage in platforms. Even so, the firepower balance still favored *Gerechtigkeitsgeschwader.*

Probably favored the Andermani, Travis cautioned himself. Basaltberg's three battlecruisers should be a decent match for the enemy's four, and his two battleships—*Friedrich der Grosse* and *Vergeltung*—outnumbered *Preussen* two-to-one. He had an edge in the cruiser components of the two forces, as well: three heavy cruisers and five of the big *Drachen* and *Reiterei*-class frigates against the enemy's five cruiser-range hulls.

On the other hand, the frigates were spread around the hyper-limit's periphery. Only three of them were close enough to join Basaltberg's formation if he continued straight into the attack. On top of that, the insurgents enjoyed a better than two-to-one advantage in destroyers. It was unlikely that would be enough to offset the second imperial battleship's firepower, but it was far from impossible.

"Put me through to Korvettenkapitän Scherzer," Basaltberg told Westgate.

"Jawohl, mein Herr."

A few moments later, a small, dapper korvetten-kapitän appeared on the main com display.

"Guten Morgen, Herr Graf," he said, bending his head courteously to Basaltberg.

"Guten Morgen, Fregattenkapitän," responded Basaltberg. "It would appear we have our work cut out for us."

"It would, indeed, *mein Herr,*" Scherzer agreed.

"How likely is it, in your opinion, that these people know that you detected their reinforcements' arrival?"

"Impossible to know for certain, *mein Herr.* They've known we're here, and they probably know our numbers fairly accurately, given the sensor platforms they've undoubtedly deployed. On the other hand, we've maintained strict emissions control and kept our wedges to minimum power, so I doubt they know precisely where any of us were at the moment of their arrival. They were actually tracked inbound by *Langschwert*, the only ship in passive sensor range of their alpha translation. I would say they almost certainly assume we detected their arrival footprint, but *Langschwert*'s wedge was completely down at the time, so whether they know we were close enough to get a source count or identify ship types even tentatively is another question."

Basaltberg nodded and raised an eyebrow at Schlamme. "Your assessment, *Herr Fregattenkapitän*?" he asked the staff tactical officer.

"From what Fregattenkapitän Scherzer's just told us, I'd say the odds are they don't know *Langschwert* was close enough, *mein Herr*," Schlamme said. "With the hyper limit's circumference well over a light-hour, we were unexpectedly fortunate to have *any* of our ships in position."

"It has been said that good officers make their own luck," Basaltberg said.

"Indeed, *mein Herr*," Schlamme agreed. "I would anticipate that the insurgents don't know *Langschwert* was able to identify any of their ship classes. At the same time, I would hesitate to adopt tactics based on that assumption."

"And they definitely know that *we* have arrived," Basaltberg pointed out. "Fregattenkapitän Scherzer is correct that they must have deployed sensor platforms sufficiently sensitive to detect our hyper footprint."

He considered that for a moment, then looked at the navigation display and nodded.

"Very well. We will execute Plan Alpha. Fregat-tenkapitän Scherzer, I see *Schwert, Drachen,* and *Kurzschwert* are close enough to match velocities with us. We won't delay long enough for *Langschwert* and *Reiterei* to join us."

"*Jawohl, mein Herr,*" Scherzer said.

Basaltberg turned back to his chief of staff. "It would appear we have a great deal to do today, Kapitänin der Sterne. Best we begin."

"At once, *mein Herr.*" Kranz turned to Westgate. "Korvettenkapitän Westgate, send the message."

☆   ☆   ☆

"... and so His Majesty has instructed me to give you this final opportunity to surrender your persons and your ships immediately," the gray-haired, iron-faced man on Kapitänin der Sterne Hansen's com display said grimly. "Those who have committed crimes will be held accountable for them. If you fail to comply, you will be attacked by the forces under my command, and many of the units—and people—you were given the trust and the honor to command will be destroyed. I await your response. Basaltberg, clear."

For a moment *Preussen*'s bridge was silent. On the surface, Llyn noted, Hansen's face was completely expressionless.

But Llyn could see more deeply than most. He could see behind the face to the quiet heartache that had begun with her first view of Basaltberg's face and only grown deeper as he delivered his message.

Surreptitiously, Llyn checked his chrono. It had taken that message seventeen minutes to reach *Pre-ussen*, arriving five minutes after the deployed recon platforms had reported his arrival in Tomlinson space.

At the moment, he was headed in-system at a steady eighteen thousand KPS, putting him 1.3 light-minutes closer to Tomlinson than he'd been when he sent it. At that velocity, he would reach Tomlinson orbit in just under four and a half hours.

Of course, there was little point in simply blowing past the planet and its defenders at high speed. No, he'd be decelerating at some point.

The question was when.

"The hidden cost of defection," Quint murmured at his side.

"What?" Llyn murmured back.

Quint nodded toward Hansen and the face frozen on the com display. "Turning your back on people you've spent your career with," she said. "You never expect just how much of a gut-punch it is to see them look at you like that, or to issue that kind of ultimatum."

Llyn nodded. In that respect, at least, far better to be a mercenary with few such ties.

Or a Black Ops agent for a transstellar corporation with no ties at all.

"What are you going to tell him, Captain?" Bajer asked quietly from beside her.

Hansen turned to him, her expression visibly wrenching itself out of memory and back to the present. "Excuse me?"

"I asked what you were going to tell him," Bajer repeated.

Llyn looked at the man, wondering yet again what kind of relationship the two of them had. Bajer had been offered a ship of his own, Quint had told him, his choice of the dozen destroyers Bryce had talked PFT into supplying to the Tomlinson rebels. Instead, and to Quint's surprise, he'd chosen to remain in his post-mutiny position as *Preussen's* executive officer.

Of course, like the other Tomlinson-born members of the battleship's crew, he now held his rank from the Provisional Free Government of Tomlinson and no longer used the hated German rank titles. Quint had told Llyn about that, too, voicing her concern that mixing ranks and titles could throw just that little extra bit of sand into what needed to be a smoothly running command structure.

"The dice have already been rolled, Commander," Hansen said, turning her eyes from Bajer to Quint and Llyn. "The only thing now is to see how they fall."

Her nostrils flared as she inhaled deeply. "Ober-leutnantin Braunstein, record for transmission," she ordered *Preussen's* com officer.

Braunstein tapped an icon at her console.

"Live mic, *meine Kapitänin.*"

☆   ☆   ☆

"Incoming transmission, *Herr Graf,*" Korvettenkapitän Westgate reported.

"Display it," Basaltberg replied.

The face of a gray-eyed, brown-haired woman in the uniform of the Imperial Andermani Navy appeared on the main display.

"I decline to surrender the forces under my command or any of my allies, Graf von Basaltberg," she said with measured deliberation. "I do not recognize your authority, or that of Andrew Anderman. Neither I nor the Andermani personnel under my command owe him our allegiance—" she paused "—because I have genetic proof that *I* am Gustav Anderman's daughter."

Travis felt his eyes widen. Gustav's *daughter*? He

flashed a look at Lisa, saw her eyes had gone as wide as his own.

"I am, in fact, his eldest child, and as such, the throne Andrew Anderman currently occupies is rightfully mine," Hansen continued in the same tone of harsh, unyielding determination. "I realize Andrew Anderman was recognized by the Landtag as my father's heir. But they had not seen the evidence which I now possess."

Someone across the bridge muttered a word that had never shown up in any of Travis's language lessons. Basaltberg didn't seem to notice.

"I would also submit that my younger brother is just that: young. Too young, and completely unproven. I, in contrast, have amply demonstrated my capabilities as a ship commander and senior naval officer. I am not only the rightful inheritor of the crown, but far better suited by experience and training to wear it.

"Accordingly, *Herr Graf,* under my rightful authority as your legitimate Kaiserin, I call upon you and your personnel to surrender yourselves to *me.*"

She looked into the pickup a moment longer, then gave a brisk nod. "Hansen-*Anderman*, clear."

And as if a spell had been broken, every eye on *Friedrich der Grosse*'s flag bridge turned to Admiral Basaltberg.

For a long moment Basaltberg just sat there, his expression somewhere between stunned and disbelieving.

But only for a moment. His face went hard and cold, and he snapped his fingers and pointed to Westgate's console.

The communications officer shook himself, punched a button, and nodded.

"Live mic, *Herr Graf*," he said.

Basaltberg squared his shoulders, and spoke very, very clearly into the pickup.

"Obviously, I did not expect that response from you, Kapitänin Hansen," he said. "However, even if this evidence you claim truly exists and does, indeed, prove your heritage, it cannot excuse your current actions or the ones which preceded them.

"Even assuming that you are in fact Kaiser Gustav's daughter, it changes nothing. The Articles of Succession clearly state that the Crown passes to the eldest *male* heir. That is the fundamental law of the Empire, based upon the *königliches Erbrecht* of the original Kingdom of Prussia on Old Earth and adopted by the Landtag at His Majesty's urging. You cannot change it simply because you have learned that you are his child.

"Laying that aside, however, even if you had a *legal* claim to the Crown, the proper course of action would have been to present it before the Landtag. It was *not* to violate your oath as an officer of the Imperial Andermani Navy, and it was *not* to ally yourself with terrorist rebels against the Crown's authority. It was absolutely and a thousand times *not* to participate in and lead a mutiny which killed scores of men and women. Men and women who, unlike *you*, died loyal to the oaths they had sworn.

"For all those reasons, I reject your claim to authority over me or any other officer or spacer of this fleet, and I once again call upon you to surrender yourself and your ships.

"I can and will make no promises about your own fate, should you do so. The power to pardon or commute rests with the Crown, and while I cannot speak for *Seine Majestät's* ultimate decision, I know him well. Because I do, I know he will at least listen to whatever you may wish to tell him in justification of your actions.

"But I would also suggest that whatever he does finally decide will be greatly influenced by how many more lives his navy must spend against you. By surrendering now, you can preserve the lives of those under your orders . . . and, perhaps, some fragment of your honor as an imperial officer.

"I urge you to consider this very, very carefully, Kapitänin der Sterne Hansen. If you persist in this course, if still more Andermani lives are squandered as a result of your actions, you will leave *Seine Majestät* no honorable choice but to keep faith with his dead and see justice done in their behalf. The window in which he can extend clemency, if he so chooses, is closing quickly."

He looked levelly into the pickup.

"Basaltberg, clear."

☆   ☆   ☆

"Basaltberg, clear."

The cold, uncompromising words dropped into the stillness of *Preussen's* command deck fifteen minutes after they had been transmitted.

Llyn hadn't expected Hansen's expression to change, and it didn't. She certainly must have anticipated that response from the moment she discovered Basaltberg was in command of Andrew's fleet. The question now was what she was going to say in response.

Had she perhaps expected to be facing someone else? From what Jachmann had told Amos about one of Gensonne's fellow conspirators still lurking in the shadows, it was possible the traitor was high enough in the Navy that Hansen had expected him to be in command instead of Basaltberg.

Alternatively, if the traitor himself wasn't in a position to help her, maybe she thought there were Andermani admirals who, while still a hundred percent loyal to the Crown, might nevertheless be willing to hold off on their attack until they'd investigated her claim. Certainly there must be senior officers on Potsdam who were concerned about Andrew's ability to handle the job he'd been thrust into.

But whichever way Hansen had been aiming her dice, she'd come up short. Basaltberg was here, Basaltberg was in command, and Hansen's only hopes now were either to stop him cold or to inflict so much damage to his forces that he had no choice but to retreat.

Both were still possible, Llyn knew, but both were risky. And neither would be pleasant.

At least the light-speed communications delay, a stray part of his mind noted, meant that she'd had plenty of time to sculpt her answer.

She straightened her spine and looked at Braunstein with a raised eyebrow.

"Live mic, *meine Kapitänin*," the com officer replied to the unspoken question, and Hansen faced the pickup.

"You know I can't do that, Graf von Basaltberg," she said levelly. "I've given my word to stand beside my allies, come what may. Whatever you may think of my actions or my claim upon the throne, I will betray neither my own nor my father's honor by violating that promise. If you are equally determined to obey your orders, then hold your course and engage us. My allies and I will face victory or defeat together.

"And whatever the outcome, know well that any victory against me will be dearly bought.

"Hansen-Anderman, clear."

A tense silence fell across the bridge. No one had had any doubts as to what Hansen was going to do, Llyn knew. But knowing something and hearing it spoken aloud could be profoundly different experiences.

Beside him, Quint stirred. "I think," she said quietly, "that it's time we returned to *Retribution*. With your permission, Captain Hansen?"

Hansen seemed to come back from a distant place. "Permission granted, Commodore," she said. "Make sure your forces are ready."

"We will be," Quint promised.

"And be of good cheer," Hansen added. "The numbers may look discouraging, but such math can be deceptive."

She smiled. "Especially when not all of the numbers are visible."

☆   ☆   ☆

The message on the intricately embossed paper inside the equally detailed envelope was waiting beside Winterfall's place at the conference table when he arrived for the morning session. He read it, tucked it away in his tunic, then went back to his new pre-meeting routine of dividing his attention between his notes and the greyhound Sunna, who'd taken to lying on the floor beside his chair during the daily sessions and bounding along eagerly with him whenever he went anywhere else.

Ten minutes and a great deal of scritching later, Außenminister Shān and the rest of the Andermani arrived, and the day's business began.

At one o'clock, Shān adjourned for lunch with the announcement that, since the winds and clouds of the previous week had finally cleared away, the midday meal would be served out in the courtyard where the delegates could enjoy the sunshine and spend some time touring the Emperor's gardens.

Winterfall had finished his lunch and was watching the greyhound attendants throwing balls and an enthusiastic cluster of dogs chasing madly after them when Strossmeyer joined him. "*Herr* Foreign Minister," the major greeted him. "You seemed pleased with this morning's results."

"Indeed I did, *danke*," Winterfall said. "We're nearly finished setting up a baseline for future trade structures."

"Excellent," Strossmeyer said. "I was wondering if you'd spoken to your colleagues about my possible immigration to Manticore."

"I have," Winterfall said. "We can't make any formal commitments, of course, but there are ways to expedite entry to the Star Kingdom for specially qualified applicants, and we feel you would definitely be among that number."

"Excellent," Strossmeyer said. "And did you—?"

He broke off as Sunna loped up, clearly looking for some attention. Winterfall crouched down and gave her a pet, a moment that was interrupted when the rest of the pack charged past a dozen meters away and Sunna charged off to join them in their running game.

"Sunna seems to have taken a liking to you," Strossmeyer commented. "What's your secret?"

"No secret, and I'm just as surprised as you are," Winterfall said. "I'd have thought they would be wary of strangers. Still, my mother breeds dogs back on Manticore—maybe Sunna senses the dog lover in me."

"It wouldn't surprise me," Strossmeyer said. "Was that a letter from the Emperor I saw you handling earlier?"

"It was, and on his own special note paper," Winterfall said, touching the pocket where he'd put the note. Actual paper communications were rare these days, though given the late Emperor Gustav's obsession with Old Earth Prussia a physical note shouldn't have been a surprise. "I've been invited to spend a few minutes alone with him in his study between the afternoon session and dinner."

"In his *study*?" Strossmeyer said, his eyes going momentarily wide. "That's—do you have any *idea* what a rare honor that is?"

"I had an inkling, yes," Winterfall said. "Even more so now."

"It's the room where Emperor Gustav spent his private time," Strossmeyer said. "It's where he met with close friends and worked on *Sternenkrieg*, his definitive work on military strategy and philosophy. It's filled with mementos of his life and pictures of his associates. Aside from his private bedroom, it's probably the most intimate place in the entire palace."

"Sounds like you're very familiar with it."

"The Emperor's *Totenkopfs* are familiar with *everything* having to do with the palace," Strossmeyer said with quiet pride. "Yes, I've stood guard there on occasion. But never when the Emperor was present. That duty and privilege was for others. I envy you this honor."

"Assuming he doesn't simply want a more private

setting in which to take me to task for something," Winterfall said, scrunching up his face a little.

"I doubt that," Strossmeyer said. "Regardless, I would be most interested in hearing about the meeting afterward."

"If it's something I can talk about, I'd be happy to do so," Winterfall promised. "Speaking of meetings and talking, I'd best return to the Audience Room and look over my notes for the next session."

"I believe you have one more task to perform before that." Strossmeyer nodded over Winterfall's shoulder. "Sunna is coming back for some more petting before her nap."

☆   ☆   ☆

The afternoon session was a bit rockier than the morning one had been. The Andermani finance minister's representative had firm ideas on how balance of trade deals should be worked, while the delegate Winterfall had brought from the Exchequer had equally firm ideas, but in different directions.

But between Shān and Winterfall the two men were eventually able to draw back a little from their positions without any actual duel challenges being issued. The Empire and Star Kingdom were still a long way from agreement, but it was a start.

At five o'clock, Shān called the session to a close, and the delegates scattered to their various quarters or homes to rest and prepare for the evening meal.

And it was time for Winterfall's private meeting with Emperor Andrew.

"Don't worry, you'll do fine," Strossmeyer said as he escorted Winterfall across the Audience Room to the Music Room and the study beyond it. "Just bow and smile and agree with him. That always worked with his father."

"I'll remember that," Winterfall promised. "And if he asks something I don't know the answer to, I'll pretend Sunna wants attention."

Strossmeyer looked down at the greyhound trotting placidly at Winterfall's side. "I don't think you'll need to pretend very hard," he said. "In my opinion, you're spoiling that dog."

"My mother always spoiled hers, too," Winterfall said. "It runs in the family."

"As do so many other things." Strossmeyer stopped, gesturing to the door directly ahead and the two *Totenkopfs* standing stolid guard beside it. "This is where I leave you. Good luck, and *Gott* be with you."

"Danke," Winterfall said. Taking a deep breath, he continued forward. As he did so, one of the *Totenkopfs* detached himself from the door, meeting Winterfall halfway for a quick but thorough check with a hand-held scanner. A subtle hand signal, and the other guard pulled the door open. Nodding his thanks, Winterfall stepped through, Sunna at his side.

Emperor Andrew was already there, seated behind an old-style desk. Behind him stood two extra-tall *Totenkopfs*; in a chair to the Emperor's left was Baronesse Shenoa, her eyes steady on Winterfall's face.

"Guten Abend, Herr Winterfall," the Emperor said, gesturing to a chair in front of him. "Please, be seated."

"Danke, Majestät," Winterfall said, wincing as he sat down. After all the preparation and all the planning, it looked like the whole thing was now going to end in failure and embarrassment.

And all of them knew it was Winterfall's fault. It

had been his vague suspicions that had started the whole thing going in the first place, after all. Not only was the Emperor probably disappointed, he was very likely annoyed at what his guest had put him through. "My deepest apologies, Majestät, for wasting your time this way."

"Wasting my time?" Andrew echoed, raising an eyebrow. "Hardly, *mein Herr.*"

"But—" Winterfall's eyes flicked to Marija, back to Andrew. "But he was supposed to—"

"Give you something?" Andrew smiled tightly. "*Nein, mein Herr.* You underestimate him." He gave a short whistle and Sunna, who'd just settled down beside Winterfall, lurched back to her feet and trotted around the desk to look up in eager anticipation at the young man. Rubbing the greyhound's head with one hand, Andrew reached beneath the dog's collar with the other. For a moment the fingers seemed to be searching; and then they emerged, holding a flat lump of a clay-like substance.

A lump with a small electronic circuit embedded in it.

Winterfall stared at the clay, a fist seeming to close around his heart. Behind him, he heard the door open again—

"My only question," Andrew said quietly, "is why you hate me so much."

For a moment the room was silent. Winterfall stayed motionless as long as could bear. Then, knowing it would break the moment, he turned his head.

Strossmeyer stood behind him, the two *Totenkopfs* who'd been at the door standing at his sides and gripping his upper arms. One of the guards, Winterfall noted with the eerie feeling of a near-death experience, was holding what appeared to be a small transmitter.

"You misunderstood, Majestät," Strossmeyer said, the tone of his voice wrapping the title in contempt. "I don't hate you. Nor did I hate your father."

"Then why did you try to depose him?" Andrew lifted the clay a couple of centimeters. "And why did you try to kill *me*?"

"For the same reason," Strossmeyer said. "My love of the Empire and her people."

"For *love*?" Marija said. There was a quiet, deadly anger in her voice that sent a shiver up Winterfall's back.

Strossmeyer's eyes flicked to Marija, then shifted again to Andrew. "Your father was senile," he said. "You're weak and untested. Only with strong, competent leaders can the Empire survive."

"And you thought *this*—" Andrew waved the clay again "—would cause such leaders to arise?"

Strossmeyer favored him with a thin smile. "That leader has already arisen," he said. "She will soon come into her own and claim the crown that is rightfully hers."

"And should such hopes fail, you planned to run from your part of it?" Andrew demanded bluntly. "This Empire you claim to love—you would flee from it on the first available ship?"

Strossmeyer's face had gone to carved stone. "I need not justify my actions to you, Majestät. I'll merely repeat that another, more suitable leader will soon ascend to the throne. And if *Gott* grants me breath, I will be there to see it."

"*Gott* will grant you breath at His own pleasure," Andrew said quietly. "But you will not see your hoped-for leader ascend to anything. Admiral Donnic, whom you believed you had persuaded to your ill-advised cause, has reconsidered his rash pledge."

Strossmeyer's expression cracked long enough for a flicker of surprise and disbelief to cross his face. "You lie," he said.

"He also no longer commands *Liegnitz*," Andrew continued as if Strossmeyer hadn't spoken. "You may find it interesting that in his letter of resignation he stated that it was the Tomlinson insurrection, and my response to it, that persuaded him that I am indeed fit to be Emperor."

Strossmeyer's eyes flicked to Winterfall, back to Andrew. "He is entitled to his opinions and decisions," he said stiffly.

"As are we all," Andrew agreed. "And you will now have time to contemplate the consequences of yours."

He made a small gesture. The two guards tightened their grip on Strossmeyer's arms and turned him around, marching him back through the door. One of the *Totenkopfs* behind Andrew stepped forward, carefully took the clay from the Emperor's hand, and hurried out behind them.

"And so it ends," Andrew said. With the confrontation over, he seemed to shrink a little in his chair, his eyes unfocusing to something in the distance. Or, perhaps, to something in the past. "My father always suspected there was one last conspirator the investigation had failed to root out. Now, he can finally rest." His eyes came back and focused on Winterfall. "We owe you a great debt of gratitude, *Herr* Winterfall, for your part in exposing this traitor. Thank you."

"It was my honor and privilege, Majestät," Winterfall

managed. So there'd been *another* person besides him that Strossmeyer had been trying to manipulate? The possibility of a second traitor hadn't even occurred to him. "Ah . . . that *was* a bomb, was it not?"

"Yes, indeed," Andrew confirmed, looking at his fingers. "One sufficient to shatter this room and everyone in it. And you're right, we assumed he would plant it on you before our meeting. I didn't expect him to use one of my own greyhounds as his angel of death." He reached down and gave Sunna's head an extra rub. "May he be doubly damned for that."

"Agreed," Winterfall said, looking at the dog. To put an explosive on an innocent greyhound's collar in order to kill her master . . . "Though *angel* is hardly the word I would use for him."

"No, the honor of that designation belongs to you, *Herr Baron*," Andrew said quietly. "To accept the role of bait in a situation in which neither you nor your government has any role or responsibility is friendship of a depth that should be honored and hailed from the highest tower."

He paused, and a shadow seemed to cross his face. "I say *should* because the reality is that no one outside these rooms must ever know of your courage. The people must never know there was a deadly plot against their Emperor. Certainly not until they have learned to have confidence in me and my rule."

"I understand, Majestät," Winterfall said. "To be honest, I was wondering how I was going to put all this into my report anyway."

"Yet another problem solved," Andrew said with a slight smile. Slight, but with a warmth Winterfall hadn't seen in him before.

"Yes," Winterfall said. "One question, Majestät, if I may?"

"You want to know what will become of him?"

"I'm sure he'll receive whatever justice is called for," Winterfall said. "My question was how you knew. My vague feelings about him certainly weren't enough. I couldn't properly express them. I'm not sure I even believed them myself."

Andrew gestured to Marija. "You were the one who caught it, Marija. Tell him."

"It was when he said it wasn't as if Emperor Andrew would give him a ship of his own and speed him on his way," Marija said. "That's exactly what Emperor Gustav did for the last of the conspirators in that failed coup. The officer in question had been only peripherally connected to the plot, and partially redeemed himself at the end, so instead of imprisoning him the Emperor gave him a captured enemy frigate and allowed him to go into exile."

Winterfall swallowed. "That wasn't general knowledge, I assume?"

"Not at all," Andrew said. "But it was something the last of those conspirators would have been aware of. Something that had probably gnawed at his soul for the past eighteen years."

Winterfall frowned. "That your father had shown mercy?"

"That my father had taken away Gensonne's chance to die with dignity," Andrew said.

"I see," Winterfall murmured. "No, there was indeed no dignity to his death."

"Nor was there any honor." Andrew straightened up in his chair. "And now, *Herr* Foreign Minister," he continued in a more formal tone, "the evening meal is near at hand. I release you to return to your quarters and preparations."

"Thank you, Majestät," Winterfall said, standing up and bowing.

"And once again, I thank you," the Emperor added. "As I said, most will never know what happened here today."

He looked again at Marija. "But those of us who do will never forget. On that, *mein Freund*, you have my promise."

CHAPTER TWENTY-TWO

"COMMENCE DECELERATION AND deploy the drones,"
Basaltberg ordered.

"*Jawohl, Herr Admiral*," Fregattenkapitän Schlamme
said crisply, and looked at one of his petty officers.
"Deploy," he said.

Just under two hours had elapsed since Hansen's
last, defiant transmission, and *Gerechtigkeitsgeschwader*
was halfway across the sparse debris field that was the
system's outer asteroid belt. A little over eighty-seven
million kilometers, a little under five light-minutes,
yet to go. The squadron had already turned end-for-
end, pointing its units' sterns at the point in space
Tomlinson would occupy in the next few hours. Their
wedges came back up at Basaltberg's order, and Travis
watched the displays as the ships began decelerating
at just over two hundred gravities.

He winced a little with embarrassment. Even the
massive battleships *Friedrich der Grosse* and *Vergeltung* had an acceleration rate that was almost twenty
percent greater than even that of a relatively nimble

RMN destroyer. Yet more proof of how far behind Travis's navy lagged.

Tomlinson's magnified image was a marble on the visual display, one side bathed in the system primary's light. But that marble was going to grow . . . and when it was big enough, the battle would begin.

"I'm looking forward to seeing one of their recon drones in action," Lisa commented from beside him.

"You're going to be disappointed," Travis said. "Those drones are the next best thing to invisible."

"I was speaking figuratively," she said with the combination of mock patience and mock exasperation that she was getting quite good at.

"Actually, *I* wasn't," he said. "Their stealth technology's another area where they're light-years ahead of us. Once the drones' running and position lights go down, they really *are* invisible."

"Unless you know where to look?"

"Even then it's problematic," Travis said. "We saw one in action at Walther, remember. Once it went dark we couldn't find it on visuals and never got a sniff off of it from any of our active systems. Even when its impeller wedge went active *Casey* could barely detect it, and *that* was again knowing where it was. Hansen and her people are going to play merry hell trying to pick it up."

"Maybe," Lisa said. "But remember that unlike Gensonne's people, Hansen knows Basaltberg has at least one of them available to him. Plus, she has the full specs on the system, which gives her all of the stealth parameters."

"For whatever good that'll do them," Travis said. "Granted, the drones are pretty myopic, especially when their wedges are up. But a starship's a hard thing to hide if you have even a vague idea of the approximate volume to search in. And, as you say, the other side already knows Basaltberg's got them, so it won't cost him anything in terms of surprise even when the first one goes active."

In point of fact, he knew, the number of possible surprises still waiting out there should be fairly limited. Long-range visual observation had already located many of the Freets' ships, and he had no doubt the drone would use its active systems in its flyby of the planet. Even though it would pass Tomlinson at a fair distance, in order to avoid being successfully engaged by the planet's defenders, that range wouldn't prevent it from getting a detailed look at who was waiting for them.

Still, it was always possible to miss something. Even under strict emission control and with the wedge down, a lurking ship usually had a heat signature, but at a great enough distance that profile could disappear into the background. The Andermani fleet would just have to hope the drones would get close enough to spot any such lurkers.

"I've always hated the waiting part," Lisa said, her eyes turning distant. Probably remembering similar times on other ships, Travis thought. "I'd rather just get it over with."

"I understand," Travis said. Though for his money, things happened more than quickly enough once the combatants finally reached engagement range.

In this case, the waiting time was going to be longer than usual, or at least longer than the physics and geometry required. A least-time transit would have taken the Andermani to Tomlinson in just seventy-nine minutes, but since it would send them past the planet and insurgent forces at nearly twelve thousand KPS there was hardly any point to it. Alternatively, Basaltberg could have opted to accelerate another eighty-two minutes before starting his fleet's deceleration and they would have reached orbit five and a quarter hours after their arrival.

But the admiral was in no hurry, and had elected instead to maintain the same steady 18,000 KPS he'd brought across the hyper wall, coasting ballistically towards his objective.

Time is not my enemy. Basaltberg had said that to the two Manticorans two days ago during a private conversation in his cabin.

He'd had a point. Whatever reinforcements may or may not have arrived at Tomlinson would already be there by the time *Gerechtigkeitsgeschwader* made its appearance, and there was little to be gained by charging in any faster than necessary.

On the contrary, there was a great deal to be said for exercising extra caution during their approach. Twenty T-years earlier, another Andermani battleship, *Bayern*, had been mousetrapped and destroyed in this same system. Hansen was well aware of that incident—and of course knew that Basaltberg also knew the details—and it seemed unlikely that she would try a similar strategy. Still, it would be wise to move slowly and feel out her ship deployment, and from that her likely strategy.

There was also the possibility that the insurgents might decide to make a run for it, in which case *Gerechtigkeitsgeschwader*'s slower approach might possibly allow them to escape the Andermani force completely. But no one expected them to do that. Not the Freets, because the whole point of their existence was to free Tomlinson from Andermani control; and not the mercenaries, because that would be a betrayal of their employers and bad for future business.

And if everyone else chose to stay and fight it out, Hansen would certainly do so.

Still, there remained one crucial question, one that Basaltberg and his staff had batted around without coming up with an answer. Given that Captain Hansen commanded the insurgents' lone battleship, it was logical to assume she was in overall command of the Freet forces. But that wasn't necessarily a given. With the number of ships *Gerechtigkeitsgeschwader* already knew about, the mercenaries the Freets had hired might be led by a commodore or even an admiral, and that higher-ranking officer could conceivably have assumed overall command of the defensive forces. That would mean all of Basaltberg's insights into Hansen's character and tactical habits might be useless.

But like so much else in warfare, that possibility was a two-edged sword. Hansen was emotionally wrapped up in this whole thing—whether or not she was genuinely Gustav Anderman's daughter, she clearly believed she was and that she'd been cheated out of the crown. A mercenary chief, on the other hand, might be able to look at the situation more dispassionately, recognize how overwhelming the force was that Emperor Andrew had sent against them, and seek some sort of negotiated surrender.

Granted, the terms Basaltberg had been authorized to offer would be far less than the Freets desired. But even the most limited terms would be better than wholesale death and destruction.

That was the best-case scenario. It was the outcome everyone from Basaltberg down hoped for.

It wasn't the outcome any of them expected.

No, the insurgents would stand and fight, and the result would be an obscene cost in lives and destruction, not just for the combatants, but also for the ordinary people of Tomlinson.

And as Travis gazed across the bridge at Basaltberg, seated square-shouldered in his command chair, his face showing no sign of the anguish and regret he must already be feeling, he wondered just how obscene that cost would be.

☆   ☆   ☆

"They've begun decelerating, *meine Kapitänin*," Korvettenkapitän Kistler spoke up from *Preussen*'s tactical station. "Two-zero-two-point-two gravities."

"Acknowledged, TO," Hansen said, her image on *Retribution*'s com screen turning to the tactical plot. Llyn took the cue and likewise turned to see the same plot on Quint's display.

Not surprisingly, the solid red line marking Basaltberg's projected vector had now changed. Instead of bypassing the planet, it now ended in two and a half hours at a point still over five million kilometers short of Tomlinson. A slowly shifting amber cone continued beyond that point, displaying his possible position if he altered heading or acceleration yet again.

On the com display, Hansen snorted. "Trouble, Captain?" Quint called.

"Just noting the computer's spread of options, Commodore," Hansen said. "Gotthold Riefenstahl has many traits, but indecision isn't among them. I seriously doubt he has any intention of coming this far only to bypass the planet *or* stop five million kilometers out of range."

"He might *pause* there, though," Quint pointed out. "Take a breather to assess the situation."

"Yes, he might," Hansen agreed. "Speaking of which, make sure your people are keeping a close eye out for their drones. You probably won't see anything Basaltberg doesn't want you to see, but there's always the possibility. And I want to know how close they come to the planet, if there's any way to tell."

"Understood, Captain," Quint said. "We'll do our best. Congratulations on your insight, by the way. You'd said they weren't going to rush in, and you were right."

"Basaltberg is a methodical man, Commodore," Hansen agreed. "He's also well aware of what happened to *Bayern*. He'll come in at a low enough velocity to avoid any ambushes we might have set up."

"And to keep us from leading him *into* any," Quint said.

"Correct," Hansen said. "He's also not going to come barreling in too fast to back off if we break orbit and head for The Cloud."

"I doubt that's high on his anticipations list," Quint said. "The planet is the only truly important strategic objective in the entire star system. If we're willing to move off of it, he'll be more than happy to seize it and force us to come to him to take it back."

"Especially since Basaltberg isn't the type who just wants to kill people and break things," Hansen agreed. "He'd be more than happy to end this without a single drop of spilled blood if he could."

Quint looked at Llyn, and he could see the quiet regret in her eyes. Her own bit of bloodlust had died along with Gustav, and like Basaltberg her goal would be the cleanest victory possible.

But as Llyn had long since learned, few people if any ever got what they wanted.

"I can sympathize," Quint said. "Unfortunately, he's already rejected that option."

"Yes, he has," Hansen agreed. "Maybe once we bloody his nose a little—"

"Active sensors, *meine Kapitänin!*" Bajer cut into the conversation. "Radar and lidar."

"Source?" Hansen asked.

"Zero-one-zero, two-zero-one," Bajer said.

Llyn looked at *Retribution's* tactical. The red icon of a hostile impeller wedge had appeared at that location, barely thirty thousand kilometers from Tomlinson.

He frowned. Thirty thousand kilometers *past* Tomlinson, actually. Basaltberg had let his drone overshoot the planet? "What's he up to?" he asked quietly.

His intent had been for the question to be heard only by Quint. But the com mic was apparently better than he realized. "He's waving a big flag at us, of course, Mr. Llyn," Hansen answered. "Make no mistake: he *wanted* us to see it."

"Obviously," Quint said, as if even a civilian unschooled in proper navy strategy ought to have seen it. "Basaltberg knows that we know he has that capability, and he has two battleships out there that are both equipped to operate drones. If he didn't want us to see this one, it wouldn't have been decelerating at maximum power and giving away its position."

"For that matter, it would never have gone active in the first place," Hansen added, in the same tone.

"He wants us to see *this* one so that we know it isn't operating even deeper in-system."

"Like sweeping The Cloud?" Llyn suggested.

"Not necessarily," Hansen said.

"That *could* be what he's doing," Quint said. "But the second drone could just as easily be hanging around Tomlinson at a zero relative velocity. He could have released it outside of his alpha translation, let it accelerate to a higher velocity, then braked for a zero-zero with Tomlinson. If he timed it right, it would never have shown a wedge powerful enough for us to detect at anything above half a light-second. So it could be sitting out there right this minute, hiding only a hundred and fifty thousand klicks from us."

"Held ready in his right hand while he waves this one in his left as a distraction," Hansen concluded.

"I see," Llyn said. It was actually more explanation than he'd needed, but he'd learned that letting people finish their lectures had the dual advantage of giving them satisfaction and luring them into underestimating him. "So if it *is* sitting out there, how likely is it to have detected our surprise?"

"If it doesn't go to active sensors, not likely at all," Hansen assured him. "Not unless we do something to draw its attention. Not more likely to see anything than its friend did on its way past, at least."

"That one's in the wrong place and looking at us from the wrong angle to see much of anything," Quint added. "Especially since it would have to pick through all the freight and service platforms' shadows first."

"Understood," Llyn said. "I suppose we'll just have to wait and see."

"Which unfortunately sums up most of warfare,"

Quint said with a hint of a dry smile. "Incidentally, I'm going to be locking the spin section in about forty minutes. If you want to eat or do anything else that's easier in gravity, now's the time to do it."

"Thank you," Llyn said, pushing himself away from the bulkhead and floating toward the hatch. "There *is* something I need to do, actually."

"Just get back here as soon as you can," Quint said. "You wouldn't want to miss all the fun."

"No, I wouldn't," Llyn agreed.

But then, there was another bit of fun that Quint didn't know about. Fun that was about to happen right here in her ship.

Fun that Llyn had no intention of missing. Not for the world.

☆   ☆   ☆

Lisa was conversing with Oberleutnantin Unterberger about ship-to-ship tactics coordination when a musical tone chimed across the flag bridge.

"Alpha Drone telemetry is coming in, *Herr Graf*," Schlamme announced.

"Excellent," Basaltberg said. Pushing off with a toe, he sent himself across the flag bridge toward the tactical officer's station. He caught a handhold, brought himself to a halt, and hovered there, watching Schlamme's display as the fregattenkapitän downloaded the drone's report.

Lisa pushed off Unterberger's chair, heading for the admiral's side and noting Travis heading the same direction.

But she would get there first. Travis had already seen an Andermani drone in action, after all. Lisa hadn't, and it was only fair that she get the better of the limited number of viewing vantage points.

Sure enough, she brought herself to a stop just behind Basaltberg and nearly three seconds ahead of her husband.

Gerechtigkeitsgeschwader had begun decelerating ninety-five minutes ago, its closing velocity now down to just over twelve thousand KPS. The drones, which had traveled ballistically with the fleet's initial translation velocity of eighteen thousand KPS, had reached the planet two and a half minutes earlier.

"We have good passive data on...looks like fourteen units, *mein Herr,*" Schlamme reported, peering at the data scroll. "Confirm *Preussen,* four battlecruisers, two heavy cruisers, three light cruisers, and four destroyers. Emission signatures suggest that all four battlecruisers are *Iskra*-class. One of the heavy cruisers is probably a *Kenichi*-class; CIC's not sure about the other. None of the light cruisers or destroyers match anything in our database, although Fregattenkapitän Lindauer says at least one of the light cruisers *might* be a fairly heavily modified *Bataan*-class."

Lisa nodded to herself. She'd learned from Unterberger that Hong Lindauer, *Friedrich der Grosse*'s XO, was an avid ship completist. If he said the cruiser was modified *Bataan*-class, he was probably right.

"But only four destroyers," Basaltberg murmured.

"*Ja, Herr Graf.*" Schlamme looked up at the admiral. "It would appear the others are elsewhere."

"Indeed it would." Basaltberg glanced at the time display. "No doubt we will find out where soon enough."

He gave himself a half turn, caught Lisa's and Travis's eye, and nodded toward where chief of staff Kranz was waiting by Basaltberg's command chair. He gave himself a push that sent him drifting that direction, the two Manticorans following close behind. "You heard, Kapitänin der Sterne?" he asked as the three of them again came to a stop.

"*Ja, mein Herr,*" Kranz replied. Her lips puckered briefly in thought. "It's not what we expected."

"No, it isn't," Basaltberg agreed. "Interesting. I wish now that we'd programmed the Alpha Drone for a zero-zero with the planet. I should have liked a more extended examination of Kapitänin der Sterne Hansen's deployment."

Lisa nodded to herself. The Alpha Drone had fulfilled its assigned duty of passing by Hansen's ships and lighting off every active sensor, with the dual purpose of gathering as much data as possible while making its presence obvious to the insurgents. The up side was that it was going too fast for an effective response; the down side was that it would now take the drone over twenty minutes to decelerate to zero. If Basaltberg wanted it to then return to Tomlinson's vicinity for more data that would add another twenty minutes.

Which would be just about the time *Gerechtig-keitsgeschwader* would reach Basaltberg's planned attack position, as well as the time the Beta Drone would reach the outer edge of The Cloud to see what might be hiding there.

The hope was that the Freets would see Alpha and never notice Beta. Not until it was too late.

"So you think the other destroyers are hiding in The Cloud?" Kranz asked.

"I can't see any other place Hansen could hide them where they would still be available for battle," Basaltberg said. "Still, I'd expected better. Something more creative than a repeat of the *Bayern* ambush."

"Perhaps this offers an answer to the question as to who is in control of their deployment," Kranz said. "If the mercenary commander is unfamiliar with the *Bayern* incident, he or she might indeed attempt something similar."

"Excuse me, *Herr Admiral*," Lisa said, feeling uncomfortably like she was talking out of turn. "But I don't think Kapitänin der Sterne Hansen has yielded command."

"We've been through this, Commander—" Kranz began.

She stopped at a small gesture from Basaltberg. "Explain, please," he invited.

"Kapitänin der Sterne Hansen is driven by passion," Lisa said, mentally crossing her fingers. This had all sounded reasonable in her head, and she could only hope it stayed that way when it came out as actual words. "She has a mission, a burning desire to right what she sees as an enormous wrong. The mercenaries are here because they were hired and because it's their job."

She waved a hand toward the distant planet. "It doesn't matter that Hansen may be too involved to see things clearly. It doesn't even matter if she recognizes that fact. This is *her* operation, and she won't let anyone get in her way. Not *anyone*."

"And if the mercenary commander insists?" Kranz asked.

"Then that commander is dead," Lisa said bluntly. "I've known people like this, *Herr Admiral*. She will complete her mission, or die in the attempt. And so will anyone who gets in her way."

For a moment Basaltberg didn't speak. Then, he

gave a small nod. "I've known Kapitänin der Sterne Hansen all her life, Commander and, unfortunately, I must concur. I say *unfortunate* because it means there is little to no chance of a negotiated surrender."

He looked at the tactical. "And because I can't believe Kapitänin der Sterne Hansen will try something she knows I know about. That means she's come up with something new."

"Such as, *Herr Graf*?" Kranz asked.

"That's the problem," Basaltberg said. "I have no idea."

☆   ☆   ☆

Llyn had been waiting in Quint's private galley for about ten minutes when Amos came through the hatch.

"Oh—Mr. Llyn," the steward said, clearly surprised to see Llyn sitting quietly in the chair he'd placed against the aft bulkhead. "Sorry, sir—I thought you were with Commodore Quint on the bridge."

"I was," Llyn confirmed. "Now I'm here. Why are *you* here?"

"I heard the announcement that the spin section would be locking down in half an hour," Amos said. "I thought I'd make the commodore some tea before we lost gravity. It's much harder to prepare in zero-G."

"Very thoughtful of you," Llyn said approvingly. "Did you have any plans as to where you would wait out the battle?"

Amos shrugged as he crossed to the stove and popped the kettle loose from its restraints. "My official station is in aft damage control, but I'm going to try to also keep an eye on the commodore's cabin. Clean up anything that gets knocked loose, make sure it's ready for her return. Just basic tidiness."

"Also very commendable," Llyn said. "Though if things start getting knocked loose the entire ship is probably in serious trouble already. I don't know if you've been paying attention to the repeaters, but we've got some heavy-duty trouble coming at us."

"Indeed we do," Amos agreed soberly. He got the water heating, then crossed to the pantry cabinet and began perusing Quint's selection of teas. "I'm afraid Captain Hansen is in for the fight of her career. And Commodore Quint, too, of course." He looked over his shoulder at Llyn. "I presume you have a plan for getting us off the ship before all that trouble starts happening?"

"There are a couple of options," Llyn said. "Simplest is to forge an order giving us access to a shuttle for some sort of special mission or errand on Tomlinson. Once we're there we disappear into the population, wait for all the dust to settle from New Berlin's response to all this, then wait a little more until Axelrod sends a transport."

"Sounds reasonable," Amos said. "You have new identities for us?"

"I have a new identity for *me*," Llyn said. "I didn't know you were part of the equation when I was making the arrangements."

"Of course." Amos flashed him a smile. "That's all right. Bryce set me up before she left *Retribution*."

"I rather thought she would."

"She's one of the best," Amos said, selecting a package and turning back to the kettle. "A nice Da Hong Pao, I think. An import from Potsdam the commodore has become quite fond of since our arrival here. Captain Hansen would probably hate it just on general political principle. When were you planning on leaving?"

"Actually," Llyn said, "I wasn't."

Amos frowned, pausing in the middle of opening the tea packet. "Excuse me?"

"I'm staying," Llyn told him. "Quint is going to see this through. I've decided to see it through with her."

"That wasn't the plan," Amos said. His casual, almost light-hearted tone was gone, leaving something cool and dark in its place. "We—*you*—were supposed to get Quint's mercenaries here, stir up enough chaos to draw Andermani attention away from Manticore for the next few years, and not leave any traces behind."

"Oh, I won't leave any traces," Llyn assured him.

"Your dead body qualifies as a trace," Amos countered bluntly.

"I'm not expecting Quint to lose."

"You were the one who just told *me* how much firepower Admiral Basaltberg was bringing to the table."

"You're welcome to go," Llyn told him. "Those falsified shuttle orders I mentioned are already in place. You can go whenever you want. Sooner rather than later would probably be best."

"That's not how this was supposed to go," Amos said, his voice darkening a little more. "And I have no interest in returning to Axelrod just to tell them I took off and left you behind."

"You want me to write you a note?"

Amos's eyes narrowed. "I'm serious, Llyn."

"So am I," Llyn said. "Leave if you want. I'm staying."

Amos hissed out a breath. "Fine." He turned his back on Llyn, stepping to the cabinet beside the stove and pulling out a vacuum flask. "Just don't forget I warned you."

"I won't," Llyn assured him. "Incidentally, don't bother looking for your poisons. I've already found and destroyed them."

Amos's face was still turned away. But the sudden stiffness of his back was all the confirmation Llyn needed. "Excuse me?" the steward asked, his voice far too casual.

"Oh, and I got your scratch-stick, too," Llyn added. "Nice little gadget, that. Someone gets poisoned after drinking tea, you naturally suspect the tea. When it turns up safe, they start hunting for something else that was eaten or inhaled. No one pays any attention to a small scratch that even the victim probably didn't notice at the time."

"It has to be done, Llyn," Amos said, still not turning around. "She has to die."

"There's a fair chance the battle will do that without any help from you."

"She has to die *before* Basaltberg gets here," Amos amended, his voice still calm. "That way the insurgent battle plan collapses, the Andermani win quickly and handily, and the status quo remains."

"But if Hansen wins, the Empire collapses into chaos," Llyn said. "Then Silesia rises to the forefront, Manticore screams to Haven for help, Haven moves in to protect them, and suddenly Axelrod has a much harder time taking over the system. Yes, I've heard all the doomsaying and run all the scenarios, too."

"Then you agree it has to be done."

"I agree that *Axelrod* thinks it has to be done," Llyn said. "But for once, that's not good enough."

"I'm sorry to hear that," Amos said. "I will, of course, have to report—"

And in the middle of the threat, he spun around and hurled the vacuum flask directly at Llyn's head.

He was halfway into his follow-up leaping attack when Llyn's shot caught him squarely in the chest and dropped him to the deck.

Llyn got his arm up mostly in time to deflect the flask, bouncing it off his forearm and cheek and sending it clattering across the galley. Wincing at the sudden double dose of pain, he nevertheless kept his eyes and gun focused on Amos. At this range electric-discharge rounds were nearly always instantly lethal, while the completely silent break-apart airgun that fired them was guaranteed not to attract unwanted attention.

Still, it was theoretically possible for Amos's clothing to have muffled the shock just enough to leave him alive. And if there was anything about this that Llyn couldn't afford right now, it was leaving Amos alive.

But the other remained motionless, with none of the twitching that might indicate parts of his nervous system were still functional. Just to be sure, Llyn fired a second shot, this one into Amos's back, before crossing to the figure and confirming the man was indeed dead.

For a long moment Llyn gazed down at the body, an odd feeling in the pit of his stomach. He'd killed many people throughout his career, more than he cared to remember. But those deaths had always been necessary to complete his assigned mission. This was the first time he'd killed one of Axelrod's own.

The fact that Amos was simply trying to fulfill *his* assigned mission just made it worse.

But Llyn had had no choice. Quint was a good

commander, and she'd come into this in good faith. She'd delivered value for Axelrod's investment, and there was no way she deserved to die. Certainly not by Amos's hand. Certainly not to mitigate vague future problems that no one could possibly predict with any reasonable accuracy.

Llyn had never defied his superiors before. Never. He'd had to improvise, or change details of a plan, or sometimes scrap a plan entirely. But he'd never done anything of the sort unless it was absolutely necessary, and he'd always done it with an eye toward finding a way back around the thistles to the ultimate goal he'd been set.

Maybe he could think of this one in that same way. He wasn't defying Axelrod, but merely stopping another agent from making a tragic mistake. It certainly wasn't—

He bared his teeth in sudden anger and contempt. *For the love of a good woman* was such a horrible cliché that his mind refused to even consider the concept.

Axelrod black ops agents had no emotions. They couldn't afford them. Not hate, resentment, or joy, and certainly not love. Good agents planned and carried out their missions with calmness, efficiency, and dedication—nothing more, nothing less. Quint was merely one more in a long line of assets Llyn had used and then abandoned. She simply had too much use left in her to be discarded this soon.

From across the galley came a familiar chime. Standing up, checking his throbbing cheek to see if Amos's attack had drawn any blood—it hadn't—Llyn crossed to the intercom and keyed it on. "Llyn."

"Quint," the commodore's voice came. "Just reminding you that lock-down's in fifteen minutes."

"Thank you," Llyn said. "Do you need me to do anything before that?"

"Actually, I was wondering if Amos might be there and might brew me up a flask of tea," Quint said. "It's going to be a long couple of hours in here."

"I haven't seen him," Llyn said, looking over at the body. "But if I can figure out how to use the kettle I'd be happy to make you some tea myself. Anything in particular you'd like?"

"Surprise me," Quint said. "Thank you."

"I'll be there soon," Llyn promised.

The intercom keyed off.

Llyn checked the water, confirmed it was almost hot enough, and finished opening the tea packet Amos had chosen. The steward knew Quint's tastes even better that Llyn, and if this was the one he'd picked as the last beverage she would ever drink, Llyn was happy to go with it.

But before he made the tea, he had a body to get rid of. Fortunately, he'd scoped out the options and made the necessary plans a long time ago.

He was in a lift car with Quint's flask in hand when the lock-down alert began to sound. Somewhere down the line, he knew, he would probably be called on to explain Amos's disappearance, and he knew the explanation had damned well better be good. But that was the future, and there would be a massive battle before that question even arose.

And in the meantime Commodore Quint would be alive.

Besides, there was still the question of Quint's charge of murder against the late Emperor Gustav. Llyn had no idea how the Andermani or Emperor Andrew would deal with that when she was finally able to make her case.

But he was rather interested in finding out.

CHAPTER TWENTY-THREE

"NINE MILLION KILOMETERS, *Herr Graf*," Basaltberg's staff navigator Fregattenkapitänin Shuren Hasselreider announced.

Lisa looked at her chrono. Nine million kilometers out from Tomlinson; fourteen minutes since the Alpha Drone's report was first received. It was nearly time for Travis to leave the flag bridge and take up his battle position in CIC.

"Very good," Basaltberg said, turning to Travis and Lisa. "Lieutenant Commander?"

"*Ja, Herr Admiral,*" Travis said.

Lisa braced herself. Make that *exactly* time for him to go.

And the look on her husband's face as he turned to her was exactly a match for the one she was trying so hard to hide.

Best for her to get in the first word. "Don't worry, I'll be fine," she assured him. As if a promise like that meant a single damn thing on a ship heading into battle. "You just stay clear of trouble yourself."

"I will," Travis said, making the same useless promise in return. "And remember why we're here."

"To make sure the Andermani abide by the rules of the Deneb Agreement," Lisa said.

"*And* that the Freets and mercenaries out there do likewise," Travis added. "I can keep an eye on the data flow in CIC, but you're the one who will hear all the communications."

Lisa nodded. Which meant she would be the first one on the hot seat if the Solarian League ever came to investigate what happened at Tomlinson today and Emperor Andrew sent his two Manticoran observers to testify on the Empire's behalf.

This had looked like a wonderful opportunity when first presented, a chance to see Andermani tactics and combat skill in action. Now, with battle looming and the specter of hard-eyed men and women in Solarian legal robes picking at their memories, it didn't seem nearly as attractive.

The fact that she and Travis would be going into danger in entirely different parts of the ship just made it worse.

But that was how it had to be. They were here to make sure everyone followed the rules of warfare; and while duplicate observations and memories could be useful, overlapping ones were better.

The fact remained that, given the realities of warfare, this might be the last time they ever saw each other.

She wanted to give him a kiss good-bye. She *really* wanted to, and she could tell he did, too. But they were on an Andermani ship, surrounded by an awesome depth of social and cultural reserve, and she and Travis already felt like backwards, unsophisticated cousins.

And so they settled for a quick touch of hands, and an exchange of brave but strained smiles.

Then Travis was gone, headed to CIC and the aft engineering section of the battleship. Lisa watched until he had disappeared through the hatch, then turned her eyes to Korvettenkapitän Wuying Haberman and the TO's spread of tactical displays. She had a job to do, and uncultured cousin or not, she was damned well going to do it.

Travis would be fine. *She* would be fine.

But in the back of her mind she could hear the whispered words of doom.

Damn all those teen-age dramas and tear-jerkers, anyway.

☆   ☆   ☆

"They've stopped decelerating, *meine Kapitänin*," Kistler's voice came from *Retribution*'s bridge speaker. "Range from planet, nine million kilometers."

"Interesting," Hansen murmured, her image on *Retribution*'s com display looking thoughtful as she gazed at her displays.

"Is that good or bad?" Llyn asked Quint quietly.

"Not necessarily either," Quint said, finishing her last sip of tea and resealing the flask. "Mostly just unexpected."

"At least now I know how he plans to approach," Hansen said, turning to look at the com connection to *Retribution*.

"Walk us through it, please," Quint said.

Llyn smiled to himself. *For the benefit of our resident ignorant civilian,* she might have added. But Quint was far too classy for that.

"First, he's not going to reduce to zero where we first projected," Hansen said. "Which was, granted, always unlikely. But he's still closing at thirty-six hundred KPS, which gives him plenty of acceleration advantage to catch us if we decide to run for The Cloud at this late date."

"He still thinks we might do that?" Quint asked.

"Basaltberg likes to cover all his bases," Hansen said. "More importantly—and probably of higher priority in his mind—is that he can still kill all his remaining approach velocity in about thirty minutes, which would allow him to stop advancing before he enters our missile range."

"Sounds like the cautious type," Llyn suggested.

"He is that," Hansen agreed. "But don't make the mistake of confusing caution with timidity. Once he's decided on his move, he'll fully commit himself to it."

"Sounds like the kind of commander you like to have on your side," Quint commented.

"No argument from me," Hansen said. "Maybe when I'm Empress Florence and I've accepted his resignation the Quintessence can offer him a position."

"Let's get past this particular hurdle first," Quint said. "So Basaltberg doesn't panic. Does he expect that kind of behavior from his opponents?"

"Maybe not *expect* it," Hansen said. "But he would certainly be open to the possibility."

"Well, then." Quint looked at Llyn, a tight smile on her lips. "Perhaps it's time we did so."

"I believe it is," Hansen agreed, and her image on the com display turned in the direction of her com officer. "Oberleutnantin Braunstein, send the order."

☆   ☆   ☆

"Transmission from the Beta Drone," Unterberger announced from the ATO position in front of the enormous plot in *Friedrich der Grosse*'s Combat Information Center.

"Acknowledged," the battleship's XO, Fregattenkapitän Lindauer, said from the command chair to her left. "Let's see what we've got."

Alphanumeric data began to scroll across Unterberger's display. Floating at his assigned place behind the two senior officers, Travis took a moment to look around, trying to absorb everything.

There was a *lot* there for him to absorb. CIC was located between the battleship's command deck and flag bridge, adjacent to Damage Control Central, serving the two command centers as the primary evaluator of every sensor reading and tactical transmission from the fleet. Every scrap of information coming in was processed here, then passed on to Admiral Basaltberg or Kapitänin der Sterne Sternberger as either of those senior officers requested.

For Travis, the most profound difference between this arrangement and standard Manticoran doctrine was the deployment of the senior officers. A battleship was big enough to survive damage that would destroy or mission-kill a smaller unit, and CIC's physical separation from both flag bridge and command deck created a third command node that could keep *Friedrich der Grosse* in the fight even if Sternberger and Basaltberg were both killed.

Hence, the presence of XO Lindauer and ATO Unterberger. Not only would Lindauer be able to take up command if necessary, but being stationed in CIC also meant that he was fully up-to-date on the ship's and fleet's tactical situation. In addition, having an extra set of skilled and experienced eyes monitoring the data flow meant Lindauer could decide instantly if Basaltberg or Sternberger needed to be advised of something beyond the parameters they'd specified.

Still, impressed as Travis was, there were parts of the arrangement that he quietly disagreed with. During one of Carrino's orientation tours during the voyage, he'd been surprised to learn that CIC lacked either of the two command decks' direct ship controls. He could understand that, until a takeover was necessary, the personnel in here were to be totally focused on their primary function of processing information and presenting it to Basaltberg and Sternberger on clean, uncluttered displays optimized for quick evaluation and response. But if CIC *was* called upon to take command, that lack of direct control capability might slow the ship's maneuvers and responses.

On the other hand, as Carrino had explained—and this time without any of his usual spread of good humor—if that situation ever occurred it was likely that *Friedrich der Grosse*'s maneuverability would already be severely limited.

Travis turned back to Unterberger's display just as the alphanumeric data resolved into a cluster of angry red icons on the periphery of The Cloud. Lindauer regarded them through narrowed eyes for a moment, then punched a button.

"Herr Admiral, meine Kapitänin," he said into his boom mic, "the Bravo Drone has just detected nine—I repeat, *nine*—destroyer-range impeller wedges accelerating out of The Cloud at one-point-eight-four-five KPS squared."

☆   ☆   ☆

"So now we know where the missing destroyers have been hiding, *Herr Graf*," Kranz commented.

"*Ja*, we do," Basaltberg acknowledged. "Along with at least one more ship than we thought they had. The question, of course, is *why* they are where they are."

Lisa rubbed a fingertip absently across her lower lip as she studied the flag bridge plot and the icons that had appeared simultaneously with Lindauer's report. The admiral had a good point. From the insurgent destroyers' current position, 1.23 light-minutes from Tomlinson, it would take them just over two and a half hours to make a zero-zero with the planet. If all they wanted was a bypass, they could achieve that in less than eighty minutes, shooting past at 9,280 KPS.

But none of those numbers or strategies made sense to her. *Gerechtigkeitsgeschwader* had shaved another million and a half kilometers from their own range to the planet, which meant that even without accelerating *Friedrich der Grosse* and her consorts would reach Tomlinson orbit in only another thirty-five minutes. If the ships in company with the planet headed to meet the newly detected destroyers and Basaltberg went in pursuit at two hundred gravities from his present overtake velocity, he'd still catch them over two hours short of the oncoming destroyers.

"On the face of it, this deployment makes no sense," Basaltberg continued, his words echoing Lisa's silent doubts. "Their destroyers have lost the element of stealth, and yet they can't possibly intervene before we've decisively engaged the main force."

"Perhaps Commander Donnelly Long's reasoning for Kapitänin der Sterne Hansen being in command was flawed," Kranz suggested, throwing a quick look at Lisa.

"I don't think so," Basaltberg said before Lisa could come up with a response. "If the insurgent commander wanted to repeat the ambush of *Bayern*, they would have begun falling back from Tomlinson no more than an hour after our arrival. They didn't."

He pointed at the display. "But note the timing. They've revealed their destroyers just about the time Kapitänin der Sterne Hansen would have anticipated our second recon drone would be approaching The Cloud."

"You think they're showing themselves to us on purpose, *Herr Admiral*?" Lisa asked.

"A distinct possibility, Commander," Basaltberg said. "They could be drawing our attention there in hopes that we'll miss something more critical."

"Or else whoever is in charge simply panicked," Kranz put in. Clearly, she wasn't quite ready yet to accept the theory that Hansen was still in command. "Or else thought that if the planetary defenders hurt us badly enough, that many undamaged destroyers might be able to deal with our remnants."

"What they might be able to do afterward seems to me to be an unwise reason to leave that many launchers out of the main engagement," Lisa pointed out.

"It does indeed," Basaltberg agreed. "We'll just have to keep both our eyes and our options open. I'm sure that sooner or later the insurgents' strategic reasoning will become clear."

Lisa winced. "Perhaps at the point of a missile wedge."

"Very likely," Basaltberg said. "In the meantime, we'll carry on as planned."

"No changes, then, *Herr Graf*?" Kranz asked.

"Correct, Kapitänin der Sterne," Basaltberg told her. He paused, gazing for another moment at the display, then nodded. "No. No changes."

☆   ☆   ☆

Twenty-nine minutes had passed. The range to Tomlinson had fallen to just under a million and a half kilometers.

And the tension on *Friedrich der Grosse*'s flag deck had hardened into something thick, dark, and very cold.

Lisa sat in her borrowed chair, her helmet in her lap, her gloved fingers drumming restlessly against it. She knew that tension. Knew it all too well. It was the anticipation of battle, the sharpness of focus, the hope of victory and the dread of defeat, the last chance to mentally run through all the factors and possibilities before the heat of battle plunged everything into chaos and uncertainty and trained reflexes.

Only here, for the first time in her career, she had no role to play in what was about to happen.

She wasn't in control of even the smallest part of the ship or fleet. She had no authority, no responsibility, no way to affect the smallest iota of the outcome. She was passenger, observer, occasional sounding board.

She was dead weight.

She hadn't expected to feel this way. But she did. And the knowledge that something was about to happen that was completely out of her control was stifling.

But she was a professional, and she would do her best to act like one. If for no other reason than to prove to the Andermani that she could.

"Launch in one minute," Sternberger's voice came in her earbud, and a countdown clock appeared in the master display, the seconds ticking downward with uncaring precision.

"Launching," Schlamme said.

Friedrich der Grosse twitched slightly as fusion boosters flared and four missiles exploded from her after-launchers. *Vergeltung* and the battlecruisers added another eight missiles to the salvo, and ten seconds later, they fired yet again.

"Decelerating," Hasselreider announced as a third salvo erupted from the launchers, the waves following each other as quickly as the launchers could reload, and went streaking toward Tomlinson.

"Good telemetry on the first salvo, *mein Herr*," Schlamme confirmed, and Basaltberg nodded.

"Acknowledged," Basaltberg said. "Stand by to pitch ship."

☆   ☆   ☆

"They've opened fire," Bajer said sharply.

"Not a full salvo, though, *meine Kapitänin*," Kistler said. "We show twelve point sources and—" He broke off. "Second salvo. They're ripple firing, *meine Kapitänin*. Three salvos, twelve missiles each."

"I see," Hansen replied. "Return fire: Fire Plan Hohenfriedberg."

"*Jawohl, meine Kapitänin*," Kistler replied, and sixty-nine missiles erupted from First Fleet's forward launchers.

"They're decelerating, Captain," Bajer reported.

"Of course they are," Hansen said calmly, her eyes on the missile icons streaking towards *Preussen* and the waiting Quintessence ships. "Kistler?"

"Launching second salvo," Kistler confirmed.

☆   ☆   ☆

"They've fired," Unterberger announced. "Sixty-plus incoming." She paused twelve seconds. "*Second* salvo launched," she amended.

"Acknowledged," Basaltberg's voice came from the CIC speakers. "Main combatants, stand by to pitch on my mark."

Travis watched the icons creeping across CIC's master plot. Basaltberg had limited his attack to his after-launchers, despite the fact that doing so allowed the defenders to fire much larger, much more concentrated salvos in reply.

But there'd been method in that apparent madness. Accepting the lighter throw weight had allowed Basaltberg to begin decelerating the instant the final wave left his launchers. That meant that, with *Friedrich der Grosse*'s base velocity adding to their own acceleration, those missiles now had an effective powered range of 1,410,000 kilometers, whereas Hansen's return fire had a maximum range of only 767,800.

Had Basaltberg maintained his original base velocity, the range would have fallen to 642,000 kilometers in the three minutes the Hansen's missiles' drives lasted, putting *Gerechtigkeitsgeschwader* well inside the insurgents' missile envelope. Now, instead, the Andermani ships would be outside that range, allowing them to defend against a ballistic attack rather than one that was under telemetry control.

But this was warfare. What that advantage ultimately meant, only the next few minutes would tell.

Space was vast, and impeller-driven missiles were relatively small targets. Yet, as the opposing missiles hurtled toward and then past each other, two of them actually met head on and wiped one another from the face of the universe. Their brethren, undeterred, continued toward their own dates with destruction.

Gerechtigkeitsgeschwader's attack reached its destination first. Eleven missiles hurtled into the defending starships' teeth, and defensive fire came to meet them. Reaction-drive counter-missiles were pathetically slow compared to the incoming attack birds, with a maximum range from rest of no more than fifteen hundred kilometers, but they did give the insurgents some area defense capability. Fast though incoming missiles might be, they still had to run pretty much straight at their target over those last fifteen hundred kilometers.

The defending missiles raced outward, then detonated, spreading clouds of shrapnel in the paths of the oncoming attackers, and at the velocities involved even a relatively tiny solid object wreaked catastrophic damage. Missiles that didn't simply break up might continue ballistically onward, but their threat value would instantly plummet to something very close to zero.

A third of *Gerechtigkeitsgeschwader*'s initial salvo died as the missiles slammed into those clouds of tiny solid objects. But the other eight screamed on, all of them heading for the same target.

Preussen.

The insurgents' autocannon opened up as the remaining missiles blew past the counter-missile barricade, firing streams of rocket-propelled shrapnel shells that duplicated the counter-missiles' proximity attack, but on a smaller scale. Together, *Preussen* and the Quintessence warships mounted thirty-three autocannon forward, a formidable defense against any missile attack. But in this case, only *Preussen* had the range to reach the incoming fire.

They did their best. But despite the withering torrent of defensive fire, two of *Friedrich der Grosse*'s birds broke through. One raced down *Preussen*'s starboard side and detonated just outside her sidewall. Sidewall generators screamed in protest as the megaton warhead smashed at them, but they held.

But the second missile entered the throat of the battleship's wedge...and detonated less than a kilometer from her hull.

☆   ☆   ☆

Alarms howled on *Preussen*'s command deck and the heavily armored battleship heaved in agony.

"Missile One and Two out of action!" Kistler barked. "Point Defense Three is down!"

"Hull breach at Frame Sixty!" Lieutenant Commander Vaznys, *Preussen*'s Tomlinson-born engineer snapped. "Multiple cell ruptures in Radiator One. Radiator One now offline, Captain. And Reactor One's gone into emergency shutdown!"

"Acknowledged," Hansen said, sitting motionless like a boulder at the heart of the tumult as the second salvo tore down upon her ship ten seconds behind the first.

☆   ☆   ☆

"Pitch ship," Basaltberg ordered.

In response, both of *Gerechtigkeitsgeschwader*'s battleships and all three battlecruisers raised their bows into a climbing attitude relative to the system ecliptic.

☆   ☆   ☆

The radar and lidar of First Fleet's fire control officers had to sort through the clutter left by the first salvo, and the heavy cruiser *Crossfire* suffered a power failure and was unable to launch in time at all, but twelve counter-missiles raced to meet the second Andermani salvo.

Ironically, despite their lower numbers, they were actually more effective than the first intercept launch had been, taking down all but five of the attack birds. Those five continued their merciless charge toward *Preussen*, and then it was once more the autocannons' turn.

Despite *Preussen*'s damage and the targeting interference, the cannon killed four of the lethal quintet. The fifth got past them, and it, too, entered the throat of the battleship's wedge, but at a steeply crossing angle that passed above *Preussen*'s hull. It would have continued onward, into the inner edge of her port sidewall, but its proximity fuse detonated it at the moment of its closest approach. The battleship bucked like a frightened horse as the outermost edge of the fireball's periphery smashed into her forward hammerhead, and crimson damage control codes flashed.

"Heavy casualties in forward impeller room," Vaznys reported sharply. "Forward ring...forward ring is down, Captain."

"Missile Three and Point Defense One and Point Defense Two are gone." Kistler looked across the bridge at Hansen. "Number Four mount's the only one we have left forward, *meine Kapitänin*," he added, his voice grim.

"Understood," Hansen replied.

On the tactical, the counter-missiles launched to meet the last installment of *Gerechtigkeitsgeschwader*'s rippled salvo. Only five shipkillers got by them, but three of the attack birds howled straight down on *Preussen*, and her close-in defenses were at only quarter strength. Her single remaining forward point defense went to continuous fire, trying to fill the space between her and the threat with a solid wall of shrapnel.

Two of the incoming missiles hit that shrapnel and died.

The third didn't. It charged across *Preussen*, once again above the ship but this time angling sharply to her right. Its proximity trigger was late, not detonating until just *after* it had crossed the hull, the blast knocking out the starboard sidewall generators, stripping the shuttles off her forward small-craft hard points, and opening four compartments of her habitat ring to space. All things considered, it was incredibly light damage.

The cruiser *Black Knight* was less fortunate. She survived, but only as a hulk haloed by voiding atmosphere and a ring of spreading lifepods.

☆   ☆   ☆

"We've lost the feed from *Preussen*," Commodore Quint's com officer said.

"Not surprising," Quint replied grimly. "That ship has definitely gone through the shredder."

Llyn looked at *Retribution*'s displays, a hard knot settling into his stomach. "Is it as bad as it looks?" he asked.

"It's bad enough," Quint conceded. "But she's still there, and Andermani battleships have a reputation for toughness. Let's see how fast Hansen can clear away the mess and get on the secondary com channel."

"It had better be fast," Llyn warned. "Without *Preussen* this whole thing gets a lot dicier a lot faster."

"No argument here," Quint said.

"Wedge burnout," *Retribution*'s tactical officer announced.

Llyn looked at the tactical display. Every missile in First Fleet's first answering salvo had now gone ballistic, thirty-two thousand kilometers short of the decelerating Andermani ships, and nineteen thousand kilometers short of their counter-missile envelope.

Sitting ducks, in other words. Very fast, very lethal ducks, but sitting ducks nonetheless.

Two seconds later, the salvo ran into the Andermani counter-missile zone, and thirty-two of them died right there. The rest—

"And, damn," Quint said quietly.

"What?" Llyn asked, searching the displays for the information his untrained eye had clearly missed.

"Basaltberg's being clever," Quint said. "Normal defense for non-evading targets facing up-the-kilt shots is to pepper the whole area with counter-missiles and autocannon and hope for the best. Instead, our Andermani admiral had his major ships pitch their wedges and turn their roofs to our barrage, dumping the full antimissile responsibility onto his screening units."

"Seems reasonable, if a bit timid," Llyn said. "What's the downside?"

"The downside is that if any of our barrage had targeted those smaller ships they'd be toast," Quint said. "Without the capital ships' antimissile screen they wouldn't have a prayer of stopping that big an attack. Basaltberg gambled a large percentage of his throw weight that Hansen would order us to concentrate exclusively on his two battleships and leave the rest for later."

Llyn grimaced. "Which she did."

Quint nodded. "Which she did."

"Second salvo approaching," the tactical officer spoke up. "Wedges still active."

"But all of them still targeting the capital ships," Quint said resignedly. "And already too close for us to change them to different targets."

"Would you have done things differently if you were in command?" Llyn asked, lowering his voice.

"Probably not," Quint conceded. She considered. "But I suppose we'll never know."

Floating side by side, they watched as the missiles followed their sisters into oblivion against the Andermani capital ships' wedges.

☆　　☆　　☆

"At least two hits on *Preussen*, *Herr Graf*," Unterberger's voice came from the flag bridge speaker. "Data feeding to you now."

There was a stirring through the compartment, Lisa noted, a small lessening of the tension that had filled and permeated *Friedrich der Grosse* and everyone in it.

But only a small lessening. *Hit* was a highly elastic term when it came to missiles, after all. Two *direct hits* would have utterly destroyed the battleship, but direct hits were the exception, not the norm, and CIC was still sorting through the data in order to ascertain exactly how extensive *Preussen*'s damage was.

And even if it was as extensive as everyone hoped, *Preussen* was hardly all alone out there.

"There *might* have been a third hit," Unterberger continued. "We don't yet have clear evidence. But sensors confirm a steep drop in her wedge strength, which strongly suggests her forward ring is completely down."

"Very good," Basaltberg replied. He looked at Kranz

and Lisa and raised his eyebrows. "Thoughts?" he invited.

"It sounds like she's badly hurt," Kranz said. "And if her ring is indeed down, we may be able to assume the damage is concentrated forward."

Which, if true, would be a huge shift in the battle's dynamics, Lisa knew. Like *Friedrich der Grosse, Preussen* mounted four twin-armed launchers forward, and she had much deeper magazines than the *Iskra*-class battlecruisers the Freets' mercenaries had brought to the battle. With twenty rounds in her box launchers, an *Iskra* could throw an impressive weight in her alpha salvo, but she had nowhere near the sustained capacity of an Andermani battleship. If a couple of *Preussen's* launchers had indeed been knocked out, and if they and their magazines were no longer available, the insurgents' firepower had just suffered a significant blow.

"*Herr Admiral,* passive sensors now suggest significant loss of atmosphere from *Preussen,*" Lindauer's voice came from the speaker. "Nothing conclusive, but for us to detect it from here would suggest massive hull breaching."

"Coupled with the change in *Preussen's* impeller signature, that suggests serious damage, *Herr Graf,*" Kranz said. "The fact that they haven't already fired another salvo suggests they're reserving fire until we are closer."

"So: badly hurt," Basaltberg said. "Or at least badly enough to conserve ammunition." He turned to Hasselreider. "Put the squadron back on approach profile, Fregattenkapitänin," he ordered the astrogator. "But stay ready for additional helm orders."

"Jawohl, Herr Graf," she replied.

"And now," Basaltberg continued, looking at Lisa as *Gerechtigkeitsgeschwader* turned its bows back toward Tomlinson. "Let us see just what surprises Kapitänin der Sterne Hansen has arranged for us."

☆   ☆   ☆

"Andermani fleet is moving forward," Quint said. "It looks like Basaltberg intends to close the range before he resumes fire."

"Agreed," Hansen said calmly.

A calmness Llyn couldn't help but admire. The image on Quint's com display was not of the best quality, the mark of heavy com damage, and the fact that Hansen had donned her helmet suggested that it wasn't just communications that had taken a beating.

Yet Llyn couldn't see any of the tension or outright fear that he would be feeling under similar circumstances. Hansen was certainly smart enough to realize she was in trouble, but had chosen to hide the doubts inside, showing only confidence and determination to her officers and crew.

From everything Llyn had read, Gustav Anderman had been the same way. Maybe Hansen really *was* his daughter.

"Assuming he's correctly identified your battlecruisers, he knows you've fired off two thirds of your missiles," Hansen continued. "He's also obviously aware we've been hurt badly." Her mouth tightened briefly, a brief flicker of the darkness within her peeking out.

Again, Llyn knew, hardly surprising. He'd seen the casualty reports *Preussen* was sending over to *Retribution*, and those numbers weren't good.

"So he won't waste his own fire at extended range,"

Hansen concluded. "He's going to get closer, where he'll have better sensor coverage and less transmission lag on his telemetry."

"We always knew that Basaltberg's battleships would give him a potentially decisive advantage," Quint said. "Not just in launchers, but in telemetry capability and magazine depth. With *Preussen*'s damage, he must be feeling pretty confident by now."

"Confident, but not arrogantly so," Hansen warned. "He'll be on the lookout for surprises." Her image frowned, her eyes flicking back and forth, probably checking her displays. "Yes," she murmured. "If *Preussen* hadn't lost so many of our telemetry links, I'd recommend holding fire until he launches and we know the geometry he's committed to. Under the circumstances, I'm not sure we have that option."

"I agree," Quint said, pointing Llyn at the correct display for the numbers she'd already seen and evaluated. "At this speed, he'll be past us quickly, at which point the initiative will be back in his hands."

"And we won't be able to surprise him a second time," Hansen said. "So do we accept that even more of them will be going in blind and start hitting him early? Or hope we'll have enough time—and will last long enough—to be decisive as he over-flies?"

"For all the reasons you just stated, I vote for now," Quint said.

"Concur," Hansen said simply, and nodded to someone off-screen. "Fire Plan Bruchmüller."

"Jawohl, meine Kapitänin."

Llyn shifted his attention to *Retribution*'s tactical displays. Hansen's command went out . . .

And the launchers in Tomlinson orbit, the hidden

launchers that Basaltberg's Alpha Drone had failed to detect, came to life.

☆   ☆   ☆

"*Lieber Gott!*" Unterberger gasped.

Travis's head twisted around to the plot, his eyes widening in disbelief. What in the name of *hell*—?

"Missile launch!" Unterberger snapped urgently. "Estimate two hundred fifty—repeat, *two-five-zero*! Correction—multiple launches. We have two—repeat *two*—salvos incoming."

"Return fire," Basaltberg snapped instantly. "All ships, yaw and pitch in twenty seconds."

"*Third* launch!" Unterberger called.

And in that frozen handful of seconds, seven hundred and fifty missiles began racing toward *Gerechtigkeitsgeschwader*.

CHAPTER TWENTY-FOUR

THERE WAS NO COMPARISON between the weights of fire being exchanged this time. None at all. The sheer density of the attack streaking outward from Tomlinson was far beyond anything any naval planner could ever have anticipated, certainly not from an opposing force of so few ships.

It's not as bad as it looks, a small, distant part of Travis's horrified mind tried to reassure him. The insurgents' remaining telemetry links couldn't possibly control that many missiles simultaneously.

But the logic was of small comfort against the enormity of the disaster zeroing in on *Gerechtigkeitsgeschwader*. Even if most of the missiles were essentially in fire-and-forget mode, the relative few that *were* under control were undoubtedly targeting the two Andermani battleships.

He was still staring at the coming onslaught when *Gerechtigkeitsgeschwader* launched its response.

It was larger than the first attack had been, seventy missiles this time instead of thirty-six, and under normal circumstances the fleet would have had enough telemetry links to control all of them. But with the insurgents' missiles roaring at them the Andermani ships dared not present the throats of their wedges to such an attack. And so, moments after launch, *Gerechtigkeitsgeschwader* turned away once again, simultaneously yawing to starboard and pitching upward to twist its wedges into position.

The move cost Basaltberg the control he would have needed for accurate fire, and indeed Travis watched the icons of the Andermani missiles go virtual as *Friedrich der Grosse*'s wedge began to cut off both telemetry and sensor feeds. Like most of the insurgents' missiles, *Gerechtigkeitsgeschwader*'s would have to find their own way to their targets.

On the other hand, the insurgents' stationary position made any evasive maneuvers they might make far less effective. It could also limit their own control over the core of their alpha missile strike and badly degrade the accuracy of any follow-up salvos.

And that was clearly something they couldn't afford. This was Hansen's make-or-break bid, her best and most powerful launch. The next handful of minutes would determine whether she won the battle or lost everything.

The first wave of insurgent missiles crashed over *Gerechtigkeitsgeschwader* like a sledgehammer forged in hell.

Twenty-three of the attack birds targeted the heavy cruiser *Schreien*. Her class carried a powerful electronic warfare suite, specifically designed both to draw fire from higher-value units and to spoof the sensors of the missiles she decoyed, and she was equipped with heavy defenses to engage any missiles that refused to be spoofed.

But it wasn't enough against that many threats, especially as her shifting wedge blocked her own counter-missiles and the wedges of her consorts prevented them from providing their own area defense assistance.

Five of the missiles slammed into her wedge and died. Two more were stopped by her port sidewall. But the other sixteen raced across and into the throat of her wedge. Her desperately firing autocannon stopped six of them; the final ten detonated inside her wedge.

One of them was barely five hundred meters from her bow when its proximity fuse triggered.

Fireball and radiation engulfed her, her wedge disappeared, and the uncaring void swallowed her fragments.

The destroyer *Kunlun* died two seconds later, and *Kunlun's* sister, *Xingtian* lost her forward impeller ring, both missile launchers, and half her point defense as a near miss savaged the forward half of her hull.

Vergeltung's port sidewall took two near misses in the space of less than a second and its generators failed. The battleship shuddered as blast and radiation erupted through the sudden gap in her defenses, but the sidewall had done its job and only a tithe of the warheads' fury got through. Travis winced as he watched the telemetry flow, but *Vergeltung's* thick armor absorbed the worst of the damage, and Andermani battleships carried a third generator for each sidewall. The backup snapped to life, generating a half-strength replacement wall, leaving her combat power unimpaired.

That was all of the kaleidoscope of battle that Travis had time to see before the fury of the insurgents' attack reached *Friedrich der Grosse*.

A dozen missiles wasted themselves against the flagship's wedge. One didn't. It just scraped by the forward edge of her port sidewall, angling inward, and detonated off the battleship's port bow. *Friedrich der Grosse*'s own motion carried her forward into the blast zone, and the massive ship bucked madly as the shockwave whiplashed through her.

CIC's displays went down, then flicked almost instantly back to life as the backups cut in. Crimson damage codes glared in those displays.

"Heavy damage forward!" Carrino's voice came over Travis's earbud, even as the battleship bucked. "Cascade failure! Explosions in Con—"

A secondary shock rocked CIC. The voice cut off abruptly, and Damage Control Central was suddenly another pulsing damage code. Travis's eyes darted across the list of codes, trying to see what other areas had been hit—

He felt his heart freeze. One of the codes marked damage to the flag bridge.

Where Lisa was.

He was halfway out of his restraints before the full implications even penetrated his consciousness. Flag bridge damaged—extent unknown—casualties unknown—communication impossible.

And Lisa was there.

He could get to her, Travis knew. Even with all the damage there was bound to be a route to the flag bridge he could get through. He might not be able to do anything to help, but he couldn't just sit here and wait on someone else to do something. Damage all over the ship, but his wife was in the flag bridge, and he needed to get to her.

"CIC, this is the Kapitänin," he heard Sternberger's voice over the speakers. "We've lost contact with Flag Bridge and Damage Central."

"CIC confirms com loss, *meine Kapitänin,*" Lindauer responded, his voice almost calm.

He could afford to be calm, Travis thought bitterly. It wasn't *his* wife trapped on the devastated flag bridge. It wasn't *his* wife injured, maybe dying, in the middle of a battle that didn't even concern her or her navy or her kingdom.

And to his everlasting regret and guilt he'd been too self-conscious around the Andermani to even kiss her good-bye.

He pushed off Unterberger's chair and headed toward the hatch, his face turned to the damage-status display, his eyes looking for a path—any path—to the flag bridge. Yes, he could make it. Come hell or hard vacuum, he would make it.

"We need eyes in DCC *now,*" Sternberger said. "Leutnant Stentz is trapped in Damage Beta, and he has no communication with repair parties forward of Frame One-Niner-Five."

"Understood," Lindauer said, and out of the corner of Travis's eye he saw the XO start to unstrap. "I'll go."

Travis reached CIC's main hatch, catching the handhold to stop himself, focusing one last time on the damage display—

Abruptly, the swirling emotions seemed to vanish like flame in vacuum. The red display marks—the scrolling damage codes—the controlled chaos of orders and reports he could hear from the coms—Kapitänin der Sterne Sternberger's urgent need for someone to get to Damage Control Central—

And in that instant, Travis the husband vanished, and Lieutenant Commander Travis Uriah Long of the Royal Manticoran Navy appeared.

"It's all right, Fregattenkapitän Lindauer," he called to the XO across the compartment. "I'm on it."

He had just enough time to see Lindauer's surprised expression, and then he was through the hatchway and heading down the short passage to DCC, fighting to pull up every scrap of memory of the area that he could from Carrino's orientation tours.

The glaring red light strobing above the DCC hatch indicated vacuum on the other side, and Travis spent the last five meters of his floating dash securing his vac suit helmet. He reached the hatch, grabbed the handhold to stop himself, and hit the latch button.

Nothing happened.

He slapped the emergency override switch. The hatch jerked open, but made it only halfway before it jammed. He twisted his body down and to the side, fighting the sudden currents as the air from the corridor rushed past him, and forced his way through. Fumbling for a grip on the far side of the bulkhead, he finally pulled himself past the jammed hatch.

And emerged into a charnel house.

He didn't know what freakish damage was responsible, but something had blown a meter-long, twelve-centimeter wide breach in the inner bulkhead and sent fragments slashing across the entire DCC. They'd scythed through its ten-man crew like demented buzz-saws, and blood globules drifted everywhere in the microgravity. Two Andermani petty officers were still up, struggling to aid the rest of the crew.

A little way apart from the survivors, still strapped to his couch in front of the main displays, was Carrino. Blood oozed upward from his shattered helmet, joining the other globules as they eddied toward the breach on the wave of atmosphere Travis had brought with him.

Travis gave himself a shove across the compartment toward the couch, gazing with a fresh sense of loss at the remains of the man who'd spent countless hours guiding him through *Friedrich der Grosse*, and in the process had become the closest thing Travis had to a friend among the Andermani.

There was nothing he could do to help Carrino. But maybe he could use the knowledge Carrino had hammered into him to keep others from suffering the same fate.

He reached the couch, grabbed a handhold, and peered at the displays, distantly aware that the slow fountain of blood from Carrino's helmet was daubing his vac suit crimson. He ran his eyes down the warnings...

"*Damn*," he muttered under his breath, the knot in his stomach tightening another turn. At least now he knew where the gap in the bulkhead had come from. Plasma Conduits Five and Seven had ruptured and vented into space, but not before Seven breached DCC, sending shrapnel across the compartment and sucking out its air.

But it was worse. Much worse. Conduit Nine had been damaged, as well, not from the initial hit but from secondary damage when Seven blew.

Only that one *hadn't* vented. In fact, it was still feeding power at ninety percent of design capacity, despite its damage, because no one outside DCC knew it had been hit and no one inside DCC had cut it from the circuit.

But that fragile stability wouldn't last. The conduit's structural integrity telltales were pinned deep into the red. If someone didn't get control of it in a hurry—

He jerked the hardwire umbilical loose from Carrino's helmet and jacked it into his own helmet com interface, and a torrent of German from the two petty officers slapping patches onto leaking vac suits filled his ears as his com dropped into the dedicated DCC circuit.

"*Hör auf damit, verdammt!*" he snarled.

The petty officers' helmeted heads jerked toward him. The two of them had been so focused on their comrades, he realized, that they probably hadn't even seen him enter the compartment.

He could sympathize. Some of them might still be alive, and needed to have patches applied to their suits before the rest of their life-sustaining oxygen disappeared.

But there were priorities to be followed in combat. Duty, responsibility, the greater good for the greater number. And if that greater good required that some individuals be left to die, there was nothing that could be done.

Even if one of those individuals was someone's beloved wife.

He took a deep breath. "You can't help anyone if you're dead," he bit out in German. "This ship—this *entire* ship—will die if you don't get back to your stations."

He pointed to the blood-splashed displays. "We need to get on top of that conduit before it breaches. Understand?"

For a fraction of a second the Andermani just stared at him. Then, one of them—an oberstabsbootsmann from his helmet insignia—slapped the other across the back of her helmet and both of them came flying across to join Travis.

"Understood, *mein Herr*," the oberstabsbootsmann said as they braked in front of two of the control stations and began inputting commands. "Who are you?"

"Lieutenant Commander Travis Long of the Royal Manticoran Navy," Travis said. "I was brought aboard as an observer."

"Oberstabsbootsmann Ferber; Bootsmann Prager," the petty officer identified himself and his colleague. "Yes, we heard about you. Our *offizier*—" his eyes flicked for a moment to Carrino "—spoke highly of you."

"I'm honored," Travis said, watching the displays closely. Conduit Nine's status was starting to change...

"He said you would have made a fine Andermani *offizier*," Ferber continued, glancing at the displays and then continuing at his board.

"Doubly honored," Travis told him. "Sadly, I am not."

"No, you were not." Ferber paused to look first at Carrino, then at Travis. "But you are now."

Travis felt his throat tighten. "For Admiral Basaltberg and the Empire, then," he said. "Let's get that conduit under control and then restore communications with Damage Beta—" despite himself, his voice wavered "—and flag bridge."

☆　　☆　　☆

The single Andermani salvo reached First Fleet.

Llyn watched the attack unfold with a growing sense of fear and futility. *Preussen* was, not surprisingly, Basaltberg's primary target, but as Quint had pointed out the fleet's defensive wedge pitching had cut off all telemetry and turned the salvo into essentially blind fire.

But blind or not, there were still seventy missiles in it, and First Fleet was a non-evading target.

Quint had ordered *Revenge* to stand between *Preussen* and the incoming fire, and the battlecruiser's counter-missiles and paired point defense laid down a heavy defensive barrage. Her sisters *Retaliation* and *Spark* were close enough to lend their counter-missiles to the battleship's defense as well, but far too distant to protect her with their point defense cannon.

The attack birds roared in. Over thirty of them broke through the counter-missiles. Sixteen of those fell to the autocannon. Eighteen drove straight into First Fleet's formation.

None of them made it all the way to *Preussen* this time, and without midflight telemetry updates most of the ones that survived the defensive barrage missed, despite the vulnerable wedge throats presented to them.

Most, but unfortunately not all. Three of the missiles reached their targets, and *Revenge* and the cruiser *Saber* died as spectacularly as any of Graf von Basaltberg's ships.

Gerechtigkeitsgeschwader had completed its course change by the time the second and third of the insurgents' massive salvos arrived. The vast majority of the incoming missiles wasted themselves against the warships' interposed wedges, but there were enough of them to leak through anyway, and the same maneuver which used their wedges as protective shields also chopped off their sensors and telemetry links. They could neither track the insurgents' missiles nor intercept them, and their own missile launchers faced away from Tomlinson and the ships still arrayed against them.

The insurgents' shipkillers rained down upon them, and some of them had to get through.

The battlecruiser *Seydlitz* staggered as a proximity fuse detonated and the savage explosion shattered her forward hammerhead and a hundred meters of hull.

Her sister ship, *Yanwang*, was more fortunate. She lost her port sidewall, both of her aft missile launchers, and her after heat radiator, sending her after reactor into emergency shutdown. Personnel losses were heavy, but her forward armament was untouched.

The destroyer *Xiangfei* blew up.

Korvettenkapitän Scherzer's *Drachen* simply disappeared as two warheads detonated almost simultaneously on either side of her.

The battlecruiser *Zhong Kui* lost her Number Two missile launcher and Number One point defense, but her personnel casualties were minimal and damage control parties labored frantically to put the point defense installation back online.

The heavy cruiser *Landwehr*, unluckier than her sister *Gewalthaufen*, lurched madly as her forward impeller ring went down. An instant later, a cascading power surge took her after impeller room off-line. Only for a moment...but in that moment, she had no wedge, and at least six missiles ripped her apart.

In the space of two minutes the Tomlinson insurgents inflicted the heaviest losses the Imperial Andermani Navy had ever suffered.

☆   ☆   ☆

"Looks like we hit them hard," Quint said, studying her displays as estimated damage scrolled across it. Her voice was steady enough, but Llyn could see the anger and ache in her eyes at the loss of *Revenge* and *Saber*.

"Indeed we did," Hansen replied heavily. Her voice wasn't nearly as controlled, and even in the lower resolution of the secondary com display Llyn could see the haunted look in her eyes. Wondering, no doubt, how many men and women whom she'd known for decades she'd just killed.

She would have known, of course, that unless her claim to the throne was accepted by the Andermani fleet this slaughter among friends and colleagues would inevitably be part of the outcome. But knowing in one's head and feeling in one's heart and gut were two entirely different things.

And Llyn had long ago learned that the first never entirely prepared one for the second.

"Unfortunately, we expended all of our orbital surprise doing it," Hansen continued, her voice a bit steadier now. "We're down to our internal magazines for the next phase."

"And our battlecruisers have only eight rounds left in their box magazines," Quint pointed out.

"Plus *Preussen*'s lost all but one of her forward missile batteries." On the display, Hansen's lips tightened. "We'll just have to hope we hit them hard enough."

☆   ☆   ☆

"Flag bridge is back in the circuit, *mein Herr*," Oberbootsmann Ferber said, half turning toward Travis. "They report casualties, but none fatal."

The frozen stone which had been Travis's heart cautiously began to come back to life. At least Lisa was alive.

But they had work to do, and there was still no time to think about that. "Bootsmann Prager?" he called.

"Nearly there, *mein Herr*," Prager called from one of the control boards. She was junior to Ferber, but Ferber had sent her to deal with the ailing Conduit Fifteen while he worked to reestablish DCC's communications.

Travis could see why. Hunched over her board, her fingers moving with a speed and confidence he'd rarely seen before, she was clearly the better choice to race the clock against the last of *Friedrich der Grosse's* damaged plasma conduits. His eyes flicked back and forth between Prager and the displays...

And with a final command, the conduit safeties popped open, venting the trapped plasma to space.

Travis huffed out a relieved sigh. At least the ship wasn't going to be blown up by her own power systems. "Outstanding work, both of you," he said, sending a tight smile at each of them. "You very well may have saved the ship."

"*Danke, mein Herr*," Ferber said. "What next?"

"We get reconnected to Damage Beta and the bridge," Travis told him. "I'm sure they'll have a list of things we can do."

CHAPTER TWENTY-FIVE

"*HERR GRAF,* WE HAVE COMMS AGAIN," Westgate spoke up.

"*Danke,*" Basaltberg said, giving Lisa and the corpsman working on Hasselreider one final, lingering look.

"She'll be fine," Lisa assured him.

"We got to her in time, *Herr Graf,*" the corpsman confirmed.

"Good," Basaltberg said. His eyes touched Lisa's. "*Danke,*" he said quietly.

"*Bitte,*" Lisa said. Helping the corpsman cut open the astrogator's vac suit, after all, was the least she could do to help.

No one in the flag bridge had been killed, but it had been a close thing. Hasselreider had been the worst casualty, with blast damage from Plasma Conduit Seven blowing back into the compartment and sending fragments of her console into her vac suit in several places. It had only been through quick work by Lisa and one of the corpsmen that they were able to get her suit open and stop the bleeding in time.

The other two injuries had been relatively minor, and other corpsmen were already in the process of treating them.

Which wasn't to say either the flag bridge or *Friedrich der Grosse* itself was exactly sitting pretty. The plasma blast hadn't depressurized the compartment as it had Damage Control Central, but if this part of the ship took another hit and lost containment Hasselreider, at least, was dead. And it was likely she wouldn't be alone.

The flag bridge com section had also been temporarily lost, taking with it not just voice communications but all the tactical displays as well. Now, as Lisa looked up she saw the displays beginning to come back to life.

She winced as the reality of *Gerechtigkeitsgeschwader*'s situation began to appear. Basaltberg had gone into battle with sixteen ships. Now, he had only eight combat-effective units left, and Lisa had no idea how loosely the Andermani defined the term *combat-effective*.

As for *Friedrich der Grosse* herself...

She felt her throat tighten. The display showing the flagship's own damages had come up now, and it was even worse than she'd suspected. Only one of the forward launchers remained operable, and the telemetry and communication links were badly damaged.

The good news, such as it was, was that three of the battleship's four point defense stations had survived, although two of them had been cut off from central fire control. Those two would be firing under local control only, their crews forced to rely on the on-mount sensors for targeting solutions.

Gerechtigkeitsgeschwader's three battlecruisers had been reduced to two. *Seydlitz* remained theoretically intact, though from the sheer damage profile listed on the display Lisa could only wonder what was holding her together. *Zhong Kui*'s forward firepower had been cut in half, but at least *Yanwang*'s damage was all aft. Basaltberg's single remaining heavy cruiser, *Gewalthaufen,* was also unhurt, but his destroyers had been gutted. Only the undamaged *Mazu* and *Kuafu* remained capable of combat, supported by the frigates *Schwert* and *Kurzschwert,* and all four of them together mounted only as many launchers as a single battleship.

And speaking of battleships . . .

Lisa frowned, giving the damage listing a second, longer look. Could *Vergeltung* really have come through that hellish barrage unscathed?

"Signal all ships," Basaltberg said to Westgate. "Cripples are to remain turned away from Tomlinson. Capital ships and undamaged units will alter to open their wedges as we pass. Then get me Kapitän der Sterne Schwender."

"*Ja, Herr Graf,*" the com officer said, turning to his board.

"And us, *Herr Graf*?" Kranz asked pointedly. "May I ask which heading we fall under?"

"You may indeed ask," Basaltberg told her. "I'll decide after I've spoken to Kapitän der Sterne Schwender."

His chief of staff nodded, though in Lisa's view the gesture indicated acceptance without necessarily being agreement.

Kapitän der Sterne Chao Schwender's image appeared on the com display. "Schwender, *mein Graf,*" he said formally.

"Kapitän der Sterne," Basaltberg greeted him in return. "From what I can see here, *Vergeltung* appears undamaged. Is that true?"

"Not entirely, *Herr Admiral*," Schwender said. "We've lost one point defense, our port sidewall is on the tertiary generator, and we have minor damage to our after telemetry arrays. With that proviso, though, we are completely combat ready."

"*Herr Graf?*" Schlamme cut in. "CIC confirms the destruction of at least one of the mercenary battle-cruisers."

"Good," Basaltberg said, looking back at Schwender. "So it will be our two battlecruisers against theirs, and your *Vergeltung* against *Preussen*. Opinion?"

"I find the odds eminently acceptable, *Herr Admiral*," Schwender said. "Particularly since we know the *Iskras* exhausted much of their ammunition in those first two salvos and that *Preussen* is badly hurt."

"That was my analysis, as well," Basaltberg said. "*Gewalthaufen* will be outnumbered two-to-one, but *Vergeltung*'s firepower should more than offset the insurgents' advantage in heavy cruisers. *Mazu*, *Kuafu*, *Schwert*, and *Kurzschwert* will simply have to deal with the two remaining light cruisers and the destroyers until you can get around to them. Now."

Basaltberg paused, and when he spoke again his voice had gone a shade darker. "I believe the odds favor us, but they will still be tight. Given the state of *Friedrich der Grosse*'s forward armament and defenses, I intend to present only her stern to Tomlinson as we pass."

"I see," Schwender said, his forehead furrowed but his voice steady.

"Unfortunately, our sensors and comms have taken significant damage," Basaltberg continued, "which means I cannot form and manage a coherent picture of the engagement from here." He seemed to straighten up a bit. "And *that*, in turn, means primary coordination for the attack will rest with *Vergeltung*."

"I understand, *mein Herr*," Schwender said, his voice going a little deeper.

Not surprisingly, Lisa thought, eyeing the stiffness of Basaltberg's posture. Turning *Friedrich der Grosse*'s after aspect toward the insurgents would double her remaining firepower and allow her to deploy her towed decoy system.

But it would also further reduce the reach of her already badly damaged communications links. Whatever Basaltberg's desire to personally bring this to an end, he knew that was no longer possible.

Earlier, Lisa had felt the frustration of being in the middle of a battle where all control was with other people. Now, Basaltberg had to face the same thing, only a thousand times worse, in order to complete his mission.

Back on Manticore, in the days before her wedding, Lisa had sometimes teased Travis about his continual references to his time with Basaltberg and the Andermani. Privately, she'd concluded that her husband-to-be had probably blown Basaltberg's abilities and character out of proportion.

Now, for the first time, she realized he hadn't.

"Very well, Kapitän, you're in command," Basaltberg said formally. "You have three minutes to prepare. *Gott sei mit dir*."

"*Und mit uns allen, Herr Graf*. Schwender clear."

☆　　☆　　☆

Gerechtigkeitsgeschwader continued toward Tomlinson, its combat-effective units rotating once again to bring their forward weapons and sensors to bear. There wasn't a great deal of time to accomplish that, and Travis and his two petty officers were still fighting to restore communications with Damage Control Beta as the targeting solutions came up in CIC, DCC, and on tactical displays throughout the squadron.

The displays blinked in crimson readiness, and Kapitän der Sterne Schwender's level voice came over the com net.

"Engage," he said.

And once again, *Gerechtigkeitsgeschwader* spat death into the night.

☆   ☆   ☆

"Incoming!" Kistler's voice sounded extra hoarse over the link to *Preussen*, and Llyn could picture sweat beading the TO's forehead despite his vac suit's temperature control. "We count thirty-six birds. Time-of-flight one-eight-zero."

"Return fire," Hansen replied. "And stand by countermissiles."

"Missiles away. Prepping second launch. Countermissiles launching in . . . two minutes."

"Very good."

Quint said something under her breath, then turned to Llyn. "We hurt them, all right," she said as, on the tactical, fifty-four missiles streaked away from First Fleet. "But I don't think we hurt them badly enough."

"We *are* throwing a bigger salvo," Llyn pointed out.

"By a considerable margin," she agreed. "Unfortunately, numbers and throw weight aren't the full story here. Basaltberg's defenses are almost certainly better than ours and his capital ships are tougher." She pointed at the secondary tactical. "Worse, the destroyers' and *Crossfire*'s cell launchers have run dry. That leaves us only twenty-six missiles for our second salvo and twelve for our third."

"Which will drain the battlecruisers' launch cells?"

"High and dry," Quint confirmed.

Llyn nodded, feeling the tension of a gambler pushing his last chips onto the table. If the first two salvos did the trick, they won.

But every one of Basaltberg's launchers were fed by internal magazines. Any ships that First Fleet failed to destroy had many more reloads available.

"Second launch away," Kistler said.

Llyn looked at the tactical as First Fleet's second, smaller salvo sped away. "A little surprised she didn't hold them back a bit longer," he murmured.

"I'm sure she *wanted* to," Quint said. "You'd always like to see what the first wave does before you send off the second. But in this case, it's pretty much a *launch-'em-or-lose-'em* situation. She *may* hold back her last twelve, just in case she's still around to give them targets. But that's not much more than whistling in the dark."

In case she's still around. "So you're expecting Basaltberg to focus on *Preussen*?"

Quint gave a little shrug. "*I* would."

"*Third* salvo launched," Kistler said, his voice almost unrecognizable now. "Counter-missiles launching. Forty seconds to impact."

"And, damn," Quint said softly.

And on the tactical Llyn saw the fourth salvo explode from the Andermani launchers.

☆   ☆   ☆

Basaltberg's ships put four salvos into space—a total of one hundred and forty-four missiles—before the first one reached its target. Unconsciously, Lisa tensed, watching for the insurgents' response.

When it came, it was decidedly anticlimactic: eighty missiles in two uneven salvos. A far cry from the seven hundred fifty that had devastated the Andermani fleet.

Basaltberg's guess had been right. That single attack had been the enemy's best and last hope. Now, they had all but run dry.

She looked over at the tactical. Schwender had redirected his third and fourth salvos, she saw, switching targets from the battlecruisers and the other ships which hadn't joined into the second salvo in order to concentrate on the handful of smaller ships that still had launchers and the missiles to feed them.

The waves of missiles passed one another, and this time there were no midflight collisions.

The insurgents' remaining counter-missiles began to launch, spreading their shrapnel, building their walls in space. *Gerechtigkeitsgeschwader*'s first salvo slammed into and through that cloud, twenty of the missiles surviving. They scorched in on their targets through the final, desperate fire of the point defense cannon.

And then the surviving missiles were clear, and once again the fury of thermonuclear destruction marched through the insurgent fleet in hobnailed boots.

☆   ☆   ☆

Basaltberg's targeting had concentrated the first salvo almost exclusively on the surviving Quintessence battlecruisers, with only an afterthought for the badly damaged *Preussen*. Two of the missiles got through to *Spark*, and the battlecruiser reeled as they detonated off her starboard bow and savaged her entire starboard side. *Retaliation* ate only one missile, and it was almost past her before it detonated. Almost. It exploded close aboard her port quarter, and her after hammerhead disintegrated under its fury.

Retribution's cannon stopped two missiles, and her port sidewall smothered the damage of a third. The fourth detonated as its proximity fuse triggered, but it was too distant to inflict significant damage.

Only one of the surviving missiles targeted *Preussen*. Like *Friedrich der Grosse*, Hansen's ship had turned away, exposing only her undamaged after aspect to the enemy's fire. But that single missile eluded the pair of autocannon flailing at it with fists of flame, and unlike *Friedrich der Grosse*, Hansen's battleship had never been fitted with a decoy system. That single missile threaded the needle of her impeller wedge's kilt and exploded close aboard her after hammerhead, stripping away both of her aft launchers.

"Skew turn starboard!" Hansen barked as her ship reeled and damage signals screamed like tortured souls, and *Preussen* labored to obey her. Llyn could hear the hatred in Hansen's voice, the self-contempt at having to turn her wedge to the enemy and cower behind it.

But she had no choice. Her after defenses were as shattered now as her forward ones, and she couldn't bring her single pair of surviving launchers to bear without exposing the defenseless throat of her wedge to the waves of missiles still streaking toward her.

Eleven seconds later, even as the Andermani missiles tore into First Fleet's hulls, it was *Gerechtigkeitsgeschwader*'s turn.

☆   ☆   ☆

Thirty-one of the insurgents' first wave survived the counter-missiles, continuing on through the autocannon gauntlet while decoys tried to lure them aside. Nineteen got past the final barrage. Five of them targeted *Friedrich der Grosse*, four targeted *Vergeltung*, and the rest were scattered among Basaltberg's lighter units.

Both battleships pitched upward in the final seconds before impact. They had fewer active defenses from astern, but the geometry of their wedges made them less vulnerable from that aspect, and the angle into their kilts could be closed by a smaller pitch angle. Despite that, two of the shipkillers evaded *Friedrich der Grosse*'s wedge. One detonated on her port side, far enough away that the sidewall absorbed the explosion without further damage. The second ran up on her other side and detonated close aboard. Blast and radiation ripped through her sidewall, the forward sidewall generator exploded in ruin, and the starboard face of her locked habitat ring was turned into a tortured, half-melted landscape of ruin.

Fresh damage alarms screamed, and Lisa heard the reports flow in as the main DCC damage control team—which had somehow and inexplicably ended up under her husband's command—worked frantically to stem the tide of destruction. The after reactor was scrammed barely in time, and all three of the flagship's starboard shuttles simply disintegrated on their hard points. Thirty more of *Friedrich der Grosse*'s people died or were wounded, and Lisa found herself wincing at each loss.

Yet despite the death and destruction, all of the battleship's remaining weapons systems survived unscathed.

Vergeltung was luckier. Only one of the four missiles

that crashed in through her point defenses reached attack range. It detonated outside her starboard sidewall, sparing her crippled port side, and she came through completely undamaged.

Zhong Kui also let only one missile through her defenses. But that single shipkiller detonated barely a hundred meters astern of her, shattering her hull like an icicle dropped on a ceramacrete floor.

There were no survivors.

And then *Gerechtigkeitsgeschwader*'s second launch tore into the surviving insurgents.

☆   ☆   ☆

A cascade of destruction burst through First Fleet's all but depleted point defenses. The already damaged battlecruiser *Spark* died spectacularly and *Preussen* had barely begun her skew turn when she took two more near misses.

She survived the damage as only a battleship could. But there was a vast difference between surviving and remaining combat effective.

On *Retribution*'s displays, Llyn saw *Preussen*'s Missile Five go red, leaving the battleship with just a single launcher. He waited for Hansen to do something, or at least say something.

But for once the leader of the insurgents, the woman who would be Empress, was silent.

The Andermani's third salvo slammed home, and the battlecruiser *Retaliation,* targeted by no less than five missiles, died as spectacularly as her sister *Spark.* The *Bataan*-class cruiser *Amphitrite* reeled out of formation, her half-shattered hull shedding life pods. The destroyer *Brindle* took a direct hit and simply vanished.

Retribution once again survived, again with negligible damage aside from the near miss that stripped away half her port sidewall.

But that almost didn't matter. First Fleet had been reduced to seven units, only three of which—all destroyers—were undamaged. And aside from the *Bataan*-class *Warrior* and the heavy cruiser *Crossfire*, every one of them had exhausted their ammunition. That gave them exactly six operable missile launchers.

But the time to use them had long since passed.

"All ships: evasion!" Quint snapped.

Hansen was in command, Llyn reflected, and might well consider Quint's unilateral order to be mutiny. But Hansen had gone silent, and Llyn doubted Quint cared what she thought. The Quintessence mercenaries were hers, and she wasn't going to waste any more of their lives in a campaign that was clearly lost.

Her people knew it, too. They were already responding, pitching up or down madly, interposing their wedges against Basaltberg's fourth wave of missiles. They were lighter and more nimble than any battleship, and the emergency maneuver saved nearly all of them.

The one exception was the destroyer *Nebula*, which took a near miss that shattered two thirds of her hull, killed almost half her crew, and sent her reactor into emergency shutdown. Her wedge vanished, leaving her open and helpless.

Llyn stared at the displays, his heart pounding out the seconds, waiting for Basaltberg to fire a fifth salvo, the one that would finish them all.

But that attack didn't come. The Andermani fleet was still in missile range, yet the attack didn't come.

"Quint?" Llyn asked carefully.

"He's giving us a chance," Quint said, her voice laced with sadness. Not for the mission, Llyn knew, or even for her ships, but for her lost people. "Like us, he's a professional."

She gestured to the com officer for an open mic. "All ships, this is Commodore Quint. Strike your wedges. I repeat, strike your wedges.

"It's over."

For a long minute the bridge was silent except for the urgent murmurings of the com officer repeating and confirming her order into his own mic. Llyn watched the displays, waiting. *Retribution*'s own wedge was the first to go, but it was followed immediately by those of the rest of the Quintessence ships. For a few seconds *Preussen*'s remained active, and Llyn wondered if Hansen was going to take her people and her ship down in the blazing fire of a Wagnerian opera.

But then, her wedge, too, vanished.

Llyn took a deep breath. "So that's it?"

"Not quite." Deliberately, Quint turned to him. "The Deneb Agreement stipulates how defeated mercenaries are to be treated. There are no such rules for civilians." She raised her eyebrows. "Especially civilians who are up to their necks in provocation, bribery, and warmongering."

"So I've heard," Llyn murmured.

He could kill her, he knew. He could kill her right here, in front of her officers, without any of them seeing or hearing a thing. The falsified shuttle orders were still in place, and enough of *Retribution*'s shuttles were still in good enough shape for him to escape to Tomlinson. Long before Basaltberg's overflying ships could decelerate and return he would be hidden among the populace with his forged papers, free to wait out the Andermani until Axelrod could bring him home.

He could do all of that. But as he gazed into Quint's face, he knew he wouldn't.

"All I can say," he continued, determined to at least play it out to the end, "is that turning me in to the Andermani will cost you a *huge* amount of paperwork."

"And I *do* so hate paperwork," she said. "So here's the deal."

She seemed to brace herself. "In the closet in my cabin is a Quintessence uniform in your size. Get up there—right now—and put it on."

Llyn felt his mouth drop open a couple of millimeters. "Excuse me?" he asked carefully.

"You're Lieutenant Arnold Bax, special liaison on loan from the Vorpal Blade Mercenaries on Preston." Her lips quirked in a small smile. "Yes, I know. But it should hold up long enough for you to get repatriated with the rest of us. The ID and other documents are in the pockets."

"I—thank you," Llyn said, an odd feeling seeping into him. He'd never liked having to accept favors. In fact, he'd worked very hard his entire life not to be put in that position. But here and now, he didn't have a choice.

And to his mild surprise, it wasn't nearly as bad as he'd expected.

"You're welcome," she said. "Now go."

"Right away."

He started to turn, paused as she caught his arm. "One more thing," she said, her voice gone odd. "I assume Amos won't need a uniform?"

Llyn braced himself. "No," he said.

"Why?" she asked.

"Because he was going to kill you."

Quint's lips compressed briefly. "Yes, I thought that might be the case. Bryce wanted me dead, didn't she?"

"That was her interpretation of her job," Llyn said. "My interpretation was different."

"I'm glad," she said. "Well. Basaltberg will be here sometime in the next couple of hours to accept our surrender. The least we can do is try to tidy up a bit for him."

CHAPTER TWENTY-SIX

IN THE END, DESPITE QUINT'S COMMENT, Basaltberg didn't seem impressed at all by *Retribution*'s tidiness or lack of it. All he and the boatloads of soldiers he brought aboard cared about was collecting the Quintessence officers and crew, checking IDs, cataloging equipment and weapons—functional and otherwise—and hauling everyone and everything that was moveable across to a set of waiting transports.

At one point a large percentage of the soldiers disappeared, and Llyn caught a few scraps of conversation that suggested the destroyers that had charged out of The Cloud just before Hansen's massive ambush had finally straggled in and surrendered. Considering that those crews had been a mix of Quintessence and Freet, the pre-surrender conversations aboard them must have been loud and interesting, possibly including some judicious gunfire.

But that didn't seem to impact anything happening aboard *Retribution*. The Andermani finished their work, put everyone aboard transports for a quick trip down to one of Tomlinson's army bases, and the processing began.

At which point it was Llyn's turn to be impressed.

Axelrod had dealt with other mercenary groups over the years, and Llyn had heard his share of horror stories about defeated crews languishing in processing camps for months or even years while the winners painstakingly ran everyone's identities, checked for possible war crimes or violations of the Deneb Agreement that could be held against them, and otherwise drowned everyone in paperwork.

Andermani didn't drown in paperwork. If anything, they surfed on it.

The officers in charge of the processing were quick, precise, organized, and efficient. Almost frighteningly efficient, in fact. Within a week the first round of interrogations had been completed and Basaltberg's people were sorting out the mercenaries from the home-grown Tomlinson insurgents, with special attention being paid to those of *Preussen*'s officers and crew who had committed mutiny and treason.

There would undoubtedly be more to be done with the latter two groups. But for the Quintessence the rules were clear and straightforward. Barely eighteen days after Quint's surrender the entire company of mercenaries were aboard a pair of troop transports heading for New Berlin and their final disposition.

Of course, given Gustav's history as one of the greatest mercenary commanders of his age, it made sense that the Andermani would have gotten the whole thing down to a science.

He didn't see much of Quint during the two-week voyage to the Andermani capital. Officers and crewers were kept in separate sections, with the surviving Quintessence captains further segregated into their own block. His Quintessence uniform got some odd looks from the rest of *Retribution*'s officers, but no one went to the Andermani with suspicions or pointed fingers. Either Quint had already clued them in to Llyn's supposed mercenary liaison identity, or else they simply trusted their commodore enough to accept whatever she did without question.

There was one last round of processing when the mercenaries reached Potsdam, but it was more perfunctory than Llyn had gone through at Tomlinson and he was released along with the rest of the officers in just three days.

Only to find that Quint herself had been summarily taken to Sorgenfrei Palace. Apparently, Emperor Andrew had invited her for a meeting.

☆   ☆   ☆

In some ways, the two hours Llyn waited just outside the palace grounds were the longest of his life. Quint had desperately wanted to kill Andrew's father, to the point of extracting a promise from Llyn to do the deed for her if she failed to complete it... and now Gustav's son and successor had called for a confrontation.

Llyn had no way of knowing how much information the Andermani had on Quint's obsession. But he could think of no way a private meeting translated into anything but trouble.

He was running all the possible scenarios through his mind for the hundredth time when he spotted her and her two-guard escort leave the palace and head toward one of the garden exits. A car pulled up to that gate as she approached, presumably preparing to whisk her away somewhere.

Llyn made sure he got to that rendezvous point first.

He was waiting near the car, ignoring the suspicious looks of the driver, as she and her guards came through the gate. "Commodore," he said, taking a step toward her.

For that first second he wondered if she'd been drugged. Her eyes were downcast, her forehead wrinkled, her expression an odd mix of thoughtfulness and antipathy. Almost reluctantly, he thought, she looked up.

Her expression cleared a little as she saw who it was. But just a little. "Lieutenant Bax," she greeted him in return. Her voice was the same mix as her expression. "The Andermani have formally released me to return to our fleet train. I'd assumed you'd already left with one of the other groups."

"I was waiting for you, Commodore." He flicked a glance over her shoulder at the palace. "Your meeting went well?"

"The meeting was interesting," she said. "Come on, you can ride with me." She looked at her guards. "If that's all right," she amended.

"Of course, Flotillenadmiral," one of the guards said without hesitation. "If you'll both get in, we can be on our way."

Llyn didn't expect Quint to share her story with a trio of Andermani listening in, and he was right. Nor was she apparently interested in talking about anything except Quintessence business once they were aboard the troop carrier with the last group of her officers, instead focusing on plans once they'd gathered the rest of their now meager assets together.

But finally, late that night, they found in Quint's quarters the privacy Llyn had wanted.

"What did Andrew say?" he asked when the hatch was sealed behind them. "Did he offer any compensation for what his father did to your mother? Or even an apology?"

"Neither," Quint said, that thoughtful look back on her face.

"Of course not," Llyn said, feeling his lip twist. "But then, why *should* the son have more integrity than the father?"

"You're missing the point," Quint said. "He told me his father didn't kill her."

Llyn snorted. "So. Gremlins?"

She looked him straight in the eye. "*My* father."

Llyn stared at her. It was an obvious deflection for Andrew to make, he belatedly realized, a standard shoving of someone's guilt onto someone else.

But as he looked now into Quint's eyes, he realized to his amazement that it might actually be true.

"He says Gustav *did* come to our hotel room," Quint said, her voice going distant. Part of her believed it, Llyn could see, while another part wanted to reject the thought completely. "But he says it was to offer my mother a position with his group. They talked together for a few minutes, quiet and all very civilized. Quietly enough that I never heard any of it through the bedroom door. Then he left."

A wave of old pain crossed her face. "And then my father, who'd been sitting listening to it all, went crazy. *He* was the one I heard shouting at my mother, not Gustav." She closed her eyes. "And he's the one who killed her."

For a long moment they sat together in silence. There were questions Llyn wanted to ask, investigative poking he wanted to do at the edges of Andrew's story.

But this wasn't the time. Not yet.

"Then he came into the bedroom and told me Gustav had done it," Quint said. "We went to the police station, he made his statement, and we went back to the hotel until it was time to leave."

"And Gustav?"

"It took the police three days to track him down," Quint said. "Not surprising—he was celebrating with his people and had no idea anyone was looking for him. By the time they found him and took his statement, we were gone. By the time they did an actual investigation, we were already on another job."

"And out of reach?"

"Out of reach, and the Condotta Group was never much for personal accountability outside of the job anyway," Quint said bitterly. "Andrew told me his father tried a couple of times to track us down, but I know my father changed names at least once and merc groups at least twice before I was eighteen. And I don't remember us ever getting anywhere near Gustav again."

"It *is* a big galaxy," Llyn conceded.

"And it holds a lot of people who want someone else to do their fighting for them." Quint shook her head. "I don't know, Llyn. He could be lying through his teeth—he showed me Gustav's copy of the police report, but those things can be faked. It's just . . . why would he bother? Now that Gustav's dead, why bother? Is the old man's reputation *that* important?"

"Sometimes," Llyn said. "I've known people whose

public image was all they had. I guess *my* question is why would Gustav offering your family a position make your father go full berserker that way?"

"You weren't listening," Quint said. "He offered my *mother* a position, with me coming along as part of the package." She hissed out a sigh. "Apparently, he thought my father was too unstable."

"But she *did* turn him down, right?"

"Of course," Quint said. "But I suppose even just listening constituted treason in my father's mind. And was dealt with the only way he knew how."

Another silence filled the compartment, a longer one this time. "And there's one more bit of irony," Quint said. "After laying out that whole spin-coaster of a ride for me . . ." She shook her head. "Andrew offered me a job."

Llyn stared at her. "You're kidding."

"Apparently, the Empire recently lost a lot of qualified officers," she said with a hint of the dry humor he hadn't heard from her in a long time. "He said if I was willing to become an Andermani citizen and go through a two-year probationary and training period I could start right in as a senior officer. He also made the same offer to anyone from the Quintessence who I recommended."

"Are you going to take the job?"

"No," Quint said "At least, not now. I have the rest of my people to think about, see what I can do about getting them into other positions or settled elsewhere. But the offer's apparently open-ended." She gave him a slight smile. "You want me to recommend you?"

Llyn smiled back. "I don't think there's enough irony in the galaxy to even start ladling onto that one."

"I thought not." She took a deep breath. "I don't know who you are, Llyn, or who you work for, or, really, what this was all about. But your employer put the Quintessence back on our feet, and I appreciate it."

Llyn winced. And then, of course, Basaltberg knocked them right back down again.

But that was the life of a mercenary. That was the risk they took.

And even if the Deneb Agreement had required Quint to forfeit the warships she'd brought to Tomlinson—what was left of them, anyway—in exchange for repatriating her crews, she still had the non-combat ships of her fleet train plus the two destroyers that had been left there to watch over the dependents and other civilians. It wasn't much, but a bit of judicious hiring out of her ships and her people and she could start rebuilding her organization.

"And I also gained some personal closure, so there's that," Quint went on. "Anyway. I'll need to discuss our next destination with my officers, but you're welcome to stay with us until we reach some place that's convenient for you."

"Thank you," Llyn said. "I'll make sure I'm not a burden to you any longer than I have to be."

"No problem." She gave him another small smile, this one looking a bit more relaxed. "And if you ever come across anymore warships that have gotten lost in the paperwork, let me know."

"You'll be the first," Llyn promised.

And actually, once Axelrod finally took over Manticore, there might well be a warship or two they would want to get rid of.

Something to think about.

☆   ☆   ☆

"And so, we are met again," Emperor Andrew said, looking down the table at the assembled guests.

Marija sat quietly, following his gaze, remembering the last time they'd all been assembled this way: Admiral Basaltberg, Kanzlerin von Schwarzer Flügel, Außenminister Yuèguìshù Shān, Admiral der Flotte Berg, and *Friedrich der Grosse*'s commander Kapitänin der Sterne Sternberger. It wasn't a table aboard a battleship this time, but the personnel were the same.

And the last time they'd been together Andrew had threatened to have every single one of them executed for treason.

They all remembered that threat, certainly. And the fact that they'd been right to keep the Emperor out of battle—and Marija fully believed they'd been right—didn't change the fact that they had indeed disobeyed Andrew's direct orders to the contrary.

More to the point, she was pretty sure Andrew knew they'd been right, too.

But that might not make a difference.

There were some leaders, Marija knew, who never backed down from a position. Sometimes it was from stubbornness, sometimes from a fear their opponents would think them weak or indecisive, sometimes because they were firmly convinced they were right and to hell with logic or reason.

Andrew was keenly aware that some thought him too weak to rule, and Hansen's bizarre claim to the throne just served to underline his youth and inexperience.

Sometimes he would share his thoughts and plans with Marija. Not this time. Whatever he had to say to this assembly, Marija would hear it the same time they did.

"I assume you all remember our last meeting," Andrew said. "You'll recall I wanted to immediately attack the Tomlinson traitors. All of you stood as one to defy that order, insisting I be returned to Potsdam and safety before returning to bring them to justice, Now, because of that delay, it would appear that many more good men and women have been forced to give their lives for the Empire."

He paused, looking again around the table. Marija held her breath, noting the quiet stiffness in the others' postures and their carefully controlled expressions.

"However," Andrew continued, "I say *it would appear* because none of us truly knows what would have happened if you'd attacked as I wished. We know the insurgents received additional ships during the delay, but we don't definitively know how much of their force was already prepared. Most significantly, we don't know the state of the massive missile ambush that came close to costing the entirety of Admiral Basaltberg's force. If even a large percentage of it was already in place at that time, none of us might be here now."

He paused again . . . but this time Marija could see a hint of a smile touching his face. "An Emperor cannot afford to have his word flouted for no reason," he said. "But likewise, an Emperor cannot afford to ignore sound advice, whether or not in the heat of the moment he judges it to be sound."

He raised his eyebrows. "And an Emperor *certainly* cannot afford to destroy the voices that offered that counsel.

"I imagine some of you, at least, came here today expecting to hear a pronouncement of judgment on you. Instead, I offer my apologies and gratitude. We don't know how an earlier battle might have turned out, but we *do* know that my life and the stability of the Empire would have been put at risk. I therefore withdraw the punishments I threatened you with, and ask your forgiveness for my hasty and ill-considered speech."

"You are our Emperor, Majestät," the Kanzlerin said gravely, the weight of her long service mixing with relief. "But like all of *Gott's* servants, you are also human. We will always extend forgiveness to you for your errors if you will likewise extend such forgiveness to us."

"Thank you," Andrew said. "And now, I'll allow you to return to your duties. *But.*"

He lifted a warning finger. "In three short weeks' time I will marry my beloved. A short time after that, I expect there to be an heir to the Imperial throne.

"After *that*, if you ever again wish to keep me out of battle, you'll need to come up with a new excuse."

☆   ☆   ☆

And so, the man who was Emperor and the woman who'd sought to replace him finally met.

It wasn't the way Hansen had expected. She'd envisioned a triumphal return to New Berlin, with Flotillenadmiral von Jachmann announcing her arrival, Graf von Basaltberg and a large part of his fleet escorting *Preussen* into orbit, and Admiral Donnic aboard the battleship *Liegnitz* making sure the rest of the Capital Fleet remained calm. She'd envisioned the Kanzlerin and *Staatsministerium* gathered to meet her shuttle, and a triumphant journey to Sorgenfrei Palace. She'd envisioned Andrew humbly welcoming her as he swore fealty to the new Empress, and standing to the side as she ascended the throne that was rightfully hers.

But Jachmann was dead, his murder a crime that

would now likely never be solved. Basaltberg had rejected her and her claim, and had beaten her ships into twisted shards of debris and lifeless bodies. Her Tomlinson allies were taken or dead or scattered, the army systematically dismantling their bases and confiscating their stocks of weapons. If any of the Empire's ministers had stood up in her support, she'd not heard any word of it. The mysterious ally who'd hired the Quintessence Mercenaries and sent intel and weapons to her had vanished as if he'd never existed.

And the young man—the far too young man—seated in front of her showed not a single iota of humility as he prepared to pass judgment.

Even here, it didn't go as she'd envisioned.

"It's ironic, really," Andrew said, a sort of melancholy in his face as they stared across the two-meter gap that separated them. "All the time I was growing up I longed to have a brother or sister. But it never happened. I had to make do with the friendship of nurses like Marija, and the limited time I had to spend with my parents, and the greyhounds."

One of the two dogs that had settled down at the foot of the throne perked up a bit, as if she knew Andrew was talking about her. She paused there a moment, then laid down her head again.

"Do you know why my parents never had other children?" Andrew asked.

"No idea," Hansen said. She hesitated, but the little dig was too tempting to resist. "Maybe Gustav's lower strength wasn't up to it. He certainly had no trouble with *my* mother."

"Ironically, it was because of concerns about this exact situation," Andrew continued as if she hadn't spoken. "My father had read about the chaos that periodically erupted in Old Europe, siblings fighting among themselves for control of their various countries. He'd seen the modern-day equivalent when a mercenary commander unexpectedly died and his top lieutenants tore the organization apart in attempts to gain and solidify their power. My father thought it would be safer for the Empire if I remained an only child."

He gave her a sad smile. "I never expected my dream and their nightmare to come together this way."

"It's not too late," Hansen said. It probably was, actually, but she had nothing to lose by trying. "Surely by now you've seen the DNA evidence that I'm your older half-sister. That gives me a legitimate claim to the throne you're sitting on. And I think we can both agree that I'm better suited for the job."

"The job." Andrew smiled again, but this time there was only ice there. "Is that all you think it is? A *job*?"

"I have more life experience," Hansen said. "More military training—"

"Yes, I've seen the evidence," Andrew interrupted. "I presume it came from *Totenkopf* Major Strossmeyer?"

"He was the one who brought it to me, yes," Hansen said, feeling her eyes narrow. Andrew wasn't supposed to know about Strossmeyer.

"Did you know he was planning to run out on you?" Andrew asked. "As soon as it was clear that the ambush on my father's cortège had failed he began working on the Manticorans to let him immigrate there."

Hansen stared at him. Strossmeyer had been going to *desert* her? Ridiculous. He'd pledged to work here on Potsdam to gather support among the *Totenkopf* and government officials in preparation for her return.

"Though he adjusted his timetable a bit when we offered him an opportunity to assassinate me," Andrew went on, his smile fading, the ice turning into granite. "He apparently decided that before he ran he could finish the job you'd started."

"We were never going to kill you," Hansen insisted. "You were just going to be placed into custody while the courts and Landtag debated my claim."

"*Into custody*," Andrew repeated. "That was the same excuse used by the traitors who tried to depose my father. You *do* remember that, don't you? Because I certainly do."

Hansen clenched her teeth. "That was an attempted coup," she said. "This was different."

"No," Andrew said. "Because this wasn't just an attack on me. It was an attack on the structure of the Andermani Empire."

He gave a little sigh. "You see the Emperor's throne as a job, my sister. But it's far more than that. The Emperor is a symbol, the soul of the nation, an example the people should be able to look up to." His eyes hardened. "The soul of the Andermani Empire does not include mutiny, treason, and murder."

The excuses and explanations that had long been simmering in Hansen's heart came boiling up into her throat. But as she gazed into Andrew's face, they remained unspoken.

Because there was clearly no longer any point.

"If you'd brought this evidence peaceably to my father—*our* father—a year ago, things might have been different," Andrew continued. The sadness was back in his voice, but the steel and granite remained untouched by it. "If you'd brought it to *me* six months ago there might have been the judicial hearings you spoke of.

"But you did neither. Instead, you sought to seize the throne through violence and at the cost of thousands of Andermani who had looked up to you as their commander.

"Your actions have left me no choice, Kapitänin der Sterne Florence Hansen. In the name of the Andermani Empire, I sentence you to death."

He lifted his eyes to the *Totenkopfs* holding her restraints. "Take her away."

And as the guards walked her back to her cell, Hansen wondered if she'd been wrong. If perhaps Andrew did indeed have the resolve and ruthlessness necessary to be Emperor.

And that, too, was something she hadn't envisioned.

CHAPTER TWENTY-SEVEN

SEVEN MONTHS AGO, back on Manticore, Admiral Basaltberg had been an unexpected but welcome guest at Lisa and Travis's wedding.

It therefore seemed both fitting and proper for Travis, Lisa, and Winterfall to be guests at Emperor Andrew's.

Travis had wondered how exactly the disparate Chinese and German influences of the Empire could be brought together: whether they would complement or clash, whether one would completely dominate the other, whether the final result would be beautiful, confusing, or awkward.

He needn't have worried.

The ceremony was beautiful. The groom was young and handsome, far more so than Travis had been. The bride was radiant, though less so than Lisa. The royal gardens outside Sorgenfrei Palace, where the event took place, were precisely manicured; the music, flowers, and benediction were flawless. The guest list filling the space was undoubtedly the top tier of Andermani authority and culture.

Against such a lavish backdrop, Travis felt completely out of place. If he'd had any idea who most of the people here were, he reflected, he would probably feel even more intimidated.

Fortunately, even if he felt like he and the others were intruders, no one else seemed to share that opinion. He and Lisa were seated with Basaltberg for the ceremony, and everyone he came in contact with either smiled at him or offered small nods of greeting. He'd lost Winterfall among the rest of the throng, but Basaltberg had told him his brother had been invited to sit with the foreign minister, Außenminister Yuèguìshù Shān, and her group.

With the final marathon of diplomatic and trade negotiations taking up most of Winterfall's time in the month since the battle, Travis hadn't seen much of him. But rumor had it that the Emperor had personally stepped in on two or three of the sticking points, his rulings generally favoring Manticore. No one seemed to know why, and Travis was looking forward to grilling his brother on the subject during the journey home.

☆   ☆   ☆

"I trust you were taking notes, Gavin," Lisa commented as the three of them stood at one of the stand tables off to the side, their plates and cups crowded precariously together on the tabletop.

"I'm sure the whole ceremony was recorded," Winterfall reminded her. "We can probably get a copy to take home if you want one."

"Oh, I don't need it for *me*," Lisa said, the impish look that Travis knew all too well mixing with the underpinning of innocence he was also quite familiar with. "I'm thinking of *you*. You're going to get married someday, and this kind of wedding would be the talk of Manticore."

"And then some," Travis agreed, skipping the impishness—which he didn't do nearly as well anyway—in favor of straight innocence. "I'm sure she and her family would be impressed."

"This *she* being my nebulous future bride?" Winterfall asked. "I don't suppose you'd like to enlighten me as to her name?"

"Well, if *you* don't know who she is, *we* certainly don't," Travis said, watching Lisa carefully spear another of the wrapped shellfish from her plate and place it almost reverently in her mouth. Never mind the wedding itself—what had clearly impressed her more than the ceremony were *these* dainty little beauties.

"Speak for yourself, Travis," Lisa said, the words muffled as she talked around her bite. Apparently, she wasn't quite finished with the game. "What about this Baroness Crystal Pine you were going on and on about on the trip here?"

Winterfall blinked. "I wasn't going *on and on* about her. Anyway, Olga and I are just colleagues."

"You must be a bit more than *that* if you're already calling her Olga," Lisa pointed out.

"Come *on*," Winterfall protested, and to Travis's surprise he seemed to be actually squirming. He'd assumed Lisa was just teasing, but now he wondered if she might have genuinely hit a nerve. "I barely know her."

"Barely or not, you're fifty-three T-years old," Lisa reminded him. "If you're not careful you're going to run out the clock on other options."

"And who are you, my maiden matchmaker aunt?"

Winterfall countered. "I appreciate your concern, but I can handle my own life."

Lisa sent Travis a significant look. "Best defense . . . ?" she prompted.

"A good offense," Travis finished the aphorism, starting to enjoy this. He didn't get to tweak his older brother nearly often enough. But then, Lisa had a knack for such things. "What she means is—"

"I *know* what she means," Winterfall growled. "And I'm—" He broke off, his eyes switching to something behind Travis, his face suddenly changing. "Yes?" he said in an entirely different voice.

"Foreign Minister Baron Winterfall?"

Travis turned. Standing a meter behind him was a black-clad *Totenkopf.*

"I am," Winterfall confirmed.

"*Seine Majestät*'s greetings, *Herr* Foreign Minister," the soldier said. "Your presence and the presence of your companions—" his eyes flicked to Travis and Lisa "—is requested. Follow me, *bitte.*" Without waiting for an answer, he turned and started back through the crowd.

"Come on," Winterfall said, leaving his plate and cup and setting off after the soldier.

Travis had assumed that the invitation was to some kind of group event, and that once inside the palace they'd be joining up with some of the prominent Andermani in attendance. But the Entry Hall was deserted except for a few watchful *Totenkopfs*, as was the exquisite Marble Hall beyond it. Their guide turned them left out of the Marble Hall, through one more room, and finally to a closed door flanked by two more *Totenkopfs.*

"*Seine Majestät* awaits you," he said, stopping and gesturing ahead.

Travis looked at Winterfall, got a microscopic shrug in return before Winterfall started toward the door. Travis followed, Lisa close at his side. One of the *Totenkopfs* pulled open the door and ushered them in.

There they finally found the crowd Travis had been expecting. A small crowd, certainly, but what it lacked in numbers it more than made up in prestige.

Emperor Andrew was there, seated on a velvet-covered couch beneath one of a pair of huge mirrors, two more *Totenkopfs* at his sides. At his feet a pair of greyhounds lay curled up dozing on the floor; beside him on the couch rested a flattish rectangular box. Standing past the guard to Andrew's right were Admiral Basaltberg and an older woman in an army dress uniform who Travis tentatively identified as the Chancellor, Kanzlerin Schwarzer Flügel, the government's top official. Behind the three Manticorans, as they stepped into the room, were two more *Totenkopfs*.

"Greetings, my honored guests," Andrew called, beckoning them forward. "Please, approach. Our time together grows short, and I would speak with you before you leave New Berlin tomorrow and begin your long voyage home."

"We are honored, Majestät," Winterfall said, ducking his head in a low bow as he again led the way forward. If he was surprised or disturbed by the presence of Basaltberg and Schwarzer Flügel he gave no indication of it. "May we offer our congratulations on this, your wedding day, and also on the generous hospitality of you, your government, and especially the Andermani people."

"*Danke*," Andrew said with a smile. "Though I dare say the Manticoran definition of *hospitality* is an interesting one. Asking one's guests to put their lives in deadly danger is hardly part of the diplomatic code."

Travis threw a sideways look at Winterfall. Was Andrew saying *his* life had been put at risk, too?

"Which is why I asked you here," Andrew continued. "The official gifts have already been presented and stowed aboard *Damocles* and *Diactoros* for you to take back to your queen. But I wanted to express my personal gratitude with a few more personal tokens. Baron Winterfall: step forward."

With maybe half a second's hesitation, Winterfall complied. Andrew gestured, and Schwarzer Flügel left Basaltberg's side and walked over to face him.

"For your role in protecting the Emperor's life," she intoned, "and for your part in unmasking and putting to rest the final chapter in a dark night of Andermani history, you are hereby awarded the *Hausorden von Anderman,* an award for civilian bravery and merit."

And to Winterfall's clear surprise, Schwarzer Flügel produced a red-and-white ribbon and pinned it to his formal tunic. *"Für Gott und den Kaiser,"* she intoned.

"Danke, Kanzlerin Schwarzer Flügel," Winterfall said, inclining his head to her. *"Danke, Majestät,"* he added, turning and bowing more deeply to Andrew.

Andrew nodded in return and gestured him to step back. "Lieutenant Commander Travis Uriah Long: step forward."

Feeling his heart pick up its pace, Travis did so, watching as Schwarzer Flügel moved back and Basaltberg took her place. "For your role in saving *Friedrich der Grosse,*" the admiral said, "and for overall gallantry in the face of the enemy, you are hereby awarded the *Orden von Tischendorf."* Producing another ribbon, this one green and white, he fastened it beneath the modest row of Manticoran medal ribbons on Travis's uniform.

Which was going to look odd, a small part of Travis's brain warned, given that the dimensions of the ribbons didn't match. But that was something for the RMN leadership to figure out, not him.

"*Danke, Herr Admiral,*" he said, repeating the movements and gestures he'd seen from his brother. "*Danke, Majestät.*"

Andrew nodded in return. Travis started to step back, but stopped at a small gesture from the Emperor. "It was my father who invited you to New Berlin and who wished to meet you," he said, reaching beside him and picking up the rectangular package. "That opportunity was sadly lost; but in his memory I would like you to have this." He held out the package. "Please, open it."

Frowning, Travis stepped closer and took the box from him. It was a lidded metal container, he saw now, its black surface holding a subtle etching of the Andermani Imperial seal. Balancing it on his right palm, he swung open the lid with his left.

Inside was a book. A real, paper, printed book. And on the cover—

"*Sternenkrieg,*" Andrew said quietly. "My father's treatise on warfare and philosophy. In many ways, his life's work. This is part of the very first printing, and I would be honored for it to be an heirloom of your house and descendants."

"The honor is mine, Majestät," Travis said, stumbling over the words as he gazed in wonder at the book. A gift like this—

"Of course, you may wish to read it before securing

it in your family archives," Andrew added with a small smile. "I'm told the Star Kingdom could use some additional instruction in strategy and tactics."

"We absolutely do, Majestät," Travis agreed. He opened the book's cover.

And felt his eyes go even wider. Not just a rare paper book. Not even just a first printing. It was also inscribed.

For Lieutenant Commander Travis Uriah Long, on behalf of those Andermani whose lives he helped to save—Emperor Gustav II.

He frowned. *Gustav II?* He looked up at Andrew—

"You read that correctly," the Emperor said. "I thought you might appreciate a bit of advance notice, since you won't be present for the official announcement next week. Yes, I've decided to rule under the name Gustav II, both as an expression of continuity in Andermani leadership, and as notice to the galaxy at large."

His eyes hardened. "They must know—all of them—that the Empire is not to be underestimated, dismissed, or trifled with. Our future enemies will learn that to their regret. Our future friends—" the eyes softened "—will know it to their comfort and reassurance."

"I understand, Majestät," Travis managed. "I hope that the Empire and Star Kingdom will always find themselves in the latter list."

"As do I, Lieutenant Commander," Andrew said. "You may step back."

"*Danke, Majestät,*" Travis said, returning to his place between Lisa and Winterfall.

"And now, let us end our solemnity with one final presentation," Andrew said. He gave a whistle, and the two napping greyhounds leaped to their feet and loped over to the Manticorans. "I presume, *Herr* Winterfall, that you recognize this one?"

"I do indeed, Majestät," Winterfall said, reaching down and rubbing one of the dogs' heads. "It's my old friend Sunna."

"She who helped you defeat a traitor," Andrew said. "As a personal token of my gratitude, I would like her to be yours."

Winterfall's hands froze in mid cuddle of the dog's head, his eyes wide as he looked back up at Andrew. "Majestät?"

"And this is her mate, Glenr," Andrew said, shifting his attention to Lisa. "Do you also appreciate dogs, Commander Donnelly Long?"

"Very much, Majestät," Lisa assured him, offering her hand for Glenr to sniff and then stroking the dog's head.

"Then Glenr is yours," Andrew said. "I would hate to break up a couple, and I'm sure you and your brother-in-law must spend a great deal of time together."

Travis looked sideways at Lisa, wondering what she would say to that. But she just smiled and nodded. "We are doubly honored by your gift, Majestät. We'll make sure Sunna and Glenr never grow lonesome for each other."

"I would expect nothing less from you," Andrew said. "And since *Herr* Winterfall mentioned that his mother breeds dogs, I would like to send a breeding pair of pups as a gift for her."

"She'll be thrilled and honored, Majestät," Winterfall assured him. "Once again, we are in your debt."

"Excellent," Andrew said. "All four dogs will be

delivered to your ships this evening, along with sufficient provisions and accessories for the voyage. And now, you're free to return to the reception. Enjoy the food and drink and the music and fireworks which will follow. I wish you a pleasant and safe journey home, and I hope that on some future date we may meet once again."

"We, too, will look forward to that day, Majestät," Winterfall said.

"Oh, one more thing." Andrew pointed at Lisa. "I understand, Commander, that you've taken a particular liking to our *Gebäckgarnelen*."

Travis looked at Lisa in time to see her cheeks turn pink. "*Ja, Majestät,* I have," she admitted.

"You have excellent taste," Andrew said, smiling. "Please enjoy as much as you wish."

A minute later they were outside the palace again in the sun and scented air. "Every time I think the Andermani can't surprise me," Winterfall commented, "I find myself standing corrected. Amazing man. Amazing people."

"He's absolutely right about one thing," Travis said. "The Star Kingdom definitely wants to be in the *friend* column of the Empire's ledger."

"I just hope everyone on Manticore sees it that way," Winterfall warned. "There are some in Parliament who might feel just the *slightest* bit intimidated by them. Sometimes that manifests in grumpiness and rejection."

"Never mind them," Lisa said. "Queen Elizabeth will snap them into line. *My* question is whether Baroness Crystal Pine likes dogs."

"I suppose we'll find out," Winterfall said. "Maybe we'll even find out if she likes *Gebäckgarnelen*."

"How?" Lisa asked. "You going to ask for the recipe?"

"No, I'm just betting you'll find a flash-frozen container of the stuff aboard *Damocles* when we get back," Winterfall said.

"Right," Lisa said dryly. "I'll take that bet, *Herr* Foreign Minister."

☆　　☆　　☆

As it turned out, they were both wrong. The wrapped shellfish were instead delivered to *Diactoros*.

And there were, in fact, *two* containers of them.

☆　　☆　　☆

"It's a mess," Lady Calvingdell said heavily. "And I'm pretty sure it's just going to get worse."

Seated across the desk from her, Chomps had an awful urge to ask if she was blaming him for someone else's murder. But good sense and self-preservation won out. "I heard Crystal Pine has gone into seclusion," he offered.

"What she's gone into is house arrest," Calvingdell said bluntly. "My God, Townsend. I sent you to look into Duke Serisburg's death, not to bring down a sitting Peer and kick the House of Lords in the back of the knee."

Once again, Chomps considered reminding her that he hadn't been the one whose foot had been inside that particular boot. Once again, the better part of valor prevailed. "So I take it Masterson finally gave her up?"

Calvingdell glared at him another second then lowered her eyes to her tablet. "Not in so many words," she said, some of the frustration-born fire fading. "He was never told who hired him, so he couldn't finger her directly. But he kept some financial records in case he needed leverage down the line, and the fact that she was the only one who gained by killing the entire family was enough to get a warrant for her own records. Eventually the investigators were able to make enough connections to make the charge stick."

"Was he actually from the Solarian League?" Chomps asked. "I know that's what he said, but I never found out if that was true."

"Who knows?" Calvingdell said, shaking her head. "We've got a message ready to send with the next ship heading that direction, but it'll be at least a couple of years before we get an answer. But given that the duke's car was a Solarian model, and Masterson apparently was one of the people who helped talk Serisburg into buying it in the first place, I'm guessing that was true."

"Which suggests this whole thing was in the works for a long time," Chomps pointed out.

"At least a decade," Calvingdell agreed grimly. "Maybe more. Crystal Pine *really* wanted that seat in the Lords."

"So I gather," Chomps said. "What kind of fallout are we getting?"

"You mean SIS personally or the Star Kingdom in general?"

"You can start with the first," Chomps said, mentally crossing his fingers. If ONI was screaming for SIS's collective head, but decided they'd settle for his...

"No one's happy with us," Calvingdell said. "Our charter doesn't permit us to go poking around in internal affairs, though Masterton's self-identification as Solarian makes that edge a little fuzzier. Still, ONI's using that excuse to try to get us shut down, or at least put under their oversight. But given what we found, their heart really isn't in it. They're likely to just put it aside in their collection of things they plan to pile on top of us as soon as they figure the stack is big enough. The fact that you'd been fired from SIS and therefore not under my control also helped."

Chomps had to smile at that one. Not under her control. Flora Taylor's little visit—complete with Sphinxian whiskey—and her revelation as to what Calvingdell *really* wanted him to do in Serisburg was clearly irrelevant. "Especially when they've got such a nice, big target in the Royal Investigation Division, first for taking Masterson into their ranks in the first place and then for duffing the whole investigation?" he suggested.

"Yes, big, fat, happy targets do seem about all that ONI's capable of hitting," Calvingdell growled. "Add in *unmoving* and you've got the picture. Mind you, if you'd moved a single day earlier you'd have been one of those big, fat, et cetera targets. They were just waiting for you to do something suspicious."

"Figured as much," Chomps said. So the former NCO who'd been hanging out at the Three Corners Inn those first few weeks playing birdwatcher *had* been ONI. Chomps had been pretty sure he was, but it was nice to have confirmation. "How did they even know I was there?"

"Don't be so modest," Calvingdell growled. "You've been on everyone's radar since you got back from Silesia. That's why I had to fire you to get you on this case."

"*Pretend* to fire me, you mean, right?"

Calvingdell's lip puckered a bit. "We'll have to see," she said evasively. "If this blows over quickly enough, I can probably get you back in. If not . . . well, there are some options on the table. Some people we're talking with. Maybe we can give you a leave of absence."

"With all due respect, My Lady, I don't *want* a leave of absence," Chomps said stiffly. "I want to get back to work."

"And we want you back." Calvingdell smiled faintly. "Pain in the neck though you are sometimes. Just try to be patient."

"If I have to," Chomps said with a sigh. So maybe his Delphi career *was* down the tubes. Still, he *had* helped catch a murderer. That had to count for something.

Even if no one else ever knew.

"I assume I won't be getting any credit for this?" he asked.

"Given that there's a target already painted on your back, do you really *want* any?"

"Probably not," Chomps conceded. "Anyway, Deputy Lassaline deserves it. It's hard to do good investigative work when the suspects are people you know and like. She did a great job."

"Agreed." Calvingdell raised her eyebrows a little. "Maybe we should hire her and let you take her place in Serisburg."

"I'd rather wrestle hexapumas in a carnival," Chomps said. "Though the Whistlestop ice cream *is* pretty good. So what's the timeline look like?"

"God only knows," Calvingdell said, shaking her head. "Crystal Pine's holdings will have to be dissolved, with the Crown probably taking over her barony like it did Serisburg. The Queen will have to figure out how to sort out the holdings, but filling the seat in the Lords will be easy enough."

"The fifty-fourth investor in the original corporation?"

"Right," Calvingdell said. "There's been some occasional talk over the years about modifying the current cap on House of Lords membership, and I'm guessing this may bump that discussion up to the front burner. So that could be interesting."

"Though probably not an issue I need to worry about for the immediate future."

"Not unless you plan on marrying into the Peerage," Calvingdell agreed. "All right, here's what I can do. If you'd like, I can hire you on as a secondary analyst."

"A secondary analyst," Chomps said flatly. "Sorting through papers and numbers that other people have already sorted through."

"It's a necessary job," Calvingdell said. "Extra eyes, and all that. More to the point, it doesn't require a security clearance since you'll only get the data after it's gone through the classification process."

"We certainly wouldn't want to strain ONI's resources reinstating my clearance," Chomps said sourly. "Lower pay, too, I suppose?"

"You'd be treated exactly the same as our other secondaries," Calvingdell said. "You'd have to be. You want it, or not?"

Chomps sighed. "Sure," he said. "At least I can come in every day and give Flora someone to be irritated with. I imagine her life was pretty boring these past few months."

"She managed to survive," Calvingdell said. "All right. Give me a couple of days to push through the paperwork, and you should be back at your desk by Friday."

"Thanks," Chomps said. "I appreciate it."

"I appreciate you catching the murderer of my friend," Calvingdell said, a flicker of old pain crossing her face. "And don't worry. Sooner or later this will die down, and ONI will forget, and I'll be able to fully reinstate you."

She smiled lopsidedly. "And look at the bright side. While your friend Long was being bored out of his mind sitting through fancy state dinners and listening to long Andermani speeches, you got to investigate a crime, catch a killer, and nearly drown yourself."

"*And* get shot at."

"And get shot at," Calvingdell agreed. "For once, you'll be the one with the exciting story to tell."

EPILOGUE

THE TRIP HOME FROM POTSDAM seemed to Travis to go by faster than *Diactoros*'s earlier voyage in the other direction. Part of that was there was no anxiety about what they would face at the other end, part of it was that he wasn't spending ten grueling hours a day shoveling German vocabulary and grammar into his brain.

And part of it, the best part, was that with *Damocles* running smoothly and the XO considered a hero, Captain Marcello was giving Lisa lots of time to spend on *Diactoros* with her husband.

Granted, much of that time was also spent wrangling the four greyhounds traveling with them. Marcello had taken a single look at the dervishes that were the two pups and flatly refused to let them anywhere near his ship. Given the limited free space aboard any ship, *Diactoros* included, it was something of a challenge to find places where the animals could burn off some of their boundless energy.

Fortunately, the adult dogs seemed better under

control, or at least understood basic obedience commands and were willing to follow them. Even more fortunately, Winterfall proved to have a knack for dealing with them. He handled a lot of the caring and feeding and maintenance, and by the time they reached Manticore he had even the pups somewhat trained.

Travis had hoped to have some time along the way to talk with his brother, to perhaps start building the kind of relationship they'd never had and that Travis had always wanted. To his relief, Winterfall was not only willing to make that effort, but actually seemed equally interested in doing so.

Of course, neither of them had expected those conversations to take place over, around, and through a double pair of bouncing, attention-demanding dogs. But oddly enough, it worked. In fact, by providing a bit of a distraction, the dogs' presence may actually have helped get them through some of the more awkward parts of their talks.

Lisa, for her part, was willing to give the brothers whatever time they needed, provided that she got the time *she* needed with her husband.

The three of them also spent a lot of time sitting around discussing Emperor Gustav II, the Andermani, and what the future might hold for relations between the Star Kingdom and Empire. The topics ranged all over, though of course nothing was solved.

Still, the dogs enjoyed the extra attention.

Their arrival home was marked by muted, mostly uncaring notice by the general public, followed by closed-door briefings with the Cabinet and Admiralty, followed by frantic discussions among both groups.

Winterfall spent a lot of time with the former; Travis and Lisa spent an equal amount of time with the latter.

Travis's reunion with Chomps was mildly amusing, in a strange sort of way. Both fully expected *their* story of the past half year to be the high point of their first lunch-time get-together, and both then had their socks knocked off by the other's tale.

For Travis, the worst part of Chomps's story was the revelation of Baroness Crystal Pine's treachery. For weeks afterward he waited for his brother to say something about the woman he'd called a friend, or at least talk about how he felt about her downfall.

Winterfall never spoke of it. Travis, taking the cue, never asked.

It was three weeks after their return home that the final bombshell crashed in on them.

☆   ☆   ☆

Travis was at one of the computers in Delphi's Room 2021, temporarily back with SIS to work on a report Lady Calvingdell had commissioned, when a roar from Chomps's direction shook the entire room.

He was out of his chair and across the open space in eight seconds flat, beating out the other two SIS agents who'd been at their computers and even Lady Calvingdell. "What is it?" he snapped, giving his friend a quick once-over. Nothing seemed wrong or out of the ordinary except for the grim set to his mouth and the simmering fire in his eyes. "Chomps?" he prompted.

"I was going through the recordings you brought back from the Quintessence repatriation," Chomps said, an unnatural flatness to his voice. "I wanted to see if there was a mention of any of them in our files." He nodded at the computer. "That's their chief, right?"

Frowning, Travis stepped around behind him for a better look. The image on the screen showed two people, Commodore Quint and a man he didn't recognize, both in Quintessence uniforms. "Yes, that's Commodore Catt Quint," he identified her. "I don't know who the man is."

"Oh, yes, you do," Chomps said, an edge of frustration in his voice. "Let me back it up a couple of frames."

The picture jerked slightly...jerked again...the woman half turned to the man...the man smiled... Chomps again paused it. "Tell me I'm wrong."

Travis frowned a little harder. Okay, so the man was smiling now. Why should that make any difference?

And then, abruptly, it clicked.

"No," he breathed. "No, it can't be him. *Smiley?*"

"Bingo," Chomps said darkly. "I guess running ops against Manticore wasn't enough for him. Now he wants to destabilize the Andermani Empire, too."

"Pull up everything we have on him," Calvingdell ordered. "I'll talk to Dapplelake and Winterfall and see how fast we can get a ship organized to send to Emperor Andrew."

"Gustav II," Travis murmured.

"Whoever," Calvingdell said impatiently. "If they don't already know about this man, they'd damn well better get up to speed. Who the *hell* is he?"

"I'd settle for what the hell he wants," Chomps said.

"I'm not settling for less than everything," Calvingdell bit out. "As of right now, Townsend, you're fully reinstated. Start pulling together everything we know about Mr. Smiley and get it ready to send to New Berlin. Long will help you translate it into German—I don't want any linguistic roadblocks to slow them down. They have *no* idea what they're getting into."

"Maybe not, My Lady," Travis said, a fresh knot forming in his stomach. "But neither does Smiley. Emperor Gustav was *very* clear that he and the Andermani weren't going to be trifled with. If Smiley isn't careful, he may turn out to be the first object lesson of that policy."

"I hope not," Chomps said.

"You hope *not*?" Calvingdell demanded.

"That's right, My Lady." Chomps gestured at the smiling image still frozen on the screen. "We're the ones he started with.

"It's only fair that we be the ones who end him."

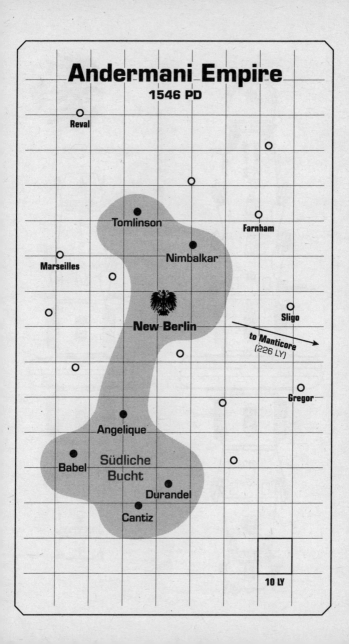

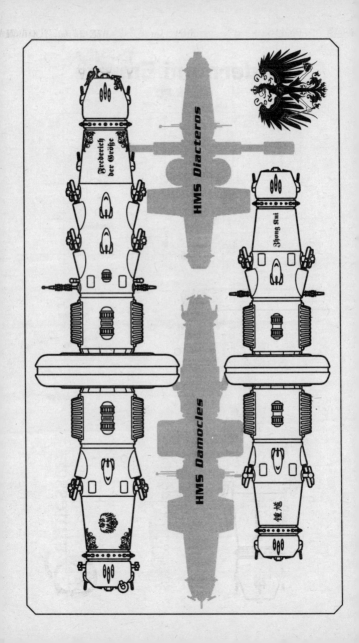

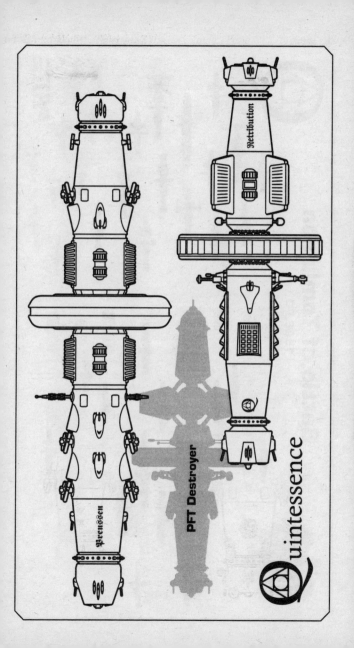

Preußen

Retribution

PFT Destroyer

Quintessence

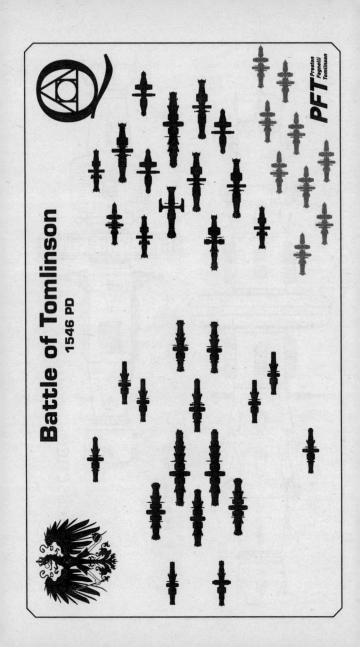

Battle of Tomlinson
1546 PD

PFT
Preston
Fagnelli
Tomlinson

A NEW ENTRY IN THE MANTICORE ASCENDANT
HONORVERSE SERIES

A CALL TO DUTY
By David Weber and Timothy Zahn

Growing up Travis Uriah Long yearned for order and discipline in his life. So when Travis enlisted in the Royal Manticoran Navy, he thought he'd finally found the structure he'd always wanted so desperately. But life in the RMN isn't exactly what he expected; and with the Star Kingdom of Manticore still recovering from a devastating plague, the Navy is on the edge of budgetary extinction. With only modest interstellar trade, no foreign contacts to speak of, a plague-ravaged economy to rebuild, and no enemies looming at the hyper limit, there are factions in Parliament who want nothing more than to scrap the Navy and shift its resources and manpower elsewhere. But those factions are mistaken. Events are in motion that will prove that the universe is not a safe place. Manticore may not be as isolated as everyone thinks, and Travis Long is about to find that out.

MM: 978-1-4767-8168-6 * $8.99 US / $11.99 CAN

"A new series set in the universe of Weber's popular heroine Honor Harrington gets off to a solid start . . . Cowriters Zahn and Weber do an excellent job alluding to events known to longtime fans . . . [T]his astronautical adventure is filled with . . . intrigue and political drama."
—*Publishers Weekly*

A CALL TO ARMS
MM: 978-1-4767-8156-3 * $8.99 US / $11.99 CAN

A CALL TO VENGEANCE
MM: 978-1-4814-8373-5 * $9.99 US / $12.99 CAN

Available in bookstores everywhere.
Or order ebooks online at www.baen.com.